# Missing Julia

CATHERINE DUNNE is the author of seven previous novels (*In the Beginning, A Name for Himself, The Walled Garden, Another Kind of Life, Something Like Love, At a Time Like This* and *Set in Stone*). She has also written about Irish immigration in *An Unconsidered People*. All of her work has been published to both critical and popular acclaim. The novels have struck a chord in several countries and have been translated into many languages and optioned for film. Catherine Dunne lives near Dublin.

*Acclaim for* MISSING JULIA

'Dunne's latest story asks tough questions,
not only of its characters but also of its reader'
*Image*

'Dunne has a great talent for making the minutiae of life
fascinating and for exploring the emotional background
of her characters with great finesse'
*Sunday Tribune*

D0493860

# Catherine Dunne

# Missing Julia

PAN BOOKS

First published 2010 by Macmillan

This edition published 2015 by Pan Books
an imprint of Pan Macmillan, a division of Macmillan Publishers Limited
Pan Macmillan, 20 New Wharf Road, London N1 9RR
Basingstoke and Oxford
Associated companies throughout the world
www.panmacmillan.com

ISBN 978-1-4472-8914-2

Typeset by SetSystems Ltd, Saffron Walden, Essex
Printed and bound by CPI Group (UK) Ltd, Croydon, CR0 4YY

Visit **www.panmacmillan.com** to read more about all our books
and to buy them. You will also find features, author interviews and
news of any author events, and you can sign up for e-newsletters
so that you're always first to hear about our new releases.

*For Paula Dunne*

## Do Paula

Ar an margadh cheannaigh tusa cruach eochraca
is póca síolta, cheannaigh mise baclainn fhocal.

Agus An Chearnóg á trasnú againn d'éirigh stoirm
ach sheas muid an fód gur ghlan an spéir.

Ar shroichint an bhaile dúinn chuir tusa do shíolta,
líon an teach le ceol. Chruthaigh mise an leabhar seo.

Oscail é agus tiocfaidh tú ar fhocail
a cheiliúrann ár n-aistear, mín agus garbh.

Breathnaigh amach gach maidin go bhfeice tú iomad
bláthanna, is cuma cé chomh dorcha an oíche aréir.

Celia de Fréine

*For Paula*

*At the market you bought a stack of clefs
and a pocket of seeds, I an armful of words.*

*As we crossed The Square a storm arose
but we held firm till the skies had cleared.*

*When we got home you planted your seeds,
filled your house with music. I crafted this book.*

*Open it and you'll find words that celebrate
our journey rough and smooth.*

*Look out each morning and see a variety
of flowers, no matter how dark the night before.*

*November, 1999*

THREE O'CLOCK, SHARP. A murky, steel-grey afternoon. Skies with one foot firmly across winter's threshold.

'You ready?' Julia asks.

Lucy nods. 'Yeah. I'm ready.'

'Bundle up.' Julia winds a scarf around her neck, pulls on her gloves. 'It looks chilly out there.'

Lucy turns up her collar, shoves her hands into the pockets of her coat. 'I'm fine. Let's go.'

Julia begins to make her way towards the door.

'Wait.'

She turns. Her eyes search Lucy's. 'What is it?' For a moment, her expression is animated, hopeful.

'I'm glad you're with me.'

Julia reaches out, touches the younger woman's face with her fingers. 'I wouldn't have it any other way,' she says.

Lucy nods. 'Well, just so you know.'

'Yes. I do.' Julia seems about to say something. Then she stops, smiles instead.

'You lead; I'll follow.' Lucy gestures towards the exit.

Julia turns and walks towards the door of the terminal building. She looks straight ahead; her stride is purposeful.

She will not look back.

\*

The car is waiting for them as they come out of the arrivals terminal. The driver is short, stocky, a corduroy cap pulled down low across his eyes. His hands look bulky in faded sheepskin gloves. As Julia and Lucy approach, he moves away from the half-open driver's door where he's been standing, sheltering from the cold. 'Mrs Delaney?' he says.

Lucy nods. 'Yes. And this is my . . . sister, Julia Seymour.'

He tips the peak of his cap at both of them. His round glasses make him look owlish. Julia can't see his eyes properly – the lenses are glinting in the low winter sunshine. The effect is disconcerting.

'I am Bernard,' he says, smiling. 'Your escort. My mother was a great theatre-goer. I am named after your Mr Shaw.' He holds out both hands to Julia. 'Please, let me take that for you.'

And she hands him her rucksack.

# PART ONE

*Ten Years Later*

# *Julia*

JULIA STEPS INTO the porch and closes the outer door behind her, pushing the handle upwards into the locked position. The darkness of the October night is thick and heavy and she turns her back to it with relief. Even the street lamps can't cope: they're haloed in grainy mist, their light a yellowed and sickly one. She struggles with her keys and the lock for a good minute before becoming exasperated. 'Oh, come on, come *on*, will you,' she says aloud, and eventually manages to elbow open the front door. As she does so, she drops some of the carrier bags that have deadened her fingers. Their contents spill out all over the hall floor.

She kicks them out of the way as the alarm starts beeping: an aggressive sound, its shrillness feeling like an assault. She jabs at the numbers on the keypad and then puts on all the lights whose switches she can reach. The porch, the hall, the upstairs landing. Only then does she exhale and lock the front door behind her. She is hardly aware that she's been holding her breath: she's been doing it so much lately that she has ceased to notice.

She bends down now and sweeps the bags over towards the bottom of the stairs, murmuring to herself as she does so. 'Just five more hours,' she says. 'Keep it together, Julia. Keep it going. We're nearly there.' She places her bunch of keys on the low table that rests to the left of the banister. There used to be a small dish here, its enamelled surface glowing cobalt blue and emerald green, drawing her deep into the memories of a childhood seascape. It has held her keys for almost thirty years. But now it is packed away, wrapped carefully in smooth plastic sheeting, criss-crossed with duct tape. Julia is determined that it will not get damaged. Her footsteps echo as she walks down the hallway towards the kitchen. Already, she thinks, her energy has been filtered out of this place. *This place*: this solid and comforting house, which has been her home for three decades and a little more.

Halfway down the hall she pushes open the door into a downstairs office. The desk is bare, the laptop already packed away. She's left most of her books on the shelves that line three of the walls. Her old medical texts, side by side with fiction and poetry; the odd gardening manual. And the coffee-table books full of lush photographs of art and architecture, a recent twin passion. She can see their familiar shapes in the light that oozes in from the hallway. Some of these volumes will interest Melissa or William, some of them will interest both. Julia grimaces as she imagines an unlikely scene: the two of them, slugging it out over their favourite titles. She reaches to her right and switches on the desk lamp. Its glass shade fires up opalescent, the light spilling onto the telephone below. She sees that the tiny red oval of the answering machine is flashing. She frowns and considers for a second the option of not listening to it, but curiosity gets the better of her. She presses 'play'.

'Mum, it's me. It's nine o'clock on Monday night?' Melissa's words have their usual interrogative edge, their usual ragged emphases. They imply that Julia has no *business* not being at home when her only child phones. *It's late*, Julia hears; *far too late for* you *to be out. Where are you, Mother?* And then, just below the surface: *Where are you* ever *when I need you?* Melissa's is a voice that is already disappointed, already tired of life. 'Derek and I are invited out to dinner on Saturday,' she goes on, 'and Chloe – my babysitter – is sick. I know you're probably busy with William, but I just wondered, if you have nothing else planned, could you stay with Jamie and Susie?' And then, as an afterthought: 'Please? Give me a call when you pick this up.'

Julia stands by the desk for a moment. She plays the message again and shakes her head at all the grievances in the undertow of her daughter's words. Then she erases it, switches off the lamp on the desk and makes her way towards the door. As she does so, the telephone rings, making her jump. It sounds much louder tonight than it normally does. She breathes deeply and stands very still in the darkness, one hand on the door frame, the other resting at the base of her throat, as though warding off attack. Fight or flight, she thinks suddenly, as she feels the adrenaline coursing through her. Its startled, tingling rush makes her hot, and the top of her head begins to pound.

'Julia? William here. Tried your mobile earlier, but no luck.' Cheerful, loving Will. 'I'm heading out now for a pint with Jack, so I'll call you in the morning. Hope all is well. You're a bit hard to catch! Anyway, shout if you need me. You know where I am.' And then, after a short pause: 'Love you.'

Julia hesitates for a moment, then steps out into the hall and almost closes the door behind her. But she keeps holding on to it; indecision is etched into her features. She runs one hand through her hair, feeling all over again how unruly it has become. She keeps forgetting that she's been letting it grow, leaving it untamed for all these months. She knows that this change puzzles William, although he never says. She also knows that it angers Melissa, who does say. But it is not for discussion. Julia shakes her head. 'Leave it, you have to leave it,' she says aloud, and wrenches her hand away from the doorknob, as though it has suddenly become too hot to handle.

She walks towards the breakfast room and pushes open the door, carefully. Tinkerbelle is inside, in her usual position. Her solid black-and-white and elderly body lies across the saddle, waiting for Julia's return. Like an old-fashioned draught excluder, William had once exclaimed, laughing, and Julia feels that that is exactly right. She pushes against the door again and can feel the cat moving, can hear the purring begin. Julia could swear that she knows something: the cat has clung to her every night for the past couple of weeks, the clear greenish eyes shadowed and anxious.

'I should change your name,' she says now, leaning down to stroke Tinkerbelle, just as she begins to insinuate herself around Julia's ankles. 'Clinging just like ivy, aren't you? How'd you fancy being called after a weed?' She moves from the breakfast room into the kitchen on the right and fills the cat's bowl with water. She pulls open the fridge door and Tinkerbelle's tail shoots up. All the fur on her body seems to stand to attention. 'What have we here?' Julia soothes, pulling some tinfoil parcels off the shelves. 'Not a whole lot, Tinky, because tonight's the night. Eh, puss? Tonight's the night.'

She mixes some leftover roast chicken with dry cat food and smothers the lot in cold gravy. Then she turns the small jug upside down so that Tinkerbelle can see. 'All gone,' she says. The cat checks to make sure and then loses interest. She's agitating for the bowl in Julia's hands. Julia sets it down by the back door, just beside the cat flap. 'Enjoy,' she says, scratching the hard little bone of cat-head that lies between the silky triangles of her ears. 'Last supper, Tinky-Wink. Eat like there's no tomorrow.'

Julia stands up and moves briskly back towards the breakfast-room door. No point in lingering. She switches off the light and steps back into the hall. She bends down and gathers up the carrier bags that she has abandoned earlier.

Quickly she scoops their contents back into them again, almost without looking. Then she starts to climb the stairs.

Once inside her bedroom Julia draws the curtains, making sure to shut out the night. There is one medium-sized wheelie-bag on the bed, a rucksack and a bulging laptop case. She upends each of the carrier bags onto the duvet. Six white T-shirts fall out, six black. Then two pairs of black chinos; two pairs of beige. Two pairs of jeans. Two pairs of casual shoes. Underwear; socks; sunblock: Factor 50.

She folds the clothes quickly and places them in the wheelie-bag, on top of the sweaters, her black bag, a half-dozen books. She closes the zip and secures it with a small combination lock. Then she hefts it off the bed and out onto the landing, where she leaves it at the top of the stairs. She comes back into the bedroom and decides to test the rucksack, heaving it up on her shoulders, trying for balance and a more comfortable distribution of weight.

As Julia does so, she catches sight of someone in the long mirror that stands in the corner of her bedroom. She freezes. So does the image. At first, she doesn't recognize herself. She has been avoiding her own reflection, she realizes, for some time now. She sees a tall figure – very tall, for a woman: almost six feet – in blue jeans and a navy sweater. Her hair tumbles to her shoulders in a great mass of grey waves. Her eyes are blue, clear, somewhat startled in a face that looks suddenly paler – almost greying, to match her hair. Julia has never lost her rangy shape: her body has that strong, wiry substance that never runs to fat. She could pass for much younger than her almost sixty years, as she well knows, but that is no longer relevant.

She shrugs off the rucksack now and places it beside the bag on the landing. She pulls a piece of paper out of the back pocket of her jeans and smoothes it with the palm of one hand.

'Check,' she says, and 'check' again, her index finger moving quickly along the neatly printed items. The list complete, she crumples the paper in her hand and tosses it into the wastepaper basket beside the mirror. Then, suddenly realizing, she takes it out again and shoves it into the back pocket of her jeans. She meets her reflection once more as she straightens up, and it gives her pause. She looks into her own blue eyes, clarity meeting clarity, focus meeting focus.

'We're sure about this, Julia, aren't we?' she says. 'Very sure?' The reflection nods and Julia draws herself up to her full height, shoulders back. 'Good girl,' she says. 'Now let's get on with it. Once more with feeling.'

She pulls open the double doors of her wardrobe. Inside is empty, apart from three pieces of clothing shrouded in see-through flimsy plastic, their dry-cleaning tags still attached. They are the only outfits that Julia hasn't been able to give away to charity. She has distributed the rest of her belongings carefully, seeking out those shops that are furthest from where she lives, where she's always lived. In the circumstances, she'd thought it best that her cast-offs not be flaunted around her home neighbourhood like some sort of rebuke. Melissa might object. And it might be the most unforgivable thing that Julia could do to her.

The pieces that remain hanging in the wardrobe are not there because of any misplaced sentiment, either. Julia feels very firm about that. It's not that she's wanted to hold onto them. It's just that she hasn't been able to decide what is the best thing, the right thing, to do with them. She has fretted over her inability to decide this most simple of issues, worries that it might be more significant than it seems. Anyway, it's too late now. Melissa will probably be furious with her for leaving them – but then, her daughter will be furious with her anyway. And Melissa *has* admired these pieces again recently, in a way that made Julia think that she was hinting at ownership. She had run her hands over the silk dress, looked wistful over the cashmere suit. Her face had filled with an expression that looked like admiration, but the twin children of resentment and covetousness had lurked beneath the surface. Julia had almost heard them whine.

Melissa's life has turned out to be not as wealthy as she might have wished. Julia knows this, feels it in her bones and knows, too, that *she* is somehow held responsible. Another failure. Another thing she didn't teach her daughter. A piece of knowledge she'd kept to herself: how to snare a rich husband. Julia sighs and moves the clothes along the rail. So, let her have them if she wants them. She no longer knows – if she ever has – what makes her daughter happy. The gold, crushed-silk dress, the sequinned jacket, the ruinously expensive trouser suit that she had worn to Melissa's wedding: perhaps they would please her. They will all suit her, Julia is certain of that. They are the same height, of similar build, and the one thing Melissa has always approved of is her mother's taste in clothes. At least, she has approved of the taste that her mother *once* had in clothes: not any longer.

The remaining loose hangers sway gently towards each other, their metal edges chinking faintly. Julia nods at them as she closes the wardrobe, pushing the doors to with extra pressure. Tonight of all nights, she doesn't want them flinging open in the darkness, the fault of the catch that seems to lose its magnetism from time to time. When that happens, Julia's heart thuds her into wakefulness and makes any further sleep impossible.

She makes her way now across the landing to the other two bedrooms. All the wardrobes, cupboards and bedside tables are cleared. She still finds it strange how the absence of a few personal belongings here and there has immediately reduced her home to nothing more than a house. In this large and chilly spare bedroom, only ever used for visitors, there used to be an old-fashioned tortoiseshell hairbrush set in front of the dressing-table mirror. A small Moorcroft vase – an unloved and unloving gift from one of Julia's aunts – had stood forever on top of the chest of drawers. And some fading photographs had dotted themselves around the bookshelves and the bedside tables. She would never have thought of any of these random bedroom belongings as being particularly significant. And so it surprises her, the way that their presence must have breathed something quietly potent into the air here, over the years. Something that is now missing.

Julia is aware that she has gradually been keeping her distance from these spaces over the previous months. Nevertheless, the sudden lack of warmth in the rooms, of a sense of belonging, of personality, disturbs her more than she would like. Quickly she pulls both doors to, and locks them behind her.

Back downstairs once more, she enters the room she has deliberately left until last. The living room, complete with its sprawl of couches, its squat coffee tables, its old sink-into-me armchairs dotted everywhere. Even the new television, the one that William had encouraged her to buy. He'd been horrified at her lack of movie education, had set about filling all the gaps. She smiles now, remembering. The evenings they spent together with Bette Davis, Humphrey Bogart, Katharine Hepburn – Julia has enjoyed them more, much more, than she's been prepared to admit to Will. She's loved his earnestness when he's tried to explain how seminal some movie was, how cutting-edge for its time.

She has left this room as it is, as it has been for the three years she and Will have been together. It is still alive, this living room. Julia can sense their presence here, can almost see

William's long outline on the sofa, her own softer shape leaning into him. And in front of the sofa is the coffee table, the ugly one belonging to Richard's mother. She has never had the heart to throw it out. On its surface rests the open chessboard, already set up as though for Wednesday night's game. The game that will never happen. Instead, she hopes that William will understand the message she has left him, hopes he will know that this is her way of preserving what there was – what there still is – between them. She wants, more than anything, to help him to understand.

She closes the door behind her, leaving the room to its silence and its ghosts. She will not set foot in here again.

She ascends the stairs slowly. This is the last time she will go back up these steps. After tonight, the journey is all one-way.

She walks into her bedroom and sets the alarm on her mobile phone for two a.m. She undresses, folding the clothes carefully, draping them across the bedroom chair, ready for the morning. Then she slips between the cold sheets and reaches over to switch off the bedside light.

The room is quiet. Outside, she can hear Peadar next door whistling for his dog. 'C'mon, fella' rises on the night air. C'mon, Oscar.' Then: 'Good dog' and the back door is closed quietly.

Suddenly, and more quickly than she has anticipated, exhaustion overtakes her. Julia is glad of its ambush: she can feel emotion gather around her in the darkness of the bedroom, luring her towards weakness. And she will not cry. She will not cry. She sighs once and turns onto her right side. Facing the future, William used to say.

She sleeps.

*

In the early morning, she wakes before the alarm sounds. She is instantly conscious, all her senses primed. For a moment, she is reminded of the first few days of Melissa's life, when she, Julia, would awaken a split second before her baby daughter's wails, ready, always ready. She would feel the let-down of her milk as the liquid rushed to her tingling nipples, searching for the small, hungry mouth.

There is that same sense of high alert this morning, that need to be fully present in herself, ready for all eventualities.

Julia showers and dresses quickly, keeping the mobile close by on the bathroom shelf. Later, she'll remove the SIM card and replace it with the new one that is waiting in the side pocket of her rucksack. Another letting-go: but one that can't be thought about now, not this morning. This is the morning when all of her movements have to be brisk, efficient. She takes her bags downstairs, one after the other, and brings them into the kitchen, leaving them at the door that leads to the garage. She does not want breakfast. She knows that her stomach will rebel if she tries to feed it. Later, perhaps; there will be time to think about such things later.

She leaves food and water for Tinkerbelle. That cat is no fool. When the food runs out, she will simply make her way to Peadar and his mother next door. She'll sit on the back windowsill and whine, looking piteous, until Mrs Mc clicks her tongue and lets her in. Julia has found her there before, has had to reclaim Tinkerbelle from her curled comfort in front of Mrs Mc's turf fire. Even Oscar, the ancient Labrador, is a reluctant host to Tinkerbelle. He accepts her presence, tolerates her fireside incursions. Julia has made sure never to greet Oscar empty-handed. She'd always sneak him a couple of doggy treats from her pocket, on the occasions when she has had to go next door to collect the cat.

Oscar has always understood the transaction. 'Good dog,'

Julia would say, stroking the golden fur. He would struggle to his feet, tongue lolling, brown eyes gazing expectantly. Peadar and Mrs Mc would pretend not to notice him nosing the treats from Julia's discreet hand. Then he'd subside by the fire again, his large body panting with the effort. Resting his head on his paws, he'd gaze up at his owners. Julia could swear that sometimes she has glimpsed triumph in his look. Then, as always, he and Tinkerbelle would continue to keep a careful, disdainful distance from each other.

It is now two forty-five; Julia is ready to stow her luggage in the boot of the car. She locks the door to the kitchen and steps out into the sudden coldness of the garage. No lights are needed: she knows her way around here in the dark. She presses the remote control and the door rolls up and back, quietly enough, onto the garage ceiling. She has made sure to oil every part of it that she could see, to stop the small metallic shrieks that would set the entire estate's teeth on edge. Here, in this quiet cul-de-sac, full of elderly couples, or widows and widowers, Julia has done her homework. She has learned about the neighbourhood dog-walkers, the restless, the terminally curious; she knows that nobody moves in or out of any of the surrounding houses before six a.m. Eight weeks of patient observation have taught her that.

*Time warp*, William has said to her, on more than one occasion. *You live in a time warp.* And Julia agrees: her neighbourhood has remained unchanged, unchanging over the years. It has stayed resolutely unsurprised, even by events that have convulsed the nation. Nothing *ever* happens here – up until now.

She struggles into the driver's seat. She'd parked badly yesterday, in her hurry to get the car in off the road. This garage had not been built for modern cars: there is barely enough room to manoeuvre herself through the car door into a sitting position. She starts the engine, but doesn't switch on the lights, not yet. She drives out onto the road, taking things slowly. Then she walks quickly back down the driveway and presses the remote once more. The garage door starts to close, the white metal panels rolling jerkily downwards. Just as the bottom panel is about to reach the ground, Julia slides the remote control underneath it, back onto the garage floor. It spins a couple of times before the door judders to a stop, metal grinding against concrete.

She looks around her, but everywhere is in darkness, apart from the eerie glow of solar lamps in Mrs Byrne's front garden. She slips into the driver's seat again and makes her way slowly towards the main road, trying not to look behind her. When she reaches the mouth of the cul-de-sac, she switches on her lights. She indicates right and swings out into the deserted street.


Once on the M50, Julia begins to breathe more deeply. It's just after three-fifteen, and the roads are clear. The black ice, threatened by last night's forecast, doesn't seem to have materialized. Nevertheless, she'll keep carefully to the speed limit. She has three hours of a journey ahead, according to the AA. The route planner, printed off the Internet weeks back, lies on the passenger seat beside her, its entrances and exits highlighted in yellow marker. She has everything worked out, building in her usual ninety minutes or so of 'getting lost' time. And even if things do go haywire today, there is always tomorrow.

But she doesn't want to think about tomorrow. Tomorrow brings Will into focus. She can see him, sitting beside her at the coffee table, with their Wednesday-night chessboard set up between them. He is a good teacher, patient and thorough. And he's proud that she has been such a good student. He even grins when she beats him. Julia knows that, by tomorrow evening, William will be really worried. By then he will not have heard from her, or seen her, since Monday morning. She hates the thought of his suffering, but there is nothing to be done about it now.

For a moment she has the wild, unbidden realization: It's not too late! You can always turn back! Your life is there, still intact. And nobody would know. But the thought wilts almost as soon as it has blossomed. Someone already *does* know, someone who has made this flight inevitable. She grips the steering wheel more tightly. Instead of thinking, she recites aloud what she has memorized. Junction 18. Newry Bypass. Banbridge Bypass. Hillsborough. Westlink. Larne.

That's enough uncharted territory to keep anyone busy, their mind concentrated. As a southerner, she'd never crossed the border up until a year ago. All her life, that bit of the world had been off-limits: more remote, more bewildering, more inaccessible than if it had been another universe. Which it was – or had been, when Julia was a teenager. Now, people crossed the border willy-nilly. Shopping in Newry had become the new national sport. Decades of finely tuned political grievances slackened and loosened in the sticky grip of economics. Julia hopes that a Tuesday at the end of October, with all the children on half-term, will be enough of a disincentive to keep mothers at home and the northbound traffic to a minimum.

Mothers. Children. Without wanting to, not now, Julia thinks of Jamie and Susie. Four and almost two. For a moment, she can feel the sweet warmth of Jamie's heavy head on her arm as she carries him up the stairs to bed. Missing him is a physical ache. And Susie – to think that she might never again . . . Julia stops herself. 'Enough, already,' she protests aloud.

She is jolted back to the present by the looming road-signs warning her of the toll-bridge ahead. She has just hit a patch of fog that is suffused by a strange saffron glow: part motorway lights, part car headlights. She'd better pay attention. The traffic will probably begin to build soon. She thinks, not for the first time, how awful it must be to spend your day – your life – in a car; on the way to somewhere, or on the way home. And the bit in the middle, into which you disappear, called work. It's all work, Julia thinks. Such a waste, all that time commuting. Melissa complains about it constantly. And she has a choice, even if she refuses to see it.

Julia slows as she reaches the toll-booth. She hands the young woman a two-euro coin, marvelling at the fact that she is fully made-up, even at this hour of the morning. Huge hoop earrings, eyelashes black and spidery, false nails. Carmela nails, Julia thinks suddenly. She'd read somewhere that the woman who played Tony Soprano's wife – Edie Falco, that was her name – had had to apply her acrylic nails before she could begin to get into character. You can't work with nails like that, she'd declared; they force you into inactivity. Nails like those were the defining characteristic of the modern gangster's moll. Julia watches as the young woman in the booth has difficulty fishing out her twenty-cent change. Her fingers falter over the coins and Julia stifles a smile. Right on, Edie, she thinks. Those ain't no nails for a working woman.

'Thank you,' she says now as the young woman glances at her. And then: 'Have a nice day.' She gets a surprised look and a small smile. Julia waves and drives off as the barrier lifts. She feels suddenly energized by the human contact. The past few days in particular have seen her withdraw from everyone around her. She's been forced to be careful of what she said, of what she was seen to do. Now she feels a sense of liberation. And the further Dublin lies behind her, the weaker becomes the pull of guilt.

# *William*

WILLIAM TRIES AGAIN.

It's not like Julia, not like her at all. She always returns his calls. And she's a demon texter. But she hasn't replied to any of the messages that he's sent her since midday. And the only message he's getting from her mobile is that she's inaccessible right now, or may have her mobile switched off. Well, that much he has just about figured out for himself.

He feels uneasy; someone has walked over his grave several times already this morning. He waits, hoping that the answering machine will not click in this time, that instead Julia's voice will greet him, maybe a little breathless from running to the phone. She's always running to the phone. William has failed to convince her to bring it with her around the house. Cordless, he used to remind her. It means what it says.

If she doesn't pick up right now, in person, he will call Melissa. He looks at his watch again as Julia's recorded voice comes down the line: 'Hi, this is Julia. You know the drill. Leave a message after the tone.'

He slams down the receiver, angry now. It's two o'clock on Wednesday afternoon and he hasn't seen, or heard from, Julia since he left her early on Monday morning. He called Monday night, last night and again today. Several times. What is she playing at? And then the lurch of fear, from somewhere cold in the pit of his stomach. What if she's had an accident? What if she's lying in a heap somewhere, unable to speak? What if she's had a heart attack, a stroke?

After a moment the rational part kicks in, chiding him, talking sense. If anything awful has happened, he'd have heard: bad news travels fast. The simple explanation is that she must have stayed with her friends in Wicklow overnight. And the mobile signal is useless there: too many mountains. There is no need to panic. But he does anyway.

He paces the room, doing battle with himself. Is he over-reacting? Should he be doing something? And why does he have such a bad feeling about all of this – whatever 'all of this' is? Underneath the ambush of questions lies another nagging suspicion, a germ of doubt that he's been avoiding ever since it woke him in the small hours of this morning. But he has no option now. It's sending forth shoots, climbing rapidly towards the light. Julia had taken his key back from him last Sunday night. He'd thought nothing of it at the time: but now he's wondering.

'Oh, before I forget,' she'd said, just as they were getting ready to go to bed. She'd been plumping up the cushions on the sofa, smoothing the crocheted throw that they often put over their legs in winter. 'The gas boiler's acting up. I want to leave a key with Mrs Mc. She's promised to let the service man in on Tuesday.'

William had crossed the living room to retrieve the DVD from the machine. He'd looked back at her, over his shoulder. What was happening on Tuesday that he'd already forgotten about?

'I'll be in Wicklow all day, remember?' she'd continued, picking up the wine glasses from the coffee table.

He'd kept looking at her, trying to dredge something – anything at all – from the sludge that he often felt had begun to settle where his memory used to be.

'The annual lunch?' she'd continued, with exaggerated patience. 'With Hilary?'

He'd nodded, with a vague sense that he'd heard something about it before. But Julia had so many friends that he'd long ago stopped trying to keep up. This one had certainly slipped below his radar. He'd been almost overwhelmed when he'd first got to know Julia. They'd been showered with invitations to lunch, dinner, surprise birthday parties. He'd never known that it was possible for one person to be so intimately connected to so many others.

'Can I have your key to leave next door? Don't know what I did with the spare.'

'Sure,' he'd said, straightening up. He'd rummaged instantly in his trouser pockets. 'Do you want me to do anything?'

She'd shaken her head. 'It's fine, thanks. Mrs Mc has already offered. I think she likes to feel useful. Besides, you know plumbers. He mightn't turn up at all and you'd have a wasted day.'

William remembers struggling to unhook his door key from the ring. He can see himself handing it to her. 'Thanks,' she'd said, smiling at him. She'd placed it in the little blue-and-green enamelled dish that always sat at the bottom of the stairs. They'd turned off the lights, locked the doors and climbed the stairs to bed. The usual routine. Julia had curled herself around him, holding him so close that he'd protested, laughing. 'You'd better let me breathe, woman,' he'd said, 'or I'll be no use to you!'

She'd kissed him. 'Make love to me,' she'd said, her voice urgent in the darkness. He'd thought, even at the time, that there'd been a suspicion of tears. But Julia was a passionate woman. He'd often been blindsided by her sudden extremes of feeling.

'Hey, hey,' he'd said, tenderly, 'what is it? You okay?'

'Yes,' she'd said. 'I love you. Just stop talking.'

Now, as William thinks about that, he feels afraid. He is missing something here. Something has happened between them that he hasn't understood, that he hasn't caught in flight. Maybe it even happened on Sunday night. He flicks open the phone book on his desk. Julia had written Melissa's number in there a couple of months back, 'just in case,' she'd said. 'Just in case what?' William had demanded. He couldn't think of any reason why he'd ever want to call Melissa. She'd never been anything but hostile to him.

Julia had shrugged, laughing at him. 'I dunno – in case the house goes on fire, in case my mobile dies, in case you can't find me.' She'd taken down Michael's number as well, that evening, storing it in her mobile. Although William had grumbled that a fat lot of use his only son would be, if anything ever happened to *him*. Stuck in the wilds of Australia. Nevertheless, Julia had insisted.

'Sod this,' William says out loud now. 'I'm going over there. If there's no answer at the house, *then* I'll call Melissa.' He pulls his overcoat off the hallstand and struggles into it. He grabs his keys off the hook and slams the apartment door behind him.


Even her front door looks different. Something has happened, something is off-kilter here. William has always thought of the air around Julia's home as open, welcoming. The house has had a vibrancy to it, an energy that was all hers. Now the blue door seems silent, sullen, closed against him. He locks the car and walks across to the porch. He presses the doorbell urgently, keeping his finger on it, pulsing the sound from time to time. Nothing. He peers in the window of the front room, shading his eyes against the glancing winter light that forces him to see nothing except his own reflection.

Inside looks normal. William can make out Julia's desk, the lamp, the bookshelves on the walls. Everything seems to be in order, nothing obvious is out of place. That gives him hope. He moves quickly back to his right and tests the garage door. It is locked. He tries the porch door once more, just in case. He is about to turn away when the postbox to his left catches his eye. He had fixed it there for her, one Saturday morning, drilling into the red brick and attaching the box securely to the wall. Cast-iron, cobalt blue: she had found it in an antique shop in Rathmines and had immediately fallen for it. William remembers her excitement. 'Oh, look, William!' she'd exclaimed. 'Exactly like the one we had when I was a kid. Even the colour! Would it be easy to put up?'

He lifts the flap cautiously now, as though something might explode in his face. Inside is crammed with envelopes. William stares at the evidence, trying to understand something that keeps eluding him. She hasn't collected her post, either. That does it. He pulls his mobile from his coat pocket, calls up the number that he'd stored earlier and then, suddenly, he remembers. He puts the phone in his pocket and walks quickly instead back down the driveway and up the neighbour's path to Mrs Mc's front door. She's there almost as soon as he rings the doorbell. Has she been watching, waiting? He wonders and doesn't care.

'Mrs McCarthy? I'm William Harris, Julia's friend. I was wondering . . .'

'I know who you are. Come in, please, Mr Harris. Don't mind Oscar. He's as gentle as a lamb.'

William bends down and strokes the Labrador's ears. He knows all about Oscar and Tinkerbelle's on-off courtship.

'Hello, fella,' he says, kindly. Julia is so fond of Oscar that, for a moment, William feels his breath catch at the memory of her anorak pocket full of doggy treats. He straightens up. Mrs Mc is waiting. 'I've been trying to contact Julia,' he says, following the elderly lady down the hall to the kitchen. But she doesn't respond. Perhaps she hasn't heard. He tries to curb his impatience. This is how it's going to be, he thinks. Slow. Courteous. It would be rude to hurry her. As she makes her stately progress, William notices her floral apron and has a brief flash of memory. His mother, up to her elbows in flour, the smell of cinnamon and warm cloves all around her. Pinny, he remembers suddenly, that's what she used to call her apron. 'Where's Pinny?' she'd say, as though it was a person in its own right, deserving of a capital letter. He doesn't think too many women wear aprons like that any more.

'I haven't seen Dr Seymour for the past couple of days.' Mrs McCarthy opens the door into the kitchen. The fire is lit and Oscar immediately makes his way onto the rug, easing his arthritic hips into position and then stretching out, resting his mournful face on his front paws.

'Didn't she leave you a key, then?' asks William.

Mrs McCarthy looks at him sharply. 'Why would she do that?'

William treads carefully. This lady is poised to take offence. 'I understood that Julia had a boiler repairman due this week, and I thought I heard her say that you had offered to let him in.' It sounds all wrong, William thinks now, even as he says it. It doesn't sound a bit like Julia.

Mrs McCarthy frowns and shakes her head slowly. 'No,' she says. 'I'd remember that. I saw her on Monday around lunchtime, when she was sweeping up the leaves in the garden. She came over and spoke to me, like she always does. But there was no word of any key.' She is starting to look worried now, as though she, too, is missing something, something she should be responsible for.

'My mistake,' William says hurriedly. 'Only, I can't reach her and I've left my own key at home.' Keep it simple.

'I have Melissa's number,' Mrs McCarthy says now, brightening. She is glad to be of help.

'Thank you,' he says. 'So do I. I think I'll give her a call. There's probably nothing wrong, but I'd rather be sure.' He pats his pockets, a polite prelude to taking his leave.

'You're welcome to use our phone,' she says, her body already turning in the direction of the old-fashioned telephone, where it squats, black and solid, in the corner of the kitchen.

'It's fine, thanks.' William is now anxious to be gone. He doesn't want any audience for his call to Melissa. 'I have it here on my mobile. I'll just step outside, if you don't mind – the signal is always better outdoors.'

Mrs McCarthy pulls open the kitchen door. 'Let me know when you reach her, won't you?' The elderly eyes are troubled now. 'Dr Seymour, I mean. She has always been so good to us, to me and Peadar.'

William smiles at her, reassuring. 'Of course. I'm sure everything is fine – we just keep missing each other, that's all. She could well be on her way back from Wicklow as we speak.'

William has already pressed the call button when Mrs McCarthy closes the front door behind him. After two rings Melissa answers, her 'Yes?' an impatient one.

'Melissa? This is William Harris.' He decides not to bother with any further explanations: Melissa knows well enough who he is.

'Is there something wrong with my mother?' she demands. 'Is she with you? She won't answer my calls.'

William lets all the undercurrents wash over him. 'I was hoping you could tell me,' he says. 'I can't reach her either. I'm standing outside her door and there's nobody home.'

'Can't you use your key?' her voice is sharp. 'Let yourself in?'

'I don't have one,' he says. What he really wants to say is: Do you think I'm stupid? Would I be standing out here in the pissing rain if I had a fucking key?

'Oh,' she says. 'Wait there. I'll be with you in fifteen minutes.'


It's twenty-five minutes since he's called Melissa and William is impatient. He can feel that old, old longing for a cigarette, like something hollowing out his gut; itching under his fingernails. He stamps his way down the driveway again, glancing towards the far corner that leads into the cul-de-sac from the main road. He is aware of a curtain twitching anxiously over his left shoulder. He has already turned down a cup of tea, a warm kitchen, neighbourly solicitude. Now he's just mad at Melissa. What the fuck is keeping her?

He stops in his tracks as wavering lights become visible in the distance. A car turns into the cul-de-sac and William exhales in relief. He walks back up the drive and waits at the porch door. He can see the rain slanting – fine, bright, glow-worms in the beams from the headlights – and only then realizes how wet his overcoat is, and his hair, plastered against his skull.

Melissa parks at the kerb and jumps out of the car. She slams the door shut and runs across the gravel, stumbling a little in her high heels. To William's surprise, she looks distraught; her hands are trembling and, when she speaks, her voice is reedy, just on the verge of collapse. 'I don't understand it,' she's saying, fumbling with a bunch of keys in her hand. 'I knew something was wrong, I just knew it.'

'We don't know anything yet,' William says, gently. He has never seen Melissa in such a state and he can feel himself warming to her. Her distress forces him to be calm. 'She may still be in Wicklow, there may be nothing at all to worry about.' But even to his own ears his reassurances sound hollow, false.

She hands him the keys. 'Wicklow?' she says. She looks puzzled. 'She didn't say.' Then she shakes her head. 'Never mind. Here, you open the door.'

He realizes that she is terrified of what they might find. Suddenly he doesn't feel so good either. Her anxiety is infectious. He can feel himself begin to buckle under its weight, even before they go inside. He gets the key in the lock on his second attempt and pushes open the inner door. Melissa hurries past him and presses in the alarm code. William feels a flash of annoyance at this gesture of ownership. He is surprised at his own pettiness. Be reasonable, he tells himself. She's Julia's daughter, after all. And she's as worried as I am.

'Okay,' he says. 'I'll try upstairs if you'll—'

'No.' She shakes her head vigorously. 'Let's do it quickly, together.' She runs towards the kitchen and flings open the door. He sees with a pang how like her mother she is. Tall, slender, with a definite shadow of Julia's strength in her long arms and legs. The light blinks into brightness as William looks over her shoulder. There are a couple of bowls sitting by the back door, one with the remains of cat food, one with a glint of water. 'Nothing,' he says. 'Come on.'

He tries the office next. Although he had seen nothing when he'd peered in through the window, now he is afraid that he might have missed something: a body slumped on the floor by the desk, a handbag spilling open on the chair. Anything.

But the room, although still full of Julia's possessions, is curiously empty. And then it strikes him: the laptop is missing. Now that is unusual. Julia never brings it anywhere with her. 'Smacks of work,' she used to say. 'And I brought *that* everywhere for more years than I care to remember.' William files the information away in case he needs it later. Melissa doesn't seem to have noticed.

'Everything here is the same as always,' she says. Her eyes are huge, shadowed. William wonders whether she has slept at all the last couple of nights. Is there something unhappy going on with her, besides this? Julia has had her doubts about Derek; William already knows this. And the girl looks exhausted. 'Living room?' she asks him now. William nods.

He starts to tremble as they open the door. The chessboard is set up, as it always is for their Wednesday evening game. So she intends to be here, then, is that what Julia's telling him? And something is preventing her? But William doubts it: this room has acquired a stillness that is not natural to it. Something has escaped from within these walls, and the nausea that suddenly fills his throat warns him that everything in his life is changing, or is about to, or has already done so while he wasn't paying attention. He hesitates, unable to step any further into the room. Even then, he is aware that he wants to do this without Melissa. Out of the corner of his eye he sees something that jars, something that is significant in its insignificance. For a moment it feels like a speck in his eye, a bit of grit in his shoe. But he can't stop to figure out whatever it might be. He can feel Melissa at his elbow, her rapid breathing unnerving him, reminding him that they have a job to do.

'Quickly,' he says. 'Upstairs.'

Melissa doesn't respond, but he senses her behind him, taking the stairs two at a time, just as he does. When they reach the landing, he misses his footing and crashes into the bedroom, the door jerking back against the bedside table. The bed is made, cushions piled high over a tumble of pillows. But no books litter the floor or the shelves above the bed; the top of the chest of drawers has been swept clean. William looks around him. He is aware of being plunged into the midst of a puzzle whose pieces don't fit together, no matter how he arranges them.

He hears Melissa cry out suddenly and takes a step towards her. She has opened the wardrobe doors and both her hands now cover her mouth, as though she is afraid of what might come out if she speaks.

'What is it?' William says. All he can see is a few garments hanging there, harmlessly. What is Melissa so upset about? And then he sees it too. The emptiness, sister of the stillness downstairs. Melissa turns to look at him, her eyes now brimming. He is shocked at how blue they are, just like Julia's. He has never noticed that before.

She points to the clothes, hanging limply in the wardrobe. 'Everything is gone,' and her voice is a whisper. 'Except for these – and she joked a few weeks ago that she'd leave them to me, when the time came.' Now Melissa begins to cry in earnest. 'I don't understand,' she sobs. 'What is she doing? Where has she gone? I'm frightened, William.' He puts one arm around her, awkwardly. He doesn't know what to say. This is a Melissa he hasn't met before. Shaky, tearful, unsure of her ground. She wipes her eyes with her sleeve and looks at him. 'Something bad has happened to her, I'm sure of it. I can feel it.'

'Let's not jump to any conclusions just yet,' he says, although she has voiced exactly what he is thinking. 'We'll go back downstairs and be more methodical. There has to be a clue somewhere.'

What he doesn't say is that this looks like no random disappearance. This has all the signs of a planned, orderly retreat. But why? And from what?

'Come on.' He leads Melissa towards the stairs. 'Let's have a stiff brandy and put our heads together.' Melissa's face is grey with shock. He's afraid she'll pass out on him if he doesn't get her downstairs, fast.

'Garage,' says Melissa suddenly. 'We haven't looked in the garage.' William sees the appeal in her eyes.

'Stay here,' he says. 'I'll go.' He picks up the key from its position under the lamp on the bookshelves. Cookery books: they're all still there, nothing out of place. The shelf is jammed, as usual. Books are upright, on their sides, even double-parked, as Julia calls it. William feels as though his perception has been heightened: that he is seeing, hearing, *sensing* more than is possible for one human being. *I am a camera.*

He opens the door and steps into the garage, deliberately pulling the door to behind him. His instinct is to protect Melissa from what he is dreading might meet him. Julia, slumped over the steering wheel, cold, staring. He snaps on the light, but even as he does so, he has already picked up on the emptiness of the garage. There is the faintly musty, earthy smell of the leaves that Julia has dumped into the compost bin. Its lid is still open. He walks over to it, looks inside. But there is nothing, nothing but leaves. What had he expected?

As though in answer, he suddenly kicks something that skitters out of his way, plastic scraping against concrete. He looks down and at first thinks: mobile phone? His mouth goes dry. His mind's eye sees ambush, struggle, kidnap. Not the why: just the fact of it. He bends down to pick up whatever it is. The remote control for the garage door. He sees at once what must have happened: Julia, crouched outside, spinning the device back into the garage, just as the door shuddered to a close. He exhales and the vision of anguish, of attack recedes. His breath frosts out smokily into the stale garage air.

He takes one last look around him. He tries to banish the other pictures of Julia, those that have hovered at the threshold. Images of all those people who kill themselves in their cars. And for the first time, he wonders, shocked at his slowness: Might Julia be ill? Is that why she has gone away like this? The thought makes him pause. He has to stop while his mind careens around their last days together. He begins to see everything in the new and garish light of her disappearance. But it's all too much. It's a sensory overload that he'll have to unpick when he gets home. Illness begins to seem like a real possibility: a new and frightening one, but at least something that begins to make some kind of twisted sense. But he will not share this thought with Melissa, not yet.

When he goes back into the kitchen, Melissa is standing, one hand on the table for support. Every fibre of her resonates strain; William can almost hear the vibrations. 'Nothing,' he says. 'Her car is gone, but there is nothing in the garage out of the ordinary.'

Melissa slumps again, resting her elbows on the scrubbed deal table that is one of Julia's many domestic delights. 'I rang on Monday night, asking her to babysit,' Melissa is saying. She is frowning, trying to make sense out of the senseless. William knows the feeling. 'But she didn't ring me back.' He pours a brandy for both of them. 'I left a message on the answering machine. I wonder, did she even get it?' Melissa has just switched on the heating. The house is cold, and she has started to shiver.

'Mrs McCarthy next door saw her on Monday morning, sweeping up leaves in the garden,' William offers. 'Julia was to go to Wicklow on Tuesday, to Hilary somebody-or-other.'

Melissa frowns. 'Hilary?'

'Yeah – something about an annual lunch. Why?'

'I think I've met all of Mum's friends at one time or another. I don't think there's a Hilary – at least, not any more. The only person I know who lives in Wicklow is Roisin, but I'm not even sure if she still does.' She pauses. 'Are you sure she didn't say Roisin?'

William curbs his irritation. So Melissa thinks he's thick as well. 'Positive,' is all he says. And he doesn't say what else he's thinking. That Julia has a life that her daughter is not aware of. Why should she know everything about her? Then he stops. What about all the things *he* doesn't know about her? If Melissa has to face an uncomfortable truth about how well she knows her mother, then he does, too, and he doesn't like it. 'Let's try her address book,' he says instead. 'I'll get it.'

He leaves Melissa and makes his way quickly back into Julia's study. He wants to be there on his own, in case Julia has left something for him here, tucked away in the pages of her well-worn address book. He used to tease her about that, too. 'Why don't you just use "Contacts"? Keep all that stuff on your laptop?'

But she had been very protective of the black leather-bound book. Each page was full of crossings-out, changes, notes to herself. 'This is more than an address book,' she used to insist. 'This is the geography of people's lives. The places they've lived, the places they've moved to. And, sometimes, the gaps that show me I've lost contact with someone who used to be important.' And she'd tapped the cover with her long fingers. 'It's a reminder to put that right. All that white space needing to be filled.'

He remembers now how that sentiment had touched him.

'Besides,' she'd said, 'it's not held to ransom by power failure, computer crashes or any of the other – what do you call them – "outages" that people talk about.'

'But you might lose it,' he'd said gently. 'At least let me make a copy of the current information for you.'

'Maybe,' she'd conceded. 'But how can I lose it, if I know where I always keep it?'

In the first drawer of the desk, William thinks, his heart hammering now. He pulls the drawer out, and the ease with which it rushes towards him tells him it is empty, even before he looks.

'Well?' Melissa's voice from the doorway makes him jump. 'Has she left anything? A note, a hint even?'

He shakes his head. 'Her address book is gone. There's nothing here.' He continues to pull all the desk drawers open, one by one. A sudden waft of perfume, Julia's perfume, is painful for a moment. He looks around at the bookshelves, the occasional tables, the ancient leather wing-backed chair. In a room once so full of Julia, he now feels her absence so keenly that he shudders. The gnawing in his gut is becoming even more insistent. He can already feel the hot, heady nicotine rush that will come with the first drag of the cigarette. He knows he's going to have to give in. It's only a matter of when, not if.

'Come back into the kitchen,' Melissa says, tugging at his sleeve. 'I don't think there's anything useful for us here.'

He follows her down the hallway, fuming inwardly. Us? Why should there be anything here for you? You gave her nothing but heartache. There is no 'us'. I made her happy, and she's left me. You made her unhappy, and she's left you. That's all there is to it. Damn you, Julia, he thinks. A sign, a message, a code: anything other than a waiting chessboard. I deserve more than that.

'Have you got a cigarette?' he asks.

Melissa looks at him. 'I thought you'd . . .' she begins and changes her mind. She rummages in her handbag, hands him a packet of twenty Silk Cut and a red plastic lighter. 'Help yourself,' she says. 'I'd better ring Derek. I want him to know what's going on.'

'I'll just step outside,' William says. He lights the cigarette first and inhales deeply. But he is disappointed. He might as well be smoking fresh air. Bloody politically correct cigarettes, he rages. He hands the packet back to Melissa. 'Make your call in comfort. I'm going to wander around for a bit. Something might come to me.' He stands up.

Melissa nods. She is sitting across the table from him, curling a strand of hair around and around her finger. He wishes she wouldn't do that. It reminds him of Jan. She looks away from him and reaches into her handbag again, this time for her mobile.

William closes the kitchen door behind him and walks rapidly back towards the living room. Now is his chance to find whatever it is that's been nagging at him, prodding him in the ribs, ever since he'd stood here earlier. He stands in the doorway again and begins to scan the room, just as he had done when Melissa was with him. It takes him a while to see it. When he does, he feels something shift inside him, something both alert and peaceful. He breathes deeply as he recognizes it for what it is: the slow, faint stirring of hope. On the innocent chessboard that awaits on the low, old-fashioned coffee table, the white queen is off her square. It is no mistake: it *can* be no mistake. A white queen on a black square? Julia would never get that wrong. He should know: he has been the one to teach her how to set the pieces up, has made her do it over and over again until she could do it blindfolded.

'Like stripping a machine-gun in the dark,' she'd teased him. 'Chess isn't just a matter of life and death for you, is it?' And he'd laughed, saying, 'No, as good old Bill Shankly said about football – it's more important than that.'

Now, he stares at the board, the blood ringing in his ears. Quickly he puts the queen back where she should be, but he's got the message. What the message is, he can't be sure, not yet. But he'll find out. And it's for *me*, he thinks, almost savagely. This is not to be shared with anyone.

'Messages,' he says suddenly, out loud, as the word makes other connections fire inside his head. 'The answering machine.' He stands up from where he's been crouched by the chessboard and hurries back to the kitchen. Melissa is still sitting at the table, her face a blank. She is holding her mobile in one hand, a tissue in the other. 'We should listen to Julia's messages,' he says. Melissa doesn't seem to have heard him. 'The answering machine, Melissa, come on.'

She puts down her brandy and follows William out of the kitchen. He can hear her footsteps, just behind his. He shoves open the door to Julia's office. It has always had the tendency to stick. He sees the tiny red light of the machine, winking away at him. For a moment he wonders whether Julia might have called her own number, just to let them know she is safe. She must know that they'll be frightened, worried about her. He presses 'play' and the first voice they hear is his. He feels a small surge of disappointment, but refuses to let it unbalance him any further. He has the queen to hold onto: the queen and her silent, cryptic message.

But he is shocked, listening to himself speak. That world he is speaking from – one where Jack calls around for a pint, where William is both sure and unaware of tomorrow, where Julia is solid and certain in his life – has all suddenly spun out of orbit and he is falling, falling into an echo. And there is no pull of gravity to yank him back to safety, to steady him on ground that is familiar and unyielding.

William wonders whether Julia has even heard this message. If so, did she sit in this room as he spoke, letting him talk and all the while she was planning never to see him again? Because that is what William now believes: that wherever she is, whatever she's doing, it is for good. The blankness of this empty house tells him that Julia is not coming back.

'About what time did *you* call her, then?' Melissa asks. As though he had no right.

William knows exactly what time he called. He decides to ignore her tone. 'At a quarter to ten.'

'Well, I phoned at around nine,' she says. 'I was surprised that she wasn't here.'

Maybe she was, William thinks. Maybe she was and didn't want to talk to you. 'Melissa only rings when she wants something,' Julia has said to him recently. 'I'll call her back when I'm ready.'

He has a moment of satisfaction that even he recognizes as childish. Melissa's message has been erased. His has not.

'We need to call the police.' Melissa's tone is flat. 'In the morning it'll be three days since anyone has seen her or heard from her. I think that qualifies as a missing person.'

'And what if she doesn't want to be found?' William asks quietly. Melissa looks at him, her eyes suddenly angry.

'What do you mean?' she says. Her tone, her eyes, her chin: all sharp.

'Look around.' He is amazed at how calm he sounds. Inside, he is churning, but he feels that he has reached the truth of Julia's disappearance. And she would not want him to flinch from it. 'Her laptop is gone. There is nothing personal here – last time I saw this office it was a mess. A normal, working mess. But now, everything is tidied away.' He pauses. 'Her clothes are gone. And when we give the house a thorough going-over, I bet every other trace of her is gone as well. Can't you feel it? This house is . . . empty. Hollow.' He stops. He will get to the bottom of it. If Julia is missing, then he will find her. It is as stark, as simple, as that.

'Did you have a fight?' Her voice is tight, angry. The blue eyes are blazing.

'No,' he says, tiredly. 'We did not have a fight. I know that you don't want to believe this: you never *have* wanted to believe it. But things were good between us. Very good. Your mother was happy when she was with me.' Now he can feel himself getting angry. He knows that Melissa has never forgiven her mother for being happy without her father. Has held it against her – against both of them – for three years now. Well, he's not going to apologize for anything. Least of all for loving Julia. Or for her loving him. Melissa is just going to have to swallow that.

'She must have had some sort of a breakdown.' Melissa is shaking her head. 'She'd never have left us – she adores Jamie and Susie.' William lets this slide. 'What am I going to say to people?' And then her voice cracks. 'Such a selfish thing to do,' she sobs. 'Leaving like this and telling no one.'

William doesn't reply. He watches Melissa absorb what is happening to her. He had felt it the moment he'd stepped across the threshold. Julia's absence was – is – a palpable presence. The only thing he can hold onto is the connection between the two of them. Him and Julia. He is consumed by it, she has acknowledged it. Somewhere between those two certainties, he must fight to keep hope alive.

Right now, all he wants is to be alone. Melissa is grating on his nerves. He can feel his patience wearing thin. All his earlier, unexpected affection for her has started to drain away. He feels weary. And anxious: he needs to go home, to think, to try and pull things together.

'I don't think we can do anything else here tonight,' he says.

'We must go to the police.' Melissa is insistent. 'It's been more than forty-eight hours.' She looks around her. 'And with the house . . . emptied like this, they'll have to take us seriously.'

With William's silence, Melissa suddenly seems to realize what she's said. 'Even if they say it's her choice, I still want to know what's happened to her.' Her tone moves from defiant to deflated in the course of the sentence: so much so that William can barely hear the end of it.

'I'll come with you,' he says. 'Of course.'

Melissa turns away from him reluctantly. She doesn't want him with her, and she doesn't want to say it. He can read it in her spine: the stiff way she holds herself, the eyes cast downwards.

Tough, he thinks angrily. I have as much right as you do. Abruptly, he walks into the hallway and begins switching off the lights. 'Coming?' he says. He stands by the alarm this time, getting there before Melissa. On guard. She sweeps past him, throwing one end of her scarf back over her shoulder. It is an aggressive gesture, redolent of dismissal.

William keys in the alarm code, locks the front door behind him and follows her out into the night.

# *Julia*

JUST BEYOND THE VILLAGE of Ballynure, the weather worsens. It's that fine, misty rain that defeats even the most enthusiastic windscreen wipers. Julia can feel herself growing more and more anxious. She slows down, conscious both of the traffic behind her and the thunder of oncoming lorries. They crash past her, on the other side of the road: line after line of them, their names looming up at her out of the darkness. McBurney Refrigeration; McMullan; McPeake; Montgomery. The number of them must mean that the ferry has docked on time. But their lights dazzle Julia and she's finding it difficult to see the road ahead. She knows she's going too slowly, can imagine the stream of invective from the motorists behind her.

And then: the signs appear. For the weighbridge, for Larne, for the harbour itself. 'Thank God for that,' she says, aloud. The tall Victorian houses start to crowd up on her left and she wonders what this town must be like on a sunny day. Their domestic elegance is a strange counterpoint to the snarling traffic making its grey way towards the sea. Talk about seeing somewhere at its worst.

Ahead, she catches a glimpse of the P&O ferry, is startled at its size. Years ago, she remembers that she and Richard took the car to France one summer – but she has no memory of the ferry itself. Didn't need to, she thinks now, suddenly. Richard would have taken care of everything: the driving, the planning, the passports. She would have been the passenger back then, observing, making conversation, enjoying the absence of responsibility.

A woman in a yellow jacket holds up her hand and signals to a stream of cars on her left. She motions at Julia to stop, holding up her walkie-talkie like a badge: an old-fashioned sheriff, brandishing her authority. Julia waits as a courtesy bus makes its way towards the ramp. She feels curious about these foot passengers: what do they do at the other end, without a car? And why not fly, instead? Surely a flight would be almost as cheap – if not cheaper, booked well in advance? The bus pauses for a moment and she can see tired, ghostly faces, heads resting against the windows. Then she spots him. A little boy, hair spiked just like Jamie's, his nose pressed flat against the glass. She feels her stomach lurch. Both of his small hands are rubbing away at the condensation on the inside, while he tries to peer out, his face bright and mischievous. She can't help herself. She waves, even if he's not able to see her. But he does, and waves back, turning excitedly to say something to the owner of the adult hands that are placed firmly around his chest. The bus moves off. The small hand continues to wave palely, and then disappears. The rain gets heavier so that Julia has difficulty even following the glow of its tail lights as it mounts the ramp in front of her. A Jeep follows, then a horsebox, all of them disappearing quickly into the belly of the ship. Across the swelling water of the harbour she watches as the tall industrial chimneys of Larne seem to shy away from her, backing off into the gloom.

And now it's her turn. Following the sweep of the yellow jacket's arm, Julia mounts the ramp at what feels like a surprising speed, enters the maw of the ship and parks where she's told to. It all feels very brisk and efficient. The yellow jackets have an air of bored competence about them that Julia finds comforting. When she switches off the engine, she can hear the announcement: 'Beware of moving vehicles', over and over again. She steps out of the car and closes the door behind her, grateful that stage one of her journey is now over.

She takes the rucksack and the laptop out of the boot. Car deck number three, she notes, as she is waved towards the stairs. She stumbles a little as the rucksack refuses to settle on her shoulder and jerks downwards into the crook of her arm instead. Immediately, she feels a hand at her elbow.

'All right, madam?' Another yellow-jacketed woman, another crackling walkie-talkie. She peers right into Julia's face. For a moment, Julia feels indignant. How dare she: does she think I'm drunk? She is reminded of the nurses in Casualty, the way they used to size up the patients who'd topple into the hospital from Friday- and Saturday-night pubs, roaring and swearing after midnight. In Your Face, they'd called it. Partly for challenge, partly for information. Who needs a blood test? they'd say. Just smell his breath, up close and personal.

'Yes, I'm fine, thank you.' Julia stiffens and is aware that she has just used her *Don't mess with me* doctor-voice. But the woman merely motions her along with one arm: another passenger, one of so many early-morning sheep. Must be losing my touch, Julia thinks. The passengers move along, silenced into submission by the presence of so many Day-Glo jackets.

Upstairs, Julia sees that the Quiet Lounge is full, some people already deeply asleep in comfortable armchairs. She passes the video area, with its garish gaming machines. A few teenagers are already installed, slouched over the screens. They are dressed almost identically in jeans, hoodies and dirty trainers. There is a sign to their left announcing that this morning's feature film is *Definitely, Maybe*. For a journey of an hour and a half? Julia stops herself. It is a sign of getting old, this recurring irritation at other people's constant need to be entertained.

Finally, she reaches the lounge, which is empty apart from a young man at the other end, engrossed in the screen of his laptop, and a young couple, each engrossed in the other. She sits at a table for two, right over beside the door. On such a dreadful morning she doubts that there will be much activity out on deck. Perhaps the occasional intrepid smoker, but nothing that's going to disturb her too much. Across the narrow corridor, people are queuing for breakfast. There is the familiar clatter of cutlery, the smell of bacon and toast. Julia finds it all strangely reassuring. It's so ordinary, so crammed with the busyness of just another day, with trays and clamour and teapots.

She settles herself into the comfortable armchair and takes ownership of the small table. If she sets up the laptop immediately, then people might be discouraged from coming anywhere near her. She has a moment's misgiving as she unzips the case. She's already broken her one cardinal rule, not once but twice: to speak to no one, engage with no one. She hopes that her friendly greeting at the toll-booth will not turn out to be a mistake. That, and talking to Yellow Jacket. Even now, she's aware of how potent, how memorable a force anxiety is – and she was certainly anxious after she'd driven the car aboard the ferry, anxious and stumbling. She's never liked boats; she prefers to have her feet on the ground. That aside, she's going to have to learn to be more contained, more circumspect, if she is to pull this off successfully.

Julia waits now for the laptop screen to come to life. She sees that her battery will probably last for the duration of the journey, but decides to charge it anyway. She plugs it into the wall-socket to the left of the table and opens up the one yellow folder on her desktop: '27th October 2009. D-day.' D for Departure. A dull day, the twenty-seventh: one lacking in any sort of anticipation. The one *after* the Bank Holiday, after all the fun; after whatever it is that's going to happen has already happened. She reflects that deciding on today's date has been really difficult. When she'd started searching first, every day had had some sort of unwelcome significance clinging to it. A birthday, an anniversary, the anniversary of a birthday, or the day when something resonant had happened in the past. Meaning could have been forced upon her choice, yoked to it in retrospect, when all that Julia really sought was an unremarkable day, a day as insignificant as any other.

She looks around her. So far, so good. The breakfast trays have stayed in the restaurant area, the tables are filling up and emptying quickly. There is now only one additional couple in the lounge, middle-aged, the man already stretched out on the vinyl-upholstered seating, arms folded across his chest. His companion is impatient, speaking into her mobile phone, cross at whatever she is hearing. Julia keeps her head down and focuses on the screen in front of her. She could have taken the boat to Liverpool, or Holyhead, could have driven down the coast road from home to Dún Laoghaire, or across the toll-bridge to North Wall. Closer, easier: but also too close, too easy. That's where they will go looking for her first. Larne will grant her a couple of extra days' grace. Nobody will suspect she has travelled North: into alien, almost forbidden territory. Cairnryan to Carlisle will give her a couple more. And then the train from Carlisle to London a couple more still. Just enough to make sure she is free and clear.

Julia looks again at her plans, checks the distance by road from the ferry port at Cairnryan to Carlisle – a journey she already knows by heart. She opens up the file that shows a detailed section of Carlisle city centre, one that enlarges all the small veins that lead to and from the railway station. She already knows where she'll be leaving the car. The station offers long-term parking and she has bought two weeks' worth on the Internet. But you never can tell: something might go wrong, like last time. A few weeks back, when she'd done a dry run, a rogue digger had forced her to take an unaccustomed right turn, and then she was done for. She'd got herself into a tangle of side streets that twisted back and forth and turned against her mischievously. She could hear William's voice inside her head urging her to think, think: but to no avail. Getting hopelessly lost when she drives is Julia's default setting. If anything like that happens again, she has a backup plan; if *that* fails, she will simply abandon ship. She has already practised the removal of her number plates, can do it in the dark. And one way or the other, she's out of there and onto the afternoon train for London. Sorcha doesn't know it yet, but she is about to get a visit.

That reminds Julia. She reaches into the pocket of her rucksack and pulls out the new UK SIM, still inserted into the original cardboard wallet for safe keeping. She takes her mobile from the front pocket of her jeans and swaps over the two SIMs, making sure to keep her fingers well away from the sensitive, technological bits. She stows the cardboard wallet back in the rucksack again and pulls the zip securely across the pocket. Then she switches on the mobile and opens up her Contacts. Sorcha's is the first name there. Sorcha O'Sullivan. It will be strange to see her again, like this. Julia hopes she's home, hopes that Sorcha—

Suddenly, there is a piercing wail from somewhere down to the left. A child's cry, full of pain and terror. There is commotion, the sound of running feet, of people shouting. Julia leaps to her feet, grabbing her rucksack as she does so. She stops for a second, glancing down at her laptop. What if someone . . . ? There is another scream and she flees. If it's stolen, it's stolen.

She races towards the source of the noise, pushes her way through the large knot of people. 'Let me through, please, I'm a doctor.' She slips on authority like a white coat. The knot unravels before her and she moves smoothly through the throng to the gaming-machine area, where a child is sprawled, his head in his distraught mother's lap. The room is now an Aladdin's cave of flashing lights and discordant beepings: all the machines are on, and the music is loud in the background. Julia sees the high chrome stools and realizes that this small boy has just taken a tumble. Right now, his legs are kicking out in pain and he is shrieking, fighting his mother with both arms flailing.

Julia instantly recognizes the spiky hair – it's the child who'd waved at her so mischievously from the window of the bus. His young mother is pressing down on what looks to be a nasty gash above his right eye, but the blood keeps on seeping through her fingers. 'It's okay, sweetie, it's okay,' she keeps saying. 'You're going to be fine.' Someone passes her tissues, a glass of ice. Julia reaches her, puts one hand on her shoulder. 'I'm a doctor,' she says. Her palm on the woman's shoulder makes her turn to look at Julia, her eyes bright and terrified. Julia holds the eye contact for a moment. 'You're right, he will be fine,' she says. 'Now, just take your hand away and let me have a look.'

Reluctantly, the woman does as she's told.

'Okay, you can put your hand back now. Can somebody get me a cold compress, please?' Julia calls into the crowd. 'More cold water and a towel – or anything at all.' She turns back to the trembling mother beside her.

'What's your boy's name?' she asks, above the shrieking child. 'Keep the pressure on there, don't be afraid.' She's already reached into the belly of her rucksack and pulled out her emergency first-aid kit. 'Can someone turn down that music, please?' she calls over one shoulder.

'Andrew,' the mother says, between sobs.

Once Julia opens the first-aid kit she can feel the crowd behind her begin to relax. She pulls on a pair of latex gloves and smiles down at Andrew, who has begun to calm a little and is watching her, blue eyes fearful, tears trembling on his lower lashes. Suddenly, the music dies and the silence is sudden, grateful. Even the gaming machines seem quieter.

'Has he lost consciousness at all?'

The mother shakes her head. 'No.'

'Hi, Andrew,' Julia says, 'now that we can hear ourselves think. I'm Dr Harris and I'm going to take a look at that forehead of yours.'

What have I done? she wonders. Harris is the name that has leapt into her head and onto her tongue without warning: it is William's name. She feels a surge of anger at herself, along with the creeping sense of dismay that follows in its wake. How could she have been so stupid, so careless? At a time when it matters most, she has drawn William closer to her, appropriating his name, implicating him in the very way she has been desperate to avoid. William, who needs to be protected. Julia forces herself to concentrate. Self-recrimination will have to wait.

'Do you prefer to be called Andrew or Andy?' She begins to probe at the gash on the child's forehead. It is nasty: and there is always the possibility of concussion. She looks into his eyes, smiling all the while. The pupils are equal. 'I have a friend who prefers "Andy",' she goes on. 'What about you?'

At least four stitches, she thinks. She'll have to get him out of here to somewhere she can attend to him properly. The boy begins to wail again and snatches Julia's hand away. Just then, she feels a touch on her elbow.

'Doctor? I'm James Murdoch, ship's officer. We have full first-aid facilities on board. Is it okay to move this young man?'

'Give me another minute,' Julia says, pressing a wad of gauze down onto the cut. The child has already lost quite a bit of blood. 'Can you hold this in place, nice and firmly?' she says to the mother, who is now weeping quietly. 'Don't be afraid to apply pressure – it's not going to hurt him. And don't worry. The blood makes it look a lot worse than it actually is.'

The woman nods, biting down hard on her lower lip.

'Andrew? Are you hurting anywhere else?' Julia begins to raise the child's arms, one after the other. She runs her fingers over the crown of his head, then down the back of his neck.

'My knee,' he sobs. 'My knee hurts.'

Julia pulls up his trouser legs and checks his knees and ankles. The knees are both grazed – old injuries, nothing too serious. 'You're being very brave,' she says. 'And you're very lucky. You haven't broken anything, you've just hurt your knees in the fall. But you've a cut on your forehead, and I expect you have a great big headache beginning. Am I right?'

He nods again.

'Okay,' says Julia, briskly. 'Here's what we're going to do, Andrew. Officer Murdoch here has a special room where I can look after that cut on your forehead and make you better. We'll go there now, with your mum, of course. And I'll need you to keep on being brave for another while. Is that okay?'

He nods 'yes' and Julia keeps watching his eyes, his colour, his face for any trace of sleepiness, any change of expression. 'Okay, then. Let's go.'

Officer Murdoch stoops and lifts the child off the floor. Julia's breath catches. He is older than Jamie, of course – this child must be five, at least – but there is something about his khaki combat trousers, his trainers with lights flashing at the heels, that makes Jamie's presence here almost palpable.

Officer Murdoch strides ahead of them, Andrew resting easily across his arms. Julia turns to the child's mother, whose face is streaked with tears. She pulls off the latex gloves and holds her hand out. 'I'm Jane Harris,' she says. The lie comes more easily this time. She notices, too, that the crowd has been dispersed. Julia and the distraught young mother are now walking side by side down the narrow corridor, and so she is the only person listening this time. Perhaps things are not so serious after all.

The woman takes Julia's hand in both of hers. 'Nice to meet you, Dr Harris. I'm very glad you were here. Thank you so much for your help.'

'Not at all,' Julia smiles. 'I could keep on calling you Andrew's mum, but I'd rather not, on balance.'

The woman smiles back suddenly and looks years younger. Julia can see her son's extraordinary resemblance to her. 'Sorry,' she says, 'I'm Lucy Molloy.' Her eyes never leave her son. 'Will he be okay?'

Lucy. Julia feels her breath catch. She has a vivid memory, a light shining in her eyes. Lucy, who'd never had the chance to become a mother. She nods, blinking away the images that threaten to blind her. 'He'll be absolutely fine. Come and see.'

Lucy follows Julia into the Quiet Lounge, where Officer Murdoch has just laid Andrew, very gently, on one of the reclining seats. Julia wonders how he's managed to evict all the Quiet Passengers so quickly. She turns to Lucy. 'Sit beside him there for a moment, till we take a look at this forehead. The bleeding has eased, but there's bound to be a fair bit of bruising.' Julia pulls on another pair of latex gloves, smiling down at Andrew, who is beginning to look a little less terrified. She can already guess how his story might be taking shape, how this will be an adventure back in the school yard, with Andrew the hero, the nice lady doctor a bit-player in his personal drama.

She nods at him, her face serious. 'You are going to have a right shiner, young man. A really fabulous black eye. Well, a black-and-blue eye. Would you like that?'

Andrew looks at her. 'Will I be able to play football?'

'Certainly,' Julia affirms. 'Just maybe not tomorrow.' Quickly she assesses the damage. Four conventional stitches would do it, but the ferry's first-aid box offers her a choice of medical glues. 'We're going to try this,' she says to Andrew. 'We're going to stick your forehead back together again. Magic! And it doesn't hurt a bit. You'll have to stay pretty quiet for the rest of the day, though. No more running around.'

'We've lots of books,' Lucy interjects. 'Andrew's a great man for the stories, aren't you, Andrew?'

He nods, but his eyes never leave Julia's face. She patches him up, glancing every now and then at his pupils. 'Are you going on holiday?' she asks. Lucy shakes her head, her lip trembling again.

'No,' she says. 'I'm bringing Andrew over to visit his dad. We'll be going back home again in a few days.'

Julia looks at her. 'He'll be fine. He fell off a stool. It was an accident. Just make sure, if he seems drowsy or nauseated, to get him to Casualty straight away. And you can give him some Calpol if his head hurts.' Julia pulls off the gloves and bins them. She sprays sanitizer on her hands and replaces the bottle in her kit. She has deliberately looked away from Lucy for a moment, seeing how the young woman's face has suddenly begun to crumple. 'Kids fall over, Lucy. It's what they do.'

Lucy holds onto Andrew's hand. 'Yes,' she says. 'I know that. I only turned my back for a moment. I don't know how he managed to climb up so fast. It's just – his dad won't see it like that.'

For a moment Julia is tempted. Then she stops herself. She cannot get embroiled here. She turns to the little boy instead.

'Half an hour here, Andrew, lying down quietly beside your mum. Then come and see me again. I think I saw some deadly puzzle books in the shop.' *Deadly.* Jamie's word. That and *wicked.* Everything that was wonderful in his small life was contained in those two words of praise. Julia can see that Andrew understands. 'You can choose whichever one you like,' she promises. 'Is that a plan?'

He half-smiles at her. Jamie's smile. 'Yeah,' he says. 'It's a plan.'

'Good man.' Julia reaches for her kit. She looks over at Lucy. 'Can I bring you back a cup of tea or coffee?'

Lucy shakes her head. 'No, thanks,' she says. 'Don't think I could take anything just yet. I'm grand.'

Julia squeezes her arm. 'He'll be grand, too. I think he bounces.' Lucy smiles. 'I'll be in the passenger area, over in the right-hand corner. Look for me behind the laptop, if you need me. And bring him to see me before we dock.' She turns to Andrew. ''Cos he and I have some shopping to do.'

'We will. Thank you, Dr Harris.'

For a moment Julia is startled, then she smiles. 'You're welcome.' She waves to the little boy as she closes the door of the Quiet Lounge behind her. He waves back. Quickly she makes her way back to where she's been sitting.

As she turns the corner, Julia relaxes. The laptop is there, just as she left it. Unlikely that anything would happen in these circumstances, but you never can tell. She's learned that most thieves are opportunists. She checks her watch. Almost an hour to go. She feels agitated. Maybe this wasn't the cleverest route. Maybe a quick Ryanair getaway direct from Dublin would have been better after all, more anonymous. And how could she have used William's name like that? Pulling him closer, when more and more distance is what he needs. She hopes he will not come looking for her immediately. She needs this time to make him safe. Melissa will be fine – she has Derek and the children. It is William she needs to worry about. She wakes up her laptop and begins to read through her files again. But she doesn't even see the print.

Besides, there is nothing new she needs to learn, nothing she has left undone.

# *William*

WILLIAM AND MELISSA are kept waiting at the Garda station. There is a man at the hatch, arguing loudly with the young recruit behind the desk. William wonders if he's drunk. And wonders further still at his audacity, if he is.

'I know where I parked it,' he's saying, jabbing one finger insistently in the air. 'And I'm telling you, it's not there. It's been stolen. Right from under *your* noses.' William can't hear what the Guard replies. All he knows is, he'd take the man's keys from him, tell him to go home and sober up and come back again in the morning. And then arrest him. Charge him with being drunk and disorderly. Or something. William feels angry on behalf of everyone waiting, particularly himself. Just then an older Guard emerges and leads the man, still protesting, to another room. When he closes the door behind them, a strange, unquiet silence descends on those who are waiting. Besides William and Melissa, there are three other people lined up on the hard bench just inside the door. A woman, who has now begun to weep, stifling her sobs with a handkerchief. Two men: one young, one old. William can hear Melissa's sharp intake of breath. She is not used to being kept waiting.

'Next,' the Guard calls, and the weeping woman approaches the hatch. William wonders what has brought her here. He feels sympathy begin to well up from underneath his increasing irritation: there is something profoundly sad and vulnerable beneath the trembling blue shoulders of her coat. And at least she's quiet. Her voice is a hoarse whisper, and William becomes uncomfortably aware that the people around her – including himself – are straining to hear what she is saying. More than ever, he wants to go home.

But he'll stick it out. Not because he thinks anything can be achieved by reporting that Julia is missing, but because he is already resentful of what Melissa is likely to say about him. He is afraid that he is going to be painted as an ogre, the man from whom her mother desperately needed to escape – look at the evidence! – and he is determined to stay, to fight his corner. The young man at the end of the bench gets up and offers Melissa his seat. She takes it, with a smile that is almost Julia's.

'Thank you,' she says. 'You're very kind.'

William is relieved. With that sort of distance between them, any further conversation is now impossible.


Finally they are summoned to the hatch, where the young Guard has a huge ledger open in front of him. Despite himself, William is amused. There is a computer screen flickering in the corner, with nobody in front of it. Here, at the old-fashioned hatch, it's old-fashioned business as usual.

'Name?' he asks, looking from Melissa to William.

'Melissa Robinson,' she says. 'It's about my mother. She's disappeared.' She sounds terse. She doesn't look at William or acknowledge his presence in any way. She stands four-square in front of the hatch, and he has the distinct impression that he has just been elbowed out of the way.

'What's your mother's name?' The young man looks at her sympathetically, but, as yet, makes no attempt to write anything down.

'Dr Julia Seymour.'

'And her age?'

'Fifty-nine, sixty in November.'

He nods, making a note of it. 'And when did you see her last?'

Melissa hesitates.

'Monday morning,' William intervenes. 'I left her around ten o'clock, and she was fine.'

The Guard swivels his head to look at William. Reluctantly Melissa edges out of the way a little so that his view is unobstructed. 'And you are?'

'William Harris, Julia's partner.'

'As in . . .'

'Life partner,' he says firmly. He can feel Melissa bristle.

'My mother would never do anything like this,' she says. Her tone is insistent, but she has lowered her voice. 'There must be something wrong, something I don't know about. It's not like her, not like her at all. She would never just . . . *disappear.*'

Melissa has taken hold of the word at its four corners, shaken it out like a tablecloth. It falls into the sudden silence, white and whispery. She has pushed her way in front of William again, and when she says 'something I don't know about' – with a glancing emphasis on the 'I' – he is aware of how she half-turns in his direction. By the time she has finished speaking, accusation fills the air around him like smoke. William hears the break in her voice, but can't summon any fellow-feeling. In fact, he can hardly summon any feeling at all. Even the top of his head feels numb, and the tips of his fingers. And his feet. Is it shock? He wonders for a moment at that: extremes of feeling, freezing the body's extremities.

'What's your mother's address?' the Guard continues. He looks quickly at William, his eyelids flickering. He writes what Melissa tells him, his script slow and laborious. 'And what makes you think she's missing, rather than just . . . gone away for a little while, for a break, like?'

'She has *not* "gone away for a little while".' Melissa's anger is palpable. 'This is not about a *break*. The house has been completely stripped of anything personal. Her laptop is gone. Her clothes are gone. *All* of her clothes are gone.'

The Guard is beginning to look alarmed. 'If this is a case of robbery . . .'

Melissa sighs and William tries to turn the volume down a bit. 'There is no sign of a robbery,' he says. 'The whole thing looks planned, deliberate. The problem is – we don't know why. Or if she went of her own volition.' He adds in that last bit as it occurs to him. He can almost guess what the Guard is thinking. That, in Julia's place, he might want to get away from Melissa himself. And perhaps from her 'life partner', too: a gangling idiot, standing there with his mouth opening and closing like a goldfish.

'Are there other family members you can call? Friends?' He looks at each of them in turn. His expression is hopeful. William wonders if he is completely out of his depth, a new small-fry flailing and flapping about in a very big pool. He wants to put an end to this, and soon.

'Yes,' he says. 'Yes, of course. We just wanted you to know our concern first. We'll contact everyone we can think of and get back to you.'

'And hospitals,' the Guard offers. 'In case she hasn't been . . . feeling well.' And he glances at Melissa, who right now is pulling her mobile from her bag.

At that moment William sees her through the young policeman's eyes. Worried, confused, angry: showing all the normal reactions of someone threatened with loss, someone already grieving. What must they think about him? He knows that he appears calm, measured, apparently accepting. He feels a sharp stab of sympathy for Melissa. 'Thank you,' he says now, taking her firmly by the elbow. The door to the station crashes open just then and a huge, towering figure in blue ushers in a young man with blood streaming from his forehead.

'Ya cunt! Ya fuckin' cunt!' the injured man screams, his voice pitched high and brittle with something other than rage. His captor's face is grim. The injured man kicks out at him, one arm waving wildly, and a scuffle begins.

'Come on, Melissa,' says William. 'Let's get out of here. We can come back again tomorrow.' Everyone else in the station seems to have frozen; even the air has stilled. And he steers her out through the swing door, reminded for a bizarre moment of the swinging doors in all the saloons of all those westerns he's watched down the years. He's grateful for the fracas, the foul language, the all-too-vivid glimpse of a Dublin underworld that Melissa has probably never even imagined. The shock makes her silent, makes her go with him willingly enough – or, at least, without visible protest.

Outside, the cold air hits him like a smack. He starts to shiver. He sees Melissa wipe at her eyes furtively. 'Are you okay?' he asks, with a gentleness he doesn't feel.

'Yes,' she wipes across her nose with the back of one expensive leather glove. The word sounds strangled.

'Are you okay to drive, or would you like me to call Derek?'

She glares at him again. 'I'm fine,' she says. 'They didn't take me seriously. I'm going to come back again tomorrow.'

William nods, suddenly tired. 'Sure,' he says. 'And in the meantime, let's make those calls, to anyone we can think of.' Including hospitals, he adds silently. He'll do those by himself. 'Talk again tomorrow? We can pool our resources when we've had time to think.'

'Yes,' she says, stiffly. 'You have my number.' And she walks away from him.

William watches her go. The challenge in her departure tells him she won't be contacting him any time soon. He waits until she is safely in her car, watches as she indicates and turns in the direction of home.

Then he walks to the other end of the car park, postponing all feeling until he is sitting safely in his own driver's seat, inside his own car, in control of his own space.


William starts to shake just as soon as he slams shut the driver's door. He has held it together all evening, something that, on reflection, he's not all that sure he's proud of. But he's kept hearing Julia's voice, her words resounding inside his skull, reminding him over and over again never to rise to Melissa's bait. 'You know what she's like. Spends her life spoiling for a fight,' Julia would say, shaking her head. 'Just walk away from it.' He remembers the way the young Guard's eyes had seemed to sympathize with her. Or maybe he'd just been trying to keep the peace. He wouldn't have seen her hostility, of course: only her natural concern for her missing mother.

William begins to feel that nobody has really seen *him* today – apart from Mrs Mc, whose kindness he had brushed off. Melissa has hardly let him speak, has spoken to him only in the tone of contempt that used to make her mother sigh.

'She's a malcontent,' Julia had said to him on the day she'd introduced him to her daughter, her only child. 'Just remember that. Forewarned is forearmed.' They'd met for coffee, the three of them, at Bewley's in Grafton Street. William had thought that the hour would never end. He'd been glad that Julia had warned him what to expect. Even so, he'd been taken aback at Melissa's abrasiveness. 'Everybody else has it better than she does,' Julia had said, afterwards, 'and everyone deserves nothing but con- tempt *because* they have it better than she does. Go figure.'

He starts the car and sits very still for a few moments, waiting for the windscreen to clear, waiting for his head to clear, because he knows that he is capable of all kinds of recklessness right now. Today is a meteorite that has slammed into his life from the skies of the future, something he could never have been prepared for. He grips the steering wheel, trying not to see Julia in the tall, uniformed woman who now crosses the car park and gets into one of the waiting squad cars. He backs out of his parking space, carefully. He makes sure not to let the rage leach from the soles of his feet onto the accelerator. All he wants now is to get away from these leafy Southside streets, to go back towards the sea, back to where he grew up. To somewhere he can breathe. Suburban streets, no matter how tree-lined and well lit, always make him feel claustrophobic. It's Howth, he wants. Howth and home.

As he pulls out onto the main road, he keeps a watchful eye on his speed. There is still a lot of anger around his knees, which have been trembling ever since he left the Garda station. He feels as though his body is defrosting: all the earlier numbness is being replaced by a feeling of dislocation. It's as though he has been breathing, talking, walking several steps behind himself. He can't keep up: can't inhabit himself any more.

'What's happening to you, Julia?' he says aloud. He is used to her sitting beside him, checking his speed, chiding him every so often when his mind drifts and the needle begins to climb without him noticing. William stops himself. He will not think about her until he gets home. 'Focus,' he tells himself. 'Think about anything else but her. Just get yourself home in one piece. Leave Julia till later.'

*

William parks in the grounds of the apartment. He feels dizzy with relief: home at last. Only then does he realize he hasn't eaten since breakfast. He'll have to have something to quell the growing nausea, although he'd prefer a stiff whiskey. He takes the stairs to his flat, rather than use the lift. Conversation with any of his neighbours is not to be contemplated, no matter how polite. In fact, *particularly* if polite. Because right now William would prefer to shout at someone, to slam his fist through a wall.

He opens his front door and drops his coat onto an armchair. The brightly coloured throw that rests across the back of the sofa makes him stop in his tracks. Julia brought it back to him from India, almost exactly three years ago: electric colours of blue, lime green, saffron. Small fish-eyes of sequins that catch the light. She'd said that he needed a bit of colour in his life: that his apartment was too bare, too functional. Too *male*? he'd repeated, teasing her. Her gift had made him absurdly happy. Somehow, it had seemed to say that she intended spending a lot of time with him. That where he lived, she'd live, too.

Back then, they'd been together only a few months. Julia had gone away with Roisin on a long-planned odyssey to Mumbai, Chennai, Delhi. Her retirement gift to herself, she'd told him. Something spur-of-the-moment had developed into months of planning, devouring guidebooks, even cooking Indian food. Roisin was the seasoned traveller, she'd told him – perfect company for a neophyte like herself. He'd watched her go, regretfully, and missed her with an intensity that had taken him by surprise. In the month that she'd been away he'd grown to realize that what he felt for her was real, significant. On her return, he'd told her he loved her. 'I don't want to waste time. I'm way too old to be playing games. I want you to know how I feel about you.' They'd been together ever since, inseparable ever since, sharing two lives and two homes.

Three years later, William knows that he has waited long enough, patiently enough, to be sure that Julia will say 'yes' when he asks her to marry him. He's already bought the ring: an antique sapphire and diamond twist that she'd admired on one of their lazy-browsing afternoons, a few months ago. He'd gone back to the shop, secretly, a couple of hours after she'd seen it. It rests now in the small black box in the small black safe at the bottom of his wardrobe. All that future crammed into such tiny spaces, awaiting Julia's birthday on the tenth of November.

But now, she has gone and he's missed his chance. He regrets that, bitterly. Perhaps if he'd asked her a year ago, a month ago, this would never have happened. Not for the first time, he curses his own reticence.

William makes his way across the large living room and stands at his window, looking out at the quiet heave of the sea. The moon is full and high and the waves swell and fall under its buttery glow. Almost at once he can feel himself becoming calmer. That's what the sea does to him: the movement somehow soothes the rhythm of his heart. 'Where are you, Julia?' he asks out loud. And then: 'Did I do something to drive you away?'

Or is it someone else, some other man maybe, that he knows nothing about? Has she run away with someone else – or even from someone else? William shakes his head. Too simple, he thinks. Too not like Julia. She's tough when she needs to be, uncompromising, honest. She'd have told him if she didn't love him any more. The queen on their shared chessboard is his only clue. Something has made Julia feel off-balance, somehow out of place in her own life.

He moves away from the window and goes into the kitchen.

Rummaging in the cupboards, he finds only a couple of cans of baked beans, some crackers, some brown bread that has seen better days. It'll have to do. He was to cook at Julia's tonight – pasta with cream and fresh salmon. On a normal Wednesday, he'd have walked down the pier, bought his fish and then . . . He shakes the thought away. This is no longer a normal Wednesday. He pulls the toaster towards him and slides in two wilting pieces of bread. Then he heats up the beans in the microwave. While he waits, he pours the large measure of whiskey that has been beckoning to him ever since he left Melissa. He hopes that it will loosen the knot of grief that has been gathering in his chest all day. Loosen it, release it, and leave in its place something to make hope take root more firmly.

The toast pops and he carries his food back into the living room. Everywhere – even his own home – has begun to feel eerily silent and still, as though it knows that Julia is missing. Missing here, there, everywhere. He forces himself to eat, and takes a large gulp of whiskey at the same time. He doesn't feel that he can swallow without it.

Sitting there, he allows himself to remember her on the first evening they'd met. It's the memory that has been hurting at him all day, insisting that he unfold it, open out its pleats, regard all the glittering contents spread before him. He can't postpone it any longer. He finishes the whiskey and pours another. He is reminded of his grandfather's wake: men drinking whiskey like this, one after the other, women saying the rosary. He resents the memory, the comparison, and pushes it away. This is *not* a wake. Julia is alive and active and in control. She is *not* dead, he thinks fiercely. She is missing: missing and dead are *not* the same thing. Not the same thing at all. He can see her face on that first night, her lively eyes, her fashionably cut hair. Jack had insisted that he come to dinner. 'Celine is doing my head in. She says it's ages since we've seen you. She wants you to stop being a hermit.' William had given in gracefully.

Even then, prepared to be really honest with himself, he'd admitted that the invitation had come at a very good time. He had just begun to feel the need for change. Nothing he could put his finger on: just a vague sense of dissatisfaction. It took the form of a restlessness, a jagged edginess that often woke him with a start around four o'clock in the morning and refused to let him sleep again. He'd had the feeling that his life was straining at the seams, that all the familiarity he'd become accustomed to was suddenly no longer able to contain him. He'd begun to sleep for a couple of hours in the afternoon, instead, when the bleariness of his vision and the low level throbbing of an almost, but-not-quite headache became too much to put up with. Now that had unnerved him. 'I'm like my bloody grandfather – he took to the bed in his sixties and more or less slept the rest of his life away. I'm scaring myself, Jack.'

Jack had looked at him keenly. 'How's the writing going?'

'It's boring me,' William had confessed. He'd surprised himself with that admission: he hadn't known he felt that way. 'To be truthful, I think I'm boring *myself*. I can't be arsed with villains and police procedure – thrillers just aren't thrilling me any more.'

'Company,' Celine interjected. 'You need company, Will.' She had the knack of entering a conversation in the same way that she entered a room. She always picked up instantly on whatever Jack and William were discussing.

'Listening at doors again, dear?' Jack asked.

'I don't need to,' she said. 'You two are transparent enough already. I don't need to skulk around corners to find out what's going on.'

And so, on the appointed Friday evening, William walked to Jack and Celine's house, about halfway up the hill, a huge bunch of lilies under one arm, two bottles of wine under the other.

'Knocking with your knees, I see,' Jack grinned at him as he opened the front door. 'Come on in.'

Julia was there already, sitting on the sofa along with Billy and Erica, whom William had met before, at some of Celine and Jack's casual, good-humoured dinner parties. She turned to look at him as he came into the room and smiled. Her whole face seemed to be illuminated: as though she had a light under her skin. She regarded him with frank curiosity. William wondered whether they'd been talking about him before he arrived. He felt a jolt of attraction the minute he saw her smile. Bolt of lightning, he told her afterwards. I was smitten from the first moment I saw you.

She extended one long hand to him. 'Pleased to meet you, William,' she said. It seemed that everyone was pleased with everyone else that night. The evening lifted and lightened at once, the conversation became more animated, the laughter frequent. William was aware of a sudden rush of panic when he realized, sometime around one in the morning, that it was all over. He saw, out of the corner of his eye, the way that Celine was grinning at him in delight.

Julia looked shocked when she saw the time. 'Oh, I didn't realize—' she began and Jack interrupted.

'Sign of a good time, Julia – told you it was too long since we'd seen you.'

She smiled at him. 'You're a bad influence, Jack. Richard always used to say so.'

*Richard always used to say so.* William listened intently to her use of the past tense. He thought – hoped – throughout the evening that she was divorced, or separated, or in some way, any way at all, a free agent. The silence that followed her remark was not exactly awkward, but it was a resonant one. William realized that she must be a widow. Almost ashamed of himself, he felt relief flood him – along with hope. He would have pursued her anyway, he had already decided that, but this was a cleaner, less complicated way than he could have hoped.

Then her taxi arrived, and Billy and Erica got up to leave at the same time, and suddenly, after goodbyes and nice-to-meet-yous and handshakes, William was on his own in the living room. Celine and Jack were crowding at the narrow front door, waving goodbye to their departing guests.

'Nightcap?' Jack asked, rubbing his hands together as he came back into the room. He pointed to the bottle of Rémy Martin on the sideboard.

William nodded. 'Why not?' He felt deflated, now that she'd gone. And irritated at himself. Why hadn't he done something? Even walked her to the door, shown her some degree of interest. He'd always been the same: tongue-tied, suddenly and stupidly shy when it mattered most.

Celine followed Jack to the sideboard and rummaged for a moment in the top drawer. Then she handed William a piece of paper torn from a spiral notebook. 'Take it,' she said. 'It's Julia's number. She liked you.'

He stared at it, taken aback. 'What?' His eyes focused on the tiny bits of confetti still clinging whitely to the top of the page. He didn't even see the numbers, scrawled in Celine's confident hand.

Celine sighed. 'I know her. I'm telling you, she liked you.'

'Did she say that?' William looked up at her. He felt as though he was sixteen again, hanging around the back of the hall, too terrified to ask a girl to dance. He could still hear the jeers of the others around him, see the way they'd pull

on the fags shielded by nicotine-stained fingers. He was almost
too afraid to hope. Celine held his gaze.

'She didn't need to say anything. Trust me. We go back a
long way.'

For a moment William didn't know which was the stronger
emotion. Relief that he would see Julia again, or annoyance at
Celine making him feel transparent, reading his mind.

'You can tell her you asked me for it,' Celine said, eyes
mocking, innocent. There was the faintest shadow of a smile
around her mouth. 'She doesn't need to know that I like to
steal your thunder, from time to time.' Then she smiled, and
he forgave her. 'Just go for it, William. You've been on your
own far too long.'

William didn't reply to that. 'How do you know her?' he
asked instead, folding the piece of paper Celine had handed
him and putting it in his pocket. Curiosity was getting the
better of pique.

She jabbed her finger in her husband's direction. 'When
Jack worked with the medical supplies company, he met
Richard. We went out as a foursome, on and off, for a few
years.' Celine paused. 'Richard was a lovely guy. He died far
too young. Julia was devastated. She and I kept in touch.'

William wanted to ask what had happened to Richard, but
stopped himself. He had the absurd feeling that he might be
trespassing on Julia's privacy. There was that, and there was
also the small shot of jealousy across his bows that he wasn't
prepared to admit to at the time. 'Are you sure she's not . . .
involved with anyone else?'

'Positive.'

Jack interrupted. 'Don't even ask, William. Women know
these things. Celine certainly knows these things.' And he
grinned at his wife.

She shrugged at him and said airily, 'Yeah. We know these things. Imagine: we ask each other, and we tell each other. We *talk*. That's how we know these things.'

William called Julia the very next evening. The following weekend she came back to Howth, confessing that she'd never been in the harbour, or walked along the high wall of the pier towards the lighthouse. William thanked the gods of weather that the evening was a glorious one in mid-August. Julia had taken the Dart from the city centre and he met her at the station, his pulse racing as he watched her slow, confident walk along the platform. 'Hello,' she said, and kissed him on both cheeks. Immediately he felt it was going to be okay. His nervousness fizzled away and he returned her smile, a little lopsidedly.

'Great to see you,' he said, and meant it. 'Let me show you my domain. Usually, we like to keep it a secret from you southsiders.'

She slipped her arm through his. 'So I'm privileged, then.'

He pulled her closer to his side, delighting in her warmth, her friendliness. 'Better believe it.'

He brought her first along the pier, a bracing walk even in August. Finally they reached the harbour, the sun slanting on the water, the boat-rigging chinking in the swell. William had booked a table in the chic new restaurant beside the fishing boats. They sat at a table by the window and watched the greenly lit water lapping against the rocks below.

'This is so lovely,' she said. 'I didn't realize it would be so nice.'

Howth, or me? William wondered. But what he said was: 'You mean the north side?'

And she laughed. 'You're obviously the one with the complex. Not me.' Whatever she meant, it gave him hope. He liked the decisive way she ordered her meal that evening, chose the wine. She made everything easy.

And they talked. Without stopping, it seemed, for hours. She came back to the apartment with him, as he'd hoped, and it was there that she told him about Richard. That was the first time he heard Melissa's name, too, and saw the anguish that came with it even then.

'Richard died when Melissa was thirteen. He'd had a massive stroke and lingered for almost six months. It was agonizing. It was the last thing anyone would have expected. He was only fifty. And healthy. Didn't smoke, didn't drink, played golf, sailed.' She shook her head and William saw the disbelief still, the pain in her eyes. 'He couldn't speak, couldn't move. He must have hated having everything done for him, done *to* him.' Julia paused. 'He was so . . . stricken that he couldn't even rage properly.' William watched as she fought against tears. 'It was cruel. He was trapped, locked inside his own body. He'd just lie there and weep, silently. I really wish I could have done something to help him. It was such a difficult journey.'

Julia stops for a moment. William doesn't know what to say.

'Melissa idolized him. The rest of the world just hasn't measured up to him, I'm afraid.' Julia looked away. 'And she was furious at me, too. I was a doctor and I couldn't fix him. She raged enough for both of them. In Melissa's eyes, I had failed her father. Failed all of us. I think she still feels that way.' She looked steadily at William. 'She was a teenager venting her grief, I know that. But somehow, we've never been able to come back from that, she and I.' William took her hand. Julia's words made him feel, all over again, how he might have been a better father to Michael.

'And you have a son,' she said, as though she'd been reading his mind. Her face became composed again. William wanted to say something to her then about Richard, about Melissa, but opted instead for caution. Another time, he thought. Something felt very delicate, like a filament shimmering between them, and he didn't want to risk breaking it.

'Michael,' he said, pouring more coffee. 'His name is Michael. He went to Australia for a gap year fifteen years ago and never came back. His mother, Jan, and I had divorced and I don't think he was sure where home was. He's doing well, though, he's happy; we keep in touch.'

Liar, he thought, almost as soon as he said it. William was aware of how peripheral he had allowed Michael to become – to him, to his life – over the past five years. It was quite a shock: seeing his relationship with his own son through another person's eyes. What did he mean: 'We keep in touch'? Certainly not what Celine meant when she'd spoken about keeping in touch with Julia. William knew that he hadn't been much of a father recently, not even a long-distance one. Contact had all but tailed off between himself and Michael. He'd made one visit to Sydney, twelve years back, and after that, nothing. He had the sudden thought that perhaps his son had got fed up being the one to do all the running. Listening to Julia, William had a strong impulse to leap on a plane to Sydney right away, to put that right. Michael had invited him often enough.

'You're a free agent, Dad,' he used to say. 'And you can write your thrillers in Sydney the same way you can in Howth. The spare room is yours. Phone line, broadband. Even your own coffee-maker. Just say the word.'

He'd do it, William resolved, there and then. And soon. Maybe he'd even go there with Julia. Together. It was a nice word, rounded and solid and comforting. He felt suddenly grateful that he had a son who wanted him.

At eleven, Julia stood up to leave. 'Will you walk me to the Dart?' William felt disappointed. Their earlier conversation in the restaurant, and now the shift he'd felt happening between himself and Michael as he listened to her speak about her daughter, made him feel a deepening undertow of intimacy between them. It was something that he hadn't felt in a long time.

On impulse, he reached for her hand again. 'I don't want you to go,' he said, astonished at hearing his own words. The Silent One; William the Reticent; the Quiet Man. He'd heard them all, from Jack, from Celine. From Jan. But Julia's presence was enough to put words into his mouth. 'You need a girl,' his mother used to say, hands on her hips, pinny full of flour. 'To bring you out of your shell.'

Julia's hand was warm in his. 'I don't want to go, either,' she said, softly.

He pulled her closer and then her arms were around him. He kissed her, hardly able to believe his luck. Then he stumbled and they both ended up in a heap on the sofa, laughing. The kiss was the catalyst – or maybe it was the stumble that did it. Something loosened between them, something that blossomed into warmth and a strange familiarity. William felt as though he'd known her all his life, or had spent his life getting ready to know her. Julia stayed with him that night. They made love, tentatively at first.

'It's been a very long time for me, William. I had one kind of serious relationship about eight years ago, but it didn't work out.' She stopped. 'I haven't really been able to be with anyone properly since Richard.' She stroked his hair back from where it still fell across his forehead. 'I want to be here, with you. It feels right, but it also feels . . . strange.'

'Then we'll wait,' he said, 'until it feels right and not strange. We have all the time in the world. I have no intention of letting you get away from me.' Her skin was soft, warm, and he loved how she hugged him to her. There was trust in the way she held him. At first, William was afraid that the stern ghost of Richard might hover somewhere between them. He was careful of Julia, slow and tender.

Afterwards, she cried and he held her. 'It's not you, William, it's just . . .'

'It's okay,' he said. 'I don't take it personally. Grief still does that to me, from time to time. Lies in ambush where you least expect it.'

'Thank you,' she said, a little later, calm again. 'I don't know what I'd have done if you hadn't understood.'

He kissed her, suddenly filled with a delight that felt like music. There had been a test and he'd passed it. 'Champagne?' he said, pulling on his dressing gown. He'd bought a ridiculously expensive bottle earlier, filled with a heady anticipation that had made him feel youthful. He had hardly been able to admit to himself that he had bought it for exactly this moment.

She laughed. 'Absolutely! Bubbles at three in the morning! Such decadence.'

And he told her about Jan, about London, about life before he met her. A life that had now receded so completely that it felt like the shadow of a story he had once known. A story that had grown so familiar in the retelling that it had shed all its substance along the way: only the shape remained. The beginning, the middle, the ending.

'Do you still miss her?'

William shook his head. 'No. By the time she left, Jan and I had been kind of . . . missing each other for years. We'd just drifted apart. Ships in the night, that sort of thing. With Michael grown, it was as though the last bit of glue that held us together just sort of dissolved. Nothing dramatic happened – things just weren't right any more, and there was nothing left to distract us from noticing.' William refilled their glasses, delighting in the two of them, naked, propped up against the pillows of his bed. It felt as though Julia brought with her another life, another chance for him to get things right at last. 'I have to say – even though it didn't feel like it at the time – Jan had a lot more courage than I did. She was the one to call it a day. And part of me was relieved: it meant I didn't have the responsibility to do it.'

'That's honest. But it can't be nice to be left.'

William shrugged. 'No, and I wallowed for quite a while. But time on my own showed me that I'd have been prepared to lurch along forever, letting life slip past, day by day. Routine can be comforting like that. Safe, unremarkable. I was well on my way to becoming one of those old and disappointed men sitting in a corner somewhere. Leading a life of quiet desperation – isn't that the phrase?'

'I was lucky,' Julia said. 'I fell for Richard during my first term at university. He was one of my teachers – he was a good ten years older and we all looked up to him, all of the medical students. He was inspirational. I couldn't believe my luck when we got together.'

'Lucky for both of you, then,' William said, feeling an unworthy wave of jealousy that ebbed and flowed with Julia's words. 'After all, he got you.'

She smiled. 'We had a very happy marriage.' She paused, her face clouding over. 'Life can be very brutal. Suddenly, he was gone and I had to learn how to cope alone. And then there was my poor, grieving, angry daughter.'

William reached for her, pulling her close to him, facing her. 'This is another chance, for both of us. I will do everything in my power to make you happy.'

They made love again and, this time, she didn't cry. William shivers now as he remembers. She'd held onto him, kissing him, pulling him closer. 'You know, I feel as though I've just come home. This feels so peaceful. I'm glad I stayed.'

They slept, curled like spoons. He'd never been able to sleep like this with Jan: it had felt awkward, knees and elbows in all the wrong places. But with Julia, they fitted each other easily, sleepily.

William decided to take that as a good omen.

They woke late the following morning, he just a few moments earlier than Julia. He checked at once to make sure she was still there, fearful that he might have dreamt her. He watched her sleep, was still watching her when she opened her eyes and smiled at him. 'Good morning,' she said. There was something almost shy in the deep blue of her gaze.

'Yes, it is: it's a very good morning. Best morning I've had in many years. It's wonderful to have you here,' he said. 'I was afraid I might have imagined last night.'

'Well, if you did, then we've imagined each other. That could be handy: like a genie in a bottle. We can conjure each other up whenever we want to.'

William raised the blind and August sunlight streamed in the bedroom window. 'And just look at the day you've magicked along with you.' The sea rustled and glowed beneath them.

'You are a sweet man,' she said. 'It's nice waking up beside you.'

Joy was what he felt, William decided, as he made breakfast to bring to Julia on a tray. He went out and got the works: fresh croissants, *pains au chocolat*, newly ground coffee. And a single rose for the slim, cut-glass vase that he had never used before. He pulled it out from the back of the cabinet, dusty and unfamiliar. One of Jan's treasures that had somehow ended up in his resentfully packed boxes. But he was glad of it now. Even his apartment felt different to him on that morning. Strangely bright and calm, complete, as though something that had been missing had finally been found.

They walked across the headland at midday, had lunch in one of the sophisticated new restaurants along the pier. He pointed out to Julia where he used to work when he was a teenager. 'That restaurant there,' he said. 'The new one – it's not open for business yet. Used to be where you could buy fish straight from the boats.'

'A fishmonger's,' she said and William laughed.

'Nothing nearly as posh as that. Just a space, with a marble slab for a counter. A callow youth, I was. The others used to take the piss out of me – I was the youngest by far.' And they peered in the window together. 'The counter was there – if you can call it that . . .' William gestured over to his right, 'And the fish boxes were stored over there, when it was a kind of open yard.'

'What do you remember most?' she asked.

'The cold,' he said, at once. 'Cold stone, cold weather and bloody freezing water. And the mackerel. Tons and tons of mackerel. Haven't eaten it since. All those guts must have got to me.'

The mobile rings.

William is startled. It takes a moment for him to untangle his thoughts, knotted around the past like fishing line. He is yanked, flailing and writhing, back to the present, back to his still and empty apartment, back to his still and empty life. He glances at the screen before answering. Even before he reads her name, he knows it's Melissa. The knowledge makes a shifting feeling in his stomach. Beans and whiskey and bile don't go too well together.

'Melissa,' he says.

'Have you made any calls yet?'

'No,' says William, feeling guilty. There is accusation in her tone. 'I'm making a list,' he offers. Silence greets this, and he curses himself for making excuses. 'What about you?'

'Derek and I have phoned every hospital we can think of,' she says. 'There's no record of Mum anywhere. Or of anybody matching her description. I just thought you should know, in case you were thinking of calling. I've left my mobile number with all of them. If I hear anything, I'll let you know.'

'Thank—' William begins, but she cuts him off.

'I have to go now, Susie's crying.' And she's gone.

William sighs. And then he recalls what he'd been remembering before the phone rang. Julia on his arm, Julia across a table from him, Julia in his bed. He is filled with something raw and hot and hollow. His eyes prickle and he weeps hoarsely, unable to stem the tide any longer. That first weekend together becomes luminous with his remembering. He knows what he has lost. Where Julia used to be there is a gaping hole, an open wound, made all the more painful because he doesn't know the *why* of it. Melissa can give him all the grief she likes – spoken and unspoken – William knows that he made Julia happy. Or, at least, that Julia had been happy when she was with him. Whatever it is she is running from, it's not from him.

The realization seems to energize him. He paces the floor of the apartment, thinking, remembering, trying to find resonances in their last, affectionate meetings. He pulls a notebook from his desk and decides to list the names of everyone that Julia has ever mentioned to him. Starting tomorrow morning – it's far too late now, even for indulgent friends – with Jack and

Celine, then Roisin, then Hilary in Wicklow, if she exists. Then he'll do a search for Julia's former colleagues: he will track down every single one of them, pick their brains, force them to speak to him. Whatever Julia is running from *has* to be rooted somewhere in her own past, before their lives collided. Nothing else makes any sense. Their shared present has always been joyful, companionable, comfortable.

He writes down 'Mater Hospital', where Julia used to work, then the health centre where she'd practised as a GP until she retired early, just over four years ago. And suddenly, too, by her own admission. The heart had gone out of it for her, she'd said. He stops, angry at himself again for not asking: *Out of what?* or *Why?* or *What had changed?* He underlines the address, places a star beside it. Maybe some of her colleagues are still around. He'll need to talk to them. After that, he lists airports, ferry terminals, train stations. And banks. Surely there are credit-card checks that can be done, bank statements that can be combed for clues about Julia's sudden departure? And if they won't talk to him, he'll have to force the police to do it for him. He'll assume nothing. He'll even put up Missing Person posters on lamp posts around the city, in cafes and bookshops. He is not going to let her go without a fight. He'll let Melissa know as a courtesy, of course, that he will be doing all of these public things: but one thing is sure. She will never treat him again as she treated him tonight.

From now on, he's running his own show, and she can either like it or lump it.

# *Julia*

JULIA MAKES HER way down to the car deck, trying to hide the trembling of her hands. Officer Murdoch had finally come to seek her out, as she'd been afraid he might.

'Dr Harris?' he'd said, his handsome face all smiles.

'Yes,' she'd replied, already resigned.

'We need to fill in our paperwork.' He'd tapped the clipboard in his hand. 'We can do it here or we can use my office, if you like?'

'Here's fine.' Julia's mind had begun racing the moment she'd become aware of his approach. What was she going to say? Should she make up some story and appeal for his discretion? And then she'd realized that he was never going to find her again, no matter how hard he looked. The thought had made her brazen. She'd held out her hand for the clipboard. 'I'll drop the report into your office when I'm done.' And she'd smiled – one of her most winning ones.

Murdoch had hesitated, just for an instant. Then he'd handed over the paperwork. 'Of course. I'm sorry for disturbing you.'

'Not a problem.'

Julia had felt a sudden, guilty rush of exhilaration. It was a powerful feeling, this not being herself. Was this how everyone felt who disappeared from their lives? It was strange, the rush of transformation that came with deception, with secrecy.

It was only afterwards that she'd begun to tremble. After she'd signed the Accident Report Form as Jane Harris, not Julia Seymour. And she'd added her new signature with a flourish, too. Daring anyone to challenge her.

Now, she drives slowly down the ramp to the quayside, the sudden metallic bumps and heaves unnerving her. She can't help the feeling that she's only *just* getting away with something. She keeps glancing in the rear-view mirror, expecting to see somebody come charging after her. She keeps waiting to be caught. But no: there is no shouting, no running figure, no siren wailing.

It could have been worse. She might have had to accompany Andrew and Lucy to hospital. She follows the signs for the A75 and Dumfries, making sure to keep to the speed limit. The rain is relentless. This stretch of the road is very narrow and she soon becomes stuck behind a lorry. It throws up fat splashes of muddy water, so she keeps her distance. There is no hurry. There is a train to London from Carlisle every hour or so and she has bought an open ticket. If she misses the one she's aiming for, there'll always be another.

'Feeling better, Andrew?' she'd asked, just before the ferry had docked. Lucy had brought him to her table in the lounge, to say thank you. 'Are you enjoying the puzzles?'

He'd nodded, shyly.

'Good man. You were very brave. Just do as Mum tells you and you'll be fine.' She'd stroked his face. His colour was good, there was no temperature and he seemed bright and alert.

'Thanks again, Dr Harris,' Lucy had said. 'You've been great.'

'A pleasure. Take care, now.' This time, she hadn't even blinked at her new name. And Julia had watched as they'd walked away, tiny red lights flashing at Andrew's heels. Once again she'd felt a sharp twist of grief. Whether it had been because Andrew was so like Jamie, or because his mother was called Lucy, she had had no idea. All she had known was the stark presence of loss in the way they'd walked away together. Pain for her; pain for the other Lucy, all those years ago.

The lorry in front finally pulls into a lay-by and Julia relaxes. Now that the muddy throwbacks have stopped, she can see the vivid colours of autumn all around her, despite the rain, which is definitely getting heavier. She must now keep an eye out for Three Lochs camping ground, about fifty miles or so from Dumfries. All being well, she'll pull in there for a half-hour. There are several camping and caravanning parks along this route, all of which will be deserted at this time of year. Any one of them will do.

She has decided to call Sorcha once she has parked the car, before she boards the train for London. That will be just enough notice, if she is at home. If she's not, there's a bed and breakfast on Greenwich High Road that Julia has found on the Internet.

She'll find a room somewhere. Have credit card, will travel.

Julia arrives at Carlisle Station with two hours to spare. She's tired, sleep prickling at the back of her eyelids. And the adrenaline is beginning to drain away, too, she can feel the lack of it. Along with its absence, she can feel the presence of William and the startled rush of guilt that comes with him. He will never forgive her for this. He will never understand. She pushes the thought of him away from her. There is only so much anguish that can be coped with at any given time and, right now, she can't afford the luxury of tears.

She parks the car in one of the designated long-term spaces, between a sparkling new two-tone Mini and an ancient Volvo.

In Three Lochs camping ground, she'd pulled over into a secluded, wooded spot, even though the whole place had seemed to be deserted. She'd left the driver's door open and any casual observer would have seen a tall woman in a dark anorak and a woolly hat, rummaging for something in the boot. The woman was just like any ordinary traveller, stretching her shoulders from time to time, easing out the aches of a long journey.

What they would not have seen, a few minutes later, was the same woman kneeling quickly on a black plastic sack, hands busy at the registration plates back and front, screwdriver trembling a little in what looked to be competent hands. She'd already done most of the hard work at home, concealed behind the friendly doors of her own garage. Here, it was simply a matter of yanking out the temporary screws and affixing the false number plates as securely as possible. Then she rubbed a bit of mud and grass over them – not too much, just enough to look natural. She stood and looked down at her handiwork. It would do: fit for purpose.

She has a momentary pang about Mr or Ms whoever from Mayo whose identity she seems to have stolen, along with their discarded number plates. She wraps the old plates securely now in the black plastic sack, concealing them in the boot, just on top of the spare wheel. By the time anybody finds them, they won't matter, anyway. Julia has been amazed, right from the start of all of this, at the things one can buy when money is no object and no questions are asked.

Now Julia locks the car and slips the keys into the pocket of her jeans. She eases herself into the straps of her rucksack and slings her laptop over one shoulder. People are coming and going with bags and suitcases and shopping. A busy station. A day like any other. She snaps the handle of her case briskly into position, pulls down the woolly cap further onto her forehead and begins to walk purposefully in the direction of the main entrance.

Inside the station, Julia makes her way to the Buffet. She sits under one of the high Victorian windows and has a pot of tea and a sandwich. The food feels like dust in her mouth and, as she pours the tea, she can no longer help herself. The tears come and there is no stopping them. Her mobile is on the table beside her. It would be so easy to call William now, to hear his voice, to beg him to understand. Just to *tell* him, at last.

But where would she begin? How do you tell the man who loves you – and whom you love – that you are a sham, that you've never been the person you've pretended to be, that you have kept the most significant thing about yourself a secret from him? She shakes her head, wiping her eyes with one of the flimsy serviettes that have come with her sandwich. I can't, she tells herself. I just can't. Numbness begins to crawl into all the hollow places inside her. She feels suddenly limp, without substance. She focuses instead on the huge cast-iron fireplace to her left. Its black-and-white diamond-patterned tiles remind her of Sorcha's house in Greenwich. Sorcha.

Julia is grateful to have something to distract her from William. She'll think about Sorcha instead. Sorcha and Roisin. Roisin and Julia. Like Venn diagrams, their friendships had overlapped down through the decades. They could call each other after a lapse of months, sometimes even years, and pick up the threads of their lives wherever they'd left them, no matter how tangled they'd become. This time, though, Julia is not at all sure of what she is going to say to Sorcha, how she is going to explain this sudden arrival, and an equally sudden departure.

She leaves the Buffet and collects her pre-paid ticket from the machine in the concourse. She tears up yet another PIN number that she no longer has any use for.

And then she finds a relatively quiet corner in the station and the signal is good. The Buffet had been much too empty of customers, and Julia hadn't wanted the two or three sitting around her to be able to listen to her call. 'Sorcha? It's Julia.'

'Julia! How lovely to hear from you. Where are you? Is everything okay?'

Julia smiles as Sorcha's voice veers from delight to doubt to consternation in four short sentences. 'I'm fine. I'm on my way to London. Should be in Greenwich around half-past ten tonight. Is that too late to call?'

'Of course not! You're welcome any time. You know that. Do you need picking up?'

'No, thanks,' Julia says firmly. 'I'll make my own way to your place. It's not a problem.'

'Let me collect you at Greenwich, at least,' Sorcha urges. 'The weather is filthy.'

The thought of more rain, more cold on the walk to Sorcha's, makes Julia relent. 'Okay, then, thanks. I'll text you when I'm at the station. See you later.' Julia hangs up. People are already edging towards the platform for the London train. Her legs feel spongy; she can't wait to close her eyes. The potent cocktail of tension, tiredness and grief is making her edgy, on the verge of tears. 'Keep it together,' she murmurs and a woman to her left looks at her sharply.

Julia moves away and joins the queue further down the platform.


She faces the direction of travel. The last thing she needs is to be made to feel nauseous. She settles herself on the upholstered seat and leans her head against the window, looking out into the deepening darkness. She cannot turn away any more pointedly from the other occupants of the compartment. Everything is going more or less according to plan. She's well on her way. To London. And to Sorcha. So far, so good.

So far, so lonely, too. But Julia doesn't want to think about that.

# William

At EIGHT-THIRTY the following morning William calls Jack on his mobile. He's been up since five. The night has been a long and restless one. Julia has seeped into his dreams, her presence and their past spreading everywhere, so that he doesn't know any more what is memory, what is dream, what is wishful thinking.

'Jack? William here. Something has happened. Can I come over?'

Once more, he is grateful for Jack's response. No questions, no surprise, no probing. Just 'Sure thing. I'll have the kettle on.'

He makes his way up the hill, his notebook stuffed into his jacket pocket, along with his mobile, a pen, and his phone charger. His battery, wouldn't you know it, has just begun to die. Jack is already at the open door, and William can smell coffee and the delicious scent of something baking.

'Celine's just gone to work. She sends her love. She's put some croissants on.' Jack is about to take William's jacket and stops. 'Maybe you'll want to keep that on for a while. Bit chilly today for just a shirt. Forget your overcoat?' William looks down for the first time at what he's wearing.

'Jesus,' he groans. 'No wonder I was cold.'

'You can have one of my old-man-cardies, if you'd like. There must be six Christmases worth stashed above in the wardrobe. Kids these days are a disappointment: no imagination.'

William smiles. 'I'll just keep the jacket on, thanks.'

'Come on through.' Jack makes his way towards the kitchen and William follows, blowing on his hands. 'You'll warm up soon enough.' The table is already set for two, complete with napkins and good china. The stuff that Jack always grumbles can't be put in the dishwasher or the microwave, because of its poncy gold rim. William sits and pulls his notebook and pen out of his pocket. He motions towards his mobile: 'Do you mind?' and Jack takes it from him, plugs the charger into the socket just beside the toaster. 'Right,' he says. 'What's up?' and pours the coffee.

'Julia's done a runner.'

Jack slops some coffee into the saucer. He stops in mid-pour and stares across at William. 'What do you mean? She's left you? Walked out on you?'

William shakes his head. 'No, well, yes. In a way. It seems that she's left all of us. She's gone. Her house is empty. Her car is gone. She's disappeared without a trace.'

Jack sits down opposite him. 'Why?' His face has drained of colour. He doesn't waste time asking: Are you sure? How do you know? Maybe she just needed a break? And William is grateful to him for that, too, as for so many other things.

'I wish I knew. I spent yesterday evening with the Daughter from Hell. We went through the house together. I spoke with the next-door neighbour, and then Melissa insisted we went to the cops. Nobody has seen Julia since Monday morning – at least, nobody that we know of. She was fine when I left her.' He shrugs. 'It's all been very carefully planned, by the looks of things. She meant to do it, Jack. There's no doubt about it. She wants to go missing.'

Jack considers this for a minute. Then he stands up abruptly and pulls the croissants from the oven, dropping them into a basket. He pushes them across the table at William. 'Eat,' he commands. 'Or Celine will kill me.' William realizes how hungry he is. The beans and toast are a distant memory, but the whiskey lingers like a dark, throbbing shadow across the top of his head. He eats and welcomes this bit of normality. In Jack's comforting presence he begins to feel the optimism that had eluded him for all of yesterday.

'Any kind of trouble between you two?' Jack asks carefully, spooning sugar into his coffee. 'I think I already know the answer,' he adds, looking up quickly. 'I'm only asking to get it out of the way.'

William nods. 'It's what everyone else will be thinking. And why wouldn't they? It's what I'd be thinking, too, if this was somebody else's problem.' He looks his oldest friend in the eye. 'Absolutely no trouble. In fact, if you'd asked me last week, I'd have told you to get ready for a wedding. I was just about to ask Julia to marry me.' He pauses. 'I was waiting for her birthday in a couple of weeks. And I had no indication that she'd say anything other than "yes".'

'Jesus, Will. What's going on?'

'I have no idea. But I'll tell you this. I'm going to find out.' He taps his notebook. 'I want a list of everybody you can think of who knew her – knows her – Christ, what tense are we supposed to use here?' He is angry at himself, at Melissa again, at Julia. 'Every time I think about her in the past, it's like I'm killing her.'

'Everyone who knows her,' Jack says evenly. 'Let me get my address book. And Celine's. Her stuff is far more up to date than mine. Just give me a sec.' He stands up from the table and walks out into the hallway. William can hear his stolid tread on the stairs. Just then, his mobile beeps and he rushes towards it, almost knocking over Celine's best china in his hurry to reach it. A text from Melissa. He opens up the tiny yellow envelope, his fingers not at all sure of what they are doing. 'Have appt with guards @ 2. Let me no if u r free. M.'

Okay, he thinks. At least she's not freezing me out. He replies. 'Yes. See you there. Thanks. William.' It's one of his things. He will not use text-speak. He hates the abbreviations, the 'l8er' for 'later', 'de' for 'the', 'r' for 'are'. Jack teases him about it, the perfect punctuation, the syntax, the uptight-ness of his messages, but he doesn't care. Language matters to William. He wants to do his bit to preserve it.

Jack comes back into the kitchen carrying two address books. He puts them down on the table and fumbles in his top pocket for his reading glasses. With his other hand, he pushes the more battered book towards William. 'We'll go through both,' he says. 'Systematically. We'll start with Celine's and then we'll match them with mine. And she has more stuff on her laptop. We can look when she comes home.' He scratches his head, a gesture William knows well. 'In the meantime, something should jog my memory, somewhere along the line. I've phoned Celine, by the way. She's on it. Says to come for dinner and we'll put our heads together tonight. You okay?'

William nods. 'Yeah.' He pauses. Now, in the light of day, in Jack's warm and cluttered and ordinary kitchen, William suddenly begins to doubt the only thing that has been giving him hope, the one thing he has been holding onto.

'What is it?' Jack asks. 'Whatever it is, spit it out. It'll only bug the hell out of you if you don't. And you'll end up telling me anyway.' He refills both of their cups.

'This may be nothing – I thought it was yesterday, but . . .' William falters.

'Go on.'

'I've been teaching Julia to play chess. For over a year now. She's really good. She's even beaten me a few times.'

Jack grins. 'Good for Julia.'

'Yesterday, when Melissa and I were going through the house, there was nothing of Julia left. I mean, all her personal stuff was gone. She'd done a really thorough job. But . . .' He looks Jack in the eye, afraid of his friend's sensible scepticism, seeing his one forlorn hope now disappearing like Howth fog. 'She'd set up the board for our game last night, before she left for wherever she's gone. And the queen was off her square. I think she's trying to tell me something. Don't know what it is, but it's all I've got.'

'Julia's an intelligent woman,' Jack says at once. 'So it can't be a mistake.'

William exhales. 'That's what I'm clinging to. Something has happened to make her run, something that isn't me.'

Jack pauses. 'Can I ask you something?'

'Sure.'

Jack strokes his beard. 'It's just . . . is there any way that Julia might be, you know . . . ill? I mean, seriously ill? And not want all the fuss that would come with it here?'

'Maybe,' William concedes. 'It had occurred to me. But why wouldn't she tell me, if she was? I'm not the hysterical sort. I'd have been able to keep that as quiet as she wanted. So no, I don't believe this is about illness.'

'What about money?'

William is startled. 'What do you mean?'

Jack waves one hand in the air. 'I'm just flying kites here, trying to figure out why people might drop out of their lives like this.'

William answers slowly. 'Julia never worried about money. Said she didn't have to. That Richard had left her a wealthy woman.' He looks at Jack. 'I never even thought about that as a reason.'

'I'm just throwing it out there.' Jack signals towards the

newspapers at the end of the table. 'People are coming unstuck every day. It was just a thought.'

'No, no – it's good to think about all the angles. But no,' William shakes his head. 'Money isn't it. I'm certain. She told me a few times how comfortable she was. I think she even felt guilty about it at times. Made her a really soft touch for a pile of charities – too many, in my view. But it was none of my business.' He stops, remembering Julia's generosity to Melissa, to her grandchildren. To him.

'So it's not love and it's not money and it's not illness. All the more reason to start digging. Let's get going.' Jack pulls the laptop towards him and starts typing.

'I had a text from Melissa while you were upstairs,' William says. 'I've got to meet her at the police station in Rathfarnham at two. Then I'll be back. It's good to have all this concrete stuff to go on. I can't stand moping around doing nothing.' He shakes his head. 'It's just not an option.'

'Right.' Jack looks at him over the top of his old-fashioned glasses. 'And when we get to the medical people, I still have a few names I can pull out of the hat if we need them. Although most are retired, like myself.'

William opens up his notebook. He writes 'Friends' across the top. 'Let's start with friends and acquaintances. I really need to know if the name "Hilary" appears anywhere – Celine might know. That's who Julia was going to see in Wicklow – that's what she said – the day before she disappeared.'

Jack frowns. 'Doesn't ring any bells with me. But that doesn't mean anything. Let's start trawling here first and see what we come up with.'

On top of the gnawing sensation deep in his stomach, William is aware of a tiny flicker of relief. It seems to gain in strength as he watches Jack across the table, being what Jack does best. Solid, dependable. Here. Somehow, in this room,

Julia doesn't feel to be quite as missing as she is from every-where else. In this house, where he'd first met her, William feels he might be able to begin to draw her back to him. One way or the other, he will have to face learning about why she left. Part of him dreads that knowledge.

But the other, stronger part of him is keen to find out, and keen to put right whatever is wrong.


William reaches the car park of the police station just before two. The traffic all the way across town has been nightmarish and he's been terrified of arriving late. He dreads meeting Melissa again. She is getting to him: just the memory of her presence is enough to remind him how far short of her expectations he falls. Easy, William, easy: he hears Julia's words inside his head. You know what she's like.

Melissa is waiting for him, just outside the door. Fleetingly, he wonders why. It's freezing today, with occasional flurries of fine sleet. Why doesn't she stand inside where it's warmer? 'Any news?' he asks as he walks up to her, knowing already by her white face that there is nothing.

She shakes her head and lights a cigarette. He notices that she doesn't offer him one this time. Mind you, she hadn't offered him one last night, either; he'd had to ask. But still. She looks strung out. He'll have to tread ever more carefully here. The last thing he wants is a scene.

'Did you manage to get any sleep?' he asks.

Melissa doesn't reply. She stands there, at the entrance to the police station, smoking and looking off into the distance. He wonders if she has even heard him. He glances at his watch. 'It's almost two,' he says, gently. 'Perhaps we should go inside.'

Still she doesn't reply.

'Melissa?'

'I've been in already,' she says, tossing her cigarette butt onto the ground and grinding it with her heel. 'I got here earlier than I expected. They weren't busy, so I went ahead. Sorry.'

William is stunned. It takes a moment to absorb what feels like a deliberate affront. It is almost as though she has just slapped his face. The blood rises to his cheeks in sympathy, hot and stinging.

'Why didn't you tell me?' he asks her. 'Why didn't you keep to the time we'd agreed?' He feels a sense of outrage spreading downwards into his fingertips and shoves his hands deep into his jacket pockets. He is afraid they might leap to her throat and throttle her, if he leaves them to their own devices.

'Because I saw an opportunity and I took it – I can't hang around here all afternoon.' Her tone is sharper now. 'I have children to collect.' She stops. 'Besides. There is nothing new. They don't know anything.'

He wants to know what she's told them. But he will not ask.

'And,' she says, 'it's probably better that we don't meet them together. You have your story, I have mine.' Her gaze is defiant. But there are dark shadows under her eyes and, although he knows it is impossible, she looks thinner, frailer than yesterday.

His fury is checked by her words. Now, he is bewildered. 'Story?'

'Yes,' she says. 'You should know all about stories.'

William doesn't reply. Let her get it off her chest, whatever it is. And in a way, she's right. He can write her script, see it with his eyes closed. He promises himself silently that he will keep a lid on his anger. Melissa has just moved the goalposts and he is not going to play her twisted game any longer. Pool resources, my arse, he thinks, anger fizzing away despite himself, threatening to brim over. He waits for the tirade to begin.

'You *say* that everything was fine,' Melissa almost hisses. Her voice then begins to climb, to become shrill. It had always made Julia wince. 'All I know is that since she got together with you, my mother changed.' William watches as she struggles for control. 'For the last six months she hardly ever kept in touch with me – hardly even saw her grandchildren. I had to *beg* her to babysit. Even her appearance changed. Why would she let herself go like that, if she wasn't deeply unhappy?'

William rebels against her words, feels the hard core of their untruth. Nevertheless, he is stung. He takes a deep breath, the way Julia used to advise him to. 'I can't convince you, and I'm not even going to try. You can't handle the truth.' His tone is harsher than he intends.

'*I* can't handle the truth?' She rages at him, blue eyes blazing, equal amounts of fire and ice.

He holds her gaze. 'That's what I said. You can't handle the truth that your mother got a second chance to be happy. And she took it.' He lets that hang between them for a moment. 'Whether *you* like it or not.' She doesn't reply, just keeps glaring at him. 'She loved your father and he died. She didn't choose that. It's life. Shit happens. And years and years later, she loved me. She got tired of being on her own. Deal with it!'

Still she is silent. Hostility surrounds her like a coat. William decides that this is hopeless. 'I'm going now. Thank you for my wasted journey.' He wants to say more, but checks the words as they rise, from somewhere deep and bitter. Instead he says, 'You know where I am. If you hear anything, please do me the courtesy of letting me know.' He speaks stiffly. It is that, or take hold of both of her shoulders and shake her until her anger shatters. He turns and walks away towards his car.

'You don't deserve her, you never deserved her!' she shrieks to his departing back.

He wheels around. 'Well, that must make you very happy, then! It must do – because I don't *have* her any more!' He slams his way into the driver's seat and screeches out of the car park, wheels spitting gravel.

'Jesus Christ!' he says, and thumps the steering wheel. Then 'Jesus!' again. Somewhere, a voice whispers to him about a blessing in disguise. You won't have to have anything to do with her now, the voice soothes. You can look for Julia on your own – no interference from the Daughter from Hell. By the time he reaches the city centre, he is almost calm again.

And by the time he pulls into his apartment complex in Howth, he is relieved. He feels as though he has just discarded an awkward, heavy burden. His shoulders feel lighter, his head clearer.

He parks and locks the car, glancing up at his window to make sure the lights have switched on. He has a couple of lamps, dotted around the apartment, that are connected to timers. There are too many robberies these days. And Julia's disappearance has made him begin to feel vulnerable in a whole new way. Life suddenly appears to be very fragile – a thin crust under which catastrophe heaves and roils, erupting hotly without warning, scattering all in its path. Is this what old age feels like? he wonders. Is this the start of a disconnected and solitary and fearful life? He keeps glancing over his shoulder. It is as though everything he has known is up for attack. Nothing is what it seems.

He takes the stairs again, at a run this time. It helps him discard the last of the cobwebby feeling that's been clinging to him ever since his meeting with Melissa. He puts the key in the lock and for a moment has a flash of hope that Julia will be waiting for him inside. The apartment is empty, as the rational part of him has already known it would be. He avoids looking at the sofa, at the colours that remind him so vividly of her. He picks up his coat from where he'd thrown it on the armchair last night and puts it on. Then he locks the door, checking everything as he leaves. He puts his head down, turns up the collar of his overcoat and shoves his hands into his pockets. Then, at a very brisk pace, he makes his way up the hill to Jack.

Jack. That, at least, is something that doesn't change. Friendship, and the old familiar solace that comes with it.


Jack pours him a glass of wine without even asking. 'You look as though you could do with this.' His kitchen is a pleasantly foggy place, smelling of garlic and peppers and parsley and something roasting in the oven. 'Celine will be home in about an hour. She's finishing up early. We'll eat around six. Do you want something to keep you going?'

William shakes his head. 'I'm fine, thanks. This'll do the trick.' He raises his glass. 'Here's to both of you. To good friends.'

They clink glasses. 'How'd it go at the police station?' Jack has his back half-turned. He's peeling potatoes into the sink and William watches as their bone-white insides emerge from underneath their claggy skins. He shivers. Something about their pale, cold nakedness has reawakened that sense of dread that Jack's kitchen had begun to dispel. For a moment he doesn't know what to say. How do you explain Melissa?

Jack stops what he's doing and looks at him, his whole face a question. 'You okay? Sit down, by the way. You look a bit shook.'

William pulls out a chair, its legs scraping across the tiles. He sits, heavily, and Jack reaches across and puts the bottle of wine at his elbow. 'Melissa had a go at me,' he says. 'Seems to think I drove Julia away. That if she was happy she'd never have left like this.'

'Bollocks,' says Jack, matter-of-factly. He's resumed his potato-peeling. He doesn't let William's revelation put him off his stroke. If anything, he becomes even more focused on his task. William understands the language. He understands that Jack doesn't agree, that Jack is firmly on his side, as solid and substantial and down-to-earth as peeled spuds. 'If Julia wasn't happy with you,' he goes on, tossing the potatoes into cold water, 'she'd have kicked you out. End of story. Whatever it is, it's much more complicated than Melissa might like to believe.' He wipes his hands on the tea towel, looking William in the eye. 'Only met the girl a couple of times, but I know enough to know that she gave her mother a bellyful of trouble.'

'Thanks,' William says. It is good to hear someone else say: No, you are not mad; yes, your life – your love – has been as you've believed it to be. Something cataclysmic has happened to fracture it, that's all. It's a huge 'all', whatever it is, but it's a lot better than 'She never loved you anyway'. 'One way or the other, Melissa is not going to be my ally. I'm going to have to do this on my own.'

'Do?' says Jack. 'What, exactly?' He pushes place mats and cutlery across to William. 'I mean, once you contact friends and family and colleagues, what do you propose to do then?'

William starts to set the table for three. 'Follow her,' he says, firmly. 'Find her. I don't care what it takes. I have time, I have money – none of the usual excuses for not doing something. I love this woman.' Jack looks at him, quickly. 'And I am going to get her back. I'll help her fix whatever it is that's wrong, and I am prepared to chase her to the ends of the earth.'

'And if she really doesn't want to come back?' Jack's question is a quiet one.

'Once I understand why, I think I could even learn to deal with that.' William's thoughts are forming as he speaks. Talking to Jack is like talking to himself. And he feels he has come a long way since last night. Twenty-four hours, he thinks suddenly, as the clock chimes four. All this in twenty-four hours.

'Okay, that's honest. And reasonable. I wasn't sure how . . . you might cope with that.'

'If something has changed, I'll learn how to handle it. I know that what we've had is real,' says William. 'For both of us. I'm certain of it.' He pauses. 'Nobody could fake the past three years. Nobody.' He shakes his head. 'Something that I can't imagine has happened to make her do this. I need to find out what it is. Then, if she wants me to go away and leave her alone, well, that's what I'll have to do. Not without a fight, though.'

Just then the kitchen door is pushed open and Celine enters, her laptop slung over one shoulder, arms laden with shopping. William leaps to his feet.

'Wait,' she says. He stops. 'William, I can't believe what Jack's told me. It's so unlike Julia. You must be beside yourself. I've thought of nothing else all day.'

'Let me take these – then we'll talk.' William begins to take some of the bags from her, surprised at their weight.

'Careful,' she warns, 'the reinforcements are in that one. It'd be a shame if any of them got broken.' He takes out the bottles of wine and places them carefully in the rack beside the back door. He reflects that Jack and Celine's kitchen is as familiar to him as his own, or Julia's. He remembers Melissa's face and feels suddenly very glad to be here.

Celine goes over to the sink and gives Jack a hug. She kisses him, and then holds him at arm's length. 'How's the superannuated man?' she asks.

He pretends to huff. 'Superannuated, my arse. The washing's done, the ironing's up to date and the dinner is on. Some retirement!'

'Such a little treasure.' She turns to William. 'Have you had any news at all today?'

He tells her about the police station, about Melissa. Her eyes widen. 'Well,' she says, 'nothin' like knowin' where you stand. And' – she pulls the laptop off her shoulder, lays it on the table and unzips the case quickly – 'look what I did, just before I came home.'

She enters her password and waits for the programmes to load. In the meantime, she rummages in her handbag and takes out a photograph. She hands it to William. His mouth goes dry. It is of Julia.

'I had Jack courier it to me while you were with Melissa,' she says. 'Of course, he couldn't find this one, so he sent the whole box.' She grins at her husband.

William stares at the photo, unable to take his eyes off it. Julia's hair is short, dark, cropped just as it was on the first evening he'd met her. She is smiling into the camera, her face relaxed, her eyes bright and curious. He feels the lump gather in his throat.

'You'll need a photograph,' Celine says. 'A recent one.'

William nods. 'Yeah,' he says. 'I've been thinking about that, but this one is . . .'

Celine puts a hand on his arm. 'Hang on,' she says. Then: 'Look, the wonders of Photoshop.' And she points to the screen of her laptop.

William looks. 'Jesus!' he says, 'where did you get that?'

Julia looks out at him from the screen, an altered, up-to-date Julia. The face is as luminous as ever, the eyes as bright. But there are some changes, subtle ones. The lines around her eyes are finer, but there are more of them. Her mouth is not quite so smiling. And her hair: her hair is now long, a little wild, a lot greyer than in the photograph he holds in his hand. It is Julia: the Julia of now, of last Monday. He looks at Celine, not understanding.

'I got one of the designers at work to help me. I thought it would be useful. I only have a few photos of Julia, most of them with other people at parties and receptions and things.' She taps at the photo in William's hands. 'But Katie at work said she'd be able to do something with this one. And we did.' Celine is triumphant. 'I sat with her, told her how Julia's hair had changed, how the original photo is over three years old. I said that we wanted something that was a great *likeness*, rather than a great photo. She tinkered about a good bit and I think we've got it.'

William is so moved that for a moment he can't speak. He squeezes Celine's hand. 'Thank you,' he says, finally. 'You have no idea how useful that is going to be – and how glad I am to have it.'

'We can print off as many copies as you like. You are going to put it up on lamp posts, aren't you, the way other people do, all around the city?' Celine asks. 'And on the Internet, as well?'

'Steady on,' Jack interrupts. 'Let the man draw his breath. We're going to have dinner first and thrash out a proper plan. No point in going off at half-cock.' He takes a chicken out of the oven and places the pan on the draining board. He turns the roast potatoes and puts them back into the oven. Then he covers the steaming chicken with tinfoil. 'We need to be methodical about this, make sure we do things in the right order.'

Celine nudges William. Her expression in mischievous. 'There speaks the Works Supervisor. Never guess he used to do planning for a living, would you?'

'While you,' Jack says, motioning towards her with a fork, 'couldn't plan the proverbial in a brewery. Now take your laptop off the table, woman, and let's get on with it.'


They sit, the remains of Jack's dinner all around them. Celine has typed a long list of 'to dos' and several names and addresses. 'I'll email them to you,' she says to William. She shakes her head. 'I still can't believe it.' She gestures towards her screen. 'I think all these people are long shots, but we have to start somewhere.' She taps at her screen. 'I have no idea where this woman, Sorcha, lives. Julia spoke about her a few times, and how she used to visit her in London. Don't even know her surname. Sorry.'

'And no Hilary,' William says, rubbing his eyes. 'No one in Wicklow.' He is beginning to feel exhausted, his eyes raw from lack of sleep and staring at the computer screen. He can feel them straining against the harsh light.

'No,' agrees Celine, 'but I have a suspicion that Roisin lives in Wicklow. I can't be sure. You've met her, haven't you?'

'Yes. I met Roisin a couple of times when Julia and I first got together. We had dinner at her sister's house in Dún Laoghaire, I remember, with a few other people as well. I think the sister's name was Grace, or something like that – no, Greta. That's it, Greta.' William is suddenly delighted at the memory. He'd forgotten all about Greta. 'I can go there, find Roisin through her.'

'And maybe Hilary, too? Maybe this Greta might know her as well?' Celine suggests.

'Yeah – Julia said she was meeting her for some sort of annual reunion. I didn't question her.' William stops. Why would he have questioned her? It is only now that some of the things Julia has done are suspicious. Why would he have doubted her at the time? He wonders at how different every-thing now looks in hindsight. Like looking at your own reflection through a cracked glass.

'She definitely spoke to me of Sorcha and Roisin. They were all at college together. I'm sure of it.' Celine pulls her hair back into a ponytail and twists it into a bun at the nape of her neck. It is an unconscious gesture, a purely feminine one, and it reminds William instantly of Julia. She used to do that, too, once her hair had grown longer. Celine catches him looking at her. 'What?' she asks.

'Nothing.' He shakes his head. 'Just thinking.'

'What year did Julia leave university?' Celine asks suddenly.

William has to think for a moment. '1974, I think. Or maybe '75. One or the other.'

'Class yearbooks,' Celine says triumphantly. 'They may even be online.'

'I'll do that if I have to,' William says. He puts his hand on hers, stopping her. 'But I suspect I might have to go looking in person. You've done enough, Celine. It's nearly midnight. Time I went.'

'You sure?'

William watches as she stifles a yawn. He smiles. 'Positive. You've done more than enough, both of you. Don't know what I'd do without you.' He picks up his coat from the chair where he'd draped it earlier.

'Keep in touch, ya hear?' Jack says. 'And come any time. Two heads, and all that guff. Don't try and struggle along on your own, okay?' He helps William into his coat.

William nods. 'I won't. Particularly if you keep cooking like that.'

Jack grins. 'Never too late to acquire new talents.'

They stand, he and Celine, at the front door, watching as William walks down the path. He turns and waves and then sees the oblong of warm yellow light disappear as they close the door behind him. It's close to freezing, and he can see the pavement sparkle treacherously underneath his feet.

He walks carefully down the hill towards home. He thinks, not for the first time, how much everything has changed and how, all around him, everything still remains the same.

# *Julia*

JULIA SEES SORCHA at once, eyes anxiously searching the platform. As lovely as ever, she thinks; her small body wrapped in a camel coat, a perky red scarf at her throat. And no hat. Julia smiles to herself, filled with affection. Sorcha has always hated hats, has never believed in the fiction that most of the body heat is lost through the head. 'Rubbish,' she used to say. 'An old wives' tale, absolutely no medical foundation.'

Julia moves towards her and sees her friend's eyes widen in surprise. For a moment, she is taken aback. Then she remembers how she is dressed. Jeans, sturdy walking boots; anorak, woolly hat. This is not how Sorcha would have expected to see her elegant friend. But it only takes a moment for the expression to soften and then Sorcha's arms are wide open. 'Sweetie,' she says. 'So good to see you.' Julia walks right up to her and they hug each other, hard. She feels a sob escape her as she rests her chin on the top of Sorcha's head. She holds onto her for a moment and inhales the perfume that Sorcha has always worn, even when a penniless student. She would save from a very meagre allowance to buy herself her precious quarter-ounce of Chanel No. 5: 'You cannot beat quality.'

Julia pushes Sorcha away, arm's length, and looks at her. 'You look terrific, as always,' she says. Looking at the brown eyes, the smile, the slightly quizzical expression, Julia has the extraordinary sensation of watching more than forty years fall away from the small face, revealing the shy, uncertain teenager she had met in the halls of UCD all those years ago.

'And you, you look exhausted,' Sorcha says, reaching down to take the handle of Julia's wheelie-bag.

Julia grins at her. 'Still can't tell a lie, eh?'

'Tease all you like,' Sorcha says firmly. 'You look in need of a good meal and a decent glass of wine. Follow me.'

Once out of the station, the air is chill, biting. A fine, cold rain is falling, making the travellers put their heads down, huddle further into their collars. 'Here we are,' Sorcha says, and the hatchback of a sleek, dark-grey car opens automatically. Julia wonders what sort of a car it is. She has never been one to take much interest: all the shapes look the same to her, apart from the obviously different ones, like Beetles, Minis and the Fiat 500s of her youth. She is curious about this one, though: William will certainly want to know. And then she stops herself, overwhelmed by a wave of grief and loss that makes her choke – another half-sob, half-cough that has Sorcha immediately at her side.

'Julia, what is it?' Her concern is palpable through the gloved hand she places on her friend's forearm. 'Get into the car, I'll put the case away. Please, sit down. You're like a ghost.'

Julia obeys. All the strength seems to have left her feet and hands. They have trouble obeying her in moving to the left, pulling on the handle of the door. Eventually, she stumbles her way into the passenger seat, leans her head down into her hands and weeps.

Sorcha says nothing. She squeezes Julia's hand, starts the engine and drives in the direction of home. Julia tries to breathe deeply, to quell the nausea that has begun to storm her insides. She keeps her head down, fighting the growing darkness that is threatening to snatch her away from Sorcha's kindly presence. Gradually the pinpoints of light become brighter, her stomach settles. She exhales, feeling that there is nothing left inside but gratitude.

'You're telling me that nobody knows where you are? Nobody knows you've *gone*?' Sorcha's voice is incredulous. She has brought Julia straight to the kitchen and sat her beside the fire, throwing a cashmere wrap around her shoulders to stop her trembling. 'What are you doing?' But her hands are gentle. 'Julia, tell me quickly: are you ill?'

Julia shakes her head violently.

'Then what? What is it? Has something happened between you and William?' Sorcha pauses. 'Or between you and Melissa?'

'No, nothing like that.'

'Then what is it? Please, Julia. You're scaring me.'

Julia opens her mouth and then closes it again. Sorcha does not disturb the sudden silence. 'You must promise me not to tell.' She clutches at Sorcha's wrists, making her wince. 'I'm sorry,' she says at once. 'Sorry to put you in this position, but if you won't give me your word, then I'll have to go now, immediately and not come back.'

Sorcha sits down beside her. 'I promise to listen,' she says. 'And I promise not to judge. I can't let you go anywhere, not in this state. And I give you my word that I will try my utmost to do whatever it is that you want me to do.' She pauses. 'For the rest, you are just going to have to rely on forty-two years of friendship. I would never do anything to hurt you, Julia.'

Julia nods. She can't ask for more than that and she is too exhausted either to leave or to do further battle. 'Okay,' she says. 'I trust you, of course I do. That's why I'm here. It's just that . . .' she can't stop her eyes wandering in the direction of the kitchen door.

'Hugh won't be home tonight,' Sorcha says. 'We have the house to ourselves.' She stands up, all business. Her tone is firm. Julia is reminded of their student days. 'I'm going to get you another sweater, a glass of wine and some food and then you're going to talk to me.'

Julia nods, leans her head back against the cushion that Sorcha has placed behind her head and closes her eyes, watching as Sorcha leaves the room. Twenty minutes or so to gather her thoughts, she thinks. Twenty minutes, after so many days and weeks and months of fretful activity. That would be good.

It takes Julia a moment or two to realize where she is. The light is dimmer than she's used to, and the fire crackling quietly is not something that she recognizes. Startled, she sits forward and the chair rocks violently. Sorcha is at her side at once.

'It's okay, it's okay,' she soothes. 'You fell asleep and I didn't want to wake you. You're with me.'

'Oh, God, of course. Sorry, I'm a bit jumpy.' Julia sits back in the rocking chair, pressing both hands to her eyes, which have begun to sting.

Sorcha looks at her, her expression mild. 'A bit jumpy. I'll say. Here, I have something light ready for you. Eat it, and then you can tell me what's going on.' She places pâté, crackers and some cheese on the table by Julia's elbow. 'There's a bed ready for you upstairs and the electric blanket is on.'

'Thanks.' That one word is all Julia can manage right now. She is aware that Sorcha is waiting. She eats a little and sips at her wine. Then she can't postpone it any longer. 'I've thought it all through very carefully,' she says. 'This is no snap decision.' She is beginning to feel better, warmer. And Sorcha's presence makes her feel in some way optimistic. She is glad that she decided to come here. 'And I can't give you too much detail, either. I don't want to cause you any trouble.'

Sorcha is shaking her head. 'You're talking in circles, Julia. Give me something I can understand.'

Julia takes a long breath and exhales, steadying herself. 'I did something, a few years ago. Something I believed in. But it has had . . . repercussions. I need time to come to grips with what might happen to me. And I can't do that at home.'

Sorcha looks down into her wine glass. 'Do you want to stay here? Do you need to stay here?'

Julia smiles. 'No. That's not why I've come. I've already arranged where I'm going. I just needed to see you before I went. To tell you. No matter what I decide eventually, I feel that there is something I need to . . . reflect on, perhaps even atone for. I don't know. Sometimes, I don't think I know anything any more.' She stops, aware that she is racing ahead of her thoughts. She pauses for a moment, conscious of the delicate balance she needs to maintain. 'Anyway, I wanted you to know that. Face to face. In case something happens and I don't see you again.'

Sorcha looks at her. 'What sort of repercussions?'

Thank you, Julia thinks silently. Thank you for not asking where, or how, or what it is I've done. 'Serious ones. Or potentially serious ones. I'm not sure. All I know is that I need to come to terms with things, to clear my head, to take decisions.'

'Are you planning to come back from wherever it is you're going?'

'I don't know. I am *preparing* not to, because that might be the best option for everyone, and that's the truth. But "planning" is a different matter. If I've learned anything, it's that life has no certainties.'

'If you're not coming back, what about Melissa?' Sorcha's tone is that mix of compassion and challenge that Julia knows so well.

'I've provided for her. I've left her my house, everything I own. She doesn't know it yet, but I've left instructions with my solicitor. That gives her options. It's up to her what she chooses.' Julia can feel her eyes fill, battles the tears back fiercely. 'I don't know who Melissa is. I don't know what she wants. She has never seemed to want me in her life. Especially since Richard died. You know that.'

'That's no reason to abandon her.' Sorcha's voice is sharp. 'You're still her mother.'

Julia looks at her in surprise. 'Abandon?' she says. 'She's thirty-three years of age. She doesn't need a mother.'

'I question that,' says Sorcha. Her gaze is steady, holding Julia's. 'Think about it. You suddenly disappear out of her life. No warning, no explanation. At the very least she'd be frantic about your safety. You can't do this to your child, Julia.'

Julia looks at her, helpless. 'But I can't stay. It would be worse. For her. For the children – for everyone.'

'Then at least let me contact her. Once you're on your way to wherever it is you're going. I can reassure her that you're well. Don't do this to her, Julia. You'll regret it.'

Julia nods. 'Not before the weekend. Just give me a few more days. Then you can tell her I'm safe.' She meets Sorcha's gaze, warning her. 'But nothing else.'

'What can I tell her? I don't know anything else.' She pauses and they both allow the silence to gather. Then Sorcha speaks again, more softly. 'What about the other important person in your life. What about William? I thought you loved him.'

Julia is stung. 'I do love him!' she cries. 'More than any-thing.'

'But you're still walking out on him without a word,

according to you, with no explanation. Whatever you will or won't tell your daughter, don't you trust William enough to tell him whatever it is?'

Julia looks at her. 'I can't, no matter how much I trust him. For the same reason I can't tell you. It would implicate you, both of you. All of you, but especially you.' She looks away from the questions in her friend's eyes. 'And I can't do that.'

'Do you need a lawyer?' Sorcha asks bluntly.

'Not where I'm going,' Julia says. 'And if I do decide to come back, I don't know if I'd want one. I might want to handle the consequences myself. Courage of my convictions – isn't that your phrase? My plan right now is not to need a lawyer, not to want one. I'd rather control my own fate.'

Sorcha stands up and walks around the room. She touches things, straightens glasses, books. She doesn't look at Julia. Watching her, Julia is reminded all over again of their student days, the ones when exams loomed. This is how Sorcha used to untie knotty problems of anatomy and physiology as they revised together. She would take control of the 'information logjam', as she'd called it, the unwieldy masses of knowledge that they'd had to absorb and regurgitate every three weeks or so. It was Sorcha who'd impose order on all that chaos, who'd dismantle the edifice of facts brick by brick and, together, they'd put them back in their proper place, igniting understanding as well as memory.

She'd pace the flat, rearranging their few possessions, straightening the towers of books and papers. Julia would fire the questions and Sorcha would organize her thoughts towards a solution as she made slow progress around the room. When it was Julia's turn, their roles would reverse, but not their positions. Sorcha would pace, asking the questions. Julia would sit by the hissing gas fire, often closing her eyes as she reached for the answers. They knew each other so well that often a word or a number or an allusion was just enough to bring the required response tumbling to the surface, dragging all that knowledge with it. She was the best teacher Julia had ever known. As she watches her now, she can see that Sorcha is doing the same thing all over again.

'If you are telling me what I think you're not telling me,' she says, 'are you aware that, right now, things are changing?'

'Even if they are,' Julia answers carefully, 'this is England, not Ireland. There is a whole different . . .' she stops. 'Things change more slowly,' she says softly. 'And right now, I don't believe I have the luxury of waiting.' She lifts her glass again, notices that her hand is still shaky. 'I'm not going to say any more. I just need you to understand that there are things I need to come to terms with, perhaps even to make up for.'

'Have you changed your mind?' asks Sorcha. The room is suddenly very still. 'What you believed in then, is it still what you believe in now?'

'I don't know. I really don't know.' Julia grapples with the question. She hasn't articulated this to anyone, even herself. She's not sure what the truth is: not sure that she even understands 'truth' any more. 'Part of me says one thing, another part says something else. Part of me feels guilty for running, another part feels full of conviction. I don't know anything.' She shakes her head and looks at Sorcha appealingly. 'It doesn't feel like running away. It's much calmer than that. In a really strange way, I feel as though I'm running *towards* something.'

'And what about those who love you?' asks Sorcha quietly. 'What do I say to them, if they come looking?'

Julia looks at her, blankly. 'Why would anyone come looking to you?'

Sorcha smiles. 'For exactly the same reason you've come. Because we have been friends forever. Melissa is not stupid and neither, I suspect, is William. They'll put two and two together, either with one another or on their own.'

Julia won't meet her eye. 'But I've left no address book, no laptop – nothing.'

Sorcha sits down beside her again and takes her hand. 'You've never really understood the sort of loyalty you inspire. I saw it with friends at university, with patients when you were a junior doctor, with colleagues. You make strong connections with people, Julia. I very much doubt that William will want to let you go. Or Melissa. At least not without a fight.'

Julia draws her hand back from Sorcha's. 'I'm not telling you any more,' she says, suddenly. 'That way, you won't be able to give any information, no matter who comes calling.' She stops, aware that she is withholding something important from Sorcha. Telling her will only make it real in a way she's not sure she can admit, but she can't evade it any longer, not with her friend sitting so close, looking at her with such sympathy. 'And you're right, of course. William will come looking for me. I was too cowardly to make the sort of complete break I should have.'

Sorcha waits.

Julia rushes on, words tumbling now. 'I've left him messages – oblique bits and pieces that only he will understand. I'm hoping that by the time he finds me, I might have a better idea of what to do.' She draws one anguished breath. 'And if he doesn't come, then the break will happen of its own accord.' She looks at Sorcha. 'I told you I was a coward.'

Sorcha shakes her head. 'I don't believe that for a moment. And I still don't understand why you couldn't have trusted him. It feels as though you're testing him. Are you testing him?'

Julia feels grief gather again at the base of her throat. 'I don't *need* to test him. It's not that at all. Something has happened to push me. If it hadn't, I might have told . . .'

'I thought you said you'd thought all this through?' Sorcha's tone is challenging again. 'That it wasn't a quick decision? Now you're saying—'

'I've said enough. More than enough. Please, Sorcha. Let me come to grips with this in my own way. I feel I've made a morally responsible decision. If I haven't, then I'll have to live with it, but I have to work it out in my own way, my own time. Please, don't put any more pressure on me.' Julia is aware of the warmth and the strength of Sorcha's presence beside her. Neither of them says anything for a moment. Even the crackling of the fire seems to have stilled. The air around them is holding its breath. It is Sorcha who breaks the spell.

'I'm not trying to pressurize you. Forgive me if it feels that way. I'm just afraid that your thinking is . . . tangled.' She looks thoughtful. 'I think it's important for you to know that it's not too late to change your mind. But whatever you decide, I'll support you.'

Julia absorbs this. Tangled. It's a good word. And she can't deny that there is truth in what Sorcha says. But above all the tangle is a realization, one of luminous clarity. Julia knows that, right now, there is no going back.

'I told you I'd listen, and I have.' Sorcha looks at Julia. 'And I've listened very carefully. What you've told me could hardly be construed as information. Certainly nothing of any practical use to anyone trying to find you.' She pauses. 'Is there anything at all I can do for you, at this point?'

Julia shakes her head. 'Nothing. I've taken care of everything.' She evades Sorcha's glance. And there is an almost perceptible shift in Sorcha's attitude. She tucks a long strand of Julia's hair behind her ear. 'By the way, what's with the long locks, Rapunzel?'

'I'm not telling you that, either,' says Julia. Her eyes are defiant. 'You don't need to know. And thank you, but I don't need anything. It's important that you don't help me.' Julia puts her glass back on the table. She is glad to see that her grip feels firmer this time, like her sense of purpose. 'I'll be gone early in the morning.' A beat. 'Do you have to tell Hugh I've been?'

Sorcha nods. 'Absolutely. No secrets: that's our promise to each other, always has been.' She pauses and looks away from Julia. 'For what it's worth, I think you're making a big mistake about William. Whatever about protecting Melissa, William will not thank you for it.'

Julia stands up. 'You don't understand.'

Sorcha does the same. 'You said it's in the past. William has nothing to do with your past. William is your *present*. Your future, too. You can't shut him out.'

Julia looks at her for a long time. 'I've already said too much.'

Sorcha's face blenches. 'Oh, Julia.'

'I won't see you in the morning. I'd prefer it that way. I'll let myself out.'

Sorcha shakes her head. 'I want to say goodbye. You don't need to linger. I understand that. We'll make it quick.'

They stand and embrace. Neither says anything. Julia makes her way out into the hall. At the bottom of the stairs she pauses, waits for Sorcha to reach her. 'You've been a wonderful friend,' she says. 'I can't thank you enough.'

'Promise to let me know you're safe. I don't care how – email, third party, phone call. It doesn't matter. I won't try to find you.'

Julia hesitates and then nods her head. 'On our birthdays, okay? You'll have word on our birthdays.'

Sorcha tries to smile. But she is so transparent that Julia can see what she's feeling. Before either of them says anything more, Julia climbs the stairs to bed.

Just after five, Julia wakes. She has accepted that this is now the pattern for the way things are going to be. She sleeps lightly, if she's lucky, from about midnight. Then, any time after four a.m. she wakes, her heart pounding and her mouth dry. Often she pulls herself out of a nightmare about falling, or being pursued, or suddenly, horrifyingly, finding herself naked in public. Once, she dreamt she was pedalling her way into UCD for her finals, along a stretch of coast road that was at the same time both strange and familiar. The only question she needed to answer was propped up in the straw basket in front of her, scrawled across the bottom margin of a huge, old-fashioned projector slide. Everything was oversized in that dream – the bicycle, the basket, the road along which she was cycling. She'd felt dwarfed and terrified. When she'd lifted the slide, she'd seen that the blue acetate was in fact the ocean, wave after wave of it crashing against the white cardboard sides. Dismay had engulfed her as she'd read the one question for which she had no response: 'How do you measure the incandescence of the sea?'

She'd woken, drenched in sweat. It was the one question she couldn't answer. It feels like that again now. She remembers shaking uncontrollably afterwards in her small, dimly lit bedroom, vulnerability wrapped around her as tightly as a shroud.

She moves quietly about another bedroom now, an unfamiliar one, hoping not to disturb Sorcha next door. She will let herself out of the house, as quietly as she can. She has no wish to revisit last evening's conversation, and she suspects that Sorcha won't want to, either. She pulls the small plastic folder from her rucksack and takes out the two sheets of paper, stapled together, that detail the next phase of her journey.

If only everything could be as easily managed as the physical distances between A and B. Greenwich to Waterloo; Waterloo to Paddington; Paddington to Heathrow. At least these were values that didn't change: like mathematically sound principles that didn't bow or bend under the force of love, or guilt. Or grief.

She opens the bedroom door and winces as she stands on a board that suddenly creaks underfoot. In the stillness of the early-morning house, the sound is abrupt, sharp as gunshot. Sorcha's bedroom door is opened at once and she stands there on the landing, tying the belt of her dressing gown. 'Should have warned you,' she says. 'That was always a great alarm bell if the girls were trying to sneak away in the night. You can avoid it on the way in, it would appear, but not on the way out.'

'I'm sorry,' Julia says. 'I didn't want to disturb you.'

Sorcha shakes her head. 'You didn't. It won't surprise you to know that I haven't slept.'

Julia feels immediately guilty. Sorcha sees her expression and comes over to where she is standing. She squeezes Julia's hand. Her eyes look tired, dark-shadowed.

'That's not an accusation,' she says. 'I'm worried about you. Really worried. Particularly because you won't let me help you.'

'I shouldn't have come . . .' Julia begins.

Sorcha raises both hands in the air, a gesture of surrender. 'Stop, stop. I won't say any more. Come on, let's have breakfast together and I'll drop you at the station.'

Julia begins to protest and Sorcha stops her. 'This conversation is over. You know where I am. You know that if ever you need me – need anything – all you have to do is get in touch. I'm repeating myself, but I need you to promise.'

'I promise,' Julia says.

They make their way downstairs to the kitchen. Sorcha puts on toast, scrambles some eggs and Julia makes the coffee. They move around each other in the gleaming kitchen, talking only of the next half-hour. Breakfast is brisk, businesslike. Slipping her arms into her jacket, Julia feels how surreal this all is. She hefts her rucksack onto her shoulders and tries not to think of William, who gave it to her.

She follows Sorcha out to the car. In silence they load the rucksack, the laptop and the wheelie-bag into the boot. Also in silence they drive to the station, where Sorcha stops outside. At this early hour there is only a trickle of people making their way to the platforms. Julia wonders what they would see, had they bothered to pay any attention to two women sitting there in a fancy car, unspeaking, the engine still running. On the surface, two old friends, perhaps – one still in her dressing gown – saying goodbye, holding onto each other a little longer than is usual.

Eventually they would have seen one – the taller one – scramble out of the passenger seat, wiping one hand hastily across her eyes. They'd have watched her wrestle with a rucksack, making an abrupt gesture towards the driver that is very clear: I don't need any help. Then they would have seen her struggle with the wheelie-bag, while attempting to sling a laptop case over one shoulder. All the movements are jerky ones, as though this woman is somehow at odds with herself.

They'd have seen her back turned, and a half-wave towards the sleek grey Lexus, already beginning to turn out of the station grounds. They'd have seen the driver crane her neck for one last look, then pull out reluctantly into the steadily building morning traffic.

# *William*

WILLIAM LURCHES AWAKE, somewhere around four. He's been dreaming again: that same dream, two nights running. He's in a coach somewhere, crossing a bridge – the Chiang Mai, or the Golden Gate: altered in all sorts of dream-logical ways, but still recognizable. The bridge spans a vast blue space. It has been constructed at an impossible height, shearing upwards from some invisible earth below. Its lattice-like struts gleam loudly in the sunlight. He feels queasy: he was never one for heights. Suddenly, the coach begins to gather speed. He clutches uselessly at the armrests, looks around wildly at the other passengers. But they are indifferent.

When William looks ahead, he sees that the driver is no longer at the wheel. He is paralysed with fear. Somewhere, somehow, he knows he is dreaming – but he can't wake up. And then, the clear thought comes slamming up from the terror below: This coach is out of control. At the same time: This *life* is out of control. The coach races across the bridge, which has now transformed itself into some mad fairground spiral. Faster and faster, light glinting everywhere until the inevitable happens. The coach crashes through the flimsy metal barriers and plummets towards the sea, a slow-fast, silent, graceful arc of death.

William comes to, sweating. 'Jesus!' he says. He is trembling, can hear his heartbeat fill the quiet room. He throws back the duvet and plants his feet solidly on the bedroom floor. He rests his elbows on his knees, his head in his hands. 'Fuck this, I need a drink,' he says. He stumbles towards the light switch and sees, to his relief, that all the familiar surroundings come into focus. For a moment there, he literally hadn't known where he was.

He pours himself a large whiskey and notices that the bottle is almost empty. That will need to be rectified. And he'll need to buy food, too. Or else his ulcer will start acting up again, and that is something he can do without.

He pulls back the curtains, following an absurd impulse to check that everything is where it should be. And it is: the pier stretches wetly away from him, snailing towards the squat red-and-white lighthouse. Street lights shimmer and blur in a fine fall of rain. The cars parked below look sleek, rounded: metal dolphins waiting for the next tide. He leaves the curtains open, despite the darkness outside, and sits at the small table. He opens up his laptop. He knows he's not going to go back to sleep now – maybe a nap this afternoon, or maybe not. In the meantime, he has plenty to do.

True to her word, Celine has emailed him the photograph of Julia. He opens the attachment now and checks that there is plenty of paper in the printer. He'll start with twenty copies. He pulls his notebook towards him and begins to make a list. Whiskey. Food – ready meals. Paper. Printer cartridges. Cash. He'll add to it as the day goes on. He doesn't want to be caught out.

The first photograph begins to shudder its way out of the printer. William pulls it towards him. Seeing Julia's smile, he feels the familiar ache begin all over again. His chest seems to open, to swell with grief and guilt. He doesn't know what he's done, what he's guilty of – not yet – other than missing her, but guilt seems to be the inseparable companion of loss. 'Get used to it,' he tells himself, grimly. 'There's a lot more where that's coming from.' Three years of memories, of hopes for the future, of *happiness*, goddamit.

He waves the thought away. He forces himself to focus on the day ahead. At seven, he'll shave and shower and dress, have breakfast at the cafe around the corner as soon as it opens. After that, he'll start his search at the airport: it's closest. If Julia has parked the car there, it will have been photographed as she went in. He'd rung the Garda station late last night, just before he'd gone to bed. He'd recalled, suddenly, that neither he nor Melissa had remembered to give them Julia's car registration number. William realizes that any information would have to go through the proper channels. But at least asking the question is a start, and he has to do something.

After that, he'll drive to the ferry port at the North Wall, talk to people, distribute photographs and see if he can jog someone's memory. Finally, he'll do the same at Dún Laoghaire's terminal, before paying a visit to Greta and Gerry this evening. And he'll contact the Guards again – this time to ask about credit-card checks, bank traces, whatever they do in the case of missing persons.

That's if they're doing anything at all. William has the suspicion that a grown healthy woman, missing only for a couple of days, will not be top of the police priority list. They'll assume that she's done a runner, probably with another man. Nevertheless, he's not letting them off the hook. And, this time, he'll go and see them on his own.

He's working on the assumption that Julia has left the country. Ireland is too small to hide in: not even the farthest reaches of Donegal or Kerry can offer any meaningful anonymity. We're just an overgrown village, William thinks. She'd be spotted in a flash: someone with Julia's physical presence cannot be ignored, would not be ignored.

He needs to sit and work out what he wants to say at all of these official points of departure: he doesn't want to come across as a madman. He's aware that all of people's sympathy is likely to be with Julia. Women don't run away from their men for no reason.

Wife-beater. Control freak. Unfaithful husband. Self-centred lover. The list of his putative crimes is endless. He'll have to develop some sort of a plausible story in order to defend himself – plausible to others, that is. A story that keeps to the essential truth of her abrupt disappearance, but perhaps suggests some instability on Julia's part. He needs something that will arouse people's compassion, something that will make bored officials want to help him. In a way, he wishes he could believe that story himself. It might help to explain her extraordinary flight from her life. But he knows that the last thing Julia is is unstable. Above all she's grounded: sensitive and sensible, both feel solidly planted on this earth.

He begins to write.


At eight, his mobile rings. Jack. 'Get any sleep?'

'Nope. And there's no news.' William replaces his coffee cup with a clatter, knocking the spoon onto the tiled floor. He curses.

'Want to join me for breakfast?'

'Thanks – just finishing up in the caff. Cupboard is bare at home.'

There is a pause. And then: 'You okay?'

'Pretty much. I've a packed schedule for today – if I don't keep busy I'll go insane.' William tells him his plans. He can almost see Jack nodding in approval, stroking his recently bearded chin. He's always liked order.

'Okay. Good luck and keep in touch.'

'Of course. I'll call tonight after I've spoken to Greta.'

'Righto. Stop by for a pint when you're done. Or food. Or both. Whatever. Just call.'

William smiles. 'Will do. Cheers.'

Jack: one in a million. They go all the way back to National School together, to the days when they were five. Two small and terrified boys in grey sweaters and short pants, the serge already chafing madly at their skinny legs just above the knee. They understand each other now, and they had understood each other even then. They'd looked over at one another, cautiously at first, and William still remembers the childish recognition of so much of himself in the boy sitting beside him on the wooden bench. Along with the grey serge, they each had a shock of black hair, with a cow's lick that refused to lie down. Deep blue eyes, noses splotched with freckles, knees scarred and scabbed. They might have been brothers.

That day they'd both obeyed at once when the first order was barked from the top of the room: *Lámha trasna*. They'd folded their arms quickly across the desk in front of them, never taking their eyes off Sister Joseph. That's how it was in those days: you sat, still and silent, wherever Sister had put you, your index finger on your lips for emphasis. *Ciúineas*: silence. Speak only when spoken to. Keep your *clár dubh* neat, your printing regular and upright. And have your *glantóir* at the ready – mistakes must be erased at once, lest they become habitual. Fifty small boys crowded into a freezing classroom. It had taken William only a very short time to learn that he'd been the good boy, seated beside the wild one as a steadying influence. He and Jack had laughed about it, years later.

'You may have been the quieter one,' Jack has often reminded him, 'but you were as much up for devilment as I was. You just got away with more because you never gave any lip. I couldn't keep my mouth shut.'

Almost sixty years. These days – and for a long time now – Jack and William can say 'yes' or 'no' to one another and there's no more to it. No explanations are required. You agree; you disagree. You take as you find.

There's a whole lot of comfort in that.

William pays the bill for breakfast and walks briskly, head down, back to the apartment car park. He's already left an envelope on the front seat, filled with photographs, a brief description of Julia, a new notebook. He eases his long frame into the driver's seat, turns the key in the ignition and sets off purposefully towards Dublin airport.

# *Julia*

JUST LIKE THE first time, the noise strikes Julia like a physical blow. But now she welcomes it. It means she's almost there, she's almost made it. This time, she can push her way through the throng with a practised air. Make no eye contact, make it seem as though you know exactly what you're doing, where you're headed for. Julia already knows the price to be paid for looking lost. Even now, the memory of that first time has the power to make her fearful all over again.

Three years ago – a lifetime ago. The lifetime that had begun and ended with William. She and Roisin had arrived here off the flight from Heathrow, just after midnight. And she had not been prepared for the wall of sound that had slammed against her inside the airport terminal. And the colour: saris of lime green and kingfisher blue. Deep ochre and vermilion, saffron and emerald: all in stark contrast to the brown-uniformed officials who had tried then, as now, to marshal thousands of people into orderly queues. Then, as now, they had failed.

'I'm going to find someone to tell us how we get to the domestic terminal,' Roisin said, finally. 'This is hopeless. Keep an eye on my rucksack.' And she hurried off into the crowds. Minutes later, she was back. She nodded to their right. 'Over there,' she said. 'There's a shuttle bus every half-hour. Let's go.' The bus was ready to leave, the driver just about to close the door. 'Wait!' Roisin cried.

'No room, no more room. Next one, you wait next one,' the man called back, waving them away.

'I'd kill for a cigarette, anyway,' Roisin said, as the driver gunned the engine and the door shuddered to a close. Seconds later, the bus shambled off into the sticky night. Roisin pulled cigarettes and a lighter from her rucksack. Julia looked around them. 'There's no one smoking, Ro,' she said. 'You sure you want to risk it?'

'Taxi, taxi, madam, you want taxi?' Out of nowhere, a man appeared at Julia's elbow. Her eye was instantly drawn to his official badge, his standard brown uniform.

'No, thank you,' Roisin said. Her voice was firm, polite. 'We'll wait for the bus.'

But he shook his head, pointing to his watch. 'No bus, no more bus,' he said, his voice rising. He shrugged his shoulders, spreading his hands to emphasize the depth of their predicament. 'Not for one hour.' He pointed at Roisin. 'No smoking here. It is not allowed to smoke. I take you, I take you.'

'Shit!' Roisin replaced her cigarettes and lighter, then zipped closed the front pocket of her rucksack. 'How much?'

'Fi' hundred. Only fi' hundred.'

Julia watched as Roisin did a quick calculation. 'Absolutely not,' she said, her voice rising. 'We'll wait for the bus.'

'Okay, okay, three hundred. I show you where you smoke okay?' He began moving in the direction of the taxi that Julia could now see parked behind him. His hands waved them on, excitedly, urgently.

'No. Two hundred,' Julia called after him. The prospect of another hour's wait was not an appealing one. But they'd been warned: don't let anyone rip you off.

'Okay, okay, two-fifty, we go now,' he insisted, walking back and grabbing at Roisin's rucksack.

'I'll take that,' she said.

Julia remembers now the speed with which everything started to happen once they got into the taxi: like pressing the fast forward on a DVD. As soon as they clambered into the back seat, the driver slammed the door closed and started the engine. At the same time he shouted something through the open window. As he began to move away, the passenger door was wrenched open and another man leapt in.

Julia turned to Roisin at once, seeing her own alarm reflected in her friend's eyes. 'I don't like this,' she said.

'Neither do I.' Roisin leaned forward. 'Domestic terminal, Jet Airways,' she yelled.

The driver slammed his hand on the steering wheel. 'Yes, yes, we go, we go now.'

But Julia remembers the terror as the buildings of Mumbai airport sped past the windows of the taxi, blurred, dizzyingly, as the driver accelerated to breakneck speed. She remembers noticing half-finished constructions, diggers operating under searchlights, ancient buses criss-crossing each other. They all acquired a sudden significance, a heightened presence, as though she was seeing these ordinary things for the last time. They insisted on being remembered. She was aware, too, of Roisin shouting, of her own sudden inability to move, of the streets rapidly becoming alleyways as the airport receded into the background.

Roisin's fist punching the driver's headrest suddenly made Julia snap to. 'Stop the car! Stop the car!' she yelled.

And then it was as though someone had turned up the volume. 'Pull over, pull over!' Roisin was kicking, shrieking, at least one fist making contact with the back of the driver's head. The car screeched to a halt. The driver turned to face them, his expression ugly, angry. So did the man in the passenger seat. He grinned at them, yellowly, and both men started shouting at the same time: 'Money, money, you give me money!' The noise was terrifying.

'Fuck you!' Roisin was beside herself, sobbing, choking, raging. Julia could feel her shake. All she wanted was to get out of this car, get away, go anywhere, be anywhere rather than here. She ripped four five-hundred-rupee notes from her purse and flung them at the driver. By that time they each had a door open, had one foot each on solid ground. They stumbled out of the taxi at the same time, yanking their rucksacks after them.

And then the passenger door flung open. 'Something for me! Something for me!' the accomplice yelled, starting after them. Julia can still remember Roisin's expression: the look of astonishment mixed with fear, puzzlement, anger. The car engine revved madly in the background.

'You little fucker!' she raged. 'I'll tell you what I'll give you. I'll tell you.' And Roisin waved her mobile in his face. 'I have your photograph – here – and your taxi number. I'll give you the police! That's what I'll give you!'

The car horn started blaring. For one terrifying moment the man hesitated between attack and flight. 'You fuck off!' Julia yelled, adding her voice to Roisin's, both of them stepping towards him as though at an agreed signal.

Just then, the taxi began to pull away from the kerb and the man raced after it, yelling back at them, shaking his fist, his official badge flapping against his chest.

In the sudden white silence that descended, Julia began to shake. And then, Roisin's voice. 'The cheeky little bastard. Something for me! Something for me!' She began to laugh, tears rolling down her cheeks. They stood there, clutching at each other, laughing helplessly, drunk with relief and safety.

'I didn't know your mobile had a camera,' Julia finally gasped. 'That was really clever.'

Roisin lit a cigarette, her fingers trembling. 'Maybe it has, but I don't have a clue how to use it.' And they were off again, choking, sobbing with laughter, unable to stop. Finally they sobered up. 'Let's start walking,' Roisin suggested. 'The airport is back that way – he didn't turn either right or left. I made sure to watch where we were going. I think it's a pretty straight route.' She stamped on the remains of her cigarette. 'Jesus, that was something else. Come on, let's go. Good job we've six hours between flights.'

Julia remembers how grateful she'd felt to Roisin. Had she been on her own . . . 'You were great, Ro. I don't know what happened to me – I kind of froze. It was as though it was all happening to someone else.'

'I've had a couple of near-misses before.' Roisin shook her head, angry at herself. 'I should have known better. That was not the behaviour of a seasoned traveller.' And she grinned at Julia. 'You keep telling me. Cigarettes will be the death of me.'

Julia struggled into her rucksack. 'Taxi, anyone?'

'No more taxis for me,' Roisin said, grimly. 'How much did you give him, anyway?'

'Two thousand rupees. I wanted it to be enough so that he would *go*. Make it worth his while just to go off home, or whatever. I was terrified he'd come back for more.'

'Hope he shares it with his passenger,' Roisin said. 'Hate to think he'd be mean. Sharing is caring.'

It was a nervous walk, Julia remembers, although perhaps not as nervous as it might have been. Adrenaline coursed through her, making her feel alert, powerful. It was as though her spine had been strengthened, her muscles made more responsive. Even her stride grew longer. She nursed the feeling, making sure to look behind her, around her, glancing constantly to her right and left, as she watched Roisin doing. Once, a dog snarled at them from a smoking rubbish dump on the side of the road. Teeth bared, hackles up, intent on guarding its territory against intruders.

'Keep walkin',' Roisin advised. 'Don't even look at it.'

When they passed, and the dog returned to its nosing, Julia had a brief, heady feeling that they had become invincible.

The airport lights then began to grow brighter, throwing out huge pools of garish white. Julia could see the high fence, covered in barbed wire, coils and coils of it strung along the whole length of the perimeter. At the same time she began to make out some strange, shadowy structures. Low, ramshackle affairs, built to abut the perimeter fence. Some leaned to the right, some to the left. All sagged somewhere, making them look dejected, like abandoned sheds. They appeared to be covered in some sort of material that shone strangely in the light – a dull, almost metallic sheen. As she got closer, Julia realized that the shiny roofs were in fact tarpaulins. And then she heard a child crying: that high, reedy, new-baby wail that reminded her at once of Jamie, then almost one. She stopped, shocked. Roisin turned to look back at her, puzzled.

'What?'

Julia pointed to what she now realized were houses: made out of packing cases, corrugated tin, blue plastic. But houses nevertheless. 'People *live* here?'

'Yeah,' Roisin nodded. 'All around the airport perimeter.' She shrugged. 'Anywhere there's work. Get ready to see a lot more of it.'

But Julia wasn't able to leave the image behind. She wondered about the baby whose cry had been silenced so quickly. It haunted her – haunts her still.

She and Roisin arrived at the domestic terminal forty-five minutes later, sweating, exhausted. Julia knew even then that this night was something she would never forget: it was seared into her memory.

And that memory is enough to galvanize her now.


She moves forward with hundreds of others, her long stride confident, purposeful. Bodies press against her on all sides. Clutching her passport and her swine-flu form, she approaches the desk. The woman is wearing a face-mask, as are most of the officials around her. Julia wonders – and not for the first time – how devastating an attack of swine flu could be here, among the elderly and the children in the vulnerable shanty towns of Mumbai.

The woman stamps her form and waves her away. Julia walks towards the exit. She knows exactly where she is going. She steps outside the door, where a shuttle bus to the domestic terminal awaits. To her left she sees maybe half a dozen men seated on a low wall. She sees the badges, the uniforms.

'Taxi, ma'am?' someone asks, his tone soft, respectful.

Julia shakes her head. 'No, thanks,' she says. 'This time, I'm taking the shuttle bus.'


Now Julia watches as the lights of Mumbai grow more distant and fade away into the blackness. She closes her eyes, her head tilted towards the aeroplane window. The man to her right is eager for conversation, but she is having none of it. Now that she is here, so close to where she needs to be, she feels all at once swamped by wave after wave of misgiving.

What on earth has she done? What has she been thinking? To walk out of her life like that, to flee for cover, leaving God knows what emotional wreckage behind? All the rubble of a lifetime, to be sifted through by those she loves. The sensation is as powerful as drowning: it feels as though oxygen is lacking in the air around her. She is being slowly strangled, suffocated by a sense of loss and guilt that is overwhelming.

She is startled by a sudden touch on her arm. 'Madam? You would like some water?'

It is her Indian neighbour. He is looking at her, the concern in his eyes magnified by the thick lenses of his glasses.

Julia realizes that her gasps must have been audible. She feels embarrassed; her eyes well up at this unexpected kindness. 'Yes, please,' she manages. He presses the call button.

'I am not very fond of flying, either,' he confesses to her. His lilting cadences remind her of the reassurances of child-hood. 'But we are perfectly safe. Please do not worry.' He hands her the glass of water and a napkin. She smiles her thanks and gulps at the water. It gives her something to hide behind: something to displace the rising tide of panic.

'Please.' The man beside her holds out one hand and takes the glass when she's finished. He nods at her encouragingly. Courtesy itself, she thinks, feeling ashamed at her earlier lack of friendliness.

'You rest, now,' he says. 'All is well.'

'Thank you.'

All is well.

She repeats the phrase to herself, over and over, hoping it will calm her. She breathes deeply, trying to access the emo-tional certainties that have kept her going for six months now, ever since that awful day at Greta's. She remembers the stifling air of the drawing room, Greta's unyielding back, the creeping inevitability of a past come back to punish her. And she remem-bers, too, clutching a loaf of bread, a packet of Bewley's coffee as she stumbled up Grafton Street later that afternoon, feeling with every step that her life was moving away from her, slipping out of her grasp.

But it was William's tenderness on that day that she remembers above everything else. The way he took care of her, anticipated her every need. His unknowing vulnerability confronted her every time she looked at him, making her flinch. She remembers with painful clarity the moment she made her decision. As she'd tried to struggle awake from an exhausted, sticky sleep that had brought no rest, he'd appeared at her side, looking like a rumpled guardian angel.

'Fell asleep myself,' he smiled. 'We're a right pair,' and handed her a cup of tea.

No, she thought, the word coming at her out of nowhere, falling like a stone through space. That's what we can never be. What we cannot be any longer: a pair. I'm much too dangerous for him. And that was it. Everything else flowed from that: every decision had its roots in that moment of illumination. She remembers its brightness, the way it seemed to hover in front of her eyes, making it impossible to see anything else but the glaring simplicity of resolution.

I have to go, she thought. I have to disappear and not come back. It's the only way to protect him. And Melissa. And the children.

And then came the feverish start of her preparations. She remembers how the focus on practical arrangements consumed her. Six months of planning, of concealment, of becoming a person other than herself. Tying up the loose ends of her life. Ends that almost became undone on the evening she'd asked William for his key. No matter how she'd agonized over it, she knew that she couldn't take the risk of a surprise visit. This had to be done – and done now. She can still see his puzzled expression as he'd reached into his trouser pockets.

'Do you want me to do anything?'

Julia could see by his eyes how he was longing to be asked. He had never said, but over the last months she had watched as William struggled to accept a new and subtle distance between them. The blue postbox that he had affixed to the wall during their early days together now struck Julia as a reproach. It reminded her of how she'd enjoyed his eagerness to be of use, to be the man around the house. And how he'd enjoyed the cosiness of their evenings together: home-cooked food in her ample living room. 'A proper house,' he'd declared. 'None of this poky "bijou" crap.'

She'd had to steel herself on more than one occasion, pushing him back when what she'd wanted was to pull him closer, hold him fiercely. Stop it, she'd told herself, raging inwardly when she could feel her resolve weakening. This is life: not some cosy TV sitcom. Real people don't get to play house. It was an illusion, an interlude. Get over it.

'It's fine, thanks.' Julia had practised the lines. 'Mrs Mc has already offered. I think she likes to feel useful. Besides, you know plumbers. He mightn't turn up at all and you'd have a wasted day.' She remembers the way her heart had thudded, expecting him to resist, just a little. But she had done her work well: he'd just unhooked his door key from the ring and handed it to her.

'Thanks,' she'd said, smiling at him. His complete trust in her, his love, his concern: all were symbolized by the key that now rested in her palm. She closed her fingers over the potency of its presence. On that final day before her departure she came close – so close – to telling him. Instead, she'd turned away and placed the door key in the little blue-and-green enamelled dish at the bottom of the stairs. She can still feel the desperation in the way she had curled herself around him in bed that night, holding him so close that he'd protested, laughing.

She'd kissed him. 'Make love to me,' she'd said, her voice urgent in the darkness. If he didn't, she knew that she would weep, crumble into small pieces beside him. She needed him to hold her together.

'Hey, hey,' he'd said, tenderly, 'what is it? You okay?'

'Yes,' she'd said. 'I love you. Just stop talking.'

The following morning, after he'd gone, Julia wept until she was empty. She'd sat in the living room for hours, remembering, staring at the chessboard. Her courage was failing her. She couldn't leave him; she had to leave him. She loved him; leaving him *was* loving him. She dug her fingers into her hair, pulling at the roots: anything to displace the pain that was threatening to destroy her carefully crafted resolve.

And then she saw it. The white queen. Something shifted inside her, releasing the knot of grief that had been tightening all morning. She knew at once that this was what she would do: leave him messages that only he could understand. She felt relief so intense that it was almost pain. She moved the white queen to a black square: shifted her universe so that she no longer belonged. He would understand this. She'd lead him to Sorcha, too, and somehow all the rest would follow. He would find her. She had to believe that.

Julia sighs and settles herself more comfortably. She glances at her watch. Only another hour or so to go. She should sleep.

It's around seven o'clock in the evening at home. Jamie and Susie will both be sleepy, fragrant after bathtime. Julia feels their small hands clutch at her heart. And sees Melissa's expression: quizzical, critical. Just as she had been all through Richard's illness, and down all the years since. It was as though her face had become fixed, formed during that teenage time, and no longer capable of softening.

Julia closes her eyes. One thing at a time. She can only deal with one thing at a time. When William finds her, then it will be time for Melissa. But only when he is safe – safe and with her.

She sleeps.


At Chennai, things go smoothly. The flight is on time, her luggage arrives.

'You are feeling better?' her neighbour enquires as he helps her lift her case off the conveyor belt.

'Yes, thank you. You've been very kind.'

He inclines his head, that unconscious gesture of courtesy; old-fashioned, gallant. 'I hope you enjoy our city.'

They shake hands and Julia delays for a few moments, waiting until she is sure he has gone. What she wants now is to rest, to sleep all the way through for three nights, before the final part of her journey begins. She leaves the airport terminal and hails a taxi.

'Hotel Sea Breeze,' she says. 'How much?'

'One thousand rupees,' the driver says.

She shakes her head. 'I'll give you eight hundred and fifty.' Her voice is firm, authoritative. 'That is the correct fare.'

'Okay, ma'am,' he says. He leaps out and helps her with her bags. Julia immediately relents. His eagerness to please is almost tangible in the night air. She'll give him the other hundred and fifty as a tip. Make his day. She stops, struck once again by how badly divided the world is. Make someone's day for less than three euros?

If only everything were as easy.

# *William*

ONCE AGAIN, William has trusted his sense of direction. He finds Greta and Gerry's house in Dún Laoghaire without any difficulty. He hopes they're home. Hopes to salvage some-thing, because so far today has yielded nothing – not that he'd expected it to.

People at the airport had been courteous, promising to 'get back to him' if anything were to emerge. And the same thing had happened at the two ferry terminals. He hadn't been able to help feeling that people were humouring him. It is high time he lit a fire under the Guards' enquiries. It's forty-eight hours since he and Melissa reported Julia's disappearance. And, from what he's learned from trawling the sad, grief-stricken 'missing person' sites on the Internet, the first seventy-two hours are crucial. He is quite prepared to make a nuisance of himself if he has to. And it also might be time to put Julia's photo up on lamp posts. He quails at this, though: apart from Melissa's predictable reaction – how dare he make so public her mother's private life – he knows that sort of scattergun approach would bring all sorts of nut-jobs out of the closet. The world is full of strange people, even stranger motives. He should know: he's made a good living for thirty years writing about oddballs, petty thieves, criminals.

He turns off the engine and sits quietly for a moment, looking out at the deserted street. This is definitely the one: he remembers the pretty green space in front of the row of elegant houses. It looks different tonight, of course – now that the trees and shrubs are no longer bathed in the sunshine of late September. Nevertheless, this is the one. It used to baffle Julia, this ability of his to find his way back to anywhere he had once visited, no matter how briefly, no matter how long ago.

'How do you do it?' she'd asked him, way back when they'd first met. 'I used to keep a notebook in my handbag, always, with directions to every single one of my patients' houses. I nearly *always* got lost, no matter how many times I'd been.' Her expression verged on the bashful, as though she'd just confessed to some terrible sin and wanted to know how to avoid it in future.

'Really?' William was surprised. It didn't fit with his brand-new impression of the public Julia: a competent woman in control of herself and her own life. He felt an absurd sense of relief, once she told him. His mind's eye watched as the brisk, capable fantasy Julia dissolved, leaving behind something altogether more tender and vulnerable in its place.

She nodded slowly. 'I don't tell too many people that. In fact, I've never told *anyone* that.' And then she smiled, shrugging a little.

'Bit of a dodgy admission, all right,' he agreed. 'Not the best tag-line: the doctor who loses her patients – no pun intended.'

She looked at him. Even at the time, he thought her gaze uncertain, almost troubled. It puzzled him in the long moment before she spoke again. What have I said? he wondered. Have I offended her in some way?

'But I'm not a doctor any more. Just a humble locum, from time to time.'

He leaned across, relieved, and kissed her. 'Don't worry,' he said softly, one hand on her shoulder, pulling her closer, 'your dark secret is safe with me.'

And then, as William now remembers it, she seemed about to say something else to him. She hesitated before releasing the seat-belt, one hand resting on the strap as she pulled it out and away from her shoulder. And William had waited. He liked the considered way she'd give her opinions on things. Measured, never one to rush to judgement. But whatever it was, she changed her mind and opened the passenger door instead. 'You ready for this?' she asked, turning back to look at him.

He nodded, squeezing her hand. 'Bring it on.' Her edginess puzzled him. These people were her friends, after all, they went way back. It struck him all at once that she might be nervous about *him*: afraid that he might be gauche, or get drunk, or get into a row with someone and embarrass her. Not things he normally did – at least, not any more – but he could see how she mightn't know that. And so he reassured her. 'I'll be on my best behaviour, I promise. Even if they're all raging Fianna Fáilers, I'll keep my powder dry.'

And now he wonders. What was it that he'd missed, even back then? What might he have learned, had he waited a little longer, probed a little deeper under the cloak of vulnerability that he'd just discovered?

Instead, he made her laugh at his earnest expression, as he hoped she would. He curses himself for that now. Mr Funny; Mr Bloody Quick Wit. He remembers her again as she looked back at him over one shoulder: and now he sees – or imagines he sees – something else in that gaze. Something asking him to be patient, or understanding. Maybe even asking him to *ask* her something. But how could he have known what it was? Might something as simple as 'Is there something wrong?' have done the trick? He brushes these questions away; he hasn't the time, not now. Anyway, it's all very fine: twenty-twenty vision and hindsight, and all that.

They'd walked up to the front door together – this same front door – hand in hand, and she'd rung the bell just as he is doing now. The house is one of those solid Victorian ones that Julia has always loved. He reminds her of that now. He keeps on talking to her inside his head, continuing the conversation he'd started from the moment he'd woken around four this morning. It is his act of faith – that, and speaking about her to others in the present tense. He is determined to do this, to keep her with him.

That dinner party in the spacious dining room of this spacious house had done what all dinner parties are supposed to do. Supplied plenty of good food, plenty of good wine and plenty of animated conversation that had, at once, set about sizing up the new boy. As William thinks about it now, he can see Julia again, so vividly that he can feel his palms begin to sweat. His breathing is obstructed: her presence beside him on this doorstep, here and now, is an intense, physical one, and it hurts. He lets his right hand fall to his side, pretending he can still feel her fingers in his, imagining he can still smell her perfume. He sees the short dark hair, swept back, stylish. The blue silk blouse that he'd admired; the pencil skirt that empha-sized her shapeliness. Those long legs . . . He stops. Get a grip, he says. You have work to do.

He presses the doorbell again and waits. This time, he can hear it jangling inside the house, missing a beat here and there, but still surely loud enough to be heard. He glances at his watch. Seven o'clock in the evening. Dark and miserable, but still a respectable time to call at someone's door. At least now he is doing something that has a defined, specific sense of purpose to it. It feeds his sense of moving forward, even if it's only with his feet.

What is keeping these people? The lights are on in the hallway – he can see that, through the leaded panels on either side of the door. And the house *feels* occupied. To hell with this: he's waited long enough. He lifts the brass head of some deity or other and knocks once, hard. The door is answered almost immediately by a small girl. He can see by her size that she must have had trouble reaching the lock.

'Hello,' he says, smiling down at her. 'My name is . . .' And she flees, leaving the door open behind her.

'Granny, Granny,' she calls, 'there's a strange man at the door.'

He hears footsteps approaching rapidly down the hall. A woman's voice. 'Gráinne, I told you not to answer the door. You must call me, or Granddad.' A face appears around the door, one that William recognizes.

'Greta?' he says. 'We've met. I'm William . . .' and he gets no further.

Is it his imagination, or does her face cloud over? He watches as she seems to recover her natural politeness and holds out her hand. 'Why, William, how are you?' She glances over his shoulder quickly, nervously. 'Is Julia with you?' Something in his face makes her stop. 'What is it? Has something happened to Julia?' One hand goes to her throat. She starts to finger the small gold cross that hangs there, on a fine gold chain.

'Maybe we could talk inside?'

'Of course.' But she hesitates. It's only for a second, but William notices. Then she seems to make a decision. She opens the door wider. 'Please, come in. Let me take your coat. Gráinne, go and get Granddad, please. Hurry, there's a good girl.'

\*

William sits on the overstuffed sofa that he remembers and waits for Gerry to arrive. Greta sits opposite him, perched on the edge of the wing-backed chair. She immediately reminds him of one of his maiden aunts: her posture is too stiff, too formal, belonging altogether to another generation. Surely she can't be as old as she acts? There's only a few years' difference, if he remembers correctly, between Roisin and Greta, and therefore between Julia and her. This woman's attitude, the way she carries herself, makes her seem a whole lot older. He doesn't care. It doesn't matter: he's interested only in what she might tell him. And this house is as good a place as any to start. This was where it had happened, the first party that Julia had ever brought him to, the first time he'd met any of her friends.

'Are you keeping well, William? It must be, what, three years since we met?' Before he has a chance to answer, she rushes on again. 'Life just seems to get busier and busier.' She tries to smile, but William thinks her face looks troubled. 'Somehow, one loses touch with people.'

William hears a heavy step in the hallway and the door is pushed open, groaning a little. Gerry stands there, backlit from the light in the hall, grey hair all in disarray. William wonders whether he's just been rudely woken from sleep. He stands up, extending his hand.

'Gerry, this is William Harris. You remember, Julia's friend.' It is not a question. Greta keeps glancing at her husband, and William wonders what it is that's worrying her. She looks anxious now, and her fingers play constantly with the cross at her throat.

Gerry takes William's proffered hand and shakes it. The contact is brief and cursory. A handshake without any warmth or welcome to it. 'William,' he says. 'What can we do for you.' And that's not a question, either, William thinks. Or if it is, it's one without any enthusiasm in the asking. He decides to keep it brief, get right to the point. Maybe a bit of bluntness might shake them up.

'Julia's gone missing. No one has seen her since Monday. She has vanished without a trace.' He watches as the two faces before him shade from shock to uncertainty, and finally to a wariness that he thinks he can understand. Why should they trust *him*? 'And it looks as though she planned it, as though she was determined to leave.'

'Really? Does anyone know why? And are you sure she's missing? I mean, she hasn't just taken herself off somewhere?' Gerry is patting his pockets as he crosses the room to sit on the arm of Greta's chair. William is taken aback at the lack of curiosity in his tone. It's almost as though the man is reluctant to be given any information. William feels his resistance, but plunges ahead, regardless. In for a penny.

'Yes, we're sure. Neither Melissa nor I know of any reason why she'd do something like this.' William pauses. It's good to mention Melissa here – makes it sound as though they're allies, makes his presence here somehow more acceptable. 'We've been to the police, of course, but there is no sign of coercion, no sign that she wasn't in control of herself. And we've also called the hospitals, just in case.' He pauses. 'The problem is that what we can't know is her state of mind when she left.'

'And why do you come to us?' Greta's question comes at him, sharply.

He looks at her, feigning more surprise than he feels. 'Because I know you are old and good friends.' A bit of an exaggeration, but still. 'I was hoping that you might be able to help me.' He stops, feels the air in the room begin to chill around him. 'To be honest, I don't even know how,' he confesses. '*Anything* you can tell me would be useful, because right now I've got nothing.' He pauses again, feeling grief engulf him. All the disappointments of the day, the past three days, crowd around him, leaving him hardly enough space to breathe. 'And I'm desperate to find her.'

Greta moves even further forward on her chair. 'We haven't seen Julia for some time. I'm afraid we don't know anything about her whereabouts.'

She's guarded, William thinks. She's definitely suspicious of me. And he tries to see the situation from her point of view, hers and Gerry's. What reason do these people have to believe that he's sincere? Why should they tell him anything to help him find Julia, when they can't be sure he's not the reason for her leaving? He tries his best to reassure them.

'I know you've known Julia a long time, and you know me hardly at all. Please believe me when I say that things are good between us, very good. I love Julia and I want, at the very least, to know that she's safe.' Even to his own ears, his words sound at best hollow, at worst unconvincing. Why, he wonders silently, do I always sound as though I have something to hide?

Greta inclines her head. 'Of course. But there is really nothing we can tell you. As I say, we've kind of fallen out of touch.' She glances at her husband, seeking confirmation.

'Can you remember the last time when you *were* in touch?' William asks. 'It might be important.' He sits forward on the comfortable sofa. He can't help the eagerness he feels, but strangely, telling Greta and Gerry about Julia's disappearance is making it all feel less, rather than more, real. It feels like a story, one that he is making up as he goes along. Guiltily he sees Melissa's face, accusing him of just that.

'I'm not sure.' Greta's face has closed now. Her eyes follow her husband as he stands up abruptly and walks over to the tall window, his hands shoved into his trouser pockets. He has removed his presence, William thinks. He is no longer with them, not in any meaningful way. William can feel the hostility seeping from that corner of the room, and he's baffled. Does he look like a wife-beater, an axe-murderer? Would Julia have stayed with him for three years if all she'd wanted to do was await an opportunity to escape, to run screaming from him and seek shelter in some women's refuge? Calm down, he tells himself. That will get you nowhere. And these people know her. All they want to do is protect her.

But somehow, what he sees before him does not strike him as protectiveness – at least not of Julia. Christ, he thinks suddenly, they're protecting *themselves*. What have I stumbled on here? But he decides to forge ahead, as if nothing has occurred to him. He's good at playing dumb.

'Weeks or months?' he prompts into the sticky silence.

Greta looks at him, startled. 'Oh no, not weeks,' she says, quickly. 'Months. Several months, at least. Perhaps even as much as a year.'

William sits up straighter. 'Are you sure?' he says. The expression on Greta's face tells him it is the wrong thing to ask. But he can't help it. He knows that she is lying. His mind leaps back six months: the telephone call from Greta in the early morning, saying she was ill. And Julia's mercy dash to look after her. That day is seared into his memory: he knows now that it has been one of the many times he has missed something significant about Julia. He should have dug a little deeper, probed a little harder. The image of her sad face on that day haunts him now.

'Of course I'm sure,' she says, stiffly. 'In fact, I think I can remember when I got her text. I was in Wicklow at Roisin's, my sister's house. Her new grandchild had just been christened. And he's nine months old now.'

William feels a fizz of excitement. Now he has a connection, a lead – however tenuous – that can be followed. So Celine was right: Roisin does live in Wicklow, maybe along with Hilary?

At least he has a first name, two first names, a location. He tries not to react: he is sure that Greta has no idea about the gift she has just given him.

Gerry clears his throat. William glances in his direction, but the man is looking out the window, his gazed fixed on something very interesting on a neighbouring roof. He's not going to speak, William thinks. The throat-clearing is his way of telling Greta to stop talking, that that's enough. No more information. William knows this because he used to do it with Jan when she'd become voluble after too many glasses of Chardonnay. He can feel that his time here is coming to an end; one way or the other, he'll be shuffled out of the room before he gets much more out of either of them. And they're withholding something from him, he's sure of it.

He latches onto the memory of Roisin that is now burning a hole through his skull. He remembers a pleasant woman, soft-spoken, but not remarkable in any way. He wonders if he'd even know her if he met her in the street.

'Roisin?' he says quickly. 'Would Roisin have kept in touch with Julia?'

'Perhaps,' says Greta. She is looking at her husband. 'But I really can't answer for my sister.'

There is movement over by the window and Gerry finally steps onto centre stage, out of the wings. William has the strongest sense of a man playing a part, inhabiting a role. But he hasn't rehearsed it enough: his performance is unconvincing.

'I really don't think we can be of any help to you,' he is saying. He waves one hand vaguely in the direction of the door. 'Greta, we need to get ready to take Gráinne home. I'm sorry, William, but we can't help.'

'Can't or won't?' William asks. He feels reckless now. It doesn't seem to matter: he's not getting anything here, anyway. He stands up.

Gerry takes a step towards him.

'May I at least ask where Roisin lives?' William directs his question to Greta.

'No, you may not,' Gerry says, testily. 'You've outstayed your welcome, Mr Harris. This is family business and I'd ask you not to interfere.'

'What business?' William asks. 'And whose family? How can my questions interfere in your "family business"? I'm not interested in you, Mr Fitzpatrick: all I'm doing is trying to find Julia.' Steady, steady. Out of the corner of his eye, William can see that Greta is distressed. Maybe if he were to return when she is on her own . . .

'It's just that she mentioned visiting Hilary on Tuesday. And I'm wondering if Roisin might know who Hilary is, even if you don't.'

Greta looks at him as though he has just struck her. Suddenly there is commotion in the room. Gerry is moving him swiftly towards the door, Greta's mouth is opening and closing, but no words are coming out. What does come out is a low moan.

'That's it, Mr Harris. I insist that you leave.' Gerry's grip is surprisingly firm. William winces as the man's fingers dig into the flesh of his forearm. Gerry marches him down the hall, towards the front door. By the time they reach it, William has retrieved his arm from the other man's grasp. He tries to speak, but Gerry is not listening. He raises one hand to stem William's protests. 'And I further insist that you do not come back.' He wrenches William's overcoat from the hallstand and shoves it at him.

Before he can answer, William finds himself standing outside on the doorstep, his 'Wait, please' unacknowledged. Gerry has slammed the door shut behind him. William's heart is hammering. He can feel the blood pounding in his ears.

What is going on here? What are these people so frightened of? And who the hell is Hilary?

He opens the car door, his hand trembling a little so that he misses the lock at first. Once inside, he sits for a few moments, unable to move. He is aware of curtains being drawn in the house he has just left: or rather, in the household that has just ejected him, forcibly, out onto the pavement and into the night.

But then it starts. A little ripple of exhilaration. His instinct has been right, after all. Find Roisin. Find Hilary. And they will lead him to Julia.

First thing tomorrow he will hit the road to Wicklow.

# *Julia*

THE AFTERNOON FOLLOWING Julia's arrival, Deepak waits for her just outside the entrance to the hotel. It hadn't taken long for her to warm to him the previous night: by the time they'd reached the Sea Breeze, they were chatting like old friends. Pictures of his grandchildren littered the dashboard, marigolds hung from his mirror – 'for Lord Shiva', he told her. Now, he leaps out of the taxi as soon as he sees her and opens the passenger door.

'Good afternoon, Deepak,' she says.

'Good afternoon, ma'am. Are you fine?'

Julia smiles. Sometimes the use of English here makes her feel as if the language approaches her from an acute angle. It creeps up on her when she isn't looking. She remembers a notice from three years back, around some hotel pool or other. 'Do not swim under the influence of alcohol,' it had warned, earnest in its use of bold and italics. 'Alcohol makes you whimsical.'

'Yes, thank you, Deepak,' she says now. 'I am fine, and you?'

'I am also fine,' he says.

She waits until he is sitting beside her and hands him the piece of paper. 'This is the hospital I would like to visit. I have a colleague there – a friend from a long time ago.'

He glances down, sees where she has printed the name

clearly. He nods at once, recognizing it. 'Yes, ma'am. I know the Adyar Institute. It is a very good hospital, even for those who are not paying.'

'My friend's worked there for almost ten years. I'm looking forward to seeing her again.' Alicia, she thinks. Still tireless. Still radiating energy and kindness and competence, even by email.

'Come and see me,' she'd written. 'Let me show you what a few dollars can do in India.'

As Julia makes her way there now, she wonders at the trajectory of her life, the lives of others. All these years later, the same people are still significant to her in the different ways they have always been: Roisin, Sorcha and now Alicia, whom she hasn't seen in almost forty years.


As soon as Julia steps across the threshold of the hospital, she can feel it. The sense of purpose that is everywhere: one that vibrates with an energy that is almost incandescent. She is drawn back at once to her days as a junior doctor, realizes with a jolt how keenly she can still miss them. Things had seemed so much simpler then, even in their complexity. There had always been an answer, no matter how elusive: a certainty that could be believed in, striven towards. Nothing was ever hopeless.

She approaches the information desk. 'Good morning.'

'May I help you?' the young woman looks up at Julia and smiles in welcome. Her face is smooth, her eyes and lips heavily made up in shades that exactly suit her dark skin.

'I am here to see Dr Alicia Newcomer. My name is Julia Seymour. She is expecting me.'

Soraya – according to her name badge – looks down and searches for Alicia's name in the plastic-covered pages of the hospital directory. She frowns as her glossy red fingernail scans the lists of numbers. The telephone rings behind her. The queue of bodies pushing towards the desk is growing longer, denser. Impatience is in the air.

On impulse, Julia leans forward. 'Please,' she says, 'let me find her. I'd like to arrive unannounced. Just tell me which floor.'

Soraya hesitates.

'I'm a doctor,' Julia says. 'Dr Newcomer and I were colleagues.'

To Julia's left, a woman in a wine-coloured sari says something sharp, impatient, almost spitting her words across the desk. Julia turns just enough to see an agitated profile, a hand tapping on the desk in front of her, dozens of glass bangles jangling. Soraya nods briefly at Julia, doing her best to hide her irritation. 'Fourth floor,' she says, pointing to her left. Julia turns to go and, as she does so, her place at the desk is immediately jostled for. The space is filled before she has even begun to push her way back through the crowd.

She follows the signs for the lifts, making her way down the hallway where women are dusting, brushing, rhythmically mopping the gleaming floors. The lift is crowded, the press of bodies sticky and uncomfortable. Julia looks upwards. She tries to blot out the curious glances of the women, the conversation bouncing back and forth among three or four of the men, all of them hovering at the level of her shoulders. She doesn't know what they're saying, but their voices are loud enough to carry across a crowded street. When the lift stops at the third floor, Julia suddenly decides to escape. She'll go the rest of the way on her own.

Just before she opens the door at the top of the stairs, Julia stops and smoothes her blouse. It has become crumpled in the heat. For a moment she fears that her face, too, has become crumpled in the heat. She worries that Alicia will judge her on how she looks, on how much she has changed. On how much older she has become. But surely Alicia must have changed, too? Tireless does not necessarily mean ageless. Stop it, Julia, she tells herself. She settles her rucksack more firmly across one shoulder and pulls open the door to the fourth floor.

The contrast with downstairs could not be greater. Here, there is a hush, an atmosphere of calm that is intensified by the quiet clicking of the fans. The air is moving. Julia can feel its cool trickle across the skin of her face, her arms. She approaches the nurses' station.

And then, she sees her.

Striding across the bottom of the corridor, white coat flying, is the Amazon Julia remembers from her youth. They both stop, Alicia spotting her at almost the same time. As though at a given signal, they begin to move towards each other, Julia a little hesitantly, Alicia at a run. They don't call out, hardly speak above a whisper: when they meet, they collide, each of them grappling in her urgency to embrace the other.

'Julia, Julia! It's really you! I can't believe it.' Alicia hugs her, then pushes her away, making sure her eyes aren't deceiving her. Her face is shining. Her gaze is intense, just as Julia remembers. She hugs her again, harder this time. 'Irish, oh, Irish, it's so good to see you!'

And Julia clings to her. She buries her face in the warm, sweet-smelling skin of her neck. The tears come and she finds that she is unable to speak.

'Whoa!' Alicia holds her at arm's length. 'This isn't the bit where you're supposed to cry. That comes later – at least a bottle of wine later.'

Julia tries to gather herself, aware of the doctors and nurses orbiting Alicia, some grinning, all curious. 'What an entrance,' she says, laughing now. 'Please, accept my apologies.' She wipes away the tears, finding that she doesn't care at all. The faces are open, friendly: one or two just a little guarded.

Alicia drapes one arm over Julia's shoulder, wheels her around to face her audience, introduces her to one white coat after the other. 'This is my old colleague and friend, Julia Seymour. We studied together in Ireland. She answers either to 'Julia' or 'Irish' – whatever way the spirit moves you.'

'Pleased to meet you,' Julia says, over and over again, feeling the warmth of each handshake, feeling Alicia's welcome wash all over her.

'Come with me,' she says, tugging at Julia's hand once the last person has been greeted, the last cheek kissed.

She waves her hand in the air, an expansive gesture that makes Julia remember the fusty halls of UCD, and this electric Californian presence – a red-haired powerhouse who had swept her way through them all, kicking up a lot of dust in her wake.

'I can hardly believe you're here,' she's saying. 'We've so much to catch up on. How long can you stay?' She unlocks the door to an office and gestures Julia inside in front of her. Julia stands and looks around her in amazement.

The room is tiny, made to appear even smaller by the three computer desks that are crowding for space. The walls are lined with shelves, and towers of books rest against each other in all of the four corners. But it is the order that amazes Julia. Everything is neatly accommodated, there are no stray papers, no overflowing in-trays. This is not the messy student she once knew. She turns to look at Alicia, unable to help the slow smile that she can now feel spreading across her face.

Alicia pushes her towards one of the desks. 'I know, I know,' she says, 'I've finally become an anal-retentive. Would you believe it?'

Julia laughs. 'You put me to shame.'

Alicia shakes her head. 'Survival,' she says. 'The bureaucracy here is so overwhelming that if I don't get my shit together on the paperwork, I've no time for my patients.' She shrugs. 'So I've become organized. It's my karma.' And she grins. 'C'mon, honey, sit down. No standing on ceremony here.' She pulls an insulated jug off the shelf behind her, grabs two plastic cups from a tray. Julia watches her, sees the familiar sense of purpose that radiates from Alicia's every movement. She has the air of a woman present in her life, fulfilled in her work. For a moment, Julia feels a surge of envy, of regret.

'You're happy here,' she says now. 'And you haven't changed a bit.'

Alicia nods. 'Yeah. I am happy. I'm home.' She pushes her chair back from the desk, puts her feet up on its shiny surface. 'Oh, man, that's better. I've been standing since seven-thirty.' Then she looks at Julia. 'You still lie beautifully, by the way. I dye my hair.' She unscrews the top of the jug, peers inside. 'It's my one last bit of vanity. The rest I've just handed over to middle age.' She shrugs. 'I think I'd hate even more *not* to have changed.'

Julia shakes her head. 'No,' she says softly. 'That's not what I mean. It's got nothing to do with your hair. It's you. Your enthusiasm. It's everywhere.'

Alicia hands her a glass of water. 'Here. It's hotter than hell today.' Julia drinks gratefully. 'And what about you?' she looks across the desk at Julia, her head to one side. Her eyes are curious. 'I like the cropped look. Short hair really suits you.'

Julia smiles. 'It's a long story.'

'Well, I have a little time now, and a lot longer tonight. I'm free as a bird.' She gulps her water, refills both their cups. 'Once I knew you were coming, I roped in some favours. A lot of favours. I'm all yours, kid. Tonight – and some of tomorrow morning, with any luck. Now shoot.'

'I can't believe I'm actually here,' Julia begins. And then it happens again. Grief in its potent, subtle treachery swamps her words. Her careful, rehearsed sentences have all been swept away. Where does she begin? How does she begin? She looks at Alicia, her eyes full of appeal.

'You need my help?' Alicia has put her cup down. Her feet are once more on the floor. She is wearing the expression that Julia knows so well. Serene; compassionate; competent.

Out of the corner of her mind Julia has noticed, too, that the Californian cadences have become blurred, softened. Slowed. She looks at Alicia, trying to pick through so many strands of memory that appear suddenly brighter, clearer, more discrete than they have in many years.

She looks her friend in the eye. 'Yes,' she says. 'Yes, I need your help.'


'So,' Alicia says. 'Tell me why you're really here.'

It is later in the day. They are sitting in Alicia's apartment, the city spread out below the large picture window. The Arihant Majestic is clearly visible against the evening skyline. Alicia is sitting just as Julia remembers: her long legs tucked underneath her on the sofa, cushions scattered everywhere. The cool interior is like a blessing after the heat of the streets. Marble floors, exotic rugs, paintings that shimmer in the low light.

Julia was taken aback when she first arrived: this was not – or never had been – Alicia's style. She caught Julia's look and grinned.

'Forty years have passed – what did you expect? That I'd still be living like a student in some damp and dingy basement in Rathmines?' And she shuddered. 'Jeez, nobody does damp like the Irish.'

Julia smiled. 'No, of course not. I'm just . . . surprised. It's so . . .' She couldn't find the right word.

'Opulent?'

'Yes. If you like.' Julia stopped, dismayed. 'I'm sorry – I seem to be making a habit of saying the wrong thing.'

But Alicia laughed at her. 'Sit down, relax. I'm glad you like it.'

'It's stunning. I love it.'

Alicia spun around, taking in the whole apartment with that generous gesture that Julia remembers so well. 'It's my refuge.'

'From the hospital?'

'Yeah. I discovered pretty early on that I couldn't do this kind of work' – she nodded vaguely to the city below, teeming beyond her windows – 'if I didn't have a space like this to come home to. It's walking distance from the hospital, as safe as it gets, but at the same time it's a million miles away.'

'Functional luxury,' Julia said. 'That's what Richard used to call it.'

Alicia looked at her quickly. 'That's absolutely right. Smart man, your husband.'

'Yes. Yes he was.'

And now Alicia waits, her direct question hanging in the air between them. Julia looks at her. 'I *will* tell you what I'm doing here. I promise. But right now I have to explain how it's for a whole lot of different reasons.'

'I told you already. We have all night.' Alicia opens a bottle of beer. 'You're still a wine freak, right?'

Julia nods. 'I suppose I am. White, please.'

Alicia pours and sits back, watching Julia closely. 'Okay.

I'm on call from six tomorrow morning, so that gives you' – she glances at her watch – 'eight hours, ten hours at a stretch. Talk twice as fast and we might do it in five.'

'Okay. First, I have to tell you about someone you never met. Her name was Lucy.'

'Shoot.'

Julia can feel something inside her start to unfold as she begins to articulate the memory that has haunted her for ten years. 'Lucy was Richard's sister,' she begins. 'She was thirty-eight. She took her own life, in a clinic in Zurich, ten years ago. I was with her.' She pauses. 'I've never told anybody that. And there's more.' She looks at Alicia, can't help the knot that gathers at the base of her throat.

'You're safe,' Alicia says. 'You're safe and you're here. Just let it out. The Catholics say that confession is good for the soul.'

Julia smiles. 'There speaks the unreconstructed atheist.'

'Keep talking, Irish.'

She draws one deep breath and plunges into the unspooling memories.


Julia handed Bernard the rucksack and felt Lucy's weight sag against her other arm. She turned and helped her into the back seat of the car, swinging her legs in after her. It was all done swiftly, with fluid, practised movements.

'Thank you,' Lucy murmured. She closed her eyes and leaned her head back while Julia fastened her seat-belt.

'Sleep now,' Julia said. 'Are you comfortable?'

A nod, almost imperceptible.

Julia kissed her on the forehead. 'It won't be long now,' she whispered. 'I promise.'

She made her way around to the passenger door, almost colliding with Bernard as she did so. Then she realized and smiled. 'Wrong door,' she said. 'I'm sorry: old habits die hard.'

The drive from the airport to the suburbs brought them through an urban landscape that grew increasingly bleak. Or perhaps it's just me, Julia thought. Perhaps it's today.

Bernard pulled up outside a nondescript apartment block. Grey. Concrete. Smaller windows than Julia had expected. She turned to see that Lucy was awake. Her eyes looked suddenly huge, luminous against the pallor. 'We're here,' she said.

Inside the building Bernard called the lift. Julia focused on the mottled green floor, the subdued walls. Lucy's hand in hers.

The lift doors opened. 'This way,' Bernard said. 'We are just here, at the end of the corridor.'

Lucy's eyes followed him as he inserted the key, opened the door, turned back to them, almost in welcome. 'Like Alice in Wonderland,' she murmured to Julia. 'We're off to an afternoon tea party.' And she giggled.

Julia looked at her sharply.

Lucy smiled. 'It's okay. You always said I had a strong sense of the absurd.' Her grip on Julia's hand tightened. 'No regrets,' she said. It was not a question.

Julia didn't answer, could not answer. All she could see before her was the mischievous eight-year-old she'd first known, the youngest by far in a sprawling, chaotic family. Bright-eyed, curious, adored by all her older brothers. A charmed life, Julia had once thought. She wondered if she might have been even a little jealous of her, of the affection that always sought her out – filings to a magnet. She crossed the threshold now, guiding Lucy in before her. She noticed a couple of paintings hanging on the wall above the circular table: bright, oranges and yellows and reds.

Lucy sat on one of the ladder-back chairs that faced the small window.

'I will leave you for a little time,' Bernard said. 'You can become settled.' He placed a single key on the oilcloth-covered table. Then he left and closed the door quietly behind him. In the silence that followed his departure, Julia hung up coats, opened her rucksack, looked around the room to see what else she could do.

'It's okay,' Lucy's voice came to her softly, stilling Julia's hands that were suddenly unsure, restless. 'Come here and sit beside me.'

Without a word, Julia crossed the room.

She helped Lucy undress and lie down on the single bed. They said little, and both looked out the window. The sun was beginning to set. The skies above the city were a dirty orange, streaked with grey and the occasional flash of cobalt blue. 'I think it's going to thunder,' Lucy said at last. 'That's a very stormy sky.' And then she turned to Julia and smiled. 'Kind of fitting, isn't it? It's what I used to tell my students to call a "pathetic fallacy".'

'That rings a distant bell,' Julia said, handing her the cup of tea she'd just made for her. 'Not sure I ever completely understood it, myself.'

'Ah – but you were like my big brother: the scientist. Mr Fact Man.' Lucy looked at her, archly. 'I don't think Richard's lexicon ever ran to literary terms. Golfing ones, yes; and sailing; and, of course, medical. But I don't think he had a poetic bone in his body.'

Julia laughed. 'No, Richard was a doer. He couldn't sit still long enough for poetry.' She paused and said softly, 'But he was very proud of yours. Thrilled to bits at all the prizes you won. And your books. He treasured them.' Julia could see his pride, still. And the way his face used to light up every time Lucy came to call. Part of this family, he'd always told her. You come and go as you please. And she had come and gone: a frequent visitor throughout the fifteen years of their marriage. And then afterwards, bringing companionship and comfort to Julia's home. A house that had become divided against itself.

Lucy looked away, out into the sky-filled dusk. Julia sat back, allowed the silence to fill the room again. She'd seen this before: this thoughtful need to focus on detail, to engage with memory, to move back and forth between stillness and speech. Picking up threads; weaving; letting go.

'We're not a long-living family, are we?' Lucy asked, suddenly. She didn't turn around from the window. 'Richard at fifty, and here am I, thirty-eight. And a more active bunch of siblings you couldn't meet. What would you call that, Dr Julia?'

'A cruel irony,' Julia said quietly.

Lucy nodded. 'I'm ready now. To ask about Richard. Tell me, please.' And she turned to face her.

Julia breathed deeply. This is what she'd been waiting for, for months. Ever since the afternoon Lucy had landed on her doorstep. 'Out of the blue,' she'd said cheerfully, standing in the porch, rucksack at her feet. 'Here I am again.' True to her nature, she hadn't tried to soften her presence, either. 'I'm dying,' she'd said.

Julia had looked at her, appalled. 'What?'

Lucy had sat in Richard's chair, in Julia's kitchen, her hands spread out on the table in front of her. The usual cup of tea just within reach. Julia could still see the pale beauty of her skin, the nails pink-shaped and delicate, like shells. She concentrated on that, instead of on what Lucy was saying. She wasn't able to look at her: at that open, blunt expression that reminded her so much of Richard.

'It's true. No doubt about it. Three months at the outside. I want you to help me.'

'What? How?' The alarm must have shown on Julia's face.

Lucy held up her hand. 'I'm going to choose my own time, my own way.' Seeing Julia's expression, she said quickly, 'Not in Ireland, of course. I wouldn't expose anyone to that, least of all you. The where isn't important – I'll come to that in a minute.' She stopped. 'It's you I want. I love my brothers to bits; they're all sweethearts. But I couldn't ask them. It would be too much. Too much.' And she shook her head.

Julia tried to speak then, but Lucy stopped her. 'I won't change my mind, so don't even try. I've already made all the arrangements. What I want to know is: will you come with me? That's all I'm asking: just that you are there *with* me – nothing else.' And she smiled her crooked smile. 'You're the sister I never had. I'm not brave enough to go on my own. And I'm not brave enough to be with my brothers, either. Help me, Julia, please.'

And then she crumbled, weeping through the fingers that now covered her face. Julia went to her, put both arms around her. 'Of course I'll be with you. I'll do whatever I can, I promise,' she said, moved beyond tears.

'I don't want to suffer like Richard,' Lucy said, sobbing. 'I can't. Even now, the pain is unbearable.'

They sat for hours until the light dimmed. First in Julia's familiar kitchen, then outside, among the fragrant hollyhocks and jasmine of her silent summer garden.

'This is so tranquil,' Lucy said, smiling. 'I knew it was right to come here. It's where I want to be.' Her face clouded for a moment. 'Am I asking too much of you, Julia? Please be honest.'

'No,' Julia answered. 'Not too much at all. I wish I could

make it better. But I can't.' The bitterness of those last words surprised even Julia herself. 'I wish you'd consider other options. There is so much—'

'We've just been over all that,' Lucy interrupted, her voice sharp. 'At least three times. I'm not here to be fixed.' Her words became softer. 'I don't buy into the philosophy that doctors can fix everything. I've come to terms with what has happened to me. Oh,' and she shrugged, 'sometimes I still get mad as hell. But mostly I've accepted it. I don't see death as a defeat, Julia. You don't need to go to war on my account.'

'Nevertheless,' Julia tried to keep her voice even, 'it's . . . just . . . it's not fair.' She didn't trust herself to say more. You're pathetic, she thought, angry with herself. *Not fair*: just like a toddler stamping its foot. Fat lot of use you are, to a dying woman. To a dying husband. To anyone.

Lucy sipped at her tea, watching a tortoiseshell cat prowl along the back wall of the garden, leap gracefully onto the roof of the shed and land in the flowerbed beneath. 'Look at that,' she said admiringly, 'that's one of the things I'll miss.' And she turned to Julia. 'Ordinary things. Tea. A garden. A cat's casual elegance.' She smiled. 'I'm cheating. It's from a poem I'm working on.' She doubled over suddenly then, her face a white mask of pain. The china cup and saucer fell from her lap in slow motion and shattered into dozens of pieces on the flag-stones.

Julia stood up at once. 'Is your medication in your rucksack or your handbag?'

'Handbag,' Lucy gasped, perspiration beading all across her forehead.

Afterwards, Julia helped her up to bed. Lucy insisted on going upstairs, did not want, she declared, the invalid status of the couch.

Just before she slept, she caught Julia's hand and said, 'I've wanted for so long to ask you about Richard. About whether he wanted your help? Asked for it, even?' But her eyes clouded over, her grasp become slack.

'Sleep,' Julia urged. 'Ask me tomorrow. Ask me anything tomorrow and I promise I'll tell you the truth.'

Lucy nodded, allowed her eyes to close. But the next morning she hadn't asked. Nor in the days that followed. Julia waited, expecting it, once Lucy felt ready. Her questions had continued to hover in the air between them, unspoken until this moment: but their presence had always been palpable.


'No,' Julia said now, meeting Lucy's clear gaze. 'Richard was adamant. He did not want help. We'd spoken about it many times; we each wanted to know what was right and appropriate for the other, if catastrophe ever struck.' She swallowed; that last conversation with Richard was now more vivid than ever, the familiar ache hollowing out her insides again. Although whether the pain was for Richard or for Lucy, or for herself, she no longer knew.

'And strike it did: catastrophe.' Lucy said.

'Yes. In a way neither of us ever imagined. We were thinking long term – you know, shuffling along one day in our eighties, we might have to worry. But not before. Not at *fifty*.'

'What did he say?'

'He'd always said that life was precious. And that he wanted to experience the "fullness of everything". That was his term.'

'Yes.' Lucy looked at Julia, suddenly animated. 'That's *exactly* what he used to say.'

'He said that's how he was living his life, and he wanted to greet death, when it came, in the same way. But it wasn't that simple.' Julia could see her husband on the evening before it happened. His shock of grey hair, falling onto his forehead. His tanned face, after a summer of sailing out of Dún Laoghaire. His hand in hers.

Larger than life, they'd said at his funeral. Tribute after tribute saying the same thing. It had made her bitter. All that largeness, and how it had reduced, suddenly, to nothing. A handful of ash and bone in a blue Chinese urn.

'You must have been tempted, though.' Lucy looked down at her hands. 'I mean, you're here with me? So it's not that you have a profound moral objection to ending life when there's no quality left.' She glanced up, then said quickly, 'I'm sorry: that sounds like a judgement, and that's not what I meant. I just feel . . . this is so important: I need to get to the heart of things. My gorgeous big brother. And you loved him, I know you did.'

Julia pulled her chair closer. 'I adored the ground he walked on. It's been ten years, Lucy, and I still haven't met any man who even comes close to what Richard was. I don't believe I'll ever love again in the same way.' She paused. 'This – here with you – this is different from what happened to Richard.'

'How?'

'Because you have made a decision. You. On your own. And I am respecting that. Richard also made a decision. It was a different one, but I had to respect that, too. No matter how much I wanted to ease his suffering, I couldn't. Because he couldn't ask me. He couldn't ask me to err on the side of comfort.'

Lucy shook her head. 'But the way he looked, sometimes, the way he appealed with his eyes.'

'You think that didn't break my heart?' Julia demanded. 'But I am not God, Lucy. No doctor is. What you saw as an appeal could have been anything – any emotion at all. Or none. I did not have the right. And Richard couldn't ask.'

'It's why I'm here,' Lucy said. 'I can't go through that –

can't wait until I can no longer ask for what I want. He taught me that. And I have so little time.'

'That's why I'm here with you.' She stroked a strand of hair back from Lucy's forehead. Perspiration had begun to build across her eyes. 'It's time for your medication.' She stood up.

'No,' Lucy took hold of her sleeve. 'Leave it. Bernard will be back soon.'

'But . . .'

'No. This is for Richard.' She smiled. 'A little bit of fullness, just for him.' She stroked the back of Julia's hand. 'Tell me something else?'

'Go on.'

'Did Melissa really understand what was going on?'

Julia sighed. She had never discussed this with anyone. Until that day it had been forbidden territory.

'Who am I going to tell?' Lucy's smile was suddenly crooked. 'I can take your secret with me.'

'Melissa was angry – no, furious with me. Everything for her was black-and-white. She was a hormone-charged, grieving teenager, and she could not see why I couldn't fix her father.' Julia had to stop for a moment. It still hurt to remember. 'She'd scream at me to give him something – but Richard was paralysed, not in pain. There was nothing I *could* give him. She couldn't understand that reasoning. I had to hold the line. And I don't think she's ever forgiven me.' Julia felt her eyes fill. 'Jesus, Lucy – what a time for self-pity. I'm sorry.' She wiped one hand abruptly across her eyes.

'No,' Lucy said, softly. 'Not self-pity. Pity for all of us.'

There was the sound of a soft knock on the apartment door. Julia stood up as Bernard entered. There was another man with him, tall, dark-coated. He approached the bed, nodded at Julia. 'Mrs Delaney? I am Dr Brandt.'

Lucy reached out and shook his hand. 'Pleased to meet you,' she said, 'this is my sister, Julia.' He shook hands, looked puzzled.

'Sister-in-law, really,' Julia said.

'No time for silly distinctions,' said Lucy. 'You're my sister.'

'I'll step outside for a moment,' Julia said. Lucy nodded and Julia left the room, needing to escape. Outside, she sat on the bottom step of the upward flight of stairs and rested her head in her hands. She was unaware of the city noises beyond the window, of the cold creeping around her.

All she knew was that she had never felt so empty in her life.

The air inside Alicia's apartment has stilled. Even the whirr of the ceiling fan feels more muted.

'She went through with it.' Alicia's words startle Julia. She has been miles away, ten years away, reliving Lucy's last evening. She is amazed to find herself sitting here in another world, surrounded by the kind comforts of Alicia's home.

'Oh, yes. She never doubted it was what she wanted. She'd no children, she'd put her house in order, as she said, and she'd even had the time to be reconciled with her ex-husband. That was important to her.' Julia smiles now as she hears Lucy's last words.

'Remember the wedding?' Lucy had asked suddenly. 'Philip's and my wedding?'

Julia nodded. 'Of course.'

'I gave him all the photographs, just before I came to you.'

Julia couldn't hide her astonishment. 'You *met* him?'

Lucy nodded. 'Yeah. Thought it might be time to mend *some* of my fences, at least.'

'How did it go?'

'Fine, good. Neither of us had any anger left. It's all burnt away. We had a nice time.'

Julia stroked her hair. 'I am really glad of that.'

A beat. 'He has two little boys.'

Julia waited.

She shrugged. 'I was sad. He'd never wanted children with me. It hurt, but I was still glad I saw him. Saw them.'

'You're one brave woman.' Julia mopped her face.

'I knew it wasn't going to hurt for too long,' Lucy said.

'What about you?' Alicia asks, softly, now. 'Is her death still hurting you?'

Julia nods. Alicia doesn't speak for a moment. When she does, she says, 'You've done nothing wrong. You know that.'

Julia doesn't reply.

'You said there's more.'

Police sirens wail outside the window. Julia looks up, startled. The sound has broken the spell, the illusion of separateness, of security all around her. She sees Alicia, watching her, and shakes her head. 'No,' she says. 'Not tonight.'

Alicia makes no comment. Instead she stands up. It is a brisk, no-nonsense movement. 'Come on,' she says. 'You are exhausted. Sleep.' And she hauls Julia to her feet.

Julia allows herself to be led to the bedroom. Alicia hands her a pair of cotton pyjamas. 'Bathroom's through there. I'll see you in the morning.' She pulls Julia towards her, kisses her on the forehead. 'I'll be as quiet as I can. But I'll need to be ready to go from six, if there's an emergency.' She pats the pocket of her cotton trousers. 'I'm married to my bleep. And he's an early riser.'

She leaves and Julia sinks into the bed. Watching her friend leave, she has another vivid flash of memory. The police, the coroner, the investigation, the video-tape: Lucy. All routine, all very Swiss: organized, matter-of-fact. Clockwork.

On that night Julia had gathered up their belongings and taken a taxi to the hotel: to the room she and Lucy had never shared. Upstairs, she'd looked out of her window onto the dark waters of the lake. And at the lights of Zurich shimmering below her.

Tonight, on the other side of the world, she takes an envelope from her handbag. She places it on the small carved table beside the bed, so that she'll see it the moment she wakes up in the morning. Then she pulls a cool cotton sheet up over her head and allows sleep to drown her.

# *William*

THE MOMENT the door is opened, William knows he has struck pay dirt. Roisin stands before him, her expression quizzical. She has opened the door only slightly. He approves of her caution. She looks slimmer than he remembers, frailer. 'Yes?' she says. Now he is able to see her the way she was on the night of Greta's party, in some sort of flowery dress. Julia had greeted her affectionately, pressing William's hand into hers.

'Ro, meet William. William, Roisin. Roisin and I go way back – a bit like you and Jack. We met at secondary school. And we more or less lived in each other's houses.'

Roisin shook hands, smiling at Julia, at William. 'Pleased to meet you. It's lovely to see both of you.'

'William's a writer,' Julia said. 'You'd like his books, Ro: thrillers and corrupt cops, and murder and mayhem.'

William was surprised. It seemed unlikely that such a gentle, feminine woman would be drawn to gore. But Roisin's eyes widened in delight. 'Brilliant!' she said. 'You must tell me all about them.'

'Sure, I can bore with the best of them,' he said, cheerfully. 'And Julia tells me you're a lecturer?'

'Yes, at UCD. Liked the academic life so much I never left. But I was never the star Julia was – more earnest, more plodding, that's me.' And she nudged her friend in the ribs.

Julia laughed and put one arm around Roisin's shoulders.

'Don't you believe it for a moment. She has all her chemistry students eating out of her hand.'

It was just one of many such conversations that evening. William remembers Roisin the best, probably because she was the first person Julia had introduced him to. All the rest have since faded from his memory. Apart from Greta and Gerry, of course. He has more reasons than he can count for remembering the two of them.

He wonders now if Roisin will remember him. He holds out his hand to her, smiles in what he hopes is a friendly manner. Because right at this minute he is feeling strained and tired. His optimism has been filtering away slowly throughout the day. It's taken him until now to find where she lives: a full twelve hours of false starts, bum leads and wrong turnings.

'Roisin, I'm William Harris, Julia's partner. We met at Greta's some time ago, and again at . . .'

Her face clears. 'Yes, William. Of course. Of course I remember you. I've read all your books. This is a real surprise!' She fiddles for a moment with the chain and then opens the door wide. She smiles at him and glances over his shoulder. 'Isn't Julia with you?'

'No. That's why I'm here.' He stands in the doorway, watching Roisin's face. 'Julia's gone missing.'

Her smile fades, like someone dimming a light. 'What?'

'I'm afraid so. Since last Monday, or maybe Tuesday. We can't be sure. I was hoping you might be able to help me find her.'

Roisin stares at him. Then she seems to gather herself together. 'You'd better come in.' She stands back and he steps into the narrow hallway. He follows her into a neat, cheerful room. The curtains are drawn and a fire is lit. A book lies face down on the nest of tables. William strains to see its title. *Road Dogs.*

'Still a fan of Elmore Leonard?' he asks, keeping his voice light.

She nods, distractedly. 'Can I offer you a cup of tea, coffee?'

'Nothing, thanks.'

She gestures towards an armchair. 'Please, sit down. And tell me what's happened.' She reaches for a pack of cigarettes. 'Excuse me, I shouldn't, but I do. Do you smoke?'

It takes all his willpower, but William says no. He is too anxious to plunge into his story, doesn't want anything to distract him. He tells her everything that has happened since last Monday. He omits no detail, and feels in the retelling – at least to Roisin – that some of what he says is now accompanied by a sense of acceptance. This loss is something that has really happened: to him, and to Julia. He feels that at last his cells are absorbing the impact of his grief. And in this quiet, homely room he feels the blunt force of all his loneliness. 'And the last conversation we had,' William goes on, 'Julia said something about an annual lunch here, in Wicklow, with someone called Hilary. As you live in Wicklow, I just thought . . .'

Roisin is looking at him, shocked. Her face has now drained of colour. 'With who did you say?'

'Someone called Hilary. And as I've never heard her even mention—'

'Jesus! Oh, my God.'

'What?' William looks at her. What is she about to tell him? 'Roisin – what is it?'

He can see her distress. She begins to stand up, and William holds out one hand to steady her. But he is determined not to back down. 'I'm sorry to upset you, but I need you to help me.'

She sinks back into her armchair and covers her eyes with one hand. He notices that the other one is trembling.

'Help me, please. I'm desperate. Whatever you tell me will

remain in this room. That I can promise you. The only thing I care about is finding Julia.'

She nods. William thinks she looks defeated. He feels sorry for her. The tranquillity of her evening has been shattered. The fire, the open book, the music playing softly in the background. Rachmaninov, he thinks, waiting.

'What do you want to know?' She won't meet his gaze. Instead she smokes, looking intently at the cigarette in her hand. At that moment he thinks how like her sister she is. Younger, of course, but shock seems to enhance the family resemblance.

'First of all, who is Hilary?'

She doesn't answer. Jesus, how hard can it be to tell him who the hell Hilary is? He feels angry again: it is an emotion that lurks barely below the surface these days, and he feels increasingly powerless to mask it. The long drive, the hunger gnawing at his insides, his growing sense of frustration at all the doors that are closing in his face: he goes for broke. 'Your sister, Greta, said that you would tell me.' The lie comes easily. By now, he doesn't care.

'My *sister*?' she says, sitting forward. 'You've been to see Greta?' Now the brown eyes are filled with alarm. Her whole body is alert, alive.

'Yes. Last night.'

'What did she say?'

'Nothing. She – they – more or less threw me unceremoniously out onto the pavement. That's why I'm here.'

'They told you to come *here*?' Her voice is incredulous.

William shakes his head, relenting. 'Well, no; not quite. They told me nothing. But Greta did let slip where you live. I don't think Gerry was too thrilled about that. I've been driving around Wicklow all day, looking for anyone who might know a college lecturer called Roisin, maybe still working, maybe retired. I didn't even know your surname.' He meets her eye. 'I even drove to UCD last night, visited the Chemistry Department. But they'd tell me nothing – understandably. I didn't really expect them to.' He can still see the alarm on the student's face, sees her plunging her hands into the pockets of her lab coat. 'They told me to go to the Library, but it had just closed.' He must have appeared deranged, looming up out of the night like that. 'I've been in every hole and corner in Wicklow town since seven this morning. So you can see how determined I am. I am going nowhere until you tell me what I want to know. Please. Help me.'

'There is not a lot I can tell you, William.' Now she looks at him. 'But I will tell you that Hilary is – was – my mother.'

'Was?'

'She died four years ago.'

William looks at her, not understanding. Not understanding anything. 'Then why would Julia say she was going to meet her?'

'I don't know.' Roisin's face has closed.

'Yes, you do. You looked horrified when I mentioned her name, and your sister had exactly the same reaction. Something is going on, and I want to know what it is.' He doesn't mean to threaten, but he can't help his tone.

'My sister and I had a falling-out some months ago.' Roisin stubs out her cigarette. 'One of those not-to-be-mended fallings-out. It's to do with things about my mother – my mother's . . . estate.' She shrugs. 'You know how it is in families. Where there's a will, there's a fight.'

William regards her cagily. He doesn't know how much to believe. There is still something missing, something she's not telling him.

'Julia and I are very good friends,' Roisin continues. 'But you already know that. What you probably don't know is that Julia and my mother were also very good friends.'

'No,' he says. 'I didn't know that. Which surprises me. Particularly as Julia never once mentioned her name.' Or had she? William wonders now. He realizes, guiltily, that he'd often tuned out when Julia had spoken about her friends, or what her life had been like before he'd met her. As far as he'd been concerned, real living had begun that day on the pier in Howth when she'd walked arm in arm with him. He'd wanted her for himself, he'd known that even then, back when the two of them were just beginning. He can still remember his delight when she'd seemed to want it too – when she'd been content for there to be just the two of them. Maybe if he'd paid more attention, he wouldn't have missed so much. He might have known about Hilary. He should have listened more. He might have heard this coming.

'I am not really sure why Julia would mention Hilary now,' Roisin is saying. William has the impression that she is judging her words carefully. 'She died before you even met Julia.' She sighs. 'Are you sure you heard right?'

William doesn't feel sure of anything any more. But he senses that this is not the time to admit it. 'I'm certain. It's not a name I've heard too often. I don't think I could have made it up.' He thinks about how best to phrase what he wants to say next. The last thing he needs is to be pushed out into the icy Wicklow night, his overcoat fired after him like a full stop. 'I still don't understand Greta's reaction when I mentioned your mother's name. Or yours, come to think of it.' Roisin is about to say something, but William stalls her. 'Please. I'm not trying to pry into your "family business", as Gerry called it. I'm simply trying to find some kind of connection between you all that will help me find Julia.' He waits until that sinks in. 'And if there's anything to do with Julia in your falling-out. Otherwise, it's like trying to box with one hand tied behind my back.'

Roisin stands up. 'I don't know about you, but I need a drink. Whiskey?'

William nods. 'Please. Lying makes me thirsty.'

'Lying?' She looks puzzled.

'All day today. I said I was an old friend of yours. But that I didn't know your married name. Just that you had settled here in Wicklow and had at least one child and one grandchild.'

'Did Julia tell you that?' She looks curious.

'No,' says William. 'In fact, she stopped telling me anything about you – you or anybody else – around six months ago. I've only just realized that today. I was so wrapped up in her that I didn't care that she didn't see her friends any more. To be truthful, I was happy that I seemed to be enough for her.'

Roisin hands him a large whiskey. 'I think you were. You made Julia very happy.'

William shakes his head. 'No, Roisin, I *make* Julia happy and want to continue to make her happy. Now, will you please help me do that?'

'You must be hungry,' she says suddenly. 'Driving around all the highways and byways of Wicklow. Can I make you a sandwich to go with that?'

William sighs. He wants to shout, 'Will you just tell me what I want to know, for Christ's sake?', but he *is* hungry and he doesn't want the after-effects of whiskey on an empty stomach. Particularly as he has to drive home. 'That would be very good, thank you.'

'Back in a minute.' Roisin doesn't so much leave the room, as escape. William watches her go, takes in the quick, decisive steps, the way she closes the door behind her. Is she phoning someone, he wonders, or is she just off to the kitchen to gather her thoughts? He can't open the door, so he'll just have to wait.

He knows he's on the verge of something and tells himself to be patient. He looks around, taking in the pictures, the furnishings, the book-lined alcoves. It must have been a calm space before his arrival. There are photographs of an infant dotted around the room: some with its smiling parents, some with Roisin, its proud grandmother, some with two older children. This is a room made for one, William thinks. He knows the signs.

Roisin comes back into the room carrying a tray. 'I haven't eaten either, so I'll join you. Rough and ready, but dig in.'

William's mouth waters at the sight of buttered baguette, cheese, salami, salad. He realizes that the last proper meal he ate was the dinner that Jack cooked on Thursday evening. He'll have to do better than that. Hunger clouds his judgement and he needs to think straight. 'This is great, Roisin. Thank you.' He allows a silence to gather. He is content to wait until she breaks it.

'Okay, William,' she says after a couple of moments. 'I would like to help you. But this is a very long story and, frankly, most of it's private. What I will tell you is that Julia and my mother were very close. Greta resented that, always. But when my mother was ill, Julia looked after her like an angel. That party, where we met, was Greta's way of saying "thank you" to everyone who had been kind to us during Mum's illness. It was also a way of getting over the first anniversary. We didn't tell everyone that, of course: didn't want to dampen anyone's spirits.'

'Did Julia know?' William asks, seeing her face again in the car that evening, asking him for something he didn't know how to give.

'Yes, of course,' Roisin nodded. 'And whether Greta liked it or not, she'd had to invite Julia.' Roisin stops. She seems to be breathing deeply.

'Go on, please.' William's tone is quiet now. He doesn't want to disturb what still appears to be profound grief. He wonders at himself, briefly, for never having had such depth of feeling about either of his own parents.

'Mum – Hilary – had a massive stroke six years ago. Julia was wonderful to her, everybody acknowledged it. Mum could do nothing for herself. She couldn't feed herself, wash herself, even hold a book. She had to be hoisted into bed. It was a living nightmare, for all of us, but for her most of all. Her mind was clear, though – and she could still speak, although sometimes it was difficult to understand her.'

Just like Richard, William thinks. Poor Julia. Having to live it all over again.

'About six months ago, my sister Greta found some letters among my mother's papers. They were to me, and to Julia. They'd somehow got packed away with her things and didn't surface when they should have.' She looks at William, her gaze direct and clear. 'Their contents are private. They belong to me and to Julia. Greta read them, of course, and all the old . . . jealousies reappeared. And that's all I'm going to tell you.'

William's mind is speeding ahead of her words. He feels like a character in one of his own books. He phrases his question carefully. 'I accept that their contents are private. May I even ask the subject of them?'

'No,' Roisin says firmly. 'No, you may not. They're Julia's business, not yours.'

He nods, accepting that. 'Tell me,' he says. 'If your mother was so incapacitated, how did she write these letters?'

Roisin regards him steadily. 'She dictated them. She had carers, around the clock. One of them, a woman called Eileen, used to sit with her and take dictation, night after night. She was lovely, very fond of my mother. And she – Hilary, that is

– dictated dozens of letters: to her friends, to us, to her grand-children.'

'And to Greta?'

'Yes, of course. The problem was that Greta also read those that were not meant for her. And that really is all I'm going to tell you. Because it's all I *can* tell you. I'm sorry. Truly.'

'Have you and Julia kept in touch these past few months?' He asks the question quietly, not wanting the answer.

'Yes,' she says. But William has noted the briefest of hesitations in her reply. 'But before you ask, I had no idea she was planning to do what you've just told me. Last time we spoke was about three weeks ago, on my birthday. But we didn't meet. Julia seemed to have lots going on. With Melissa, particularly. I understood: Melissa has always been a difficult girl.'

I'll say, William thinks. 'Was there anything else in that phone call, anything at all that you can remember now, even if it might have been insignificant at the time?'

Roisin frowns. 'There might have been something. Let me get my diary. It might jog my memory as to what we talked about.' For a moment William thinks she looks wistful. 'We always used to celebrate our birthdays together.' She stands up. 'I'll be back in a minute.'

She leaves the room and William feels the world spin. What has been happening in Julia's life that he knows nothing about? What has he kept missing? He doesn't understand any of this. Has he not been present in her life in the way that she has been in his? Suddenly he feels very peripheral to the substance of Julia's existence. It's as though he has just orbited her planet, like a small universe composed of equal parts bliss and ignor-ance, moved and shaped by her gravitational pull. While she, on the other hand, did her real living, her significant living, when he wasn't around, spinning off somewhere into outer space. God, he wishes he'd paid more attention.

Roisin opens the door. Her diary is open in her hands. 'There is something,' she says. William sits up straighter. 'I didn't think it odd at the time, but in the light of what's happened . . .' She kneels on the floor beside him and points to a yellow Post-it note, clinging to the last day of December: '22nd January 2010' is written on it, in neat black script. And underneath, a name: 'Sorcha.' William feels something leap to life in his chest, the stirring of a caged bird. He's heard that name before.

'Julia insisted I write it down, in case I forgot.'

'Who is this Sorcha?' asks William.

'We were all at UCD together,' Roisin says, 'and Sorcha was a medical student along with Julia. They shared a flat together for a few years. They were really close. I'd probably have minded more, if we hadn't all got on so well together. Anyway, she said that Sorcha was coming to Dublin that weekend and that we'd have a get-together.'

'And?' William prompts.

'Here's the odd thing. She asked me: Did I still remember Sorcha's surname? I said that of course I did. Sorcha O'Sullivan. And she said: Isn't it strange that the least feminist of the three of us was the only one to keep her own name after she'd married?' Roisin looks at him.

William feels hope surge again, almost cruelly. Another name, another lead. He thinks he vaguely remembers having heard it, or perhaps it's ringing in his ears ever since Celine mentioned it. Either way, he clings to it. The drowning man, and yet another pale and fragile straw. He pulls out his notebook from his jacket pocket and his pen, prepares to write.

'The thing is, that's a kind of standing joke.' She smiles at

William. 'That's the last thing I'd need to be reminded of. Julia and I were both swept off our feet at the same time, married within months of each other. And we were both so besotted and head over heels in love that we relinquished our own names without even a second thought. Our husbands were old-fashioned kind of men.' She stands up and moves back to her chair by the fire. 'Mind you, mine didn't last. Peter, my husband, packed his bags just as soon as Roma was born. Peter Pan, Julia used to call him. Couldn't hack the responsibility.' She shrugs. 'Or my divided attention.' She looks at William. 'If I were you, I'd pay a visit to Sorcha O'Sullivan. She's the sort of person Julia would have gone to, if she needed help.'

'Help?' asks William quickly. 'What kind of help?'

Roisin shakes her head. 'Just go and see her, William.' Her words are clear, emphatic. He knows that their clarity is hiding something from him. Something is swimming underneath their surface that he cannot grasp: fish darting silverly among the rocks.

'Where does she live?'

'In London. In Greenwich.'

William writes it down. He knows he could never forget, but it gives him something to do while Roisin is talking.

'The three of us met there once, at her house, not too many years ago – maybe five? I know it was before Julia met you. We were supposed to do it every so often, but life kept getting in the way. You'd think you'd have more time on your hands when you get to our age, but the opposite is the case. Either that, or the years just go a lot faster.'

William wonders how quickly he can get a flight. 'Is she still practising as a doctor?'

'Yes, at Great Ormond Street – unless something has changed recently that I don't know about. Google her. I think her email is on the Net: her professional one, obviously. I have her home one, but I couldn't pass it on without her permission.'

'Of course, of course, I understand that.' William allows elation to course through him, head to toe. 'Roisin, I really appreciate this. You've been fantastic.' He tucks the notebook back into his pocket. 'It's the first time I feel like I'm getting somewhere. I must apologize for crashing into your evening. Can't tell you how grateful I am – and for this.' He gestures to the tray between them.

She waves it away. 'No problem. Let me give you my mobile number and an email address. Keep in touch, and if there's anything I can do, just shout. If I can help you at all, I will.'

'There is something,' he says suddenly. 'Could you email Sorcha, by way of introducing me, and my bona fides, as it were? Don't want to turn up on her doorstep unannounced.'

'Sure,' she nods. 'I'll do that tonight. And leave me your number, too – here, write it in my diary. I'll fumble with my mobile later. Roma gave me a present of a new one and it has me driven demented. I don't want all these bells and whistles. It's like learning a new language.'

William grins. He hands her back the diary. 'I know the feeling. And Julia certainly knows the feeling, too.'

The present tense again. He does it deliberately, as much for himself as for Roisin. And for Julia. To keep her alive. To keep her safe until he can get to her.

He stands up and holds out his hand. 'Once again, many thanks.'

'You take care,' she says, handing him his overcoat. 'Wicklow roads are treacherous when they're icy.'

'I will,' he promises. He can't wait to be in his car, to be on his way home: to book a flight, to google Sorcha, to follow in

Julia's footsteps. He thanks Greta silently for propelling him in Roisin's direction. And Julia must have known, too, that eventually he'd find his way to her oldest friend. Sorcha's name and the date in Roisin's diary were meant for him. Another message from Julia. He's certain of it.

He reverses carefully and waves back at Roisin, standing in her doorway, surrounded by light. Suddenly William thinks how solitary she looks.

Aren't we all, he thinks, as he points the car in the direction of home.

Aren't we all.

# *Julia*

As JULIA WAKES, all the sounds around her feel familiar: William, moving about the Howth apartment, opening cupboards, filling the kettle, whistling as he makes breakfast. At first, the strength of the illusion almost takes her breath away. She doesn't want to open her eyes. She knows that when she does, he will disappear and she will find herself surrounded instead by the quiet domestic chatter of Alicia's apartment.

She lies still for a few moments more. When she opens her eyes, she sees the sunlight ripple across the ceiling. Then she remembers. She looks down, quickly, at where she'd placed the envelope the night before. She reaches for it, holds it in her hands, turns it over a couple of times. There is a muffled knock on her bedroom door; one that allows her to respond or to ignore it, as she wishes. 'Yeah – I'm awake,' she calls.

'Breakfast. Ready when you are.'

Julia struggles into a sitting position, tries to ground herself in the reality of yet another morning. But William is a constant. Last night, she dreamt of him yet again, this time as she sped away in some nameless getaway car, slamming the passenger door shut just as he was about to get in. She can see his fading smile, the way he spreads his hands, questioning her: silent, baffled. She shakes her head and pulls on the dressing gown that hangs on the back of the bedroom door. Carefully she folds the envelope in two and slips it into the right-hand pocket, making sure that none of it is visible. Then she goes out to meet Alicia.

'Sleep well?'

'Yes,' Julia lies.

Alicia pours tea, pushes a bowl of fruit salad across the table. 'Help yourself. Is green tea okay?'

'Lovely.' Around her, the room is unhurried. Julia wonders how Alicia manages this: a marriage of potent energy and receptive calm. 'Thanks again for last night.'

Alicia butters toast. 'Not a problem. Kinda hard, carry-ing all of that around with you for a decade.' She sips at her tea.

Julia is tempted to say something, but resists.

'You said there was more?' There it is again: the quietness, the heart-of-the-matterness. Alicia doesn't look at Julia as she asks, and Julia is grateful. Right now, she doesn't believe that she would be able to withstand the probing clarity of those grey eyes.

'Not right now. There is. But I will be keeping in touch.'

'Are you going away?'

'Yes. In two days' time.'

'May I know where you're going?'

Julia shakes her head. 'Not yet, just in case.'

Alicia nods, doesn't question this, doesn't ask, 'In what case?' 'Are you safe?' is all she says.

'Yes.'

'Okay, then. You know where I am. If I can't find you, you at least know where to find me.'

'Yes.' Julia allows the silence to gather around them for a moment. Then: 'You remember the summer we spent together as students? Our hospital practice at the end of third year?'

Alicia looks at her, questioning. 'Sure do. May to September 1970, right?'

'Right. God, I was green!'

Alicia laughs. 'I wasn't much better. Just better at hiding it, I guess. Besides, Los Angeles was my home. I got to show you around. That allowed me to feel superior.'

Julia hesitates.

'Why don't you just ask me?' Alicia leans forward, touches the back of Julia's hand. 'Straight out. Whatever it is?'

'Because I'm not sure *how* to ask it.'

Alicia stands up and moves away from the table. Julia recognizes the gesture: she is impatient. This is wasting *time*. Her customary bluntness is being kept under control, but only just. She stands, leaning against the cupboards of her kitchen. Her arms are folded. Julia braces herself.

'I don't see you for forty years; then you appear out of the ether. Great! I'm more than happy to see you.' Julia knows Alicia's style. They used to call it the Velvet Hammer. Start nice; hit hard. She waits, almost wincing at whatever is coming next. 'You tell me a story about coming here that is only half the truth – if even that much. You won't tell me where you're going, or why.' She regards Julia steadily. 'Don't bullshit me – that's all I ask.' She turns her back, puts more water on to boil.

'Do you remember what we talked about endlessly, all that summer?' Julia says suddenly. 'Do you remember how obsessed we both were, particularly me? I was questioning all of it, every- thing: medicine, quality of life, quality of death. Euthanasia, assisted suicide: the whole issue of how much control we should have over our own lives – not as doctors; I mean as people. Do you remember any of that?'

Alicia turns around to face her. 'Yeah. I remember. They were some important discussions. Got pretty heated, too, with some of our colleagues.'

'Do you still believe in what we were fighting for back then?'

'What does it matter what I believe?' The force of Alicia's question takes Julia aback. 'It's obviously something you're struggling with. Why does my opinion matter?'

Julia looks at her, sees the challenge in her face. 'Because I don't know what I believe any more.'

Alicia comes back to the table. She sits down, looks Julia in the eye. 'Well, Irish, you'd better start trying to figure it out. Particularly in India. There's not a whole lot of time for sitting on the fence.'

'Tell me, then. From California to Chennai. What has brought *you* here?' Julia watches as Alicia weighs up her reply. When she speaks, her tone is considered, thoughtful.

'Ten years ago I had what I'll call a shift of emphasis. Some people call it a mid-life crisis.' She grins. 'I don't. It was nothing as dramatic as that, just a gradual realization that I didn't want to deal with "lifestyle diseases" for the rest of my time on the planet.' She shrugs. 'I got tired of fighting the healthcare war in the States. I wanted to be "useful" ' – here she grimaces – 'at the risk of sounding like an adolescent.' She pulls the teapot towards her and stands up. The water is boiling on the hob, sending up great clouds of steam. 'I attended a conference here, ten years ago at the Adyar – and . . . my medical train-ing suddenly started to make sense to me. I never went home.'

Julia watches her intently.

'Well, I went back to quit my job and put my apartment on the rental market. But essentially I never went home, not in any meaningful way.'

Suddenly the kitchen is filled with a high-pitched beeping: urgent, repetitive.

'Shit!' Alicia reaches into her pocket. 'Gimme a minute,' she says and pulls out her mobile. 'Okay,' Julia hears her say. 'I'll be there in twenty.' She snaps the phone shut. 'Sorry – I hoped I'd get away with it for a bit longer. It's a potential emergency. I gotta go. You wanna stay, or come with me?'

'I'll stay,' Julia says. 'I'll make sure to lock the door behind me.' She starts to stand up, her hand clutching at the envelope in her pocket.

'Just pull it to – give it a good hard tug. It locks automatically.' Alicia is rummaging in her handbag, checking glasses, phone, keys.

Julia steps towards her. 'I'm sorry – I didn't mean to do this so bluntly: but this is the other thing I need to ask you. I mean, for your help.' She thrusts the envelope at Alicia, who looks at her, raising both eyebrows. Then she takes it and shakes her head at Julia. Her expression is one of fond exasperation. 'I know, I know, I'm sorry. Should have got to it earlier.'

'Jeez, Irish, why can't you just be up front? I don't have time to look at this now, honey. Might be sometime this afternoon, if I get a chance to—'

Julia puts out her hand, stops her. 'Not now, not even today. Tomorrow will be fine. I'll call you.'

Alicia looks at her, her eyes troubled now. 'You wanna call by later? Or I could meet you at—'

'No,' Julia says, firmly. 'No. But thank you. I'll call in in the morning.'

Alicia turns to go, reluctance all over her face. 'Promise? As early as you can? Before things get crazy?'

'How early?'

'My first patient's scheduled for seven a.m. Come see me at five-thirty? I'll be at the Adyar. You know your way there.'

'Okay.'

Alicia puts one arm around her, hugs her with a briskness that makes Julia smile. 'You always were a deep one,' she says. 'Stay outta trouble till tomorrow.'

'Will do.'

She starts to run, waves one hand over her shoulder at Julia. 'Love you.' And slams the door behind her.

'Love you, too,' Julia says softly to the empty room.

She sits back down at the table and fills her teacup to the brim.

Calm. She feels calm.

Now, the last part of the jigsaw is in place.

# William

WILLIAM REACHES for his mobile to book a taxi to Dublin airport. Just last night, Sorcha had agreed to see him. Now he is impatient to be on his way. His overnight bag is already on the table. Coffee with Jack, a quick trip to the bank for some sterling, and a taxi at two, that's the plan. His day is clear; the way ahead fills him with energy, purpose. Things are about to start happening: he's getting closer.

But before he can make his call, the screen lights up with Melissa's name. His first reaction is not to answer. They have had no contact for the past few days – not since Thursday afternoon at the Garda station. He hesitates. But he knows that any official information about Julia will go to her first, as next-of-kin. He answers the call, fuelled by hope and animosity in equal measure. 'Melissa?'

Let's not bother with any formalities, he thinks. Let's not pretend.

'I need to see you.' Her voice sounds strangled.

William sits because his legs suddenly refuse to support him. Weak at the knees ... He used to joke to Julia that that was how she made him feel. Mocking is catching. Something inside him now goes into freefall. For the first time he feels real fear, fear that no amount of rationalizing can quell. His response is urgent. 'Tell me, Melissa. Please. Just tell me. What's happened?'

She sobs. 'Not over the phone.'

'Is she dead?' His tone is harsh, blunter than he intends. But this woman just keeps doing that to him: making him behave in a way that is foreign, not natural to him.

'No, no – it's not news like that. Please, William, just come.' Her voice rises. He can feel the jagged edges of her hysteria grating against his ear.

'I'm on my way.' He grabs coat, keys, wallet and slams his front door behind him. He races down the stairs to the car park. On the way he can't help thinking that he has all these women pulling his strings: he's been turned into a puppet, jerking his way through some sort of mad dance. Julia, Melissa, Roisin, Greta, Sorcha: all of them sharing the remote control, passing it from one to the other and back again. If he wasn't so terrified right now, he'd be bloody furious.

He curses loudly as he starts the engine. Nine-thirty on a Monday morning: it'll take him ages to get to Rathfarnham. Typical. Bloody typical. He swings left out onto the coast road and heads for the city centre.

Derek opens the door to him. The man looks dishevelled. He's wearing a pair of tracksuit bottoms and a hastily pulled-on sweater. William can see the label, the seams, the bulky stitching that all proclaim its inside-outness. This is not the Derek he's got to know: a bit flash, full of himself, in the middle of mysterious business breakthroughs that never seem to happen. 'All style and no substance,' Julia has said on many occasions.

'What's going on, Derek?' William stumbles over the step that leads from the glassed-in porch to the hallway. He's in such a hurry he hasn't seen it.

'The cops have been. I'll let herself tell you.'

*Herself.* What a strange, old-fashioned term. William's father used to refer to his mother in that way, in all matters domestic. Herself. The Boss. The Clerk of Works. Somehow, it didn't fit Derek. He seems to have reverted to some previous self, someone William no longer recognizes.

They walk together in the direction of the kitchen. William can already see, through the open door, that Melissa is seated at the table, smoking. Her eyes are red, raw, her hair is stringy and uncombed. It must be something really bad. 'Melissa?'

She looks up, startled, almost puzzled to see him standing there.

'What is it? What's happened? Please tell me.' He sits beside her, keeping his voice low, his movements quiet. She looks as though she might shatter.

'The police have been,' she says, stubbing out a cigarette. She immediately lights another. 'They're looking for Julia.'

I know that, William thinks impatiently. At least, I should hope they are. It's been a week already since anybody's seen her, and still they've come up with nothing. Not a word, not a sign. Nothing. He waits, feeling his jaw begin to clench.

She looks at him. 'No, I mean they're *looking* for her. To "help with their enquiries". Isn't that the phrase?'

The room appears to veer away from William. It feels strangely full of silence, although he knows that Melissa has just spoken. There are thoughts of his own here, too, spinning around the kitchen like dust motes. He tries to catch them, to help him understand. But whenever he is about to take hold of one, it slips away from him, hovering just out of his reach. 'Enquiries?' he repeats, stupid even to his own ears. 'What sort of enquiries?'

But Melissa has begun to weep, resting her head on her folded arms. Derek stands behind her, his hands on her shoulders. William is struck by his sudden solidity. His expression is tender. Maybe Julia has been wrong about him, after all.

William looks at him, spreads his hands in a gesture of help-lessness. 'Derek?' he says, pleading.

'Apparently, the cops are looking for Julia because an . . . allegation has been made against her. By a woman called Greta Fitzpatrick. Melissa says they used to be friends.'

Now William can feel the blood begin to sing in his ears. He has the extraordinary sensation of regaining consciousness: as though a clean, clear light is shearing through the top of his head, strengthening his spine. He sits up straighter. 'Go on.'

Melissa lifts her head a fraction, her chin still resting on her forearms. 'She is accusing Julia of assisting at her mother's death. Four years ago.'

'Hilary?'

Melissa looks at him, shocked. 'You *knew* about this?' She places both hands on the table, steadying herself. She begins to stand, but Derek presses on her shoulders and she slumps again. Her expression, as she gazes at William, is incredulous. 'You knew?' she says again.

William raises one hand. 'Hang on, Melissa. I know nothing other than what I've found out in the past week. I know that Greta and Roisin's mother was called Hilary, and that Julia looked after her when she'd had a stroke. That's what I *know*.' He pauses. 'Now, please, tell me what the police are saying, and let's see if we can make any sense of this.'

He knows he sounds calm, reasonable, but inside he is churning, filled with impossibilities. Julia, Julia, what have you done? And then: Why didn't you tell me? And again: Yes – why *didn't* you tell me? What was it about me that you couldn't trust? The pain of that question almost takes his breath away. He has failed her in some way that he doesn't understand. Has she been sending him signals for the three years they have loved one another – signals that he's kept on missing?

Melissa sighs. The sound is hoarse, ragged. 'Some papers

have come to light. It seems they have evidence that Julia helped Hilary to die.'

'Helped her, how?' William's heart has quietened. Somehow, he is not as shocked as he might be. Ever since Melissa has started speaking he has been putting the clues together. Papers coming to light: are these the letters that Roisin has already spoken to him about?

Melissa shakes her head. 'They won't say how. All they would say is that helping someone to die is illegal – even if they ask you. And because she used to be a doctor, it's even worse. *Julia – could – go – to – jail.*' She gives each word here a separate emphasis, as though repeating them clearly for someone with diminished understanding. 'For as much as fourteen years.' She stares at William. 'How could she kill someone?' Her voice is bewildered, shot through with anguish, disbelief. 'How could she do that?' And she breaks down again, a fresh storm of weeping convulsing her shoulders.

William lays one hand gently on hers. She looks at him, blue eyes liquid. 'Listen to me, Melissa. If there is any truth at all to these allegations – and I say *if* – anything Julia might have done would have been motivated by pure compassion. From what I understand, Hilary was terminally ill, and suffering.' He stops. He doesn't want to give away too much of what he knows, not yet. He can never be sure of his ground with Melissa. It shifts too often underneath his feet. 'But at least we now have a probable explanation of why she left in the way she did.'

Melissa keeps staring at him. She doesn't get it, he thinks. And then, suddenly, why should she? She has had no Greta, no Gerry, no Roisin to prepare her for this revelation.

'Why? I don't understand.'

'To protect us, all of us,' he says firmly. 'You, your family. Me.'

She flinches at that. William plunges on, regardless. 'As I see it, in the light of what you've just told me, Julia would have left in the way she did because her silence means that no one else can be . . .' he searches out the word, carefully, 'involved. By association. And now that we know that, or at least suspect it, we can start to help her.'

'How?' Melissa is frowning at him, but at least the weeping has stopped.

'I've been making a few enquiries,' he says, deciding to say nothing just now of his meetings with Greta and Roisin. 'I understand that Julia has a good friend in London, Sorcha O'Sullivan?'

Melissa nods. 'Yes, she and Mum go way back.'

'Well, I've managed to contact her, through Google.' Not quite the truth, but it will do for now. 'She's agreed to see me. If Julia has left the country – and I think we both feel that she has – then it's likely she'll have gone through London. I'm going to find out.'

Suddenly, urgently, he wants to make that flight this afternoon. Sorcha will give him another piece of the jigsaw, he's sure of it.

'Were you going to tell me about this, if today hadn't happened?' But Melissa's voice is softer. William feels sorry for her – all the fight seems to have deserted her. And he has his answer ready.

'Yes, but only after I'd seen Sorcha. I didn't want to raise any hopes.' He leans forward. 'I'm going to find her, Melissa. Find her and, if I can, bring her home. And if not, help her, wherever she is. Above all, I want to know she's safe, for all our sakes.'

Greta's face comes into focus, and Roisin's, and William is flooded with relief that he finally understands. All of it. He feels elated. Now that he knows the *why* of her disappearance, all he has to do is follow her. The *how* is not such a difficult question to answer: that's merely a matter of logistics, of trains and boats and planes. Patience, guesswork and shoe-leather are all that is required. And time, of course. He has plenty of that. He also has the sweet knowledge – his and his alone – that Julia wants him to find her. He sees again the chessboard, hears her voice urging him on in the direction of Sorcha and London. Things are out in the open. Now he can force the issue. And the last thing *he* wants is to be protected.

Melissa is different: he'll make sure to tell her nothing that might expose her. That's what Julia wants.

As for him, minding the woman he loves is his job, not the other way round. He needs to make her safe again, back on solid ground: give the queen back her square.

Melissa nods, as though following what he is thinking. 'We'll need to keep that a secret, though, won't we?'

Despite himself, he smiles at the word. *We.* 'Yes, I think that's best. Absolute discretion from all of us. And I mean absolute. The fewer people who know, the better. Silence is our best ally.'

As though just given a cue, William notices that the house is curiously quiet. Instinctively he looks around. Derek sees his glance, answers it. 'Jamie and Susie are with my sister,' he says. 'We called her as soon as the cops left. We don't want them here for any of . . . this.'

William nods. 'Of course. Kids pick up on things.'

'What will you do?' Melissa's voice is calmer, only occasion-ally catching on the downbeat of a sob.

'Go to London,' he says, at once. 'Today.' He looks at his watch. Only half-past eleven. He can easily make it. He wonders at the cataclysms that can be fitted into an hour. Time has telescoped, he feels: hours stretch away from him, fuller, denser than they have ever been before. It might be years since Melissa's call at nine-thirty this morning.

'Sorry, William. Never even offered you coffee.' Derek still hasn't moved from behind his wife's chair. Standing guard. Julia will be pleased to know that.

William stands up. 'Don't worry. We've more important things on our minds.' He turns to Melissa. 'I'm going to head off to the airport,' he says, 'but I'll keep in touch. That's a promise.'

She spreads her hands helplessly. 'I can't go, it's just not . . .'

'Of course not,' he says, quickly. He hopes not too quickly. 'Your children need you here.' And he is grateful that they do.

'Call when you've spoken to Sorcha?' She's standing now, leaning into Derek. Some of the colour has returned to her face.

'Absolutely. And beforehand, if I've anything at all to report.'

'Thank you,' she says, holding out her hand. 'I'm really grateful.' And her eyes fill again.

'We all love her,' he says, taking in Derek with his glance. 'I'll find her, for all of us.'

She nods, unable to speak.

'I'll see myself out,' he says. 'Take care of each other.' He nods at Derek. 'You'll hear just as soon as I've met Sorcha, but in any event, no later than this time tomorrow.' And he makes his way down the hallway, his heart lighter than it has been in the thousand years since Julia's disappearance.

Traffic should be lighter across the city now. And if there's any problem with a taxi, he'll just call on Jack. He'll start to gather his thoughts as soon as his mind stops racing, speeding ahead of him.

*

As he pulls out of Melissa's street, his mobile rings. It's Roisin. He presses the Bluetooth connection on the steering wheel and her voice fills the car.

'William?'

'Yes. I've heard. I've already seen Melissa and Derek.' His tone warns her not to say too much. She seems to understand.

'We need to talk.'

'Where are you?'

'Just leaving Dún Laoghaire. You?' Her voice is clipped, wary.

'On my way back to Howth. I've a flight booked to London for five this evening.'

'Let me take you to the airport. We can talk on the way.'

William can hear the strain. He can't even begin to guess at the conversation that must have just taken place with her sister. And brother-in-law. 'Family business', wasn't that what the stiff old bugger had said? And how much does Roisin know? What is her part in all of this? He starts to recall their conversation in Wicklow, begins to hear a different resonance around some of the things she said. It is like listening to a new arrangement of a familiar melody: there is more light and shade now, a change of emphasis. It's as though he has just turned up the volume. No more *piano*, all is *fortissimo*.

'Fine,' he tells her. 'That's a really good idea.' He gives her his address, some clear directions and they settle on a time.

He feels strangely calm. It's as though something inside him has been waiting for this: some interior space already furnished, waiting to receive it. What he treasures above all is that Julia has not fled from him. But what saddens him above all is the realization of everything that he must have missed. So many cues, so many opportunities to probe a little further, dig a little deeper.

But that is for later. Now, nothing else matters. Nothing.

Except finding Julia.

As he drives across the untangled city, memories come crowding. Things said and half-said, a glance, a hesitation, an unexplained reticence. He missed them all. He needs to comb through the last several months, pick over conversations, be alert to a change of rhythm.

He needs to tune his ear to a different music.

The intercom shrills at exactly half-past twelve. William jumps, startled at its impact on the silence of his apartment. He answers, sees a small, distorted Roisin standing in the court-yard below. 'Just a sec,' he says. 'Push the door when you hear the buzzer. The lift is to your left. I'm on the third floor.' He presses the button, hears the metallic echo of a door clanking open.

'I'm in,' she says. And the door judders closed behind her.

He walks down the quiet, carpeted corridor towards the lift. He knows very few people who live on this floor. People who are gone each day long before his first cup of coffee, who return when he's already had a meal, tidied up, a pleasant evening with Julia stretching out in front of him . . . He stops. The lift doors open, sliding back smoothly from their centre.

Roisin has dark glasses on. Not that there is much sunlight to be had, on a drizzly November Monday. 'This way,' he gestures back down the corridor towards his apartment. She follows without a word.

Once inside, he takes her coat, points towards the sofa. 'Sit down. I'll make us coffee. Would you like some lunch?'

She shakes her head. 'No, thanks. Don't make any food on my account – just tea, if you don't mind.'

'Peppermint? Camomile? Green tea?' He'd spotted some of

Julia's leftovers a couple of days back, when he'd made up his shopping list.

'Camomile would be great.' She starts rummaging in her handbag. She is crying, soundless tears that splash onto the fabric of her dress, tears she doesn't bother to brush away. He turns and walks towards the kitchen, giving her a moment. When he comes back, she is more composed. Her face is dry, her hand clutching a scrunched-up tissue. He hands her the tea and waits for her to begin. She sips, and he can see her struggle for words. He doesn't help. She has to find them for herself: this time someone owes him the truth – all of it.

'I don't know where to begin,' she says. 'This is all so awful.' She rummages in her bag again and takes out cigarettes, a lighter. 'Would you mind?'

In reply he gets up and hands her an ashtray. Again he waits.

'I didn't know that this was going to happen,' she says. 'At least, not now.' She lights her cigarette, draws on it deeply. 'Greta called me late last night, told me what she'd done. I drove up from Wicklow immediately and we've basically been up all night.' She looks over at him. 'I couldn't warn you, I'm sorry. And I'm sorry for Melissa too.' She sighs. 'What I told you the other night is all true. But I left out certain things because I had to.'

'The most significant things,' he says.

'Yes – and for exactly the same reason that Julia has disappeared without a word to you or to anyone else.' Her gaze is steady now, her voice full of conviction. 'There are things you can't know, William – things that are too dangerous for you to know. Ignorance is your best protection right now, and you know it. And Julia knew it, too.'

He can't argue with that. Hasn't he just said something

similar to Melissa about the need for silence and discretion? 'All right – I hear you. But let me ask you some questions. Just say whether you can or you can't answer them. Would that be okay?'

'Yes.' She answers after a pause, her tone cautious.

'You say you didn't know what was going to happen this morning – but you would have expected it sometime?'

'I knew it was a possibility, yes – but issues were still "under discussion", to use Gerry's term.' Her voice is dry. 'The official route was by no means a certainty. At least, that was my under-standing.'

'So Greta went to the Guards without telling you?'

'Yes.' Emphatic. 'The first thing I heard was last night when she called me. Deliberately too late for me to do anything about it.'

'Melissa mentioned papers being discovered. Are these the same as the letters you told me about last Saturday?'

'Yes. They should never have got packed away. They were to me and to Julia. I didn't know that Mum had written – or rather, dictated – them. She'd given me all the others for safe keeping. The personal ones to us, and the grandchildren.' She pauses. 'I'd absolutely no idea there were more. Those last few days when Hilary was alive are a blur. I know that some of the carers came and helped afterwards, cleaning up, packing up medicines, that kind of thing. One of them must have given the box of personal stuff to Greta.'

'Do you know what is in the letters? Have you seen them for yourself?'

She lights another cigarette, her hands trembling. 'Yes. Greta read one of them to me, about six months ago. My one.'

'Read it to you?' William is puzzled.

She sighs. 'I was summoned to Dún Laoghaire – there is no

other word for it – and I sat at one end of the table while she and Gerry sat at the other.'

William has no trouble imagining this.

'She said I had to sit and listen. She would not hand me the letter to read for myself because she didn't trust me.'

'In case you destroyed it?'

She nods. 'And she was right about that – I would have done.' She shakes her head. 'I never dreamt Mum would . . .' she stops.

'I presume the contents of both letters are the same?'

'I imagine so. Julia refused to let Greta read hers aloud. She got really angry.'

Good for you, William thinks. 'So whatever is in the letter is the basis of the allegations against Julia?'

'Yes.'

William is careful with his phrasing. 'Is Julia the only person who is the subject of these allegations?'

She looks at him directly. 'For the moment, yes.'

'To your knowledge, is there any truth to them?'

'I'm not going to answer that.'

'I think you just have.'

'Be careful, William. Just remember how careful Julia wants you to be. For her sake, as well as yours.'

He does think about it. And at the same time, he wonders if his visit to Greta and Gerry's has been the catalyst for this morning's events. Once they knew Julia had disappeared, had the news catapulted them into action? Has he precipitated this? He hopes that wherever Julia is now, she is far enough away that they can never reach her.

'You said on Saturday that Greta has always been jealous of Julia. Was that just a smokescreen?'

She shakes her head. 'No, it's the truth. Everything I told you on Saturday is the truth – it's just not all of it.'

'So, what motivates her to do this, then? Is she looking for justice – or is she out for revenge?'

'That is a big part of the problem.' Roisin sits forward. 'That's what we've been fighting about, arguing endlessly about, for the past six months.' She stops, grinds her cigarette into the ashtray.

William ignores the craving that has just ignited in his chest. He leans into the smoke that hangs in the living room, inhales briefly.

'She and Gerry are ardent churchgoers. They both came back to it rather late in life – like most of us, they'd stopped practising for years. But somehow, once their grandchildren came along, all the old rituals seemed to become incredibly important to them, and they took to their faith with the zeal of the converted.' She shakes her head. 'I'm not criticizing faith, genuine belief, conviction. But with these two, I just don't buy it. Most of it seems to me to be about the outer show. For what it's worth, I believe that what they've done – at least what Greta has done – is motivated by jealousy and guilt. It just masquerades as righteousness. Self-righteousness, as far as I'm concerned.' She pauses, and William sees her eyes fill again.

'Guilt?' he asks quickly, not understanding.

'Greta couldn't handle what happened to Mum. Once it became obvious that round-the-clock care was needed because of the stroke, Greta came over all sensitive and delicate.' Roisin's tone is bitter. 'That sounds harsh, I know. None of us found it easy. But in terms of Hilary's physical care, Greta just bowed out. So tell me: what's holy or spiritual about that kind of an attitude? She told me I was "so much better at that sort of thing" than she was. And after all,' her eyes are angry, 'I was single, wasn't I? Plenty of time on my hands, ever since my husband walked out. I didn't have a Gerry to look after, did I?'

William lets the silence grow. He thinks about his own

parents: dying as they had lived. No trouble to anyone. His father had had a massive heart attack in his late seventies, just after his weekly poker game and his glass of Jameson. And then his mother, fading away quietly two years later, after a short illness. He'd never had to face what Roisin is describing. But he does recognize, guiltily, something of himself in Greta. He'd been in London during his parents' final years. He remembers feeling comfortable about his mother's illness, secure in the knowledge that Margaret, his then-single sister, would look after everything on behalf of all of them. His own life could continue, undisturbed. And it did. He has the grace to feel ashamed of himself.

'And Julia?' he asks quietly.

'I told you. She was an angel. She'd been through it all with Richard. She just . . . took over. Taught me, made me competent. Together we worked out a system of carers, and she and I would always share at least one of the shifts. She came every day. She'd just retired that year, said she had lots of time on her hands. I know it must sound strange,' and she smiles, 'but we actually had great fun on many occasions. Hilary had a brilliant sense of humour. They were precious, those days. I am very grateful we had them.'

William sees her eyes light up for a moment, filled with memory. He is glad for her. 'Forgive me if this is insensitive, but had you never considered a nursing home for Hilary?'

Roisin smiles. 'If you'd ever met Hilary, you wouldn't dare to ask that question. She made me promise to keep her at home, if ever anything happened to her. And you know, I think she had a sense of what it was going to be. Three months before the stroke, she gave Greta and me Power of Attorney over everything she owned. She was a wealthy woman, she'd put by more than enough to be cared for in the way that she wanted. After my dad died when we were very young, she took over his clothing business and made a huge success if it. She was fiercely independent, bolshie, downright difficult at times.'

William is curious. 'Did Greta visit her?'

'Oh, yes. Mondays and Wednesdays and Fridays from seven to eight.' Roisin imitates her sister's accent, a clipped, business-like tone. 'Always in the evening, you see, once Hilary was settled for the night. No coincidence that Gerry plays bridge on Mondays and Wednesdays, and they go to the golf club for dinner every Friday with their golfing buddies. Eight-thirty for nine.'

William wants to draw back from such dangerous emotional territory. He can see Roisin is furious. He might be able to use that fury, to elicit some unguarded comment, to find something of all that he has missed about Julia.

'Did Hilary ask Julia for any kind of help?' He gazes at her, steadily.

She lights another cigarette. 'Come on, William, I'm not going to answer that.'

He nods. 'We're having two conversations here, aren't we? The surface one, the words we're using, the things we're saying to each other. And then there's the other one, the one that's underneath: the one I'm hearing loud and clear.'

'The one that is silent,' she agrees. 'And will always remain so. No matter how tempted you are, William, please don't ever give it a voice, for all our sakes.'

'Don't worry,' he says, grimly. 'I've got far too much to lose.'

'And if anyone comes calling, you can truthfully say that you have no knowledge of anything. Julia has made it easy for us.'

'Yes,' he says. 'She has.'

Roisin kneads her eyes with both fists. William is startled. It is something he remembers from childhood, that desperate craving to stay awake. 'You're seeing Sorcha tonight?'

'Yes. And I'll be asking her the same thing I'm now going to ask you. Have you any idea where Julia might have gone? Any idea at all?'

Roisin shakes her head, slowly. 'I've been racking my brains about it, ever since Saturday. California is one possibility – a remote one, but still a possibility. She used to know someone there, a woman called Alicia something-or-other. I remember her: a powerhouse of a woman, but I can't remember her surname. She was a medical student, and I didn't have a lot to do with her. She and Julia were close for a while. That's all I know. But Sorcha will be able to tell you more than I can.'

'Okay.' He sees that exhaustion has now overtaken her. Her face has that crumpled look that comes with sadness. She seems to have aged years since Saturday. 'Are you all right? Why don't you lie down for a while? We've at least an hour and a half before we need to leave for the airport.'

She smiles at him. 'That's not a bad idea. A whole night of Gerry and Greta is just about more than a body can take.'

He stands up. 'Come with me. Spare room is through here. I'll call you at three.'

She follows him, pausing at the doorway. 'Will you be all right? You've had one hell of a week.'

'Yeah – but now I have a purpose. I know what I need to do. I'll be fine.'

The truth is, he can't wait to get going. He feels Julia pulling him closer. And the feeling makes him joyful. Now he understands why she's been pushing him away, ever so gently, ever so gradually, over the past six months. It's not that she doesn't love him: he hasn't lost her, not in any real way. She's missing, that's all, but no longer missing in the way he'd feared. She is simply not where he is.

And he's no longer performing a mad dance: he is now walking deliberately, carefully, in the direction that Julia has ordained. And he will find her. He'll keep to the path, however narrow, however treacherous.

He will find her and they will face whatever has to be faced, together.

# *Julia*

IT'S HOT. AND DUSTY. The windscreen is shrouded in the stuff. Dead flies cling to the glass, their bodies baked hard in the heat. Julia pulls the baseball cap out of her rucksack and settles it firmly on her head. She tilts the brim downwards to block out the worst of the glare that she knows will assault her as soon as she steps out of the car. She hates baseball caps, but anything else makes her look like a genteel lady tourist straight out of E. M. Forster. And, here, she is neither genteel nor a tourist. It's only eleven o'clock, and the children will still be at school. Perfect timing.

'Here's fine,' Julia leans forward and speaks to Deepak. He glances across at her, his expression anxious.

'Are you sure, ma'am?'

She can feel his puzzlement. She has had him stop a good twenty metres away from the squat white house that marks the start of the village. 'I'm positive, thank you. I would like to surprise the person I'm visiting.'

'I watch,' he says firmly. 'I wait.'

'Thank you, no.' Julia pulls out four one-thousand-rupee notes. Deepak has been with her for almost two days now. He'd brought her to see Alicia at half-past five the previous morning, waited until she'd finished, driven her back to the hotel, picked her up again. Two days and one overnight. He'd refused the guest-house accommodation Julia had offered him, insisting that he had a sister who lived nearby. Julia had allowed the fiction, knowing full well that he had slept in his car. She hands him the notes, pressing them into his palm. 'Thank you very much, Deepak. You have been very kind.'

He stares down at the notes. He stiffens slightly. 'Three thousand, ma'am. My price was three thousand.'

I've offended him, Julia thinks. She has a fleeting memory of that other taxi ride, the one with Roisin at Mumbai airport. She shakes her head, smiling at him. 'You have no idea how much I appreciate the way you have taken care of me. Please, allow me to say thank you in my own way.' She waits. 'This is a very important journey, and you have made it easy and safe.'

Finally, he smiles. 'Thank you.' He accepts the money with that strange nod of the head – almost a wobble – that Julia has been learning to interpret. Diffident, dignified, grateful. He shakes hands with her. Then he pulls a grubby piece of paper off the dashboard. 'My card,' he says, loftily. 'My number is here, any time, day or night. You need help, I come.'

Julia meets his gaze. She knows that he means it. 'That's very good to know.'

'You have mobile?'

'Yes, thank you – with the SIM you got me. Everything is fine.'

He turns off the engine and gets out of the car. Julia waits until he opens the passenger door for her. She's made that mistake once already, has been chided gently for it. He helps her ease her shoulders into the straps of the rucksack, hands her the laptop, snaps the handle on the wheelie-bag into place. Then he inclines his head again, this time a little regretfully. 'May God go with you, ma'am,' he says, quietly.

'And with you, Deepak. I hope we meet again.' She holds out her hand, he shakes it warmly. Julia knows that he sees himself as her protector, knows his concerns about leaving her 'in the centre of nowhere'. She waits until he turns the car, waves until he disappears from sight. Then she turns and walks at a steady pace towards the village. She remembers Alicia this morning, white-coated, sitting behind her tiny desk.

'You will call, won't you, if you need anything?' Dawn splashes the sky outside the small, barred window.

'Of course I will. And I really appreciate your doing this.'

Alicia brushes away her thanks. 'I won't insult you by asking if you're sure you know what you're doing.'

'But you're asking anyway,' Julia says. They both laugh. 'And *you* did it. Don't forget that. "I never went home" – that's what you said to me the other night.'

Alicia sighs. 'This is a complicated country. I have colleagues, a structure, a system that gives me some sort of safeguards.' She lets the question hang.

'So do I, where I'm going.'

Relief floods her face. 'A hospital?'

'Of sorts.'

'Okay, Irish. I can see you're determined.' She taps the envelope – Julia's envelope – that lies on the desk in front of her. 'And I'll run these for you. I'm on it.'

'I know,' Julia smiles. 'That's why I asked you.'

'C'mere.' Alicia stands up, opens her arms wide.

Julia goes to her.

'Love you lots. You take care.'

They stand in silence for a moment.

'I will. And I'll call in a week. You sure that's enough time? I know how busy you are.'

Alicia grins. 'Remember the Matron in Holles Street? Sister Davis, Davison, something like that?'

Julia's face lights up. 'Yes. Battleship Beryl! My God, I haven't thought about her in years.'

'Remember what she used to say? And we all used to snigger behind her back?'

'Go on.'

With perfect mimicry, her mouth a prim line, her arms folded as though across an ample bosom, Alicia intones: 'When you want something done, ask a busy person.'

Julia nods in delight, student memories flooding back. 'Yes. Talk about a mantra.'

'Well, Sister taught me well. A week is fine. Call me.'

'I will.' Julia picks her rucksack off the chair.

'You got everything?'

'Yes. Deepak is waiting downstairs. And before you ask, yes, I'd trust him with my life.'

Alicia grins. 'You're learning.'


Flies buzz lazily. The occasional curious cow swishes its tail and regards Julia steadily as she passes by. The wheels of her case send up a small storm of ochre dust. A youth on a moped stares, openly. So does his girlfriend, seated on the pillion. Neither of them speaks. The girl is incongruously dressed in a silk shift, high heels, flowers in her hair. Going to a wedding, perhaps.

Julia nods to both of them. 'Good morning.'

She can hear the sea from here. She crosses the village square now – or what she thinks of as the square. It is an open space, surrounded by squat houses, the village shop with its barred and rusty gate, a cafe with a corrugated-iron roof. The cafe's outer walls are made of packing cases: she can see the manufacturer's circular stamps from here. A faded Coca-Cola sign fights for space with an advertisement in Hindi for Vodafone. It takes up one entire wall. The square also serves as a parking lot for two or three ancient cars, a couple of modern mopeds and an upended, abandoned cart. The surface is uneven, stony. Julia makes her way past sleeping dogs, the occasional hen pecking at the rusty earth, two or three snuffling pigs.

Turning the final corner, she sees the beach, the fishing nets spread long and wide, the painted boats. Half a dozen cows make stately progress along the bright curve of sand, keeping close to the cool edge of the water, or huddling into whatever shade is available. The fishermen are gathering up one of the nets, folding it, working with the slow deliberation that intense heat brings. They stow it in the bow of a wooden boat that rejoices in the name of *Sweet Lips*. Soon, they will place wooden logs underneath the hull, back and front. Then, lining up on either side, they will lean their body weight against the caulked surface and heave the fishing boat slowly, laboriously towards the sea. New nets, she notices, new boats. The tsunami has brought devastation to this village. Its recovery has been slow, piecemeal. But at least the men are fishing again.

She turns away from the beach now and makes her way down the first side street she comes across. It is crowded with ramshackle buildings in various stages of construction, or in various stages of collapse – depending on your point of view. She turns the final corner and stops at the cheerful yellow door. She takes off her cap, steadies the wheelie-bag in one corner. She knocks.

The door is opened at once. A small woman stands there, shading her eyes against the sunlight. Her sari is lime green, small sequins glint in the sun. Julia remembers the way she glides when she walks. 'Yes?' she says, her tone doubtful.

'Sarita?' Julia says softly.

The woman stares at her: takes in the closely cropped head, the case, the rucksack. Her face suddenly clears. 'Miss *Julia*?'

she says, her tone one of excited disbelief. Her small hands fly to her face, come to rest on her cheeks. Her mouth is a comic-book O of surprise.

Julia grins. She runs one rueful hand over the stubble that covers her head. 'Yes. I'm back.'

With a cry, the woman embraces her.

Julia thinks how easy it would be to lift her off her feet, swing her around, just as she used to do with Melissa, when she was a small child. She has had to bend almost double to meet Sarita's arms. She is so slight, so finely made – but there is a strength to these bones that Julia knows well.

'You have come, you have come,' she says, sobbing, holding on tight.

'Yes,' says Julia. 'I am here to keep my promise.'

# PART TWO

# *Julia*

'YOU LOOK DIFFERENT.'

Julia is sitting in one of two armchairs, facing Sarita. Between them, on a low table, two cups and saucers contain the remains of the *chai* that Sarita has prepared, with great ceremony.

'My hair,' Julia says. 'I had it all cut off when I arrived at Chennai.' She rubs her hand over her head, enjoying the feeling of lightness. She can still see the young hairdresser's bewilderment, her insistence that madam was making a terrible mistake. 'Please,' Julia had said, 'I know exactly what I want, and why I want it.' Afterwards, the effect had been one of extraordinary freedom. Like a renunciation, she'd thought; a shedding of all I've left behind.

Sarita shakes her head. 'Of course, your hair is looking different. But it is *more* than that. It is also you. You are looking sad.'

Julia is taken aback at her directness. Her eyes fill. It's as though Sarita knows what she cannot possibly know. William. And, in a different way, Jamie, Susie, Melissa. She half-laughs. 'Well, I suppose I am, a bit. But I truly want to be here.'

Sarita's gaze is steady. 'How long do you stay?'

'I have no plans to go back.' Julia drains her cup. 'If that changes, I will tell you.' She glances at her watch. She allows a small, not uncomfortable silence to develop. 'Will the children be here soon?'

Sarita nods. 'The little ones, yes.' She has accepted the new direction of the conversation, will not push Julia any further, at least not now. 'Come, let me show you all that we have done in three years.' She stands up. 'Will you stay with us here, or do you wish a room in the village?'

Julia hesitates. 'If possible, I'd like to stay here, just for a couple of nights. Then I'll look for somewhere close by.'

'Of course. You are welcome to stay with us as long as you wish. It is a room for our guests, which we are using only from time to time. An attic, a little small for you, perhaps,' and she smiles. She is as fascinated by Julia's height as Julia is by Sarita's lack of it. 'You will be needing to bend your head, I think.'

Julia laughs. 'Don't worry: after the first time, I'll remember.'

'And you know Mr Kapur? He owns the village shop?'

'Yes, I've seen Mr Kapur's shop.'

'He has ready an apartment, on the first floor, beside his shop. Underneath is his storehouse, always locked. There is a room completely private from everywhere. I have seen it. One big room, a bathroom, a very small balcony. You would like me to ask?'

'That sounds almost too good to be true! Yes, yes, please: I would love you to ask.'

'I will do today.' Sarita holds out her hand to Julia. The earlier moment of awkwardness is smoothed away by the warmth of her touch. 'Let's go now. We are going to see the children's room first.'

Julia follows her down the long corridor into a large airy room. Bunks crowd against the walls on all sides. Scattered here and there across the terracotta tiles are plain, woven mats. Julia gasps. 'Sarita! This is wonderful! How you've grown!'

She smiles, her eyes proud. 'We have forty children now,

Miss Julia. The youngest is one and one half years, the oldest ten. Twenty-seven girls, thirteen boys.'

'You've done it,' Julia says. 'Just what you told me three years ago. What a great achievement!'

'We are pleased,' Sarita acknowledges Julia's praise with a smile, 'and sometimes, we can even give the children a small treat.' She points to the boxes under the bunks. 'Thanks to you, we are giving the younger ones one toy each with the money you sent last Christmas. We are very grateful.'

Julia shakes her head. She thinks of Jamie and Susie, the overflowing toy boxes, the suitcases full of barely worn clothes. She stops herself. That way madness lies. Different worlds, different rules. And she remembers Roisin's words: you can't save a continent. 'And their health?' she asks. Last time, some of the newer arrivals had been lame, or listless, or suffering from entirely preventable vitamin deficiencies. Julia had raged about that above all.

'We have five children now who are having special problems.' Sarita pauses. 'We make sure they have food, water, comfort. We are trying and trying, but the government does not help.'

'That's why I'm here,' Julia says lightly. 'To help.'

Sarita nods. Julia can see her questions: her face is full of them. She also knows that Sarita will not ask them until she feels the time is right. She opens a door that leads immediately onto a tangled, briar-filled space and gestures to Julia to follow her. Beyond the brambles and the choking growth, there is a clearing. A large rectangular patch, surrounded on three sides by rubble.

'What is it?' Julia is curious.

Sarita's face lights up. 'Next year, or perhaps the following: we shall have to see.' She pauses. Julia can almost taste her excitement.

213

'More children?'

Sarita shakes her head. 'No,' she says. 'This is for the mothers, the women who come to us. A refuge. Somewhere for them to be staying.'

Julia isn't sure what question she should be asking. 'To be close to their children, you mean?'

'Not always.' Sarita looks around her, sweeps one graceful arm at the empty space. 'This will be for the women nobody wants. The ones who are burnt by fire, or by acid. The widows.' She shrugs. 'The outcasts.'

For one vivid moment, Julia can't speak. Her first visit here comes flooding back to her. She remembers the dusty drive, the road-workers, the assault on her emotions. And, afterwards, the impotent rage that would not let her forget.

'I told you I'd be back,' she says, quietly. 'And now you have given me yet another reason to stay. I can help you build this; you know I can.'

Sarita looks at her, her expression frank, curious. 'But why now, Miss Julia?' The brown eyes are intelligent, searching. This woman is no fool.

Julia draws a deep breath. She has to tell her something: enough to stop any more probing, to satisfy until the time is right. 'Because I feel that I may be able to do good here, things that I can't do anywhere else. My life at home has become . . . complicated. I need things to be . . . simpler.'

Sarita nods. 'Sometimes, when we run away,' she pauses and Julia is startled at her use of language, 'we are taking our . . . complications with us. We cannot will our lives to be simple. And poverty is not always simplicity.' She leads the way back inside again. Julia follows in silence, waits while Sarita locks the door behind her.

'I don't mean to offend,' Julia says, softly. 'I am asking you for the gift of time to unravel those complications. In return, I would feel privileged to be your doctor. Please don't send me away.' She looks around her. 'Particularly with all this about to happen.'

Sarita smiles. 'We understand one another. We give, you give. That is equal – that is good. Charity is another, more complex matter.'

'No, I don't see this as charity.' Julia is adamant. 'This is an exchange. As you say, an exchange between equals.'

Suddenly, they hear high, excited voices outside the front door.

'We will speak again,' Sarita says. The door bursts open and a group of children holding hands more or less fall into the room, squealing, giggling. They stop when they see Julia, fall instantly silent. She stands up, sees their crisp navy shorts and dresses, their immaculate white shirts and blouses. She sees amazement gather in their faces as they take in her full height. They gaze at her, their brown eyes wide.

Sarita is immediately at her side. 'Children, this is Miss Julia. She has travelled a long way to see us. She is going to be our guest. Now, come and shake hands.'

One by one the children approach, their faces shy, uncertain. They are marshalled by an older girl of about eight. She is like a little mother, Julia thinks. The air of responsibility she carries with her is already adult.

'This is Priya,' Sarita says. 'She is in charge of getting the younger ones to school and home again. She is very good at her job.' Priya beams and Julia takes both her small hands in hers. 'I'm delighted to meet you, Priya. And I might need your help, too.'

She grins and brings the children to Julia. They each shake hands with a seriousness that is almost comical. Until the last little boy, who walks towards Julia with difficulty, one foot dragging behind him. His face is alert, mischievous. He looks to be about six.

'I am Anand, madam,' he says, grandly. And gives her a high five.

'Pleased to meet you, Anand,' Julia says, and high-fives him right back, the way Jamie taught her. The children scream with delight. The air is instantly lighter, brighter. 'My name is Julia.'

'*Miss* Julia,' Sarita intervenes, firmly. 'Now, children, go and sit outside. Anuradha will be with you in a moment to give you lunch. Miss Julia needs to rest for a time. She will be seeing you all later.'

As she speaks, Julia realizes how right Sarita is. Perhaps her fatigue is showing in her face. It's been a long day, a very long week. And even the smallest memory of William threatens to unravel her. 'Sleep would be good,' she says.

Together she and Sarita bring her case, her rucksack and her laptop up an unsteady staircase to a room that is spartan in its simplicity. 'I hope you will be comfortable,' Sarita says. They stand at the doorway and her sweeping gesture takes in the whole room. 'Please ask for anything you are needing. There is a bathroom at the end of the corridor that the children will not use. While you stay with us, it is yours.' She switches on a large ceiling fan. It starts whirring immediately.

It's all here, Julia thinks. A monk's cell.

'It's perfect,' she says. 'Thank you. I will rest for a little while, but then there are things that you and I must discuss.'

'There will be time,' Sarita says, 'but not today. We will wait for any discussions.' Her tone is firm. 'Now you must rest. Afterwards, you will take food. Work can begin tomorrow.' She leaves, closing the door quietly behind her.

Julia sits on the bed. It is narrow, and short. She sees at

once that her legs will have to dangle over the end. No matter. There is a curtained space in one alcove with a rail and half a dozen wire hangers, some of them bent out of shape. She'll unpack after she's rested.

The window is shaded by the overhanging tin roof, and the fan helps to make the temperature bearable. Julia pulls a large bottle of water out of her rucksack and places it on the floor beside her. Without undressing, she lets her head sink into the pillow and closes her eyes.

When she wakes, it's dark outside her window. The ceaseless chatter of the cicadas fills the air. She can hear the children downstairs, guesses by the amount of noise that it is time for their evening meal. She can see them, just like that first time, taking their places on either side of the long wooden table. She remembers the scraping of chairs against the tiled floor, the high-pitched excitement, and then the silence that abruptly descended at Anuradha's command. There was no pushing or shoving around the table, no fighting. Julia remembers how surprised she'd been at the way the children had waited, quiet and patient, as their food was set before them. Nobody moved until each child had been served. In a way she couldn't explain, their obedience had made her feel sad.

She decides now to wait a while longer, until the noise level climbs again: until the clatter of dishes and scraping of chairs tells her that dinner is over, and another day begins to wind down towards bedtime. Julia still has a keen sense, a vibrant memory of the events of the first time she came here, three years ago now. It still feels hyper-real, its sounds and shapes and colours of a startling intensity. And now there is the reality of this return, too: a coming back that feels final.

She remembers how she felt when she'd first stumbled on

the reason to visit. She'd come across a child's drawing: some stick figures of smiling children, a building, the sun burning in the background of an empty, cloudless sky. It was crudely printed, a flyer about an orphanage that Julia had found in the drawer of her bedside table. It had obviously been left behind by a previous hotel guest: names and numbers were scrawled in biro across the back. Quickly, without knowing why, she'd tucked it into the pocket of her trousers while Roisin wasn't looking.

On their second day at Chennai, Roisin had planned to visit the temples of Hampi with a group of other guests, but Julia had declined. She'd done so on impulse, stood her ground in the face of Roisin's surprise, almost disapproval.

But Julia had been fired up, curious: she'd wanted to see the orphanage for herself. Instinctively she kept her plans quiet; the last thing she wanted was conflict with Roisin, who had a very different view of orphanages, about people seeking donations, about begging. A sensible view, she'd told Julia on the day following their arrival. They'd been sitting around the pool at the hotel, sipping a beer before lunch, relaxing in the grateful shade. Roisin had looked at Julia, her expression stern. She'd tapped away her cigarette ash for emphasis. You have to stop India sucking you in, she said. The rip-off is endemic.

But Julia was becoming aware even then that her view was a different one. It was still evolving, not entrenched by decades of experience as a lone traveller. Roisin's certainties made her, Julia, all the more determined to claim her feelings as her own, to hold onto her right to see the world reflected through a different prism. She'd curbed her irritation, knew that Roisin meant well. But for the first time in many years Julia had become uncomfortably aware of the soft contours of the life she led at home. A life that was safe, privileged; one that was able to welcome grandchildren, secure in the knowledge that they would be provided for. Here, in India, she wanted to celebrate Jamie's life by being generous. Charity it might be; it might be an effort at salving her own conscience; it might even be an unworthy way to feel, or an unethical way to act, in the bigger scheme of things. But the instinct to do *something* was strong, and she was not prepared to ignore it.

On the morning in question, Roisin was already up when Julia woke. She was able to smell the cigarette smoke that drifted in from the balcony, blue wisps of it hanging in the still bedroom air. The room already felt sticky, despite the early hour. The air-conditioning refused to work, apart from one brief chug into life around midnight. The unit had growled and rattled, startling both women awake. 'It's icing up,' Roisin said. 'We'd better turn it off.' Julia had flipped the switch and then rolled over. She'd slept at once, glad all over again to find herself within the safety of a hotel. The memory of the taxi ride a few days earlier, of the shanty towns, of the mean streets of Mumbai had continued to haunt her.

She threw back the single sheet and made her way across the room. As she did so, Roisin leaned around the brightly patterned curtain and smiled. 'Morning. Sleep well?'

'Like a log. The heat wasn't nearly as bad as I'd expected.'

Roisin put out her cigarette. 'Post-monsoon cool,' she said. 'It gets a lot more bearable at night, this time of the year.' She stepped back inside the bedroom and glanced at her watch. 'I'll have to get a move-on pretty soon. Our driver's coming at seven. You sure you won't change your mind?'

'Positive. I'd like to spend the day pottering about on my own. I'll see you later this evening.'

Roisin reached for her rucksack. 'I'm going to have a quick bite with the others before we leave. Do you want to join us?'

Julia gestured at her oversized T-shirt. 'You mean like this?' she grinned.

Roisin laughed. 'Well, no, that's not what I had in mind. But I'll wait till you throw on something more civilized.'

'No,' Julia shook her head. 'You go on. I'm going to have a shower and a leisurely breakfast. Bashir is picking me up at eight-thirty.'

Roisin paused. 'You sure you're happy enough on your own?'

'Absolutely. Bashir seems very trustworthy. And we've already shaken hands on a price.' Julia waved her arms at Roisin. 'Now shoo – go on. I'm fine.'

But Roisin didn't move. 'He's also attached to the hotel – that's another bit of security. I just want to make sure you're not apprehensive.'

Julia shook her head. 'I'm not. Not at all. Now will you please stop worrying, and just go?'

'Don't take too much money with you,' Roisin warned as she moved towards the door. 'And leave your passport in the safe.'

'Yes, Mummy,' Julia murmured. She sighed and looked up at the ceiling.

'See you later.' Roisin grinned.

'Have a good day.'


Julia was just finishing her coffee, the *Times Chennai* spread out on the table in front of her. She became aware of a hesitant presence, someone lurking just beyond her right elbow. When she looked up, Bashir was standing there. He smiled. 'Good morning, ma'am. I did not wish to be disturbing you.'

'Good morning.' Julia folded up the newspaper. 'You're not disturbing me at all.' She gestured to the table. 'Have you had coffee, tea? Do you want some breakfast before we go?'

'No, thank you,' he said. 'I had breakfast with my little boy before I took him to school.'

'Ah,' Julia was smiling as she stood up from the table. 'A little boy. How lovely. How old is he?' She gathered her rucksack, her bottle of water, her cap. As she spoke, she became aware of a rush of fellow-feeling. Jamie's arrival had ignited Julia's love of children all over again. She was glad of that: now she spoke a universal language that she and Bashir could share. He pulled his mobile out of his shirt pocket and a photograph lit up the small screen. Julia laughed in delight. The face before her was filled with glee, the smile broad and cheeky. 'What a cute little boy. What's his name?'

Bashir reached for her rucksack. 'Please,' he says, 'allow me.' And Julia did, already becoming accustomed to the old-fashioned courtesy that she had observed everywhere around her in the hotel. There was a graciousness to the place, a gentleness that had soothed her ever since her arrival. Faded gentility, she'd thought, looking around while she and Roisin booked in. Everything had a slightly shabby dignity to it that she'd liked at once. It had its own personality: filled with charm, lacking in sophisticated sameness. 'His name is Raju,' Bashir said, proudly. 'We are calling him after my father.'

'He looks full of high spirits.'

Bashir nodded. 'He is very lively. Sometimes, his teacher says too lively.' He lifted one eyebrow and Julia saw at once where his son's impishness had come from. They laughed. 'Please, if you are ready, you can follow me.' He led the way and they both stepped outside into a heat that was already glaring. The taxi was there and he opened the passenger door for Julia with a flourish. Then he hesitated. 'Ma'am? Perhaps you would prefer to be in the back?'

'No, not at all,' Julia said quickly. 'I'd like to sit in the front and talk to you, if you have no objection?'

'It would be my pleasure to speak with you.'

'Thank you.' She eased herself into the passenger seat.

'Now, you are sure about this journey?' Bashir looked at Julia closely.

She wondered what sort of test she needed to pass. 'Why? Is there a problem?'

He shrugged, looking uncomfortable. 'We drive at least four and a half hours, and I explain that I have not air-conditioning?' His tone was earnest.

Julia was firm. 'I understand. You explained that last night. And I should like to explain something to you before we go.'

He waited, his expression quizzical.

'This is a private journey, one I have not discussed with my friends.' She watched as he nodded, saw how closely he listened. She chose her words with care, already aware that language could be treacherous. 'I would like to do something while I am here, however small. A thank you, if you like, that my grandchild will have a safe and comfortable life.' She stopped. 'I am lucky. My family is lucky. I would like to help some of those who are not so lucky.'

He turned to her and smiled. 'I understand. We will go. Sometimes, my mother she says that India has too many children. We cannot look after them all.' Bashir fastened his safety belt and indicated to Julia that she should do the same. 'You are ready?'

'I am ready,' she said.


'You would like to stop?'

Two hours later and the suburbs of Chennai were only just beginning to ribbon out behind them. Rickety structures, low-slung dwellings, slum houses: all merged with elegant hotels and futuristic business parks, selling cars and property and technology. But the contrasts were exhilarating. Julia had the sense of lurching from one world to another, each of them crowded, each one fighting for space. Her mind felt like a camera, the shutter speeding, capturing the hundreds of images as they flashed past, leaving an impression on the retina of her consciousness. She knew even then that she would never be able to tease them apart. Recollected in tranquillity, their poetry would always lie in that very jumble: sounds, scents, colour, chaos.

'No, I'm fine. Please, let's keep going.'

Bashir was a careful driver, and Julia was grateful. She'd already developed her own philosophy of roundabouts. As soon as she saw one in the distance, she'd close her eyes. Traffic would converge from everywhere: a maelstrom of mopeds and motorbikes, cars and lorries. Buses were king: they'd hurtle into the eye of the storm and, miraculously, the traffic would surge away from them in waves: a parting of the Red Sea. There were no rules that she could see. No clearly defined entrances and exits, just a constant round of movement and the deafening sound of hundreds of hands on hundreds of horns. The first time they joined the throng she was aware of Bashir's quiet laugh. 'How do you do it?' she demanded. 'It is completely terrifying. I think that even if I was *driving*, I'd close my eyes.'

He shrugged, watching the road ahead. 'We must keep moving,' he said. 'To stop is a sign of weakness.'

Julia smiled to herself. William had joked in pretty much the same words about Dublin traffic, just before she'd come away. She wondered how he was getting on, looked forward to the friendly exchange of texts that had begun on the evening of her arrival. She missed him, was aware that she was storing up impressions to share with him later.

Once she and Bashir finally left the city behind, the landscape became green, lush. Small villages straggled, clustered together, the houses hiding from the sun. They crouched low under roofs made of coconut matting, tin or, occasionally, old advertising hoardings.

'What's this?' Julia asked. She sat up straighter. As they turned a corner, a sea of blue tarpaulin swam into view, reminding her with a jolt of the shanty town that had leaned against the airport fence in Mumbai.

'These are the migrant workers,' Bashir said. 'They are travelling from village to village looking for work.'

Julia looked at the cardboard shacks, the barefoot children, the ever-present dogs scrabbling among the rubbish. But before she could say anything, Bashir slammed on the brakes. Out of the sudden ochre dust cloud, a body stepped into the centre of the road, waving a red flag. Bashir said something under his breath. Julia didn't need to ask for a translation.

'What is it?'

'They are making a new road,' he said. 'We must wait.'

She watched as a dozen or so figures crossed and recrossed the pitted surface. They had rough cloth tied around their faces, makeshift turbans on their heads. Each carried load after load of stones back and forth, back and forth, metal sieves piled high. A dusty piece of machinery at the side of the road shuddered and belched out black smoke.

It took Julia a moment to see that the figures were all women, dressed in saris that must once have been brightly coloured. She sat, stilled by shock. One of the women caught her eye. Even as she walked in the opposite direction, she turned her head, holding Julia's gaze. When she reached the ditch, she turned away. Weeds grew tall on the side of the road, choking on the dust that had settled everywhere. After a moment Julia saw a small girl crouched in the shadow of a rock, a parcel of some sort on her knee. As the woman approached, she handed her a cup.

Slowly the woman reached under the folds of her sari. She rolled up her *choli* and splashed water on her breasts. Her back was half-turned and Julia knew she should look away, but she couldn't. Fascinated, repelled, horrified in equal measure, she watched as the girl handed her mother the parcel. Still standing, the woman unwrapped it and put the baby to her breast.

'Jesus Christ!' Julia said, unaware that she had spoken aloud. Suddenly, the green flag was waved. The women scrambled into the ditches on either side of the new, stony surface. They stood well back to let the car pass. Bashir turned on the ignition and they drove away, the figures behind them receding in the rear-view mirror.

She was conscious of the silence in the car, aware of Bashir's sidelong gaze. Finally, he spoke. 'My mother, she is right,' he said, softly. 'India, she has too many children.'

Julia felt her eyes fill. 'I'm sorry,' she said. 'I'm so sorry, it's just – I couldn't have believed, could never have imagined . . .'

He nodded. 'We are arriving soon,' he said. 'Maybe another half an hour.'


'We are here now,' Bashir said. 'This is Sarita's. I will come with you.'

Julia was about to protest, until she saw the way he looked at her.

'They are not always being honest,' he said, his face grim. 'These people. I go with you to make sure everything is okay. And to make sure you are safe.'

They walked together up to the yellow door. Julia still remembers the courtesy with which they'd been greeted. Bashir left shortly afterwards, nodding his approval. And Julia and Sarita talked, stumbling over their eagerness to get to know each other.

'We have fifteen children now,' Sarita had said, 'and I want room for twenty-five more.' She walked Julia around the house. It had belonged to her father, who was, Sarita claimed, a man 'born out of his time'. 'He worked all his life for the people nobody wanted. It was his wish that I would continue, that I would come back here to my village and use his house for that purpose.'

'I don't understand why there are so many orphanages,' Julia said. She stopped, aware of the way Sarita had just looked at her. 'I'm sorry, I apologize right now for my ignorance. It's my first time in India. I know very little.'

'Please do not apologize. You are right to ask. These children who come to us have parents, most of them. But they cannot look after them: they cannot feed so many, educate them, clothe them. So we do, until they are fourteen and can work in the fields. Then their parents can take them back.'

'All of them?' Julia remembers the way she had brightened at that: a happy ending, of sorts.

But Sarita shook her head. 'No. Not all. Some are here because of problems at home – those things that are more than poverty. The ones who come to us as babies, their mothers have been killed: dowry deaths, mostly.' Her tone was brisk, matter-of-fact. 'Their fathers do not want them and they have no one to look after them. Or else their mothers are widows, with nowhere to live.'

Julia nodded, as though she understood. 'You said you'd come back to do this work – where were you before that?'

'In Chennai. I was a teacher. A primary-school teacher. I came back to look after my father when he was ill. He died seven years ago.'

'I'm sorry.'

'Yes. He was a good man. And now we try to carry on his work. It is the best remembrance, I think.'

On the journey back to Chennai, Julia had wanted to ask Bashir to explain some of the things Sarita had said, but she'd held back, afraid that her curiosity might offend. She decided that she would find out for herself, that she would return.

'I don't know how,' she'd said, as she and Sarita had said goodbye at last, 'but I will come back. And I'll stay for a while and work with you, I promise. In the meantime, I'll send you money when I can. And we will keep in touch.' By the time Julia left, she felt as though she had known Sarita all her life.

And now, she is back. The circumstances have not been of her choosing, but she's here, back where she needs to be.

The noises from downstairs have stilled. The evening meal over, now it's homework time. Julia swings her legs over the side of the bed, brushes down her clothes. She realizes suddenly how hungry she is. She has slept for almost eight hours. She should go down and greet the others.

After months of anxiety, a week of constant movement, the treachery of emotions like a coiled spring, ready to unspool at any moment: she has finally arrived.

Now, it's time for the real work to begin.

# William

THE DOCKLANDS TRAIN swoons past Canary Wharf, the office windows there still yellowed with light at almost seven in the evening. There's no point working late now, guys, William wants to say. He imagines all the suited bankers and stockbrokers, beavering away inside their glass towers. Not only have the horses bolted, he thinks: they've taken the stable with them as well.

The buildings loom upwards, reaching towards a black night; pewter-coloured clouds sit lower down, threatening rain. William feels the acute embarrassment that he still experiences every time he visits England. That roll-call of death: the bombing of Birmingham, Canary Wharf, Warrington – as though he has personal responsibility for all of them. He tries to push away the feeling as the train pulls into Greenwich Station and the doors slide open, disgorging people onto the platform. Ascending passengers wait, more or less politely, until the descending throng has passed.

William makes his way towards the exit, pulling Sorcha's email out of his coat pocket. As he leaves the station, he can smell the river. Sharp, salty. He likes its tangy presence all around him. The air feels damp and somehow smoky. He could have taken the ferry across instead, but the wind was too biting. Another time, perhaps: once he has managed to reclaim his life. The life he'd once thought was his for good – his and

Julia's. A future spent together, one freed from all the tangles of the past. He will *not* give that up.

He remembers the last time he was in London; the three days that he and Julia had spent here together before flying out to Sydney, two years ago. He remembers how he'd always had the strongest sense, right from the beginning, that being with Julia had brought him to life in all sorts of ways that he had learned to forget. In the years after Jan, his system had shut down, like a reactor cooling towards inertia. Julia had reignited those energies, burned away their sluggishness. He'd suddenly started writing again, his work moving in a new and different direction, the tone darker, edgier. His characters became more complex, his stories less driven by external events.

'Your villains have become more interesting,' she'd told him. He'd sat for hours beside her on the sofa, nervously awaiting her verdict on the latest draft. He remembers how he'd pretended to read the newspaper, pretended to focus on the economic woes of the country. In reality, he couldn't have cared less. He was master of his own particular universe; master of his own 'grey dollar'; safe from the latest ravages of recession. 'These new characters are much more multi-layered,' she'd said.

He'd felt very proud at that, as though he'd embarked on something new and suddenly discovered a talent for it. And in a way, he had.

'And there's more than a hint of the redemptive power of love. I haven't seen you write about that before.'

Later, William had told Julia that loving her had unleashed a whole new wave of insight, of understanding, of creative power. That had pleased her: he can still see the way she'd smiled.

And Michael had taken to her at once. 'She's great, Dad,' he'd said, 'really great. It's so good to see you happy.' He'd looked at his father over the top of his glasses. '*And* it's good to see you here in Sydney. I know I've Julia to thank for that.' He and Michael had sat up talking for hours on the night they'd arrived. Julia had gone to bed earlier, claiming exhaustion. Together, William and his son had made their way steadily through a bottle of Bushmills, sitting out in the velvety dusk, under a huge Australian sky. Out of doors in their shirt sleeves: William still remembers the pleasures of a warm and sultry night.

'I haven't been much of a father in the last few years. I'm profoundly sorry about that.' He spoke into the darkness, chiding himself for his lack of courage.

But Michael had turned to face him, looked him right in the eye. 'You're here now. That's all I care about.'

William had been astonished at the readiness of his only child's forgiveness. The three weeks that followed had been gentle, rich with getting to know each other once more. And meeting Tanya: Michael's shy girlfriend. William had found that to be unexpectedly emotional. It was as though something had shifted between father and son, an old perspective changed. Michael was now a grown-up: he and his father met on equal terms. By the time he left to go home, William felt that he and his son had somehow become woven together again, their two lives linked in a way that would never have happened without Julia. Tonight, back in London without her, these memories are poignant enough to make him weep.

He turns right now and heads towards Greenwich High Road. Three streets from the station, Sorcha's note says, then a sharp left and second right. We're tucked away at the far end of the cul-de-sac. William walks down Nelson Close and finds number thirty-six without difficulty. The house has a bright-blue front door that he finds comforting. It reminds him of Julia's postbox and holds out a kind of promise.

As he stands on the porch step, he hesitates. He's arrived, as

Julia would say, with 'one arm as long as the other'. He hasn't even thought to bring anything with him. Confused, he turns away. He's already noticed a supermarket on the High Road. He'll go back and get a bottle of wine, a bunch of flowers — anything. But he must have been spotted. The front door opens and a woman stands there, smiling.

'You must be William,' she says. 'I've been keeping an eye out for you. I'm Sorcha. Come in, please.'

He shakes her hand, cursing himself for being on the back foot. He can see how Julia would look at him right now, head to one side, amused. 'Jesus, Will, have you *still* got no talent for the social niceties?' And the truth is, he hasn't. Never has had. He'd learned to see their value when Julia was with him, but now they all seem pointless again. And they seem particularly pointless tonight. 'Thank you,' he says, and steps into the cool green of a hallway.

'Let me take your coat.' Sorcha holds out both hands. 'And you can leave the rucksack behind here, unless you need it?'

'No, that's fine.' He shrugs his way out of his heavy winter coat and unwinds the scarf from around his neck. 'It's bitter out there.'

'Yes, it's been a particularly cold week,' she says politely, hanging up the coat and scarf on an ornate mahogany coat-stand. 'Come on through to the breakfast room. It's warmer there.'

He follows her down the hallway. When Sorcha opens the door to the breakfast room, there is the heady smell of stargazer lilies. 'Sit down,' she says, and gestures towards a chair at the long wooden table. The table is already set for dinner, three places with linen napkins, shiny crystal. An ice-bucket sits in the centre and William curses himself again.

'Red or white?' Sorcha asks.

He sees that the white is already open. 'White would be

great, thanks.' He waits while Sorcha pours. 'This is a really lovely house,' he says. She hands him the wine glass. 'Have you been here long?'

Sorcha glances back at him, over one shoulder. She's reaching for something in a cupboard. 'Thirty years. All my married life. It belonged to Hugh's – my husband's – parents.'

'It's beautiful. The proportions, the fireplace. Everything. Really.' William stops. He's beginning to sound like an estate agent.

'Thank you. We love it.' She places a bowl of olives in front of him. 'Are you hungry? Dinner will be about half an hour.'

William suddenly realizes how ravenous he is. 'I'm fine,' he lies.

She smiles again and pushes the olives towards him. 'Well, help yourself anyway.' She puts some dips on the table and a basket of breadsticks. William looks at her. 'Okay,' he says, relenting. 'I'm starving.'

They both laugh and William decides that he likes her. She is much smaller than Julia, and her body is compact and careful. Her fair hair is swept back into a chignon, secured with a blue velvet ribbon; her clothes are darkly elegant and understated. William is aware again of the third place at the table and decides to plunge ahead before anyone else joins them.

'I'm really grateful to you for seeing me,' he says.

Sorcha frowns, a quick, sudden change of expression. 'I don't know if I'm going to be of any use to you. I have to tell you that I don't know anything at all about Julia's whereabouts. She refused point-blank to tell me.'

Relief floods him with such intensity that he can barely speak. 'So she *has* been to see you, then?'

'Yes, she has.' Sorcha's gaze is direct. 'I told her you would put two and two together. That you'd follow her here.'

'How much have I missed her by?'

'She arrived on Tuesday, a week ago tomorrow. She left first thing on Wednesday morning.'

William nods. So she was here even before he knew she was missing. She'd sat in this room while he sipped pints with Jack in a whole other universe, not knowing that his life had already begun to come apart at the seams. Anger threatens, underneath the heady rush of relief. He sees himself and Melissa again, together at the Garda station, shocked, fumbling with their sense of loss. Sorcha sips at her wine and watches him. He notices how intensely green her eyes are.

'I need whatever help you can give me. I'm flying blind here.' He spreads his hands, their emptiness indicative of all that he feels he has lost.

'I'll help you in any way I can. Why don't you fill me in first. Tell me about you and Julia, about everything that's been happening. You must be beside yourself with worry.'

'Okay.' William draws a breath, steadies himself. 'I saw Julia last Monday. Everything seemed fine – everything between *us* was fine,' he corrects himself. 'Then, suddenly, she disappeared. She made up some story about going to Wicklow on Tuesday, so I didn't even start to be concerned until the next day. I've spent the last week hurtling around the countryside, calling on friends, trying to put the pieces of the jigsaw together.'

'And have you succeeded?'

'I was completely flummoxed until this morning.' He stops, feels again the elation that had coursed through him once he'd found the reason. Once it became clear that it wasn't *him*.

'What happened this morning?'

'Melissa called. The police had just been to see her. They're looking for Julia, but not in the way I'd imagined.' He watches Sorcha's face. But there isn't even the trace of an expression that he can read.

'Then why?'

'A woman called Greta Fitzpatrick has accused Julia of assisting at her mother's death, four years ago. The police want Julia to "help them with their enquiries".'

'Ah.' Something is illuminated for Sorcha. William can see it in her eyes, hear it in that one resonant syllable. He recognizes it because it has so recently happened to him. She nods, puts down her glass. She folds her hands and waits for him to continue. He plunges ahead.

'Greta is Roisin Macauley's sister—'

'Yes, I know who Greta is,' Sorcha stops him. He feels that she is urging him on, wants him to get to the heart of things.

'From what I understand, Greta has some letters, or papers, that somehow implicate Julia in Hilary's death. Roisin is frantic, but there was nothing she could do to prevent it. Greta and Gerry seem determined to pursue it.'

Sorcha frowns. 'I don't get that. From what I know of them through Roisin, I didn't think that Gerry and Greta would want such private family matters aired in public.'

William shakes his head. 'I don't know either – except that they seem to be on some sort of a crusade. And there's bad feeling already, going back years, between Greta and Julia, from what I understand. Anyway, I really don't care what their motivation is. I just want to find Julia.'

'Of course.'

'What did she tell you, Sorcha? Did she explain any of this?' He sits forward on the chair.

'She told me very little. You've filled in some of the gaps, so I can start to make sense of what she did say. She was very careful not to reveal anything significant, and I didn't push her too hard. But Julia must have known that this was coming.' She looks away for a moment, then directly back at William again. 'She was adamant that we all needed to be protected: you, me and Melissa. Obviously, I didn't know for sure what

234

we needed to be protected *from*, until now.' She smiles. 'I said that you, above all, might not appreciate such protection.'

William grins. 'Thank you. You got that right.'

'But she was insistent. I also know that she wants you to find her. That's the sum total of what I actually *know*.'

William slips his hand into his jacket pocket, feels the comforting presence of the white queen. 'Yes. I think she does, too. She's left a few – well, I'll call them messages.'

'Have you or Melissa got any idea where she might have gone?'

'No. Melissa is as much at sea as I am. Roisin suggested California.' He shrugs. 'Some woman called Alicia that Julia used to be close to. That's all I have to go on. And it's a long shot – but to be honest, everything is a long shot.'

'I remember Alicia,' Sorcha is thoughtful again. 'I remember her very well indeed.' She stops. 'I wish I could remember her name, though. Newsome, I think, or Newton.' She shrugs. 'Forty years is a long time. But we can try and google her later.'

William nods, all eagerness. 'Yeah, that would be great.'

'She and Julia were very close for a time.'

William hears something in her tone. 'And you? You weren't?'

She shakes her head. 'No. And Julia sensed it. She kept us apart as much as she could.'

'Why?'

'Differences of opinion. Differences of background, of priorities.'

William feels suddenly uneasy. 'You have to help me here,' he says. 'Julia and I met three years ago. There is so much I don't know about her.' He stops. 'And frankly, I'm beginning to feel that I didn't listen hard enough to what she may have tried to tell me. I'm missing a lot.'

Sorcha smiles. 'Julia never did anything by halves. She felt so passionately about things. And she always seemed to have everything worked out. I used to *understand* her reasons, most of the time, even if I didn't believe in them.'

'What do you mean?' William is curious.

'We didn't always see eye to eye. Certainly as students, we didn't. And our most serious falling-out began around the same time that she and Alicia became friends.'

William tries to curb his impatience. He can feel his manners straining at the leash. 'Tell me, please. It could be important.'

Suddenly, the door of the breakfast room opens and a large man enters, bringing the chill of outside air with him. He's still in his overcoat, a yellow scarf startling against his ruddy cheeks. 'So this is where you're hiding!'

William looks at him, trying to conceal his surprise. This is not the sort of husband he would have imagined for Sorcha. Big, beefy; almost too hearty.

'Hugh,' Sorcha says. 'You're early. Blue moon out tonight?' She turns to William. 'William, this is my husband, Hugh. Hugh, this is William, Julia's partner.'

William stands up and he and Hugh shake hands. 'Pleased to meet you,' he says, returning the other man's firm grip.

'Yes, yes indeed,' says Hugh. 'You're welcome to Greenwich.'

William is aware of the other man's scrutiny, just as he's sure Hugh is of his. Two deer, staking out their territory.

'Let me get out of this coat,' Hugh says. 'Please, William – sit down and drink your wine.' He returns almost at once, running his hands through his thinning hair, smoothing it into place across a bald patch. 'Any news of Julia?' he asks William, filling a glass as he does so. Sorcha has just brought in a bottle of red wine from the kitchen. Hugh asks his question without preamble.

William glances at Sorcha. Her nod is almost imperceptible. 'Well, there have been some developments.' He tells Hugh, and feels that the air of unreality around the telling is growing again; Julia seems very far away from him right now, in the company of at least one person who knows her far better than he does. The thought depresses him.

'I see. And is there any truth to the allegation, do you think?'

William hesitates. 'That's what I'm here to talk to Sorcha about. That, and where Julia might have gone.' He stops. 'If there *is* any truth, I wouldn't doubt the purity of her motives, not for a second.' He has trouble keeping the emotion from his voice.

'Of course, of course.' Hugh is nodding at him, but it is an absent kind of nod. William wonders if he really understands.

'Let's eat,' Sorcha says. 'Dinner is just about ready.'

William gets to his feet. 'Can I help?'

She smiles at him. 'If you'd bring in the roast potatoes, that'd be grand.' William hears the unmistakable echo of Ireland in the word 'grand'.

'Of course,' he says and walks quickly towards the kitchen. He has just reached for the potatoes and Sorcha is there at his elbow, standing urgently beside him.

'Please, just relax over dinner. We'll talk when Hugh goes out, in an hour or so.'


'Right,' Hugh says, rubbing his hands together. He pushes his dessert bowl away from him. 'Full as a tick, I'm afraid. Might come back and attack it later. Midnight feast, what do you reckon?'

'Don't worry,' Sorcha says. 'I won't throw it out.'

'It was all delicious, thank you,' William says. 'It's years since I've had sticky toffee pudding.'

'A good dinner and a good fire,' Hugh pronounces as he pushes his chair back from the table. 'Can't be too much wrong in life if a man has that.'

William doesn't know what to say. Neither does Sorcha, it seems, because she stays silent. Is he stupid, William wonders, or just insensitive? Hugh pats his pockets, checks his mobile phone and kisses the top of Sorcha's head. 'I'm off,' he says.

His hearty tone has begun to grate on William's nerves. 'Bridge club. Keeps the old brain cells ticking over.' He extends his hand to William. 'Very nice to meet you,' he says. 'Consider this home, any time. I hope you find Julia soon. Damned hard to be on your own.' He squeezes Sorcha's shoulder. 'Don't know what I'd do without her.'

Sorcha smiles up at him. She rests one of her hands, briefly, on his. 'Drive carefully,' she says. 'Enjoy your night.'

Hugh waves as he leaves the room. William is filled with a mix of emotions that he doesn't want to examine. He misses Julia with a ferocity that takes his breath away. And he resents Hugh. That's for starters.

When he's gone, a peculiar silence fills the room. William doesn't want to examine that, either. He stands up. 'If you'll excuse me, I'm just going to make a quick call to Melissa. I promised to let her know if there was any news of Julia. She'll be relieved to know you've seen her.'

'Of course. Give her my best. Stay where you are: I'll take these dishes into the kitchen and make us some coffee.' Sorcha gathers some of the plates and bowls and piles them onto a tray. 'It's okay,' she says, forestalling William. 'Make your call. I don't need any help.' She walks into the kitchen and closes the door behind her.

*

Melissa is subdued. She sounds exhausted, the wails of the children audible in the background. 'Has Sorcha seen her?'

'Yeah. Tuesday night last.'

'Jesus! Why didn't she let us know?' Her voice cracks.

'Well, we already know why. And Sorcha didn't know anything about anything. I've only just told her.'

'I am finding this really hard to deal with. I am so angry with my mother today that I don't know if I ever want to see her again. How could she do this to us?'

William is careful in his reply. 'It may be the wrong thing to do from our point of view. And I agree with you: it's very hard to take. But put yourself in her shoes. She thought this was best for everyone, and we just have to accept that. We are where we are.'

'I *hate* that fucking cliché.'

William winces. 'So do I. I'm sorry. It just seemed appropriate. We can't change anything here, Melissa. Hard as it is, we have to come to terms with what we've got.'

'What's next?'

'I don't know. I might have a clearer picture tomorrow. Sorcha's going to help me do some digging.'

'Okay. Thanks for letting me know, anyway. When are you back?'

'I didn't book a return. I wanted to leave things open, just in case.'

'I understand,' she says. 'There's nothing else here. I'll let you know if there is. I have to go.'

William promises to call again soon, to keep in touch.

Sorcha emerges from the kitchen, carrying the tray. 'Follow me,' she says. William does, and they make their way towards the front of the house. 'The morning room,' she tells William. 'Please, sit down and make yourself comfortable. I hate having coffee surrounded by dirty dishes.' She gestures towards an armchair set to the right of a blazing fire. She hands William a tiny cup, china so fine he's almost afraid to touch it. 'But Hugh and I sit here a lot in the evenings, now that there's just the two of us.'

'You have children?' William feels that he should make this enquiry. He sips at his coffee, not daring to hook his index finger through the handle, but holding the cup like a glass instead. He ignores the burning sensation on his fingertips.

'Yes,' Sorcha says. 'Three daughters.' She looks at him. 'Daisy, Adele and Julia.'

For a moment, he's confused. 'Oh,' he says. He thinks he's heard their names somewhere before.

Sorcha sits down in the armchair opposite him and throws another log on the fire. She leans forward and uses the poker to lift the glowing remains of the previous one. The new wood catches, bristling and crackling almost at once. William feels his heart flip over. Julia had done exactly that, one time they'd rented a cottage in Clare, in the dankness of early November. 'Let's get a good blaze going,' she'd said, and threw peat briquettes into the flames. 'Even the walls are arthritic here.' He'd laughed and opened a bottle of wine that they'd sipped together in the firelight and talked about their future.

He brings himself back, with difficulty, to Sorcha's hearth and home. 'What do they do, your daughters?' he hears himself ask, his voice strained, overly polite, even to his own ears.

Sorcha waves away the question. 'That's for another day,' she says. 'You don't need to be so polite, William.' Her voice is dry. 'It's not good for a man.'

He takes her at her word. He replaces the empty cup carefully in its saucer and leans forward in his chair. 'Tell me about the Julia you knew. Help me fill in some of the gaps.'

'We met as students. What I still remember most is how

compassionate she was. Too compassionate for her own good,' Sorcha begins. 'Even when we were interns together, she'd weep about the patients, take it personally that she couldn't cure them. I remember one of the professors spoke to her about it, and he was quite stern.

'We were doing our rounds with Professor Greene. I've never forgotten him. Back then, our training was very scientific. Things are different now: but for us, all the emphasis was on diagnosis, on finding the right treatment. Bedside manner, or empathy, hardly ever came into it. Even then, Julia rebelled against that. Professor Greene took her aside and told her that a "measure of detachment was essential for any doctor worth his salt". Otherwise, patients would see "a shadow of their own demise every time they looked at a medical man".'

She smiles. 'Those were his words. Including "medical man". Even though, that year, most of us were women. He told us he was too old to change his ways. That we'd just have to put up with him.'

'Did you hear what he said to her, or did Julia tell you afterwards?'

'Julia told me afterwards. He'd taken her into his office. We'd just been examining a young man – a teenager – with terminal pancreatic cancer. Julia couldn't bear it. None of us could: but for Julia the pain was more acute, somehow.' Sorcha looks at William directly. 'And it *was* – we all recognized that. It wasn't an act with her. It was real. With my own students I've seen the occasional attention-seeker, you know: "Look at me, how sensitive I am." But it wasn't like that with Julia. She was genuinely affected.

'So much so that, at the end of third year, she had a kind of crisis. She told me she'd made the biggest mistake of her life. That medicine wasn't for her. At least, not the sort of medicine we were being taught.'

William is surprised. 'Really?'

Sorcha nods. 'Yes. But she did go off that summer, to the States. She and Alicia. They went together to a hospital in San Francisco. I decided to come here, to work at Great Ormond Street.'

'Why? Did the States not appeal to you?'

'I already knew I wanted to specialize in children. And – ' here she looks at William – 'I wouldn't have wanted four or five months in the company of Alicia, anyway.' She stops. 'I've been thinking about this, while you were on the phone to Melissa. In fairness, I think I resented Alicia because she took Julia away from me.'

William nods. That is a feeling he can understand.

'As well as that, she came from a very wealthy background. Her father was a surgeon. She had all sorts of high-flown ideals, but I could see her going back to the States and setting up a very safe and lucrative practice, right under Daddy's wing. And I said as much to Julia.'

'How did she take it?'

'Oh, I was wrong. I didn't understand. She got quite cross with me. I think Julia was a little in awe of Alicia. And of her money.'

William looks at her in surprise. 'Wasn't Julia well off, too?'

Sorcha laughs. 'Only after she married Richard. Julia worked very hard to get to uni. Her parents had very little – and her dad died when she was small.'

Of course, William thinks. Life before Richard. Had Julia already told him all of this? Distant echoes of a similar conversation hover somewhere at the corners of his memory.

'Anyway, when Julia came back after that summer with Alicia, she was a lot more together. I was really glad. I didn't want to lose her. And medicine was the only worthwhile way to spend your life, we were all agreed on that. We were very idealistic back then.' She smiles at William.

'I remember,' he says. 'I was a journalist while you guys were slaving away over your anatomy books. We believed that we'd already changed the world. Mind you, the world hadn't noticed. But we didn't care. Heady days.'

'Yes,' Sorcha says. 'They were. And I was so happy to be sharing a flat with Julia, just the two of us. We had our own place until we finished college. We wanted our own space: our own chaos, as she said. We became very close.'

'And?' William prompts.

'She told me everything that had happened that summer. She had come across a group of activists in San Francisco. Both she and Alicia became involved in the debate around the right to die. Suicide, physician-assisted suicide, euthanasia – the lot. It's the sort of debate that's only begun here in the UK in the last year or so.' Sorcha shakes her head. 'It may have generated a lot more heat than light, but at least the unspeakable was out in the open. According to Julia, this was up-front, in-your-face debating. The "American Way", she used to call it. The confidence, and the passion, to speak your mind.

'She said the Irish apologized for themselves too much. A spurious modesty that she loathed – and that's Alicia speaking, too.' Sorcha frowns, trying to remember. 'I think the police were called a few times to whatever meetings they'd attended – you know, freedom-of-speech issues. The meetings often got extremely heated and noisy, but there was no actual violence. Then, a few years later, the Hemlock Society was set up. Have you heard of it?' Sorcha looks at him.

William nods. 'Yeah, I know about it.'

'Julia became obsessed with it – all the ethical and medical tangles. She talked about it endlessly. She wore me out. We were supposed to be studying, and instead there were dozens of journals and articles that she insisted I read. And Julia was always very persuasive.'

'Yes,' William says, 'that she is.'

'Eventually we had a fight,' Sorcha says. 'The pressure-cooker of exams every three weeks was bad enough. The amount of cramming we had to do was spectacular: I still don't know how we survived it all. And I certainly didn't need Julia forcing me to debate assisted suicide as well.' She pauses.

We never spoke of this, William thinks. Julia never mentioned it. It occurs to him only now that Julia might have been just as happy to leave her past behind as he was to abandon his. He listens intently to all that Sorcha is saying.

'I told her that as a doctor I was focused on life, not death. She insisted that we should focus on the quality of it, that doctors had a duty to understand what quality meant.' Sorcha's face looks troubled. 'You know, it's well over thirty years ago, and I can still remember how angry both of us got. I was shaking. She was lit up with – I don't know – call it righteous indignation. She was appalled at my "denial". I was angry at her certainties. Eventually I told her I never wanted to discuss it again. I slammed off into my bedroom and we didn't speak for weeks. The tension was unbearable. It's very difficult to avoid confrontation when living in a small flat.' Sorcha sighs.

'When did you speak again?' William is anxious to know.

'It was a couple of weeks after the exams. Things between us kind of subsided on their own. I was going to Scotland to work for the summer,' Sorcha says. 'We had to sort out the flat and other bits and pieces. To be fair, Julia came to me. She apologized. I said we'd agree to differ. And that was it.'

William looks at her, startled. 'For how long?'

Sorcha smiles. 'We did speak of it again, of course we did,

lots of times over the next few years. But it was different. We both accepted where the other was coming from. And after we graduated we stayed friends, even though we lived in different countries.'

'So you were both able to put it behind you?'

Sorcha shrugs. 'You can never forget about the past. It's real. But once I'd been practising medicine myself for a few years, I learned that the big decisions are never simple. Watching parents switch off a ventilator for the first time taught me that. It made me understand more about Julia's beliefs than all our arguments put together.'

'Can I ask you if you share – or even partly share – her point of view?'

'There are no easy answers to that, William. I feel very ambivalent about it. There are no winners in this.' Sorcha pauses. When she speaks again, she does so slowly, as though she is considering every word. 'What I do feel is that I would always trust Julia to be ethical. She would always do the right thing: I know it.' She looks troubled. 'But other people – even other doctors – might not be so scrupulous. Look at Kevorkian: Dr Death. It became a kind of a crusade for him – or in my view, a power trip.'

She stops again, considering. 'There is a strange sense of elation that can come with that kind of power. It's one thing to legislate for something, to make it legal or illegal; it's quite another to make sure that bad faith, or bad judgement, never comes into it. I would always be worried about that, about individuals getting out of control.'

'If Julia has done this – assisted Hilary to die – she could go to jail, you know. For anything up to fourteen years.'

'I am aware of that. There have been a couple of high-profile cases here recently – and they've been judged individually in the courts, on their merits. But the charge is still one of attempted murder. And Ireland is different anyway: this is yet another nettle that people will refuse to grasp. We've never faced up to our demons, or our shortcomings. It's one of the reasons I moved here.'

William nods. 'But this is not one that we can export as easily as some of our other nettles.'

The front door bangs. William glances at his watch.

'Hugh is uncomfortable with this,' Sorcha says quickly. 'I don't really want to talk about it in front of him.'

William stands up. 'No problem. It's late. I should be going.'

'Nonsense,' she says. 'I have a room ready for you.'

Hugh pokes his head around the door. 'Ah, still at it, I see. Well, you're in the right place, by the fire. Bloody freezing out there.' He rubs his hands together, vigorously. 'Nightcap, anyone?'

William no longer cares about being polite. 'Think I'll hit the hay, Hugh. But thanks anyway. It's been a long week.'

'Of course, of course. I won't see you in the morning: I've early rounds. But good luck with your search. I hope you find Julia.' He extends his hand, shakes William's.

'Thanks, Hugh. Goodnight.'

'Follow me,' Sorcha says to William. 'I'll be back in a tick, Hugh.'

William takes his rucksack and follows Sorcha up the stairs. He is frustrated, impatient at the lack of progress. And now is not the time to remind Sorcha about googling Alicia – although he is tempted. He is no nearer to finding Julia tonight than he was almost a week ago. And he feels almost blinded by tiredness.

'Here you are.' Sorcha opens the door.

'Is this where she stayed?'

'Yes.'

'Thanks for everything. I really appreciate it. Will I see you in the morning?'

'Yes, I'll be here. Goodnight, William. Sleep well.'

He undresses quickly, pulls the duvet over his head. Where have you gone, Julia? he thinks. At least give me a clue.

He closes his eyes, but sleep will not come easily. He sees her everywhere. And memory is cruel: it seems to offer him the images that cause him most pain. Julia in the sunshine of Krakow. In the snowstorms of Prague. By the fireside in County Clare. In his arms.

He turns onto his other side, willing her away. But she will not go. She is there, with him, willing him to keep on missing her until he finds her.

# *Julia*

JULIA HEARS THE noises of early morning below her: forty
eager children having breakfast. She'll wait until the melee
clears before going downstairs. She'd timed it badly last night:
at least half of the small faces around the room had lit up at
her arrival. Homework had been abandoned; voices clamoured
for her attention. She won't make that mistake this morning.
Josanna and Anuradha run a tight ship: the only way to get
forty children to school on time.

Later today she and Sarita have an appointment to see
Mr Kapur's apartment. Julia is already conscious of taking up
precious space here – and a bathroom – that might be better
used.

And she also needs to have a proper discussion with Sarita,
about money, among other things. She steps onto the floor,
remembering just in time to duck. The ceiling of her attic room
slopes right above her head. Keeping bent, she pulls her
rucksack towards her, kneels down and empties out its contents
onto the bed. Then she reaches into the inside pocket of her
suitcase and pulls out a small sewing kit. She can see herself,
on the Monday afternoon before her departure, sitting at the
kitchen table in her own home.

Tinkerbelle had watched her, her green eyes alight. 'It's not
food, Tinky, relax.' Julia had selected a small implement from
the kit, pulling it out of its elastic housing. She used its sharp

point to unpick all the stitches around the lining of her rucksack, exposing its insides. Beside her, on the polished surface of her table, lay bundles of fifty-euro notes. She had decided against the larger denomination: afraid that they might give rise to questions. She had carefully withdrawn five thousand a month since May, in cash, from different bank accounts, different branches, and had concealed them under the false bottom of her wardrobe, wrapped in an innocent black sack.

Sewing the notes into the lining of the rucksack had taken her most of the afternoon. Sometimes her hands had trembled too much to continue. Sometimes she had to stop to catch her breath, ambushed all over again by a searing sense of loss. She wept, for William, for Melissa, for the children; for herself. She could feel her steely determination seep away from her, weakening under the force of grief's onslaught.

'Just do it, Julia,' she said, over and over again. To keep her focus, she willed herself to keep remembering Greta, to relive all the details of that awful day. She unpicked the stitches of those memories too, feeling again all their unforgiving sharpness. She knows that she will never be able to forget them: that all the time and all the distance in the world will not weaken them.

She feels their rawness now as she sees herself standing on Greta's step, six months ago. She can see how she presses the bell for the second time, and this time she hears it ring. It misses a few beats here and there, but even its stutterings have to be loud enough to be heard inside. She decides to give it a minute or so, before ringing Greta's mobile. And then the door is partly opened. Greta is standing in the hallway, one hand holding onto the door, as though poised to close it again at once.

'Greta?' Julia says. For a moment, she's not sure: the figure in the hall is half-obscured by the door, and something about her expression is unfamiliar. 'It's me, Julia.' She waits and the door is pulled open a fraction further.

'Come in.' Greta now opens the door fully and Julia steps into the hall.

'Is everything all right? You said you needed to see me, that it was urgent. I thought you were ill.' Despite her best efforts, Julia can't hide her annoyance. A breathless call at seven o'clock this morning, on the house phone, had startled both her and William into wakefulness.

'What is it?' he'd asked, as she'd struggled quickly into her jeans and sweater. 'Is someone ill?'

'I don't know. It's Greta, sounding very strange. I can't make any sense of what she's saying. I'd better get over there.'

'Quick coffee?' William was already upright, swinging his feet to the floor.

'No, no,' she'd said. 'No time. Gotta go.'

'Let me know what's happening, won't you?'

'Of course I will. If I can get this damned mobile to work. One way or the other, I'll be back by lunchtime.' She'd leaned over, kissed him. 'Love you.' And she'd raced out of the bedroom and down the stairs. She'd grabbed her black bag from the cupboard in the hall, almost falling over Tinkerbelle, who'd mewled at her. 'Oh, Tinky, not now!' she'd cried.

William had called from the landing. 'You drive carefully, sweetheart. Don't worry, I'll feed Whinge.'

Julia had fled, laughing up at him.

But once in the car, she pulled her mobile out of her handbag. It had switched itself off again. That was the third time: no warning, the screen had just faded abruptly into darkness. She pressed down hard on the 'on' button, but nothing happened. Sighing in exasperation, she tossed it onto the passenger seat. She glanced into the rear-view mirror and pulled away from the kerb. There was no time to lose – Greta had sounded really strange. Julia tried to remember whether her speech had sounded slurred or just emotional. Either way, she felt a stab of apprehension. It was as though she was losing her balance. And there was no way she could get in touch with Roisin, not between here and Dún Laoghaire. 'Just drive, Julia, drive,' she told herself. If Greta was ill, there was no time to waste.

Now, she stands on Greta's threshold and the woman is just looking at her, her face devoid of expression.

'Yes, I do want to see you, and no, I'm not ill – not in the way you mean.' She seems to stumble in the half-light of the hall and Julia puts out her hand to steady her. She parks her irritation until later.

'Come and sit down,' she says. 'Let's get you off your feet. You're like a ghost.'

Greta allows herself to be led into the living room. Julia guides her gently to the sofa and waits until she is seated. 'Can I get you anything?' she asks. 'Glass of water or—'

Greta waves at her impatiently. 'No, no, no, I don't want anything. Sit down, Julia.' She fumbles at her hair and Julia notices that her hand is shaking. She sits beside her on the sofa and waits. The colour starts to seep back into her cheeks and Julia watches as she steadies herself.

'Take your time,' she says. 'Something has given you a bit of a shock.'

Greta turns to look at her. 'Roisin was here all night. Did you know she was coming?'

'No,' Julia says, surprised. 'No, no, of course I didn't. How would I know that?'

Greta doesn't answer. Instead, after a long pause, she says, 'We had a fight.'

Julia looks at her. She almost says, 'Well, nothing unusual there, then.' But something in the other woman's face stops her.

'A really bad fight.' She looks directly at Julia. At the same time, one hand goes to the gold cross around her neck. She starts to finger it. 'Among other things, it was about you.'

'About me? Why?'

Greta looks at her sharply. 'Has Roisin spoken to you today or not? Tell me the truth.'

Julia draws a long breath. 'No, Greta, she has not. It must be three weeks since I spoke to Roisin. I haven't heard from anyone today, besides you.' There is a reluctant silence. Julia is aware of all its awkward corners. She feels that something is threatening, about to tumble over into the abyss, so she speaks, simply to fill it. 'My mobile keeps switching itself off. It must need a new battery.' She waits now, watches as Greta seems to struggle with something. She won't challenge the imperious tone, not just yet.

'I need to ask you a question.' Greta begins to sit up straighter. She will not meet Julia's eye; instead, she turns her head sideways, her gaze drawn towards the fire that is already burning in the grate. Although late April, the mornings and evenings are still chilly: the spring air hasn't had time to warm up.

Julia's eyes follow hers. Somehow, she notes that the fire has that sagging, ashy look that means it has been lighting all night. Turf briquettes are lined up on either side of the fireplace like sentries. The observation seems to warn her of what is coming next. She needs to be on her guard.

'Go ahead. I'm listening.' A small, dormant part of Julia has been waiting for this moment for almost four years. Now, it is awake and she feels ready.

'It's about Hilary.'

Julia nods. She keeps her voice steady. 'Okay. So what is it about Hilary that you need to ask me?'

Greta stands up, moves away from Julia. She stands at the old-fashioned sideboard, resting one hand on its gleaming surface. 'I have some papers belonging to my mother. I didn't know I had them. Someone – one of the carers, I think – gave me a box of her things after she died.'

Julia says nothing, just waits for her to continue. She thinks how typical it is that Greta cannot distinguish one of her mother's carers from the other, can't even recall their names. Julia can remember all four of them: Brenda, Beth, Kathleen and Hilary's favourite, Eileen. Suddenly, in Julia's handbag, her mobile comes to life. She hears it beep, but she doesn't move. Instinct tells her it is Roisin, warning her.

'I came across the box on the top shelf of the wardrobe of the spare room. I was looking for something for Gráinne.' Greta begins to walk around the room. Julia has seen her do this before, building up to a moment, and so she presses both of her hands together. She has long ago discovered that 'sitting on her hands' like this prevents her from rushing headlong into speech. 'You see,' Greta goes on, 'I keep the dressing-up stuff there, on the bottom shelf, and the toys and colouring books for when the children come and visit. I don't know why it caught my eye yesterday, it just did. I had to get Gerry to lift it down for me.'

Julia tries to be patient. She knows that lingering over such irrelevant detail can often be the result of shock, of trying to order events, to make sense out of something that won't make any sense otherwise. She'll give Greta the benefit of the doubt. But she wishes she'd just get on with it.

'I don't know who put it there,' Greta looks puzzled, 'perhaps Gerry, although I really can't think why. And he says he doesn't remember. I don't remember too much either from the days after Hilary died. It was such a terrible time.' She shakes her head.

'And what did you find?' Julia prompts her.

'Letters,' she says. 'I found letters from my mother.'

Julia decides to choose her words carefully. After a moment, she says: 'Writing letters gave your mother great pleasure. She always said she wanted to leave happy reminders for those she loved.' She is conscious of the strain in her voice. Her words sound hollow in the charged stillness that follows Greta's revelation.

'I know that,' Greta says, not bothering to hide her irritation. 'After all, she was *my* mother.'

Julia doesn't answer. There is nothing to say to this: nothing that won't make Greta even more irritable. She knows instinctively where this is going, wishes she'd had the chance to speak to Roisin first.

'But these letters are different,' Greta says. She gazes at Julia with something like defiance. 'These aren't like the others at all, not at all.' She pauses. 'She wrote them to you and Roisin.' Her words are bitter.

'To me and Roisin?' Julia feels the air in the room begin to bristle. 'Then how do you know what's in them?' She keeps her voice quiet. There is no reply. 'If the letters were to me and Roisin,' Julia repeats, 'then how do you know what's in them?'

'Because I read them.' Now the defiance is emphatic, almost proud.

'And why did you do that?' Julia's mobile rings. She reaches into her bag and switches it off, but not before she has seen Roisin's name light up the screen. It's too late now. This is what it is, and she'll have to deal with it alone.

'Because of a suspicion I've had, that I've always had.'

'A suspicion?'

'And the letters prove it.' Greta's voice is rising now.

'Prove what? I don't know what you're talking about. Let me read the letter – after all, it was meant for me – and then we'll talk. Right now, I don't know anything. How can I discuss something with you if I'm completely in the dark?'

But Greta shakes her head. 'Oh, no. You're not going to trick me like that. Roisin tried the same thing last night and I wouldn't give it to her. I'm not giving it to you, either.'

'Then how am I to know what's upsetting you?' Julia begins to stand. It is impossible to be seated, trying to remain calm, while Greta hovers by the sideboard, looking down at her. Julia wants to lessen the distance between them, but Greta puts out one hand to stop her.

'Stay where you are.' Her tone is sharp, almost a bark. 'You'll know what's in it because I'll read it to you.' She pulls open the top drawer and lifts the flap of a white envelope. She begins to read, holding onto sheets of blue paper that Julia recognizes with a lurch as Hilary's. She, Julia, had made her a gift of a box of writing paper, a Martha Stewart collection. It had been a joke between them: two women with an enduring dislike of what Hilary called 'frilly home-makers'. Greta's voice is high-pitched, her sense of triumph palpable. '"My dearest Julia,"' she begins.

Julia is filled with sudden rage. Quickly she crosses the room to where Greta is. She stands in front of her, making sure that her feet are solidly planted, that she has a good grip on herself. 'I'm not listening to any more of this, Greta. That is my letter and you had no right to open it. If you won't let me read it for myself, I'm leaving now. How dare you intrude on something that was meant for me? How dare you!'

Greta looks up at her, startled. She looks at Julia as if she can't quite believe what she is hearing. Her expression is almost petulant: how come this moment has been stolen from me? In reply, Julia flings her bag over one shoulder, takes the car key out of her jacket pocket and makes her way towards the door.

'You killed her!' Greta screams. The suddenness of the accusation takes Julia's breath away. 'You and my sister: you killed her! I know you did.'

Julia walks right back up to her again. 'Be very careful of throwing around accusations like that, Greta. Before we discuss this any further, I demand to see that letter – *my* letter. Otherwise, I am leaving now. I'm appalled that you have not respected my privacy.'

Greta shakes her head. 'No!' she cries. 'You're not getting it.'

Julia opens the door into the hall. 'We'll talk again when you're calmer,' she says. She walks towards the front door, opens it, steps outside onto the porch, feeling her legs begin to give way.

She hears running footsteps behind her. Suddenly Greta is at her shoulder. She hisses into Julia's ear. 'Don't think you're going to get away with this! You: the kind doctor, the compassionate doctor – the one everybody trusted!'

Julia bites back a reply, walks to her car and opens the door. She drives away, Greta observing her from the doorway. Her arms are folded, she is still clutching the white envelope in her right hand. Julia waits until she turns the corner and pulls over into a narrow street, sheltered on either side by small houses, neat front gardens. Shaking, she pulls her mobile from her handbag. She waits for it to switch on, prays that it will work this time and calls Roisin. She answers immediately.

'Julia – I've been trying to get you . . .'

'I know – I've just left Greta. I know. We need to talk.'

'I'm in town. I can be at your house in an hour.'

'No. That's not a good idea. William is there. Let's meet

somewhere in town. Near the Stephen's Green Centre, or somewhere else where it's easy to park?'

'Okay, that's fine. Bewley's in Grafton Street?'

'See you there.'


Roisin is already on the mezzanine, looking down into the
street. Julia touches her on the shoulder and she jumps. Her
face is pale, shadows like bruises under her eyes. She smiles up
at Julia, relieved.

'Oh, God, I'm glad you're here.' She clutches at Julia's
hand.

Julia sits. The waitress approaches, her black-and-white
uniform reassuringly normal. 'Pot of tea for two,' Julia says.
'Thank you.' She turns to Roisin. 'What has happened?'

She shakes her head. 'It was awful. I tried to call you on my
way from Wicklow last night, and again first thing this morning, but your mobile kept going straight to voicemail.'

'Never mind about that now. Just tell me everything.'

Roisin takes a deep breath. 'Greta called, late last night, to
say some of Mum's papers had come to light – some letters. I
was surprised, because Hilary had been careful to give them all
to me for safe keeping.' She pauses. 'She knew her memory was
going, that she couldn't rely on it any more. So I was puzzled
about there being new ones. I asked Greta to tell me what
was in them.' She starts looking for her cigarettes, remembers
she can't smoke here. 'At first, the only thing she'd tell me was
when they were written.'

'And when was that?'

'The night before she died. Eileen was with her, I'm sure
of it, because Mum had asked for her particularly. Remember
we had to rearrange the shifts?'

Julia nods. 'Yes. I do. Eileen was the only one she trusted to take dictation. I remember her very well.'

Roisin smiles, her eyes filling. 'Hilary said she was the only one of the lot of them who could spell. And she was damned if she'd leave anything badly written for her grandchildren. That it wouldn't be a good example.' Her voice rises on a sob.

Julia squeezes her hand. 'So Eileen must have given the letters to Greta?'

'Yes,' Roisin struggles for a moment, 'along with some other bits and pieces. Photographs, letters from Dad that she'd have asked Eileen to read to her, a couple of books of poetry.'

'What do the letters say, Ro?'

'I only heard my own – Greta wouldn't even let me touch it. She read it aloud, said she'd put two and two together.'

'And?'

'Well, that's the thing. The way she read it, the emphasis she gave certain words, the way she injected suspicion into everything – you could interpret it as Mum thanking me for ending her pain.'

'Or?'

'Or it could be Mum being very grateful for the way I looked after her – *we* looked after her. You and me, I mean. What she says is: "Thank you for *easing* this pain." I can only assume your letter is similar. Is it?' Roisin's eyes are anxious, appealing.

'I don't know. I refused to let her read it to me. I wanted to get out of there, to talk to you first. And she made me angry. I told her off for invading my privacy.' Julia grimaces. 'I was afraid that the lovely Gerry might burst in at any moment, and I wanted to get away as quickly as I could.'

'Well, he pontificated in fine style all last night. I know it sounds odd to say that I felt at a disadvantage. That's an understatement, if there was ever one – but not being able to *see* the words as they were written, only as Greta was interpreting them, I couldn't really judge how an objective observer might understand them.' She looks at Julia. 'And I was given no real time to explain. The point is, Greta had made up her mind in advance and she was using the letters to support her case.'

'She threatened the police.'

Roisin nods. 'Yeah, to me too. But we have a stay of execution on that.' She looks at Julia, appalled. 'Oh, God! What an awful thing to say.'

The waitress arrives with tea. Julia pours. 'How did you leave things?'

'That they would do nothing until Greta had spoken to you. Then they'd go looking for legal advice. Then we'd talk again.' Roisin rests her head in her hands, briefly. 'They're looking for someone to blame, and they've settled on you, in particular.' She looks up, her eyes filling. 'They see you as the guiltier of the two of us: you're the doctor, sworn to preserve life. I was unduly influenced. I'm sorry, Julia. I'm so sorry for getting you into this.'

'You didn't,' Julia says, sharply. 'We all made our own decisions – you, me, Hilary. That was the only basis on which I'd proceed. I knew the consequences.'

'What do we do now?'

'For the moment, nothing. Let's wait and see what their legal advice comes to. In the meantime, silence.' Julia sips at her tea. Her lips feel parched, her throat hot and raw.

'I know Greta is genuinely upset, but you know, what I felt last night . . . it was as if she was happy to have finally found the stick to beat me with.'

Julia nods. 'I felt that too. Briefly, but I felt it. As though she had won.'

'Exactly!' Roisin sits forward. 'And none of it was about

Hilary, or how she'd suffered, or even about right and wrong: it was all about her.'

Julia nods. 'So nothing changes, then.'

'Are you going to tell William?' Roisin asks, after a pause.

Julia shakes her head. 'Absolutely not. What people don't know, they can't tell. And I don't want him involved in any way, even after the event. I can't expose him like that, and knowledge would expose him.'

'Would he understand, do you think?' Roisin's voice is soft.

Julia hesitates. 'I don't know. He once told me how his parents had died "without giving anyone any trouble". The phrase stuck with me.' She smiles. 'He's a very sweet man. His life experience and mine have been very different.' She stops. 'To be honest, part of me is afraid that he wouldn't understand, and that would change things between us.' She shakes her head. 'But I can't tell him anyway, for his own sake, so I'm not going to torture myself about it.'

Roisin's mobile rings. She answers at once. 'Hi, Roma.'

Julia reaches into her handbag for her purse.

'Of course,' she hears Roisin say. 'I'll be home around two, say two-thirty to be on the safe side.' She ends the call, half-smiles over at Julia. 'Babysitting duties.'

Julia pulls on her jacket.

'Are you okay?' Roisin asks.

'I don't know. I'm trying to get a grip on this. I thought I was ready, but Greta blindsided me this morning. And right now, to be truthful, I feel frightened.' Julia fights back tears. 'There's Melissa to think of, too, and the children.'

Roisin reaches her hands across the table, holds on tight.

'But most of all – selfishly – for the last three years, I have a life I love. A man I love. I can't bear the thought of having to lose it all.'

'It might not come to anything, Julia.' Roisin's voice is urgent. 'You know Greta as well as I do: she's the original drama queen. And I don't know that she'd want the "family business" to be made public. Don't lose heart.'

'I'm not going back there. I refuse to be part of their inquisition – particularly when I'm not allowed to see what Hilary wrote to me.'

'I don't expect you to. But I will.' Roisin's tone is grim. 'I'll fight the pair of them, for both of us. I said some very hard things to her last night, and I'm happy to say them again.'

Julia stands up. 'I have to go.' She pulls on her jacket and buttons it, suddenly feeling cold. 'I don't want William to worry.'

Roisin hands Julia her mobile. 'Here. Call him. Use mine.'

Julia shakes her head. 'No, thanks anyway. I need the time to gather my wits.' She smiles. 'If I call him now, he'll know by my voice that something is up.' She lifts the bill off the table. 'I've got this.'

Roisin stands up and hugs her. 'You take care. I'll be in touch.'

'Write to me,' says Julia, suddenly, 'if you need to get in contact. 'Proper, old-fashioned letters. I'll burn them. We shouldn't discuss this over the phone – any kind of phone.'

Roisin nods. 'Okay. I'll do that.'

'And enjoy your grandchildren. Give Roma my love.' Julia pays the bill and waves at Roisin, who is still sitting at the table, her face resting in her hands, staring straight ahead of her. But she sees Julia, and waves back. Then Julia goes downstairs, buys some bread and coffee and turns right, making her way towards the car park. She clutches the bread and the coffee beans tightly. She wants to hold onto something down-to-earth, solid, ordinary.

But she can't help the feeling that she is about to step off the sure ground of her life into the unknown. She has the sensation even now – of falling, falling. She holds on tighter to the rail of the escalator bringing her up, up towards the car park.

And home. And William.

Julia remembers again how William had cared for her on that day. How he'd looked like a rumpled guardian angel, standing sleepily at her side after they'd both slept the afternoon away. And how she'd decided there and then that this flight from home, from him, from everyone she loved, had become inevitable.

It has all been a straight trajectory, she thinks now, as she unpicks the stitches of the lining once again. Hilary, Greta, Sarita. All of them bringing her back here.

There is a soft knock at the door. Julia puts down the rucksack. 'Come in.'

Sarita stands at the open doorway. 'Good morning,' she smiles. 'You have slept well?'

'Yes – I've only just woken. I feel very rested. Come on in, Sarita.'

Sarita enters, but hovers just inside the door.

Julia walks towards her, closes the door behind her. 'I need to speak to you, on our own. Do you have time now, or would later be better?'

'Now is good. All the children have just left for school. I came to see if you would like to join me for a quieter breakfast. Me and the others.'

'Yes, I'd like that. But first, there is something I must discuss with you.'

Sarita waits, her expression calm, untroubled. Julia wonders what she is thinking. She has never been able to read beyond that serenity.

'Okay, I'm sorry for rushing you, but I really need to get this over with.' Julia sits down on the bed again, indicates that Sarita should sit on the single chair. 'I have brought some money with me – to live on, to use for the children, to buy whatever we need: whatever the orphanage needs.' She hesitates. 'It's cash, sewn into the lining of my rucksack.' She shrugs, laughing at Sarita's startled expression. 'It was the only way I could think of to keep it safe. My rucksack and I are inseparable companions.'

'Yes.' The word is cautious, puzzled. Sarita looks intently at Julia, as though her face might tell her what is coming next.

'It's quite a lot of money,' Julia rushes on. 'I had hoped you might be able to put it into an account for me. When I need some for myself, I'll ask. When we need something for the children, we can discuss it. Would that be acceptable?' She stops. 'It's just the whole process for me of opening an account is very cumbersome. So much bureaucracy.' She waits, hoping that is enough.

'I understand,' Sarita nods slowly. 'It should not be difficult. I will call it an anonymous donation.' And she smiles.

'It's thirty thousand euro,' Julia says quietly. 'That's almost two million rupees. Or about eighteen lakh.'

Sarita's smile fades. She looks shocked. It takes her a moment to speak. 'That is more than large, Miss Julia. I do not know what to say. We will all have to think very carefully of what we are doing with it.'

'Of course. Now let me just say something once and we need not mention it again.'

Sarita nods. 'As you wish.'

'That money stays here, even if something happens to me –

if I have to go home, to go elsewhere: anything at all. I want you to know that. You have my complete trust to use it for the children in any way you see fit.'

Sarita nods, again. Her eyes continue to search Julia's face. 'But better that the four of us – you, Josanna, Anuradha and me – that we are deciding on these things together. That way, there is responsibility and agreement first.'

'That's fine.' Julia smiles at her. 'I think that is an excellent idea. We can all share in the decisions. I promised you I would help – and this is how I want to.'

'This is more than help,' Sarita says, slowly. 'This is a transformation—'

Julia cuts her short. She wants her to focus. 'And now, with your new refuge planned, this can be really useful. The money can finally do its work. I am a very wealthy woman, by your standards. Let's do some good together.' She stops. That's the hard part over.

Sarita stands up and steps forward. She embraces Julia, her face full of emotion. 'Thank you,' she says. 'You are being very generous to us. I don't know what to say. We make sure to take good care of you.'

Julia hugs her back. 'Okay, now let's go and have breakfast. Afterwards, you go to the bank.'

'Is there anything else you need to tell me, Miss Julia?' She looks anxious. 'Is there trouble for you, perhaps at home? Are you needing anything from us, from me?'

'Yes.' Julia is firm in her reply. 'There is something. Can you call me Julia, at least when we are on our own? Leave the formality for downstairs?'

Sarita inclines her head. 'Of course. Anything else, you need only to ask.' She pauses.

Julia knows that there is more, much more, that she wants

to ask. 'Thank you. I appreciate that. Let's go and have breakfast. Afterwards, we'll go together to visit Mr Kapur.'

'Of course. He is expecting us.' Sarita points to the rucksack. 'And this,' she asks, beginning to smile. 'This comes with us for breakfast, too?'

Julia laughs. 'It certainly does.'

They leave the room together, Julia pulling the door to behind her. She watches as Sarita descends the stairs, thinking how ageless she looks. She moves with grace and dignity and seems to keep everything around her together by sheer force of will.

Julia follows, step by step down the stairs into what is fast becoming her new life.

Mr Kapur is eagerness itself. 'Very big-fine room, very big-fine room,' he keeps saying. 'And the fan, for keeping cool. Anything you are wanting, I can supply.'

Julia smiles. 'It's a very fine room indeed, Mr Kapur. I'll take it.'

His face lights up.

'Miss Julia will be working here, with us, with the children,' Sarita intervenes. 'We like to think that she is still being our guest. I will come back later, Mr Kapur, and we can then talk about the details, between us.'

Immediately his face falls.

'And you can please get some mosquito netting? For tomorrow night? Thank you.' She leads Julia away, her hand firm underneath her elbow.

'That was unkind,' Julia says. She's finding it difficult to keep her smile under control.

'Why?' Sarita is surprised. 'With me, you get the best price.

Without me, Mr Kapur will charge you too much. It is a simple matter of business.'

Julia doesn't try to explain. Instead, she is reminded of Roisin: of that practical, matter-of-fact way of dealing with poverty. It is something she, Julia, has never mastered.

'Besides, Mr Kapur is already rich, in this village. My father has had many battles with him. I prefer extra money in my building fund, not in his pocket. Yes?'

Julia has no argument with that.

The following night Julia brings her belongings to Mr Kapur's spacious first-floor room. The stairs are a little rickety, and some nails protrude from the wooden banisters here and there. But she is more than satisfied with her new home. The large bed is already made, the sheets a bright white: patched, darned and very clean. On the upturned wooden crate beside the bed, someone – Mrs Kapur, most likely – has spread a delicate embroidered cloth. Resting on the surface is a lemonade bottle holding bright-red poppies.

Julia unpacks. She hangs up her clothes in the alcove. She unwraps her green-and-blue enamelled dish from home and places it on the bedside table beside the poppies. Then two photograph frames. One with Melissa, Derek and the children. The other with herself and William. She wonders if he would even remember the occasion. Derek had insisted, last Christmas, delighting in his new digital camera.

She pushes the case well under the bed, hiding it from sight. Then the rucksack, now empty. Sarita had lodged the money in two different accounts and handed the receipts to Julia. 'Very safe,' she'd said. 'And now two banks will help us.'

Julia had started, late that afternoon, assessing the needs of the children, one by one. She'd created files on each of them:

their age, height and weight, any family history that Sarita or Josanna or Anuradha could give her. Tomorrow she'll continue, and the next day, and the day after that, until this first stage is over.

Then she'll call Alicia.

And then, she'll wait.

# *William*

WILLIAM HAS JUST drifted off, his mind full of his conversation with Sorcha. He'd been right: she has filled in the gaps, offered many precious pieces of the jigsaw that is Julia's past. It's not sleep as such that has finally captured him, but a long, thin imitation of it. He seems still to be aware of his surroundings: aware, too, that Julia has slept in this same bed only days before him. There is some comfort in that.

He becomes conscious of a strange buzzing, something that is both noise and sensation. For a moment, he is paralysed: a giant black fly lands stickily on his face, rubbing its back legs together, making a sound that has become insistent. He struggles against it, against the suffocation that comes with its dark, oozy body. He jerks awake, gasping for breath. His mobile is buzzing on the night table beside him.

He struggles into a sitting position, shaking off the night terrors that he hasn't had since he was a child. He finds the light switch, rummages for his reading glasses. A message from Roisin fills the screen. Fully alert now, William reads it, his heart thudding again in the way he is becoming used to. 'Just remembered something. Text me a landline. Could be important. Ro.'

It's two a.m. Roisin is being careful, he knows, but he is impatient to find out what it is that might be important. He glances at the house phone beside him, resting in its cradle.

The number isn't written anywhere. Perhaps downstairs ...
He'd spotted an old-fashioned one in the morning room,
one that had immediately reminded him of Mrs Mc and the
Bakelite monster in the corner of her kitchen. He throws back
the duvet and pulls on one of Hugh's plaid dressing gowns.
It's way too big around the middle, and ridiculously short,
exposing his knees.

He opens the bedroom door as quietly as he can, but a
floorboard groans loudly underneath his feet. For a heartbeat
he stands there, rabbit in headlights, not knowing whether to
go back or go forward. A moment later Sorcha is beside him
on the landing.

'Sorry – I really didn't mean to disturb you.' William feels
guilty, like a badly behaved guest.

'You didn't. I can't sleep. I was just about to go downstairs
and make some tea. Want some?'

'I've had a text just now from Roisin. She's asking for a
landline number, says it's important. We're trying to be careful
about using mobiles.'

Sorcha nods, understanding. 'Of course. Come on – I'll jot
it down for you.' She takes him into the morning room where
they had had their coffee together earlier. She gestures towards
the phone. 'I'll be in the kitchen when you're ready. Give
Roisin my love.' She leaves, closing the door firmly behind her.

Minutes later, the phone beside him rings. He answers
immediately. The last thing he wants to do is disturb Hugh as
well. 'Roisin?'

'Hi, William. Sorry for the ungodly hour. It's just something that has occurred to me, and I didn't want to wait until
morning.'

'Don't apologize. What is it?'

'Remember when you tried to get me to see if there was
anything significant about the last conversation I had with

Julia? When I told you about her mentioning Sorcha's surname?'

'Of course, I'm with Sorcha and Hugh in Greenwich now.'
He wants to say: Just spit it out, will you. But he's becoming
used to people needing to tell their own stories in their own
way: to impose their own shape, to forge order out of chaos,
reason out of uncertainty. He's learning to be patient.

'Well, there was something else, right at the end. Something
that struck me as odd at the time, but not odd enough to be
significant, if you know what I mean.'

William waits. 'Yes,' he says. 'I do. Right now, I'm finding
hindsight to be a particularly bright light.'

'Yeah, well. Now, it wasn't much, just a throwaway comment. She said something about it must be almost time to get
a taxi.'

William is baffled. He tries to think: where would Julia
usually go by taxi?

'The thing is,' Roisin goes on, 'that's kind of a code between
us. It means, more or less, that something catastrophic is about
to happen.'

'What does?'

'Taxi,' she says. 'The word "taxi". Did Julia never tell you
about our experience at Mumbai airport, when we tried to get
from one terminal to another?'

Something is stirring in William's memory. Right now, his
head feels like one of the drawers in his kitchen, into which he
tosses all sorts of unrelated things and then forgets that he has
put them there. String, almost-spent lighters, Sellotape; people's
business cards, Post-it notes, that kind of thing. A tangle of
items with discarded lives and half-lives. And then one day
he'll open it and come across something useful that has made
its way to the surface, something that is just what he needs.
He remembers a vague story about Julia having been frightened

in Mumbai; but he also remembers that he'd been so glad to have her back, so anxious to tell her he loved her, that he'd only half-listened.

'I remember something, yes,' he says, slowly. 'A rogue taxi-driver. Why is it important now?'

'Because of where it happened,' Roisin says. 'I think it was a clue, William: a message to you. There's no other context – it had nothing to do with what Julia and I were talking about at the time.' She pauses. 'I may be way off: but I think she's gone back to India.'

There it is again: that sense of something settling into a comfortable place in his interior landscape, a place long pre-pared for it. 'Jesus, I think you might just be right,' he says. 'It makes perfect sense.' He has a memory of Julia at his table, talking about children, poverty, perspective. He doesn't try to unpick it now: but he feels the truth of Roisin's words. He pulls towards him the notebook and pen that Sorcha has left him. 'Remind me – where did you guys go, exactly?'

Even as he speaks, more fragments of conversation are returning to him: shards of images, of half-remembered stories. A taxi-driver; some roadworks; village women with too many babies. Jesus, why hadn't he listened to her!

'I've already emailed you our itinerary,' Roisin is saying. 'Along with about five mails to friends – nothing as sophisti-cated as a blog, but a kind of stream-of-consciousness thing, just a mish-mash of impressions from that trip. I started doing stuff like that years back. Something concrete to do in the evenings when you're a lone traveller.' She stops. 'I thought you might find them useful.'

William is already planning ahead: call Jack, get him to look after the apartment. Book a flight from Heathrow. This is Tuesday morning: with any luck, he could be in India before the end of the week. 'Roisin, this is gold, pure gold.' He pauses. Relief almost overwhelms him. 'Just answer me one last question.'

'Sure.'

'The two of you were together for about a month, if I remember correctly. Were you always together, or did Julia strike out on her own?'

'That's just what I was coming to. She did – for one day. Said she wanted to poke about a bit on her own. I don't know where she went, William. All I can tell you is that she left at eight or nine in the morning and was back by seven or eight that night. I can't remember exactly, but I know it was around dinner-time, because she wouldn't join the rest of us. We were already in the restaurant when she got back.'

William's eyes search the bookshelves around him for an atlas, maps of India, anything at all.

'So, wherever Julia went, it was a maximum of a five-hour journey from Chennai – no matter which direction she went. That's assuming she spent only an hour at her destination – if she had a final destination. She might just have driven from place to place.' She stops and William hears the click of a lighter as Roisin smokes yet another cigarette.

'She went completely on her own?'

'Well, she went without me, but she had a driver, of course. A young man we felt we could trust. She'd hired him for the whole day. His name was Bashir.'

William's mind is getting away from him again. He has trouble keeping up. 'How was she when she came back?'

'Tired, quiet. She went to bed almost immediately. But India did that to Julia. She was appalled at the slums, the way the women worked in the fields. People scrabbling for a living on rubbish dumps.' Roisin pauses. 'I'm a lot harder than she is. And I've travelled a lot more. I think I've grown a shell. I'm not particularly proud of that – but I used to tell her, "You can't save a continent." She'd have liked to, though.'

'Tell me: where did you guys go, after you landed in Mumbai?'

'Chennai, first. And after that, Delhi.'

'And where were you when she went walkabout?'

'At Chennai. I'm certain of that. I did a bit of sightseeing with some people from the hotel. I'm absolutely sure it was while we were staying in Chennai.'

William listens hard to his instinct. 'Might she have visited any hospitals, do you think?'

'Possibly, but your guess is as good as mine. I really have no idea where she went. Julia could be very private.'

I'll say, thinks William. That private life has suddenly extended beyond anything he could have imagined. He wonders how much of what they have shared is real: so much of Julia's significant life seems to have been submerged in an ocean of silence. He feels as though he has only perched, precariously, on an icy white tip, unaware of the vast reaches beneath. The thought depresses him. It's a three a.m. thought: the darkest hour just before dawn. He stops himself, filled with indignation. He will not lose faith in her, in them. 'This is more than I could have hoped for, Roisin. I'll read your mails and get going. Thank you.'

'There's one more thing.'

'Go for it.'

'I've contacted Eileen. She was one of Mum's carers. I spoke to her son.'

'And?'

'Eileen is away until the end of November. In Boston, with her youngest daughter who's due a baby soon. I've left a message asking her to get in touch when she gets back.'

'What are you hoping?'

Roisin hesitates. 'It's a delicate one. I certainly don't want to put any pressure on her. But I will tell her what's going on.'

'All of it?'

'I'll kick to touch on that one. I'll just have to see how it goes. I'll let you know, one way or the other.'

'End of November. That's another few weeks away. Text me when you're meeting.'

'I will.'

'And I'll let you know how things are going here. Thanks again.'

'You're welcome. Just be careful of how you keep in touch. If I hear nothing, I'll know you're on the right track.'

'Thank you,' he says again.

'Night, William. Sleep well.'

'You too.'

He makes his way to the kitchen, suddenly craving a cup of tea. Sorcha is waiting. 'Good news?'

'Potentially. Julia might have gone—'

She raises one hand. 'Don't tell me, William. Just do what you have to do, and let me know if you need any help.'

He nods. 'Cuppa for starters. And then, if you don't mind, access to your Internet.'

'No problem.' Sorcha pours tea. She pushes a plate of biscuits towards him. How can I eat at a time like this? he thinks. But he feels permanently hungry, thirsty. As though the hollowed-out part of him can be filled by tea and chocolate digestives. If only.

William sits at the table, but he can't settle. He stands up, hands in the pockets of Hugh's dressing gown, hands out again. He is suddenly aware of how daft he looks. He sits.

Sorcha smiles at him. 'Why don't you take your tea and

biscuits up to the study, and you can start straight away. I don't think you're going to sleep much, anyway. In fact, take the pot with you.'

'You sure?'

'Of course. I've told you before. Don't be so polite.' And she smiles at him. She leads the way up the stairs, into the study that is crammed with books, a desktop computer, scanner, printer. 'It's not the most up-to-date, I'm afraid. It's really just a backup in case my laptop is out of action. A bit slow to start, but it will get you there.' She logs on. William watches as the Internet icon appears on the screen, and he pulls the chair closer.

'Best of luck,' Sorcha says. 'Take your time. Feel free to move about as much as you want. I'll see you for breakfast.'

'Are you working tomorrow? I mean, later today?' William realizes that other people still lead ordinary lives. Going to work, coming home again. Finding people where they left them.

'No. I don't work on Tuesdays.'

'Okay, then. See you later. And thanks again for everything.'

'Goodnight.' And she's gone, the door creaking to behind her.

William stares at the screen, waits until his email account loads, and logs on. I miss you, Julia. I really miss you, he thinks. Six emails from Roisin appear, one after the other.

He opens the first and begins to read.


William has no idea what a clue might look like, but he combs through Roisin's words, hungry for sustenance. Her descriptions of the places she and Julia visited are bright, lively, but impersonal. And he cannot find Julia in any of them. Maybe a second reading, when he is not so tired, might yield something. He prints them out and is about to switch off the machine when he remembers.

He pulls up the Google bar and, one by one, writes in all the variations of Alicia's name and probable surname that he can devise: Alice, Alicia, Alys, Alyssia. Possibilities crowd his screen once he adds surnames: Newton, Newsome, Newman. He comes across experts in climate change, swimmers, singers, statisticians. And a 'people search' engine that gives him dozens of listings in the United States. He makes a note of any that appear with 'Dr' before the name, but he's not convinced. Finally, he closes down the machine and makes his way back to his room. He takes a huge footstep over the threshold, avoiding the treacherous floorboard.

Leaving the pages of Roisin's emails on the bedside table, he lies on top of the duvet, arms folded across his chest. His thinking position, Jan used to call it. He could lie like that for hours, not moving, figuring out his stories, his characters' motives, the bungling police procedures that allowed the astute reader to keep one step ahead of the evolving plot. Readers like that, he'd discovered. They like being smarter than the average Joe, who has to wait for the last page for all to be revealed. Pre-writing, he used to call this still and silent musing. Getting ready for the headlong plunge into the next thriller. Although he does it differently now, ever since he met Julia. And, right this minute, he has a different sort of mystery to solve.

He allows his mind to wander back to three years ago, to meeting Julia at the airport after her trip to India. 'Think, William, think,' he says to himself. 'There's got to be stuff there you didn't notice first time around.' He's always been perceptive, always had a good eye for detail – or so his readers seem to think. Except in real life, he thinks wryly. In real life, the plot seems to run away from him, cantering off into an unknown future while he just stands there: unable to do more than lock the stable door. At least with his thriller characters, he could wrestle them to the ground, get them into an armlock when they threatened to get out of control. They knew he could terminate them with the lethal weapon of a full stop. Or a 'delete' key. They usually obliged, allowing themselves to be beaten into submission.

Right now, he can see Julia emerge from the throng at Dublin airport. He can see her, standing head and shoulders above the crowd. In all senses.

He moved towards her, arms wanting to be outstretched, but staying hesitantly by his side, just in case. Just in case what? his other self had raged. But he needn't have worried. Julia's face lit up when she saw him. She made straight for him, rucksack on her back, both hands occupied with overflowing bags. Her face glowed. Everything about her was redolent of warmth and sunshine. He put his arms around her and she let the bags fall, colour spilling out onto the nondescript tiled floor of the arrivals terminal.

'Julia,' he said, burying his face in her hair. It smelled faintly of spices. 'Welcome home. It's so good to see you. You have no idea how much I've missed you.'

She smiled at him. 'I've missed you, too,' she said. 'More than I thought.' She held him close. The crowds parted around them, like water around stone. Each was reluctant to let go of the other. It was William who broke the spell. He wanted to be alone with her, away from the eyes and ears of others. He picked up her bags. 'Let's go home,' he said. 'I have champagne on ice. I've decided to make a habit of it.' And then he remembered. 'Isn't Roisin with you?'

Julia shook her head. 'No. She's on sabbatical, remember? She went straight to Edinburgh from London. Friends of hers have a cottage near St Andrews.'

But William didn't remember. And he didn't care. All he was feeling was glee: he didn't have to share her with anybody, not even on the journey from the airport. But for a moment he tried to contain his happiness. 'Do you want to go to Melissa's? You must be missing Jamie.'

But she continued to regard him steadily. 'No,' she said. 'I've told Melissa I'll see her tomorrow evening.'

'So,' he said, lightly. 'Your place or mine?'

'Where's the champagne?' and she grinned at him.

'At mine. But we can easily—'

'Yours it is.'

He took her to bed and it was like their first weekend, all over again. But better. Now there was familiarity as well as love, great waves of it that carried him along, making the words come more easily.

'I should go away more often,' she smiled at him, taking the flute of champagne he handed her. 'If I can be sure of a welcome like that.'

He took one of her hands in his, traced the veins that lined its surface, admired the strength of the square fingers. They spoke of their no-nonsense capability. 'I meant it when I said how much I've missed you. I don't want to miss you like that again.'

She looked at him, arching one eyebrow ever so slightly.

William hurried to explain himself. Why did he always manage to get it wrong? 'I don't mean that I'd ever try to stop . . . I mean, it's just that I'd hope we could—'

'I know what you mean,' and she squeezed his hand. 'It would be lovely to go travelling together.'

'Yes.' He couldn't help his eagerness. And he was grateful to her for making it easier. 'And I don't want to waste time, or play games or do any of that other stuff you're supposed to do in a new relationship.' He paused, took a deep breath. He saw her looking at him, the blue gaze clear and still. 'I've never been like this, Julia, but I have to tell you.' He felt – hoped – that she was willing him on. 'I love you.' There. He'd said it. He swallowed. 'I'm normally much more cautious. Reticent to a fault, or so they tell me.'

'That's no fault,' she said, softly. 'When you tell me something, I know you mean it. I can trust you. You're a man who's true to his word.'

His word. Yes. He felt proud of himself for having spoken. And it made him daring. 'I want to be with you. I don't just mean now. I mean for the rest of my life.'

She was about to speak, but William stopped her.

'No, wait,' he said. 'I don't want to put pressure on you, or push you into something before you're ready. I just want you to know how I feel. And that it's not going to change.'

'I believe you. And I don't want to hurry us.' She reached out, stroked his face. 'I want you to know how lucky I feel to have found you. I never thought I'd have this again.'

He saw her eyes fill. 'You don't need to say any more.' He bent down and kissed her. 'Not even another word.' He stood up, pulled a dressing gown off the hook on the back of his bedroom door. 'Come with me. Bet you haven't eaten in hours. And the rest of that champagne is waiting.'

She swung her long legs off the bed and onto the floor. She smiled at him and he remembers now the way his breath caught in his throat. 'You're right. I'm starving. And after that, I think

I'll sleep for about three days.' She pulled on the dressing gown he was holding for her and then threw both arms around him. 'It's lovely to be home. To be here, with you. There's nothing that makes me happier.'

He'd forgotten that: how often she'd told him how lucky she felt, to find so much love second time around. He remembers how they sat at his tiny table, half-tipsy on champagne, looking out at the Howth night creeping in across the sea. She insisted on leaving the curtains open. It had been an evening of unalloyed happiness. William knows that he had known it even then, had recognized it for what it was. He remembers marvelling at the ordinary way that the extraordinary had entered his life. Love; all over again.

'So,' he remembers saying to her. 'You're smitten, aren't you? India has wrapped itself around your heart.'

She took his question seriously. 'I can't explain it,' she said. 'So much was awful – the poverty, the slums, the shanty towns full of children.' She shook her head. 'Animals and kids rummaging in the same dumps, poking about for rags.' She paused. 'It made me count my blessings.'

William waited. She had grown thoughtful. 'This sounds like an arrogant thing to say. It's like saying that other people's suffering is what makes you shift your perspective. But that's what's happened. I'd love to go back. Maybe work there for a while.'

William remembers that tiredness had seemed to engulf her then. He'd had no time to ask: what blessings? What perspective? What has changed? All he remembers is how emphatic she'd been, just as she'd stood up to go to bed.

'It has made me feel that my retirement was absolutely the right decision,' she said. 'Not a moment too soon.' She walked towards one of the carrier bags that they'd dumped on the sofa earlier. 'Here,' she said, 'I got you something. Well, several things; this is just one of them.' And she pulled out the multicoloured throw, glorious in its chaos of shades and sequins and beading. 'For your sofa,' she said. 'To brighten up this room – I think we'll be spending a lot of time here. And right now, it's a room that's way too male for me.' She shook out the folds and the cotton billowed away from her, coming to rest on the carpet that suddenly looked sad and tired in contrast.

'It's wonderful,' he said. And he meant it. The glinting fish and beaded elephants made him want to smile.

'I'm glad you like it. And now,' she said, allowing herself the luxury of a stretch, 'I have to sleep. Wake me on Tuesday.'

He remembers sitting on the sofa after she'd left, and feeling that the room was still filled with her presence. Now, as he tries to draw together all the disparate strands of Julia's disappearance, he becomes convinced that Roisin is right.

His decision is made. First thing in the morning he'll book his flight for Chennai. An open-ended one. Something tells him he will not be coming back any time soon.

At seven, he calls Melissa.

'Have you found her?'

William has the impression that Melissa is glued to her phone. He feels sorry for her all over again, remembers her pale and haunted face at the kitchen table. For a moment, he shares the horror she must have felt as the police arrived. 'No, not yet, but I'm pretty sure I know where she is. I have a lead that I'm following. But, obviously, I won't know for a few days.'

'I suppose I can't ask where?'

'Better not. The less you know . . .'

'I know, I know. That pisses me off, too.' She pauses. William can hear how close to tears she is. 'Is she all right, William?'

'Yes,' he says, firmly. 'I really don't think you need to worry on that score. And I'll be in touch again soon, I promise. But I'll have nothing to report for at least a couple of days.'

'Just text me – anything at all – just to let me know that you're going in the right direction. Don't fall out of contact, please. I couldn't bear it.'

'I promise. I'll send you a daily update. It won't say much, for obvious reasons, but I'll keep in touch nonetheless. Try not to worry.'

She sighs. 'I want to kill her one minute and hug her the next. She's always been difficult. I miss her.' And she breaks down, sobbing.

'Melis—' William begins.

'I have to go now.' She hangs up.

Poor kid, William thinks, suddenly. Her tears remind him of Michael, clinging to his father when he'd wake at night, terrified by the monsters that sometimes invaded his childish sleep. William looks at his watch. Ten hours' difference between here and Sydney. He dials the number. The phone is answered at once.

'Mikey?' William stops, surprised at himself. He hasn't called his son that in years.

'Dad! How're ya doin'?'

'Is this a good time? There's something I need to tell you.'

Later, William buys maps, guidebooks, spends the afternoon trawling the Internet. All he can do now is wait. Michael's words – 'Just find her, Dad' – are an extraordinary comfort to him, one he can't explain. It's as though Julia, in her absence, has again filled some of the gaps between him and his son, making each of them more present to the other.

In forty-eight hours he will be on his way. Julia is waiting. And he will find her.

# *Julia*

AT DAWN, Julia and Sarita clamber into her battered ten-year-old hatchback and begin the rocky, rutted way to the market, some twenty kilometres to the west.

'Here is my list.' Sarita hands a notebook to Julia. 'I always remember more when I am driving. If you write it down, then maybe I am not forgetting anything this trip.'

Julia looks down at the list. Dhal. Sugar. Salt. Flour. Vegetables. Rice.

Sarita looks over at her. 'Very early morning, Julia. You should be resting. Josanna could have come along with me.'

Julia taps on the notebook in her hands. 'I want to see the market for myself. I want to know what it takes to feed the kids from week to week. Then we can budget properly.'

'We are having our staff meeting tonight at nine, after the children are all in bed. We can talk about these things. The medicine, the schoolbooks, the new shoes for some who are growing too fast.'

Julia nods. 'Yes. I'm looking forward to that. It's hard to get time to talk to anybody during the day. Any of the staff, I mean. I want to get to know them.'

Sarita smiles at her. 'The children: they are keeping all of us very busy, no?'

'They sure are.'

Light is filtering slowly across the landscape. Julia can make out the shapes of houses along the roadway, the occasional temple. Random cows wander out in front of the car, making Sarita brake sharply. 'Mind where you are going!' she scolds, waving one arm out of the window, keeping her other hand on the horn.

'Mind how you go!' The words startle Julia. She looks around her, as though someone had just spoken aloud in the car. Hilary used to say that, all the time, to Julia and Roisin, ever since they were schoolgirls. 'Mind how you go, girls!' It didn't matter what they were doing: going to the cinema, to a disco, or just off to potter around the city centre. Hilary had always seemed to know what dangers might lie in wait – but she'd encourage the girls to deal cheerfully with whatever came their way.

She'd been a constant presence in Julia's life, ever since she was thirteen. Julia had been awed by Hilary: by the fact that she ran her own business, by her kindness, by the acuteness of her observations. Not much got past her steady gaze. At no time during the past six months has Julia allowed herself to be drawn back towards that time. She has feared the memories: what they might tell her about Hilary, what they might reveal to her about herself. But she can't avoid them any longer.

They are the reason she is here, halfway around the world. And, in a way, Sarita's quiet presence beside her, this unfamiliar car journey, the beginnings of a life without any known contours: the time is right for her to remember.


The room is quiet. The heavy velvet drapes have been drawn and one side has been pulled to overlap the other, so that it spills crookedly onto the floor, sagging and swirling full-skirtedly around the tall window. In the light from the hallway it looks like a shadowy ballgown whose owner has recently stepped out of it. No chinks of light are visible; the moss-green colour of the curtains now looks inky-black. And the air is stifling. Sickroom heat.

Once Julia's eyes become used to the dark, she sees the two figures she expects to see. Hilary lies in the bed, still and silent. Julia can make out the steady rise and fall of the bedclothes as she breathes, and there is an occasional movement of one pale hand that rests on the embroidered top of the sheet. Even from here, Julia can see the glint of her wedding ring. Roisin is seated beside her, her chin resting in one hand. Julia opens the door wider, standing in the rectangle of light that is growing longer under her feet. It is a useful pause: one that makes Roisin look up and register her presence.

'Hi,' she says.

'Any change?' Julia reaches for Hilary's wrist, feels for her pulse. She already knows the answer.

Roisin shakes her head. 'Nothing. She's very peaceful, I think. Her hand was clutching at the air earlier. It was like she was plucking something off a tree. But she quietened about twenty minutes ago, around the time Greta left.'

'Okay. Are you all right here for another while, or would you like a break? Need a smoke, or anything?'

'No.' Roisin's voice is emphatic. 'No, I'm fine. I want to be here. Just in case.'

Julia nods. 'Of course. I've some things I need to see to. But I'll be back in about an hour or so – two at the most. You'll call if you need me?' It's hardly a question at this stage, more a reassurance.

'Yeah. Don't worry. I'll be fine. We'll be fine.'

She leaves then, watching the spill of light contract as she closes the door behind her again. 'See you later,' she says, over one shoulder.

'Yeah. See you later.'

She lets go just before the lock meets the receiver. The heavy door swings back, creaking a little, and stops. Satisfied, Julia moves down the hall, the calm of this warm and familiar house all around her.


Later, when she returns, Julia finds that all is as she left it. She approaches the bed. Hilary is sleeping, her mouth slack, her breathing laboured. Roisin is there, holding her mother's hands, stroking the backs of them where the blue veins have recently become more prominent. Julia sees that she is using hand cream, smoothing it now over the thin fingers, working it into the creases of the palm. Roisin makes sure that this is now a long and loving ritual, part of her mother's daily routine. Hilary has always been vain about her hands.

'How is she?' Julia asks.

'Good. Peaceful. She's ready. We spoke again about an hour ago. She woke for a while, just after you left. She was in good form: stayed awake for quite a while.'

'You absolutely sure about this? It's not too late.'

Hilary stirs. She is propped up by several pillows, so that she is almost sitting upright. Roisin stands and bends over her. She places her ear close to her mother's mouth. Julia watches as the slender hands now clutch at her daughter's. She hears a jagged whisper, but tonight she can no longer make out any of the words. Roisin straightens up. She half-smiles at Julia. 'She says it's her choice, not mine.' She places her mother's arms on the coverlet. She strokes her, gently. 'Bolshie to the last, eh, Mum?'

Julia moves closer and rests one of her hands on Hilary's. With great effort, Hilary curls her fingers around Julia's. She is fully awake now, her intelligent eyes bright and clear. She squeezes and Julia feels the surprising strength of her grip. She is reminded of Lucy's firm grasp, all those years ago. Her eyes fill at the memory; and for the elderly woman beside her, for Richard.

'My dears,' Hilary says, hoarsely. 'Both of you.' Roisin and Julia look at one another, startled. The words are clear, forceful. 'I want this.'

'Yes,' says Julia. 'I know. But I need you to know that maybe tomorrow you might want something different.'

Hilary smiles at her. She shakes her head, tries to lift it off the pillow. 'Enough,' she says. 'Enough now.' She sinks back again and her eyes close. Almost at once, the rasp of her breathing fills the room.

Roisin sobs. 'She's wanted this for two years, Julia. Let her go. There's nothing else she wants. I can't bear to see her like this. Please.' She wipes her eyes, gestures towards the dressing table. 'She had me read back to her today some of the letters – the ones to her grandchildren. When I'd finished she just said, "Happy." She's done everything she wants to do. Even Eileen remarked on how peaceful she seemed last night. Help her now.'

Julia nods. Wordlessly, she moves towards the dressing table. The glass is already there, innocent, waiting. She turns to Roisin. 'Has she had the Maalox?'

Roisin nods. 'Just before you arrived. She asked for it.'

'At least six tablespoons?'

'Yes. She had no trouble taking it.'

Julia mixes the liquids carefully with fruit juice. Then she takes the cheerful striped straw that Hilary has chosen, all pink and white and flexible – mindful more of a child's birthday party than of a deathbed. She carries the glass back to the bed and Roisin shakes her mother, gently.

'Mum? It's time.'

Hilary blinks. Julia puts the glass in her hands, folding them around it with her own. Together, they lift the glass so that the straw touches Hilary's lips. Julia then withdraws her hands one by one and Roisin takes over. This is what they've planned: this is what Hilary has asked for.

Julia looks down into the still, clear-blue eyes. 'I'm going to leave you now, you and Roisin. I love you.'

Hilary nods. 'I know.' No more than a whisper: but strong, a voice still present in itself.

Julia stoops, kisses her on the forehead. She touches Roisin's hand, briefly. 'I'll be just outside.'

Roisin looks at her, eyes suddenly terrified. 'What if she vomits?'

'Don't worry. She won't. The dosage is right. Just take this time with her.' Then Julia leaves the room quietly. She glances back, one last time, and sees how Roisin strokes the hair back from her mother's forehead with her free hand. With the other, she helps her hold onto the glass. She is whispering to her, tears coursing freely now.

Julia closes the door behind her. She makes sure that it locks. It has a tendency to swing open of its own accord if it's not fastened securely. She makes her way to the nook on the landing, to the familiar chintz armchair, the Chinese nest of tables. She sits, surrounded by the bookshelves and the lamps that are as familiar to her as her own home.

And she waits, her gaze drawn to the darkness outside the window.


Two hours later, Roisin emerges. Her face is white, composed. 'She's gone.'

Julia opens her arms and Roisin walks into them. She rests

her head on Julia's shoulders and sobs with relief, with grief, with love. When she finishes, she stays there, not moving.

Julia holds her.

Suddenly, she feels Sarita's light touch on her arm. She looks at her, confused for a moment, her mind hurtling back from a suburban Dublin bedroom to the villages of south India. She realizes that she has been weeping.

'Are you not feeling well?' Sarita's concern is tangible. 'Would you prefer to stay in the car?'

Julia struggles back to herself. 'No, no, not at all.' She looks out the window. The sun is climbing, crowds of people are swarming past them. Faces peer in through the windscreen, alight with curiosity. Julia can see all the colours of the market spread out before her. She wipes her face. 'I'm fine, Sarita, truly. I'm just . . . missing somebody.'

Sarita watches her. 'You are sure?'

'I am sure,' she says, preparing to open the passenger door.

Her unthinking reply has been the truth. She is missing William with an ache that is raw, almost physical. For the first time she allows herself to urge him on. She closes the car door, follows Sarita into the crowd.

Find me, William. Find me before I lose the will to keep myself together. She sees his face over their shared chessboard, the white queen off her square.

Hurry, she thinks again. Please hurry.

# William

'JACK? IT'S WILLIAM.'

'William! How's things?' Jack has answered immediately, his voice anxious. William can see him sitting over his phone, waiting for news.

'Progress. Good progress, I think. Except – I'm sorry, but right now I can't really talk about it.'

'Okay. That's not a problem.' Jack speaks slowly, trying to figure out the signals. But he doesn't ask why, as William knew he wouldn't.

'I have to go away for a while. I was wondering – could you and Celine look after the apartment for me?'

'Sure thing. Anything in particular you want done – or just the usual: post, lights, curtains, stuff like that?'

'Yeah. Just the usual. Thanks. I don't know how long I'll be.'

'What about the car? If you want, I can keep it ticking over?'

'Yeah – that would be good. The spare key is in the kitchen drawer somewhere.'

'Don't worry. I'll find it.' There is a pause on the other end of the line. 'Is everyone well and safe?'

'I think so. In fact, I'm pretty sure. But it's complicated. I'll tell you everything when I get back.'

'Okay. We'll be thinking of you. Take care and good luck. Keep in touch if you can.'

William hangs up and calls Melissa. To his relief, this time, the call goes straight to message-minder. 'Melissa: it's William. Just letting you know I've got a flight in a couple of hours. No more news, but I'll text you as soon as I can. Take care and try not to worry.'

He pushes his way through the crowds at Heathrow and joins the queue for the Mumbai flight.

At the desk the check-in staff regard him with open curiosity. 'No suitcase, sir? Nothing at all to put in the hold?'

'Nothing,' says William. 'This is a last-minute decision.' And he smiles. 'I make a habit of travelling light.' All around him he sees people who seem to be transporting the entire contents of a house: trolleys piled high with boxes, bulky packages, parcels wrapped in paper, tied with string. His lone rucksack looks almost suspicious: a wolf among all those sheep.

'Very well.' The young man hands him back his passport. 'This is your boarding pass, sir. Boarding will commence at ten o'clock.'

'Thank you.'

William makes his way towards the long lines forming at Security. In his rucksack, along with the guidebooks and some hastily bought cotton trousers and T-shirts, he has copies of Julia's photograph.

In his pocket, he has the white queen.


William blinks as he steps out into the harsh light. It's almost midday and the heat is fierce: physically shocking after the interior of the airport. He fishes his sunglasses out of the side of his rucksack and makes his way quickly towards the taxi rank. He pushes aside the hustlers, the beggars, the hawkers who try to stand in his way. He has read all of Roisin's emails so many times that he knows their contents by heart. That is what he focuses on as he walks straight to the top of the queue of taxis. He will not allow himself to be distracted. 'Hotel Sea Breeze,' he says. 'As quickly as you can.'

'Yes, sir. No bag, sir?'

'No bag,' William says, firmly. 'Let's go.'


At the hotel William checks in, making sure to be friendly. He won't start asking questions just yet. He'll shower, shave and make himself more presentable. The last thing he wants to do is arouse suspicion. This has to be handled carefully or people might shut down on him and he'd be left with nothing. In his pocket he has several thousand rupees, all in five-hundred and one-hundred notes. He's prepared to pay for the information he needs.

'Thank you,' he says, as the young man behind the desk hands him his key. 'I might need a taxi in a couple of hours. Can you recommend a driver to me?'

'Of course, sir. We have many good drivers. What time would you like?'

'Say two o'clock?' He is anxious to get going at once, but he won't force the pace.

'Of course. And you are going where, please?'

'Oh, some sightseeing around the city. Just for a couple of hours. It's my first time in Chennai.'

'I hope you will enjoy our city, sir. I will call a driver for you.'

'Thank you.' William begins to make his way towards the lift. Then, he seems to remember something and turns back. 'By the way, and I know this probably sounds like a very strange question, do you have a driver called Bashir?'

The young man laughs. 'We have many drivers called Bashir. Which one are you wanting?'

William makes his way back towards the desk. 'Well, it's just that a friend of mine stayed here, a few years ago. She got to know a young man called Bashir and asked me to look him up. But never mind, I knew it was unlikely. I just wanted to say hello to him for her.'

'I will look for you, sir.' He is shaking his head, looking doubtful. 'But maybe you are not finding him.'

'Okay, it's not a problem. I appreciate you trying. See you later.'

William takes the lift up to his room. He empties the guidebooks and clothes out of the rucksack, leaving only a notebook, a pen and the photographs of Julia, inserted between the pages of a hardback novel. Then he undresses and stands under the shower for a good ten minutes, making the water progressively colder, trying to shake off the tiredness of the long flight and the extended wait at Mumbai airport. He has no intention of sleeping.

There is far too much to be done.


The phone in his room rings at just after two. William opens his eyes, startled. For a moment, he is in Howth. Then Dublin. Then London. And then he remembers. He reaches for the phone. 'Yes?'

'Mr Harris? I have a driver for you. He is not Bashir, but he is working here for many years. Perhaps he can help you find who you are looking for.'

'Great! Thank you. I'll be down right away.' William steps into the small bathroom, throws water on his face. He hadn't meant to fall asleep. Now he feels groggy, his head full of cotton wool. He grabs his key, his mobile and his rucksack, locks the door quickly behind him. He takes the stairs from the second floor: he is too impatient to wait for the lift.

A dark, stocky man waits for him at reception. 'Mr Harris, sir? I am Vikram. I am your driver.'

'Pleased to meet you, Vikram.' William shakes hands. The other man's grip is firm, warm. William starts to relax. It might be jetlag, it might be desperation: but he feels suddenly filled with a dizzy confidence, nurtured by the warmth of this man's grasp.

'We will go now?' he asks William, gesturing towards the door.

'Yeah. Let's do it.' He follows Vikram to where the taxi is parked in the shade. 'Have you been doing this job for long?' William keeps his tone light as they cross the gravel driveway together.

He nods. 'Oh yes. A long time now. Fifteen years.'

'That is a long time,' William agrees. 'Always for the hotel?'

He shrugs. 'Not always. First on my own. But hotel is better. They are giving more work. Please.' He opens the passenger door for William.

'Thank you.' William squeezes himself into the seat. There is not a whole lot of room to spare.

'Where you would like to see first?' Vikram's tone is eager. 'There are many beautiful places to be seeing in Chennai.' He waits, his hands resting on the steering wheel.

'I am happy for you to show me your city.' William sits back, easing his knees under the dashboard. 'Give me the highlights – your own personal tour. Take as long as you like.'

Vikram grins in delight. 'We can go to Marina Beach, to the St George Fort, to the Kapaleeshwar Temple, the oldest in—'

'That's fine,' William says. 'Just let's go.' And they pull out into traffic that seethes all around them.

*

'This is Marina Beach.' Vikram spreads one arm at the long white-gold sand beneath them. 'Longest beach in the world,' he declares. 'Thirteen kilometres.'

His pride is evident, but William doesn't care. He can't contain himself any longer, now that the car has stopped. He turns around as far as he can, looks directly into the driver's face. 'Vikram. I need your help. I am looking for somebody who came here three years ago. She stayed at the hotel. And she has probably stayed there again, maybe even in the last week.'

Vikram shakes his head. He looks doubtful. 'Very little work last week. Not so many British tourists in Chennai this year, two years now. Last week, I work only three days.'

I'm Irish, William wants to say, feeling an absurd needle of irritation. He lets it go. 'Would you look at a photograph for me, anyway? Perhaps you may have seen her?'

'Yes, I look, I look.'

'Maybe we can stand outside?' William opens the door of the car, dragging the rucksack after him. He stretches his legs with relief. He rummages inside, pulls Julia's photograph out of the book and hands it to Vikram. 'Do you recognize her?'

He shakes his head. 'No.' He looks at William. His face is a study in curiosity. 'This woman – she is your wife?'

William hesitates. 'Yes,' he decides. 'And I am afraid that she is unwell. I need to find her and bring her home, to make her better.'

Vikram looks intently at the photograph. 'This is for me? I can keep this to show to other drivers, who were working last week?'

William feels relief expand inside him. 'Yes,' he says, 'yes, you can keep it.' He exhales, grateful. At the same time, a wave of exhaustion catches him unawares and he stumbles against the door of the car.

'Sir – you are feeling well?' William can see the alarm in Vikram's eyes.

'Sorry, don't know what happened there.' He watches the pinpoints of light as they dance in front of his eyes. Jesus, he can't pass out, not here. He tries to breathe deeply. 'It's been a long few days: a long flight and no sleep. I'm sorry, Vikram – perhaps it's best to go back to the hotel.' He sees disappointment cloud the other man's face. 'It's my fault. I will pay for the afternoon, of course,' he says, quickly. 'For all of your time.'

Vikram leans into the car and hands William a bottle of water. 'Drink,' he urges. 'You must have water. I take you back now. And please, you do not worry: I will make sure the other drivers are seeing the photograph.'

William sits into the passenger seat, closes his eyes. For the first time in almost two weeks he feels that sleep is about to engulf him. He surrenders, unable to struggle against it any longer.


'Sir? We are here. At the hotel.'

William forces his eyes to open. 'My apologies again, Vikram.' He pulls out his wallet. 'How much for your time this afternoon?'

He can see that the man is about to go all polite, so he thrusts two thousand rupees at him. 'Is this enough to cover it?' He can't be bothered to bargain. He can see by Vikram's face that he has made the right choice. 'Now – don't forget,' he says. 'My wife's photograph. Show it to as many people as you can. I'm counting on you.'

Dimly William spots four or five cabs parked together outside the hotel, a couple of men playing cards, a couple of them smoking. All of them waiting. The air around them is one of expectant passivity.

'See?' In contrast, Vikram is now all eagerness. He tucks the notes into the top pocket of his shirt. He points towards where the other men are congregating. 'This is where we wait for business, all the drivers. I see some now, some more tomorrow morning.' He nods at William, a parent reassuring a child. 'You don't worry, don't worry. I come when I have news.'

Although tempted to go immediately to speak to the men himself, William decides against it. It's probably wiser to let Vikram do the probing.

He stumbles up the steps to reception. 'Can you send up three litre bottles of water to Room 204, please?' He remembers having the same problem during his travels in China. Rapid-onset dehydration, making his thinking fuzzy and his limbs lack coordination.

'Of course, sir.'

Once inside his room, William lowers the shade and throws himself on the bed, his head pounding. Barely five minutes later there is a knock.

'Thanks,' William takes the water, tips the young boy, who can't be more than ten. He drinks the first litre quickly, sitting on the side of the bed, not bothering to use a glass. Then he stretches out, leaving the second bottle beside him. He'll sip at it over the next couple of hours. Almost at once, the exhaustion starts to lift.

He'll stay close to the hotel for the rest of the day. He doesn't want to miss out on anyone coming to see him. Besides, he's not a tourist: he's a man on a mission.

And, right now, all he can do is wait until that mission comes to him.

Right now, he has some more remembering to be done.

\*

William is cooking. He likes being in Julia's kitchen. It's a space he much prefers to his own. It is large, friendly, more expansive than his. He likes its old-fashioned feel, the way it is large and functional and airy. Tinkerbelle is keeping an alert, suspicious eye on him from the windowsill. As he cooks, William feels grateful to be where he is: in the life that was meant for him. He doesn't take his luck for granted. He is old enough to know how fortunate he is.

He is making fish soup for tonight's dinner. This morning, after Julia had dashed off to take care of Greta, he'd got up, showered and dressed and fed Tinkerbelle. He calls her Whinge, because of her constant complaints, her demands for food, comfort, attention. Besides, she resents him, tries to trip him up whenever she gets the chance, leaps onto his lap unexpectedly and frightens the life out of him.

He'd driven back to Howth, had coffee with Jack and then made his way down the pier to 'Nicky's Plaice'. There, he'd bought all the ingredients for a *zuppa di pesce*, a favourite of his and Julia's, a much tried-and-tested Claudia Roden recipe. Julia has promised to be back by lunchtime. He's going to take her out, to Cesare's, just down the road. After that, they're going to the National Gallery. Julia wants to see the Thomas Roberts exhibition. 'It's free on Mondays,' she'd teased him. 'No additional expense. And just think about it: in two years, you'll have free travel. There'll be no stopping us!' William grins as he remembers the mischief in her face.

He grates and chops, feeling the kitchen grow pleasantly warm and steamy around him. They'll have dinner around eight-thirty this evening. The Chablis is already chilling. And he's just picked up *The African Queen* at the local video shop. He's succeeded in turning Julia into a Humphrey Bogart nut – as he knew he would. William loves the way that his life hourglasses before him, flowing freely from yesterday into today, today into tomorrow. And into all the days that he and Julia have still to share. A future: full of days that are bright, like sand.

Suddenly Tinkerbelle leaps from the windowsill and makes her way, a furry blur, across the kitchen to the door. At the same time William hears the chinking of Julia's keys as she drops them into the ceramic dish at the bottom of the stairs. Tinkerbelle is miaowing, her front paw frantic as she reaches the door. William tries to pull it open at the same time as Julia pushes it from the other side. They almost fall into one another, and the cat insinuates herself between their ankles, making William miss his step.

'That bloody cat,' he says, laughing, 'is determined to make me break my neck.'

Julia has bent down and is stroking Tinkerbelle's silky ears. 'Hello, puss,' she says, and straightens up. She looks pale. Under her eyes is a tracery of bluish shadows, her mouth is unsteady and she does not look at William directly. For one startled moment, he wonders if she has been crying. He opens his arms and she walks into them, resting her cheek against his shoulder. He hugs her.

'You poor thing,' he says. 'You look exhausted. Is Greta okay, or was it a false alarm? Was she drama-queening again?' He helps Julia out of her jacket.

'Oh, she'll be fine. Just a bit of blood pressure, that's all. I met Ro as well, that's why I'm later than I thought.'

He looks at her, puzzled. 'No, you're not,' he says. 'You said lunchtime, and here you are. It's only one o'clock.'

'Did I?' she looks distracted. 'Is it?'

'Hey,' he says, tenderly. 'Are you okay?'

'I'm sorry, William. I just feel absolutely wiped.' She seems to sag and he takes her firmly by the elbow.

'Have you eaten? You'd no breakfast, remember.'

'Maybe that's it,' she admits. 'I do feel a bit weak.'

He brings her across to the armchair by the fire. 'Here, sit down. I was going to take us to Cesare's for a light bite, but I think you might be better lying down for a while. And the exhibition runs for another six weeks. So don't worry – we'll do it again.'

She looks at him, looks as though she hasn't heard a word. Now he's beginning to feel alarmed. 'The Gallery?' he says. 'The Thomas Roberts exhibition?'

Her face clears. 'Oh. Sorry, William. I'd completely forgotten.'

He smiles. 'Don't apologize to me. I think I might manage to live if we postpone looking at eighteenth-century landscapes.' He watches her, his alarm growing. She stands up again, looks around her as though she has lost her bearings. Then, finally, she sits down. There is something wrong. Something that may even be William's fault, although he can't think what it might be. He waits until she seems to have settled in the armchair and then he kneels on the floor beside her. He can see the light change on her face as she turns towards the window. Tinkerbelle has resumed her position on the windowsill and is licking one careful paw after the other.

Julia turns to face him and he is shocked by how troubled her eyes are. He takes her hand. 'You're freezing,' he says. 'If you won't go to bed, I'm going to get you a duvet. Is that okay?'

She nods her head. 'Yes. Yes, I'd prefer to stay here, with you. If I sit here by the fire, I might fool sleep for an hour or so.'

He wonders what she means by that, but chooses not to ask. She looks too worn out, too fragile for questions. What has happened at Greta's? he asks himself, aware that he's never liked the woman anyway. 'Hang on,' he says, 'I'll be right back.' He takes the stairs two at a time and pulls the duvet from the bed in Julia's room. Their room. In the same way that the bedroom in his apartment is *their* room.

Now is not the time to ask her, he thinks, as he wraps up the duvet so as not to trip on it going downstairs. But it will be, soon. This two-household existence is not good for either of them. It feels fractured, transient. He wants them to settle in one place, together – preferably Howth, but if not, anywhere will do as a compromise. Anywhere he can be with her, look after her. Make sure she's happy.

When he gets back down to the kitchen, Julia is already asleep. Tinkerbelle is on her lap. William bends down and takes off Julia's shoes. He lifts the cat, which resists. 'Quiet, Whinge,' he says. He tucks the duvet around Julia, covering her from her chin to her feet. Then he makes a little hollow for Tinkerbelle and places the cat gently back onto Julia's knees. 'There you go,' he says softly. The cat curls into herself.

Julia is deeply asleep, her face looking almost serene in the firelight. William sees that the skin seems to be stretched more tightly across her cheekbones; it looks shiny, as though there is suddenly too little flesh underneath. He wonders whether she has lost weight. He feels a sharp clutch of fear, remembering how unhappy her eyes looked. Is she ill?

He straightens up and brushes Julia's hair back from her forehead. She stirs, murmuring in her sleep. He can't make out the words. He looks down at her. He strokes her hair again, wanting to give comfort, even if she is no longer aware of him. Then he places the guard in front of the fire and sits down opposite her, picking up his book from where he had left it earlier on the floor. The soup can wait. His questions can wait.

Everything can wait, until Julia wakes.

\*

At half-past three, a phone rings somewhere. William jerks back to consciousness. He has dozed off and now he can't tell where the noise is coming from. Julia is restless, struggling to the surface. Cursing, he jumps out of the armchair and then she is awake, pointing to her handbag on the kitchen table.

'In there,' she says. 'My mobile.'

By the time she has pushed away the duvet, and Tinkerbelle, and rummaged in the bag, the phone has stopped. She pulls it out and looks at the screen. 'It's just Greta,' she says. 'I'll call her back tomorrow.'

'You okay?'

She smiles at William. But it is a pale imitation of her normal smile. This time, her eyes do not light up. 'I'm fine, thanks. Much better. What time is it?'

He tells her. She looks surprised. 'Was I asleep the whole time?'

'Yeah, about two hours. Let me make you a cup of tea.' He busies himself in the kitchen, wondering how to phrase what he wants to ask her. He'll lose no sleep if she and Greta have had some sort of a spat – but instinct tells him it is something more serious than a spat.

When he hands her the cup of tea, he says, joking, 'We're a right pair. I fell asleep myself. Are you sure you're feeling okay? You looked upset when you came in.'

He watches as she turns off her mobile and slips it back into her handbag. She begins to smooth out the duvet, folding it carefully. 'Oh, it's nothing for you to worry about.'

He waits for a minute. Her reply seems to him to have turned all kinds of tables. *Don't worry your pretty little head about it.* But he's not going to be fobbed off. 'What happened today, Julia?'

She hesitates. 'Nothing, really.' She looks away from him. 'Nothing important. Greta and I had a misunderstanding. We really don't see the world in the same way, that's all.' She looks up at him, shrugging. 'But then, that's hardly news, is it?'

At that moment, William is convinced that Greta has criticized him in some way, that she has finally voiced her disapproval of Julia's unsuitable partner. He has a brief flash of jealousy. Richard looms up at him from the wedding photograph in the living room. William can see him clearly, his broad frame, his crooked, charming smile. His hand in Julia's. He has a moment of vicious satisfaction that the man's hairline was already receding, even in his early thirties.

He can tell by Julia's silence that she is trying to protect him from not being liked. He decides not to push her any further. 'Maybe,' he says casually, 'you could just be busy the next time she phones. Say I'm whisking you away to Spain, or France or Italy – which,' he raises one hand, his index finger wagging, 'is not a bad idea at all. Why don't we take a last-minute deal somewhere, next week or the week after? Get away from the April showers. Spring deluge, more like.'

She brightens at that. 'Yes,' she says. 'We don't need to be here, do we? It would be lovely to get away for a while.' She is smiling again, almost her real self again.

He reaches out to her and takes her hand. But before he can reply, she puts both arms around him and kisses him. 'I love being with you,' she says. 'I want you to know that. And more and more, I like it more and more.'

He wants to say: We don't need anyone else; you don't need anyone else. We're complete as we are. But he knows that that would be a mistake.

She pulls away from him and stands up, walks briskly into the kitchen. She takes the already open bottle of white wine from the fridge. She hands it to him and sweeps up two glasses from the table. 'Take these as well.' She turns and hugs the duvet to her. 'Bed,' she says. 'Now! Everything else can wait.'

Upstairs he undresses her slowly, kissing his way up and down the long length of her. She holds onto him, tightly, pressing herself to him, pulling him closer and closer. Then she pushes him away and looks down at him, propped up on one elbow. Her blue gaze is intense. 'I love you, William Harris. Very much. You know that, don't you?' Her eyes begin to fill.

William is alarmed. 'I love you too,' he says. 'And yes, yes, of course I know it.' He strokes her face, tenderly. He wishes he knew the right things, the perfect things, to say to her. 'What's wrong, Julia? Why are you upset? Do I make you sad?' For a moment he is filled with fear that she is about to leave him. Damn you, Greta, he thinks angrily. What have you said to her?

She shakes her head and half-laughs, half-sobs. 'Oh no, William, you don't make me sad. You don't make me sad at all. I don't know what I'd do without you.' And she pulls him on top of her, urgently, guiding him into her.

It is only now, six months later, and halfway around the world, that William remembers that afternoon in all its glaring detail. Up until today it had been a rumple, a mere ripple in the texture of the life that he and Julia had been living together.

He does recall that he'd felt a jolt of confusion that day; that he'd had a glimpse of an uncertain future. But he hadn't wanted to see it. Besides, he'd adjusted to the changes it had brought with it. Anything was possible, anything was fine by him – as long as it meant that he and Julia could be together.

It seems to him now, lying in an Indian hotel room, that that was the day, the hour, even the moment when things had started to change between them. It had happened subtly, gradually – just small things that were way too subtle and way too gradual for a blunt instrument like him to notice at the time.

But now that everything is different, he can recall the

occasional weekend when Julia seemed not to want him around; the times when she had snapped her mobile shut suddenly as he entered the room. Once, about a month ago, just after he'd bought the engagement ring, Julia had announced that she'd arranged to see a friend in Scotland. She'd be gone for the whole weekend. He'd been hurt, although she couldn't possibly have known what was resting in his jacket pocket, snug in its satin and velvet box. Lying right where the white queen now rests.

And why shouldn't she see her friends? He remembers chiding himself, warning himself about the green worm of jealousy. Thinking of that day now, seeing it illuminated by all that has since occurred, William is convinced that Julia, however fleetingly, had said something that he did not hear.

What she did say, what he later *knows* she said, was: 'I don't know what I'll do without you.'

Not 'would', but 'will'. No longer conditional, but future. Not hypothetical, but certain. But William missed it, as he missed so many other things about Julia. It can't be helped, now. But he will make it up to her, as soon as he finds her.

Now that he is where she is, it is only a matter of time.


William wakes at seven. He's slept for fifteen hours. He remembers, as though through a fog, his return to the hotel the previous afternoon with Vikram. He remembers paying him, tipping him generously; remembers, too, Vikram's promise to show Julia's photograph to all the other drivers.

An hour later William makes his way downstairs. He needs breakfast, and he needs it fast.

'Mr Harris?' A voice, soft, at his elbow.

'Yes?' William sees a man, about his own age, his driver's

jacket buttoned right to the top. Tall, grey-haired; dignified in the way he holds himself.

'I am Deepak.' He holds a piece of paper in his hands. 'I have seen this photograph.'

William steps closer. His throat seems to close over. He has difficulty forming the words. 'You have seen her? You have seen Julia?' He wants to shout, to grasp this man by the hand. Is this it? he wonders. Have I found her? He can't help his eagerness. 'Have you news of Bashir?'

'My car is outside,' Deepak says. 'We can speak there.'

'Of course, of course.' Only then, following Deepak's sidelong glance, does William notice the young man at reception. Although he is looking down, concentrating on something that cannot be seen, William knows that he is vibrating with curiosity. He moves away, following Deepak out the door.

Once outside, Deepak turns to face him. 'Who are you?' he asks. He is suspicious, almost angry. William remembers Sorcha, how she'd murmured, just before he left, that Julia had always inspired intense loyalty in others. William believes he is seeing that now. He looks Deepak in the eye, speaks calmly, firmly. 'My name is William Harris. This woman' – and he points to the photograph in Deepak's hands – 'is Julia. The woman I am going to marry.' He stops. 'It is very important I find her. I am afraid that she may be ill.' Keep it simple. 'She may need my help. That is why I am here. Have you seen her?'

Deepak doesn't take his eyes off William. 'Perhaps.'

William is taken aback. Instinct tells him that Deepak is not holding out for money. There is something else in his gaze, something that William recognizes, but can't put his finger on. 'Look,' he says, quietly, 'her name is Julia Seymour. She has a daughter and two grandchildren. I think she has come to India because she doesn't want me, or her family, to suffer because of whatever it is that is happening to her. She thinks she is protecting us.'

'What are their names?'

'What?'

'Their names, her grandchildren.'

'Jamie, who's almost five, and Susie, who's just about to be two. She loves them to bits, can't stop talking about them.' He waits, afraid that the other man is going to turn and walk away.

'I have seen her,' Deepak says at last.

William feels relief take hold of him, shake him, make him more alert than he has ever been in his life. 'Where? Here? At the hotel?'

'Yes.' Deepak is giving him nothing else. He is guarded, his eyes constantly searching William's face.

'Did you drive her somewhere?'

Deepak doesn't answer. 'Why did you lie? Why did you say that she is your wife?'

'To keep things simple. And because I didn't think people would take me seriously if she wasn't. That's the truth. Look, Deepak. I have to find her.'

'I think you are telling me the truth. But Madam Julia, she put her trust in me. I have to be careful of that trust. She did not speak of you.'

William feels a surge of admiration for the man standing before him. 'Okay, Deepak. Here's what we'll do, if you agree. If you drove Julia somewhere, then I'm asking you to drive me there. I won't try to see her. Instead, I'll give you this.'

He reaches into his jacket pocket. He pulls out the white queen, presses it into the other man's hand. 'This is a message we use between us – a kind of private language. You take it to Julia. If she says "No", then that's it.' He swallows. 'I'll go away again, I swear it. Without seeing her.'

'Is madam in any trouble? Is she very ill?' Deepak is weakening. William is relieved to see it.

'Why?' he asks quickly. 'Did she say something to you?'

'Her hair,' Deepak says. 'She cut off all her hair. First, it is long,' he gestures towards his own shoulders, 'then it is gone.' He shrugs. 'Like a boy.'

'I don't know,' William says. 'And I truly hope not. What I do know is, she badly needed some time to be alone. I will respect that. But I must know where she is, and that she is safe.'

Deepak seems to decide something. 'This must be a promise, between us.'

'It is,' William says. He holds out his hand. 'Shake on it. I promise I will go away if Julia doesn't want to see me.'

Deepak shakes his hand. 'We go,' he says. 'We go now, early in the morning. It is a long drive.'

'At once,' William says. 'Let me go back to my room, grab my rucksack. I will be back immediately.'

'I will wait over there.' Deepak indicates a Maruti Esteem. 'Just under that tree.'

'Thank you,' William says. 'Thank you for trusting me.' He turns and flees. He takes the stairs two at a time. He feels invincible, nineteen again.

And inside, he is singing.

# *Julia*

'DR NEWCOMER, PLEASE.'

Julia is sitting on the bed, the remains of her breakfast around her. Mrs Kapur has decided to look after her, despite Julia's initial protests. Breakfast arrived at seven this morning. Her laundry was whisked away yesterday evening and has just been returned, wrapped in newspaper and tied with string. Everything is carefully pressed, cared for – even a missing button has been replaced. Mrs Kapur reminds Julia of her grandmother: a woman whose housekeeping skills now belong to a forgotten era.

'Yes,' she says, into the phone. 'That's right. On the fourth floor.' She waits. 'Alicia? It's Julia.

'I'm good.

'It's a bit off the beaten track, but fine. Just what I was looking for.

'You know why I'm calling.

'No, over the phone is fine. I'm not in a position to come to Chennai at the moment.

'There are no surprises. It's confirmation I'm looking for. You've already run the tests I asked you to, so you know what I suspect.

'And now you've got the results. Tell me.

'I see.

'No, it actually makes things easier. How early a stage?

'I understand that. But that's an argument for another day.

'No, of course I won't. I want the best for me, too.

'Yes, early next week is fine.

'And do I ask for you, specifically?

'I really appreciate this, Ally.

'I know – I haven't called you that in the longest time.' She laughs, softly. ' "Irish" is just fine with me.

'Yes. Love you too.

'Of course. Talk to you over the weekend.'

Julia closes the cover on her mobile and sits, without moving. Outside, she can hear the children snaking their way towards the school. There is the sound of the occasional moped coughing into life, of Mr Kapur opening up downstairs. Of the village, coming to life all around her.

# *William*

WILLIAM IS IMPATIENT to get there. He remembers Michael as a child, his petulance on long journeys: 'Are we there yet?' He can almost hear the childish tones from the back seat. Now, William knows how he felt.

It has taken forever to leave behind the urban sprawl of Chennai. Once in the countryside, William has been startled by what he sees. Women on their way to the well for water, bright plastic jugs balanced on their heads. Women carrying children, firewood, provisions. Men and women working the fields, rice paddies stretching away for miles. Two hours, he thinks. At least another two to go.

Deepak glances across at him. 'You are comfortable?'

'Fine, thank you,' William lies, feeling strangled in the cramped space available to his long body.

'We are making a good journey,' Deepak says. 'Another two more hours and we will be arriving there.'

'Good. That's good to know.' He doesn't want to think beyond today's destination. Doesn't want to think about what will happen if Julia is no longer there, if she has moved on somewhere else. 'May I ask you a question, Deepak?'

'Yes. Of course.'

'Have you any idea who Julia was visiting in this village?'

He shakes his head. 'No. And she would not permit me to enter the village with her. I left her outside and she walked alone, towards the houses.' He shrugs. 'I stay, and I watch for a while, to see where she goes. But it is not a very large village. I will ask the shopkeeper. He will know all who are arriving there.'

William can imagine the scene: Julia walking away, focused, determined. Deepak watching, loyal, fearful. He looks at his watch. But he can't will time to move any faster.


'You will wait here.' Deepak has pulled up at the edge of a village, just opposite a well-tended white house. 'You will wait until I return.' It is not a question.

'Yes. I'll wait. I'll just stretch my legs.'

Deepak's glance is sharp.

'I won't follow – I'll wait here at the car. We have an agreement. I have no intention of breaking it.'

'I will be back soon.' He shows William the white queen. 'And this is your message, yes?'

'That's my message.' William watches him go, doesn't take his eyes off him until Deepak disappears down a street to the left. His white clothes shimmer in the almost midday sun. The village is silent, shuttered against the heat. A dog barks at William once, half-heartedly, and then slopes away. He wishes he had a cigarette. He leans against the passenger door, hands in his pockets. He doesn't want to see how much they are shaking.


And then he sees her. Running towards him. He is stilled for a second, stunned at how different she looks. Even from this distance, he can see that her hair has been cropped. But it is Julia, no doubt about it. He can make out Deepak, too, following whitely behind her.

He leaps forward, shocked into action. He runs, careless of the heat, careless of the dust, careless of everything except reaching her. And then he's there, she's there, her arms flung around him, holding on so tightly he can barely breathe.

'Julia. Julia.'

'Oh, William, you've found me, you've found me.'

He searches her face. She's smiling, laughing, sobbing all at once.

'I can't believe it.' He keeps looking at her, can't tear his eyes away. 'I was terrified I'd never see you again.' He kisses her, presses her to him. 'And I know. I know about everything. It doesn't make a difference. We'll fight it together.'

And then neither of them speaks. They stand in the middle of the dusty road, not letting go, neither of them wanting anything other than this.

Then Julia draws back, looks at William. She has the white queen in her hand.

'I've missed you,' she says. 'So very much.' Her eyes are blue, brimming.

He pulls her back to him. 'You have no idea,' he begins, 'no idea at all . . .' And then he finds he is unable to say more.


Somehow Deepak has managed to get into the car, where he waits, patiently. William hasn't even seen him pass. 'Give me a minute,' he says to Julia, 'let me look after Deepak.' He opens the passenger door and leans in. He sees that Deepak is smiling at him. The man's face is transformed by delight.

Julia walks around to the driver's window. 'Deepak, I haven't even thanked you properly for bringing William to me.' She reaches in, takes both his hands in hers.

'You are welcome, madam. He is a good man.'

'Yes,' says Julia, smiling over at William. 'Yes, he is; a good man.'

'He's a very grateful one,' William says, pressing notes into Deepak's hands. 'Thank you for everything. I will be in touch – we may need you again.'

'I have your number,' Julia says. 'I've kept it safe.'

Deepak inclines his head, looks first at William, then at Julia. 'God go with you,' he says. 'Both of you.'

They wait, standing in the shade of the white house as Deepak reverses the car and drives away.

William turns to Julia. 'Take me home,' he says. 'You and I have a lot of catching up to do.'


They are lying on the bed in Julia's room, the fan whirring above them at top speed.

'You could have trusted me, you know. I'd have lied for you. Wouldn't matter. I wouldn't have cared.' William traces the line of her jaw with his fingers.

Julia sighs. 'I know. But that's what I didn't want *anyone* to have to do.' She pauses. 'How is Melissa?'

'Angry. Missing you. But softening: I think she's actually on her way to being a real human person. Some of the armour has gone. She loves you. It's very obvious.'

Julia smiles. 'That's good. I know I've hurt her, but I just couldn't see any option.'

'So what now?' William asks, quietly.

Julia looks at him. As ever, the blue gaze is clear, direct. 'I am not going home to face years in jail when there is so much I have to do here.'

'There might not even be a case to answer.'

Julia looks at him. 'What do you mean?'

He takes her hand. 'Roisin has got in touch with Eileen, one of Hilary's carers and—'

'I know who Eileen is,' Julia interrupts, sitting up. 'Roisin can't involve *Eileen*.' She looks frightened. 'That would be wrong. I'll have to speak to her.'

'Wait, wait,' William says. 'She's away until the end of November. Nothing is going to happen before that.'

Julia stands up, pulls on a thin cotton dressing gown. 'It doesn't make any difference. I'm still not going back.' William watches her. She's agitated. There is something coming. Something else he doesn't know about. 'What is it, Julia? What is it you don't want to tell me?'

'Oh, William,' she says and begins to cry. 'I am sorry. I am so, so sorry.'


He's still holding her. The storm of sobbing has abated.

'When did you find out?' he asks, gently.

'This morning.' She looks at him, strokes his hair back from his forehead. 'I spoke to Alicia around seven. She had the results ready. I'd given her a list of what I thought was needed when we met in Chennai.' She pauses. 'And then, you arrived. The best, and the worst, day of my life. All at the one time.'

'Prognosis?'

'Good. We've caught it early. I suspected myself that something was wrong, just before I left Dublin. But it was impossible to tell if it was stress or unhappiness, or just the sheer terror of being arrested. In the circumstances I did nothing about it. That's why it was such a joy to find Alicia again.'

William hesitates to ask his next question. 'This hospital where Alicia works . . .'

'. . . Is one of the best there is,' Julia finishes for him. 'World-wide reputation.'

'Okay.' William's voice is quiet. 'Is there anything else you have to tell me? Or are we done, here?'

'We're done. I hated hiding things from you. I'm sorry.'

'We'll take this together, step by step,' he says. 'We'll deal with it little by little. A minute at a time, if necessary. And we'll get through it.'

Julia doesn't reply.

He turns her around to look at him. 'Like I said, we'll fight it together.'

'This doesn't change what I want.'

He knows that look. The focus, the determination. 'Go on.'

'I want to stay in India, afterwards. I want to work here for whatever time I have left. And so far, I don't know anything about what *you* want.' She looks at him, her eyes uncertain.

William stands up. 'Don't move. I have something with me I've been keeping for you. For some time now.' He moves towards the only chair. He'd flung his jacket across it earlier.

She waits. William sits back down beside her again. He opens the small, black velvet box.

'Marry me, Julia Seymour,' he says. 'I can't keep chasing around the world after you.'

'But . . .' She looks at him, her whole face a question.

'You asked me what I wanted. This is what I want. No matter what happens in the future.' He kisses her. 'This is my answer. Wherever you are, I am.'

'And this is mine.' She pulls him closer. 'Yes,' she says. 'Yes.'

# PART THREE

*September 2010*

# William and Julia

WILLIAM WAITS AS Julia kisses each of the children. This could take some time, he thinks. With forty kids.

He loves how graceful she looks in her red sari. He watches the way the silk fabric shimmers as she moves. A deep red: vibrant, liquid. The colour of life, he thinks. And all that gold thread; the way it glints in the sunlight. He's not so sure about his own white suit – but all the women had insisted. And so he'd given in without a fight. The combined forces of Julia, Sarita, Josanna and Anuradha were more than a man could withstand.

'William.'

He turns. Melissa is at his elbow. She has Susie in her arms. To his amusement, William sees that her hands, and the baby's, are covered with intricate designs in henna. 'This is wonderful. Congratulations again.'

'Thank you. Yes, it is. Wonderful. Above all, to see Julia so well.'

'And so happy.'

He smiles.


'My very own monsoon wedding!' Julia had exclaimed. Her hair had started to grow again, and her eyebrows. She was particularly pleased about that.

'Yes, ma'am,' Alicia had said. 'You've done very well. You've responded extremely well to treatment. Fire ahead with all your preparations. But don't *dare* arrange the date when I'm in the States.'

William couldn't stop grinning. 'Let's give these people a party to remember,' he'd said.

There had been some dark days in the hospital, Julia recalls. Some darker moments. Times when she'd just wanted it all to be over. But somehow, she'd got through them. They had got through them. William had never left her side.

'I'm going nowhere,' he'd said. 'So stop trying to look after me.' He'd taken her free hand, held it tightly.

'I need to say something to you.'

'I'm listening.'

'I'm very clear about what I want.'

'Well, you surprise me,' William had teased her. 'I've never known you to know your own mind about anything.'

'This is serious.' Julia had looked up at him, anxious. 'If things go wrong, if I don't respond to the treatment . . .' She'd paused. William had learned not to interrupt. 'I want to die in the way that I choose.'

'I'm still listening. Tell me what that is.'

'I don't want intervention. Either to prolong my life or to shorten it. I want to do this in my own way, the way that's right for me.' She'd squeezed his hand. 'With you, and the people I love most, around me.'

'We can do that,' he'd said. 'And I hear you, loud and clear. I won't allow anything to happen to you that you don't want. I promise you.'

She'd smiled. 'A man of your word,' she'd said.

\*

Julia continues to make her way among the children. As she stoops, the *varmala* she is wearing dips and sways, the orchids and marigolds a swathe of colour against the deep red of her sari. She and William had exchanged these garlands earlier, each of them bending their head for the other. The children clapped and cheered during that early part of the ceremony, even though William suspects they weren't supposed to.

They had painstakingly put the *varmalas* together – as they have made everything else – under the watchful eye of Anuradha and Josanna. Auspicious flowers are placed everywhere around Sarita's garden: roses, jasmine, with scarlet petals underfoot.


By the end of May, Julia had agreed to go home, just for a while. The humidity had been unbearable. William had only to fight her a little: she'd given in easily. 'A few months of complete rest,' he'd said. 'That's all. And you'll come back fighting fit. Particularly fighting.' She'd laughed. 'Sarita insists, and I do, too. There's not a lot we can do here for the next few months. Even the building will have to stop for a while.'

William looks down at his hands. His palms are callused, fingernails broken, knuckles skinned. Not the perfect hands for a bridegroom. Still, being project manager has been satisfying; getting his hands dirty even more so. And Julia delights in his new role.


'No case to answer,' Roisin had written, back in April. 'The DPP has given his decision, and it's final.' Eileen had taken herself to the police station, indignation personified. Nothing but the best of care, she'd railed; Hilary died because her time had come.

She, Eileen, should know: she'd sat with her all the night before, taking down dictation. The poor woman's mind was gone. She was rambling. Her elder daughter would know that, if she'd spent any sort of meaningful time with her.

Would Eileen make a statement? She most certainly would.

And Melissa had looked after Julia in Dublin with a tenderness that William wouldn't have believed possible. She's still standing beside him; they both laugh as Derek tries to keep hold of an excitable Jamie.

Across the gravel that separates the house from the refuge, still under construction, William spots him. Deepak, grinning from ear to ear. 'Come with me,' he says to Melissa, 'come and meet one of your mother's greatest fans.'

'High five,' Anand demands.

Julia obliges. Out of the corner of her eye, she sees the brisk approach of Sarita and Josanna. 'Don't make them be quiet,' she says. 'Just give them some more sweets. After all,' and she looks at Josanna in particular, 'we still don't know when the next wedding will be, do we?'

She turns and sees Roisin, Sorcha and Hugh, waiting for her. She makes her way towards them, holding onto the skirts of her sari.

'Julia.' Sorcha holds out her arms.

Roisin is unable to speak. Julia nudges her. 'That's a first.'

'Congratulations,' Hugh says, pumping her hand.

'Keep going,' Sorcha says, laughing. 'There'll be time for talking later. There's Michael, waiting for you. And Tanya. And Alicia.'

And so she's off again. How do they do it? she wonders. Indian women, every day? Twelve yards or so of red silk: she's terrified she'll come undone.

And she's very grateful for all the safety pins that Josanna and Anuradha had used this morning, giggling as they pinned her together.

'Mr William must count them tonight,' Josanna had insisted. 'We have used a dozen. Otherwise, you might tear the fabric.'

Anuradha had said something, *sotto voce*, and both of the young women had laughed.

'I understood that, madam,' said Julia, sternly, sending the two off into peals of laughter again.

'Michael,' she says, hugging him. All the time, she is aware of William, watching her. Watching over her. And we're staying on, she says to herself. Like some old colonial couple: staying on.

William makes a sign over his son's head. It says: enough. Time to sit down for a while.

My rumpled guardian angel, she thinks. She makes her way towards where he stands, flanked on either side by Jack and Celine. She walks into the circle of their arms, feeling the way it tightens around her.


Afterwards – and it's a long afterwards: the wedding seems to have lasted for more than three days – she and William spend two nights near Marina Beach, looking out on the blue of the sea. She is full of plans. He listens.

And the way he listens reminds her of that part of the ceremony that she'd liked the best. Borrowed from the Hindu, Sarita had said. But we don't mind; we are a generous people.

*Shilarohana.*

Julia places her right foot on a large, flat stone set in the centre of the orphanage courtyard. Everyone waits.

'May your foot here be as firm as the stone of my house,' William says. 'With that strength we can face our enemies together.'

Stone. Flesh. Love.

No matter what happens in the days to come – fragile, numbered, or plentiful, spinning out before her – Julia thinks she will hold onto that.

And to William.

# ACKNOWLEDGEMENTS

Heartfelt thanks to Trisha Jackson, who has championed *Missing Julia* since the very beginning. It's been quite a journey and you've been wonderful.

And to the entire team at Macmillan: Jeremy Trevathan, Thalia Suzuma, Katie James, Ellen Wood, Michelle Taylor, Ali Blackburn and Eli Dryden.

To Cormac Kinsella and Dave Adamson for hard work, cheerleading and friendship.

Thanks again to Novelshop: Lia Mills, Helen Hansen, Celia de Fréine, Mary Rose Callaghan and Ivy Bannister. Such a lot of reading.

To Dr Maud McKee for taking the time to share her memories and her medical expertise. It is much appreciated.

Many thanks once more to Shirley Stewart, Literary Agent. I couldn't do it without you.

To Eamonn, for all the techie stuff and the adventure that was Mumbai airport . . .

And to Fergus, for pretty much everything.

Special thanks are due also to our friends in India for their hospitality, their time and their conversation. Among them, Colin Breese, Rosy d'Cruz, Tess Doyle, David Pierce-wright, Anthony Vaz and family, Sr Aurora of St Anthony's Orphanage and Sr Lucy Kurien of Maher.

Finally, a big thank you to Deepak Shaym Kawalekar for a most memorable journey to Murudeshwar, and to Frankie for untangling the Konkani for all of us.

# Who is Julia?

*And where does she come from?*

These are not easy questions to answer. In many ways, they are the variations on a theme that most writers have to grapple with, in public, at different times during their career.

*Where do you get your ideas? Where does your inspiration come from? Are the people in your stories real?*

I wish I could say that there are simple answers to these questions, and to all other questions like them. Answers that don't vary; answers that lead the reader to a fixed point in the geography of the writer's imagination, so that the creative process can be pinned down, like a butterfly on a board. The truth, however, is as always, a little more complex than that.

Some writers *hear* their stories, others *see* them. Sometimes, I do both, and I'll add in another – sometimes I dream them. I wake, with a sentence that has somehow formed out of sleep, and that draws me towards consciousness with the insistence of its repetition. It refuses to let go, and out of this refusal another story wakes and draws a long, slow breath.

One thing, though, has been a constant throughout all of the novels I've written – eight so far. Whatever it is that I see, whatever I hear or dream, whatever it is that I write, the whole long process always begins with a character.

In my experience, a novel is born from a single, resonant moment of illumination. A moment that evokes a response from within, as though somehow my writer's imagination has been expecting it. It's as if some sort of internal space has already been prepared for it; a place where this new beginning can come and sit, and wait and be comfortable. It is a moment that lies somewhere between recognition, vision and intuition. I believe that *this* is the spark that can properly be called inspiration. The spark that will ignite the imagination, set fire to the story.

With *Missing Julia*, that first moment was a highly visual one. My mind's eye saw a woman walking away, leaving everything behind, propelled into an uncertain future by some force I did not yet understand. What I saw was a mature woman with a mass of grey hair, angry at being sidelined because she was of 'a certain age'.

That's what I started to write: but in the writing, a different, calmer Julia took over. No, no, no, she said. I'm much gentler than that. The force you can see is not anger: it's the power of an old and long-buried secret. I puzzled for some time over what the secret might be – but Julia refused to help me. She waited until I discovered it for myself. When I did, all of the worrisome bits of the plot that I had been agonizing over suddenly fell into place.

You've got it, she seemed to say, softly. Now just write my story.

When I began to do as I was told, I had another surprise. William grew into himself with a speed that was positively indecent. I had never intended for him to hog half of the action, but he wouldn't have it otherwise. We got on very well together, William and I. Instead of simply being there, in Julia's corner, William acted with energy and purpose – and showed great emotional intelligence in the process. I think I fell in love with him.

I'd better stop here and explain that I have never claimed that writing is the pursuit of a sane person. It has to be some sort of madness; to elect to spend your days with people who do not exist, who have no past, whose future depends entirely upon the present you decide to create for them. And there's more. These imagined people often become more real than the flesh-and-blood persons who exist patiently outside the study door, waiting for the writer to emerge from long months in 'the zone': that place where the writing becomes so compelling that all else is – almost – excluded.

And let's have a word about that word 'real'. Fiction, by definition, is not 'true' or 'real' in the same way as facts are. But stories *do* hold a different kind of truth, a different reality nevertheless. They help us make sense out of chaos; they put a shape on all the quirks and oddities of human experience; they help us to see our own lives reflected in the lives of others.

Fiction – good fiction – illuminates truths about human behaviour and motivation that are missing in, say, an analytical newspaper report. Just because something is not factual does not mean it cannot be real, or true. Writers have to exercise craft, persistence and patience while coming to grips with, and giving a coherent shape to, the stories that are peopled by characters who become very real indeed. Rich, complex, fictional characters become both themselves and the created representatives of another kind of truth.

In the grip of these demanding and often difficult characters, the writer can only do their bidding. Because it is also true that writers do not choose what stories to write: our stories choose us.

The progress of those stories is rarely linear, in my experience. I tend to write in episodes – like pieces of a patchwork quilt that I later sew together into the final, complex design. The trick is not to let the seams show.

One of the 'seams' I worried about with Julia was, once she had run away, where would her final destination be? I was wary of this – very wary. Often, when writing is not at its best, it becomes obvious that the author has imported an experience into the text, where it sits, as it were, above the page and is not absorbed into it. It's almost as though the writer grits his or her teeth and says, I've paid good money to do this research, and I'll get it in there, by hook or by crook.

I was, at first, concerned about having Julia flee to India. I had just been, and my heart had been captured, captivated and made the willing prisoner of a chaotic, glorious, sensory overload of a nation. Significant parts of the novel came to life there. But I felt that it would be dangerous, fictionally speaking, to have Julia share my experiences: that India would sit on the page as a show-offy bit of background that wasn't necessary for the reader.

In a way, the decision was taken out of my hands. While I was agonizing about Julia's fictional destination, I paid a visit to a local orphanage, close to the Indian village in which I was staying. Set back from the road, the building was long and low and somewhat ramshackle. It flooded during every monsoon, and had to be put back together again each year. Inside, more than thirty bunks crowded into one large dormitory. The children were shy and curious – staring wide-eyed at this stranger who came laden with cakes and lemonade. The staff had approved the treat: such delicacies as iced buns were not a regular event.

As the lines of children sat obediently in their places and waited to be served, it hit me. For the Julia I had created – the doctor, the compassionate woman, the woman with a guilty secret that was weighing heavily upon her – this was just the sort of place where she could come and feel at home. This was the place where she could make a difference to these small lives: a place where she might begin the process of atonement that had become urgent and all-encompassing.

The decision was made: Julia would flee to India and, at the same time, leave a complex series of clues for William. Find me here, she seems to say to him, but not yet.

In this way, a real experience of my own prompted an experience for my fictional character. But the important thing is that my 'real' experience had to be transformed into fiction in order for the story to have truth. And this process of transformation is what is so central to the whole fictional endeavour.

Fiction has to do with authenticity, too. The experiences that the author chooses for the characters in a novel must be those that are right for each one. In other words, what happens to them must work in the world of the novel. It is not enough to transport a writer's experience into the text and expect it to have authenticity. The reasoning, 'but that really happened to me' is not enough.

The writer's 'real' experience is a seed, a kernel that can grow to become something else in the writing. To do so, it has to go through a mysterious process a little like alchemy, where base metal is turned to gold. Part of that, too, lies in stepping away from the self and writing from within someone else's skin.

I was sad to say goodbye to Julia and William. Sometimes, I imagine their lives continuing outside the covers of my novel. I have to curtail such imaginings. After all, they are fictional; they are not real people.

But I hope that they are true.

# Set in Stone

An extract from Catherine Dunne's compelling novel follows

*Available now in Pan paperback*

*1*

MONDAY MORNING; three minutes to six. Lynda woke.

Her eyes were drawn at once to two pinpoints of light blinking redly on the clock's digital display. She reached over, groped for the switch and pushed it to the 'off' position, before the alarm had a chance to ring. She lay still for a moment, waiting for her eyes to become used to the dark. Something had startled her out of sleep, but she couldn't figure out what it was.

She half-turned now and checked on Robert. Had he woken her? Sometimes he called out in his sleep. Sometimes one arm would flail towards her in the dark. Lynda was disturbed by this restlessness, although Robert never seemed to remember it. He was still unconscious now, as far as she could tell, his mouth slightly open, slack, his breathing barely audible.

Lynda slid the duvet away from her and eased herself towards the edge of the bed, careful not to wake her husband. She searched along the floor with her toes but, as usual, she couldn't find her slippers. When she found them at last – surely not where she'd left them during the night – she wriggled her way into the fleecy lining. Then she lifted her dressing-gown from its hook and closed the bedroom door quietly behind her.

She liked this time of morning. The house was quiet, more or less. Over the years, she had grown used to its elderly groanings and sighings, the murmurs of wood and water.

337

Robert's childhood home: a place so familiar to him that he no longer heard its night-time mutterings, but Lynda did. They often kept her company when she couldn't sleep. And that's how she thought of them: as companions, friendly voices during the hours of darkness.

She crossed the landing now to Ciarán's room and slowly turned the handle of his door. It wasn't locked. She nodded to herself. Good. That meant he'd got home at some stage last night. Safely. No matter what, that was something to be grateful for. She paused on her way past Katie's door. It was wide open. The room had an emptiness that somehow filled it, as though it was holding its breath. Lynda still hadn't got used to her daughter's absence. At twenty-one, Katie was a passionate student of Irish and History at University College Galway. She often declared that wild horses wouldn't drag her back to live in Dublin.

Downstairs, Lynda followed her usual routine. She drew back the curtains, cleared the newspapers from the coffee table, picked up the stray mugs and glasses that littered the counters. She even took a moment to empty Ciarán's careless ashtray, before Robert saw it. It was easier to do it herself, Lynda had decided a long time ago. Much easier than nagging her son.

Katie used to help her with these chores, once upon a time. She was an even earlier riser than her mother, another addict of the slow, uncluttered hours. Lynda wished she could make it home more often. Even the occasional weekend would do: Galway wasn't a million miles away. But We Mustn't Grumble, Robert kept telling her, tongue in cheek. He liked to claim that he and Lynda had, by the standards of the day, raised two trouble-free young adults. Not many parents could say that.

*Not even me*, Lynda has thought on many occasions. *Not so sure I'd say it with such conviction.* But she had never voiced this. She believed that she and Robert saw these things differently, that sometimes even the best-chosen words were not enough to close the gaps between them.

Now Lynda opened the doors to the garden and stepped outside on to the wooden decking. The sensor light snapped on instantly. The grey-green boards were slippery underfoot; they felt treacherous. The thought came to her suddenly. It surprised her, the force of it. It was freezing out there, the January air biting and bitter. She pulled her thick dressing-gown more tightly around her, her hands gripping her elbows. But she could still feel the cold. The wind stung her cheeks, continued to bite at her feet and ankles.

No matter what the weather was like, Lynda always took this time to gaze at her garden, her creation. Just below the deck, there was a wide, undulating sea of grey, raked gravel. A few crumpled, brown-papery leaves fluttered across the calm surface; there was a stray crisp packet, too. Its shiny foil eye winked at her. And the lid of a Styrofoam cup, rolling cart-wheels around the garden. A striped straw was still attached, poking its way through the opaque surface.

Despite the high walls and hedges and railings, all of this rubbish still managed to make its way into Lynda's garden with a tenacity that baffled her. For a moment, she imagined the wilful determination of inanimate objects, the gleeful sense of malice behind these invasions of her space. She laughed at herself. She'd clear them all up later, once the day was aired.

A stone tortoise, oblivious to these foreign bodies, seemed to swim towards her across the garden, its lumbering head pushing through the gravel waves. Lynda loved the sense of stilled energy all around it, admired its blunted purpose. This, according to the oriental legend, was her rock of good fortune, her isle of immortality. Surrounding the tortoise, the evergreens threw their shadows. Soon, in spring, their growth would become luxuriant. She liked the predictability of her Japanese garden, the way that no matter how much the seasons changed, her island still stayed very much the same.

The sensor light clicked off, having grown used to her presence. Shivering now, she turned to go back inside. As she did so, she thought she saw something move, high above the garden. Just last year Robert, with Ken from next door, had had to string barbed wire across the top of the old stone wall. A rash of burglaries along the street had made everyone feel on edge. Ken had embedded rough pieces of glass into a new layer of cement, too, just for good measure.

She glanced to her right now, into Ken and Iris's back garden. She couldn't help it. It was an old habit, and old habits were the ones that took longest to die. As Lynda waited for any sign of life, a wood pigeon cooed and took flight, flapping its way across the garden. She tensed, looking up again, but the trees along the high wall were blank, dark. She felt a surge of relief. Just a bird – nothing to worry about. She made her way carefully across the deck and stepped back inside, locking the double doors behind her.

She had an hour or so to herself, before the house began to stir. She made tea and toast and sat at the long wooden table, rustling her way through the pages of yesterday's *Irish Times*. She settled into the crossword. The central heating clicked and hummed steadily, filling the kitchen with warmth. Down time, she thought. Warm-up time, before the real day began.

This was the time she missed Katie the most. She missed the clatter of their early morning conversations. And the phone, too, of course. These days, the phone hardly rang at all, it seemed to Lynda, although she knew that that was nonsense. It still rang for her. And for Robert. It was just an impression, that telephonic silence. But still. The absence of Katie was a resonant one. It made itself felt above all in these early mornings, even though more than a year had passed.

But Robert was right. She shouldn't complain. She was lucky, really. Luckier than so many other people. Particularly these days.


'Ciarán, it's gone half-past. If you don't get up now, you're going to be late again.'

Lynda heard Robert's voice booming across the landing. Automatically, she stood up and filled the coffee-maker. Strong and black: Robert said his heart wouldn't start without it. His heavy footsteps made their way downstairs, abruptly silenced by the carpet as he crossed the hall. Lynda looked up and smiled as her husband opened the kitchen door.

'Morning, love . . .' He kissed her on the cheek. 'Your man above is out for the count. Did you happen to hear what time he got home at last night?'

Lynda shook her head. 'No,' she said, firmly, not wanting this conversation again. 'I heard nothing until six o'clock. No idea what time he came in.'

Robert frowned. 'Has he lectures this morning, do you know?'

'I'm not sure.' Lynda pushed the plunger down into the coffee, wiping the granite countertop as she did so. Some of the grounds always managed to escape.

'Anyway, I've called him twice already.' Robert lifted his keys and mobile phone from the kitchen table and put them into the pockets of his suede jacket. 'I'm not going to call him again. He's big and ugly enough to look after himself at this stage.'

Lynda said nothing. She'd call Ciarán herself, later. Perhaps bring him up tea and toast, once Robert had left. Breakfast in bed helped to ease Ciarán into the day. It made the certainty of his bad temper recede a little. And that made her morning easier, too. The joys of working from home. But at least she had no need to brave the tangle of city traffic; no need to hurry up and wait. 'Toast?' she asked Robert.

He nodded. 'Yeah, thanks.' He accepted the cup of coffee Lynda offered him, but he didn't sit down. Instead, he took his briefcase from its perch at the end of the kitchen table and opened it. He handed Lynda an envelope. 'Can you lodge that for me this morning? It's a draft – I don't want to leave it hanging around.'

Lynda suppressed a rush of irritation. She hadn't planned on leaving her studio this morning, had things to do, drawings to finish. Her time was accounted for, all of it. 'Sure,' she said. 'Business account or personal?'

Robert hesitated. It was a fractional delay, but enough for her to notice. 'Personal,' he decided. 'As soon as you can. I've a site meeting in Blessington at ten and I'm tied up for the rest of the day.' He glanced in her direction, gestured towards the envelope with his coffee cup. 'I know you're busy – I wouldn't ask you if it wasn't urgent. Sure you can get to it?'

She nodded, feeling suddenly guilty. Sometimes, she thought, she underestimated the pressures he was under. Sometimes, she forgot to understand. And at least he had acknowledged her day. 'No problem,' she said. 'I'll get to the bank just as soon as it opens.'

'Great, thanks. Appreciate it.'

There was the sound of the letter box flapping open, the thud of post hitting the floor. 'Postman's early today,' Robert commented.

'Always is on Mondays,' said Lynda. She was surprised that he had forgotten that. It was one of the more enduring, predictable rhythms of their home. She began to empty the dishwasher. At the same time, she switched on the radio for the eight o'clock news. The headlines astonished her, all over again.

The last few months had been like life lived in another country. Crisis after crisis – job losses, plunging house prices. It was as though the miracle of the nineties had never happened. How come the Celtic Tiger had turned tail so quickly?

She turned around to see if Robert was listening to George Lee's latest economic forecast. The 'busiest man in Ireland', as Robert called him. More banks were toppling, lurching drunkenly towards collapse, bringing directors and shareholders with them. But Robert was no longer in the kitchen. Lynda reached up instead to open the cupboard door.

And then, suddenly, he was beside her again, looming out of nowhere. They collided clumsily and Lynda dropped one of the three mugs she was clutching, still slippery from the dishwasher. She watched as it fell from her hands and shattered on the tiled floor. The white shards dispersed everywhere, sputniks flying. She watched their starry explosion with dismay.

'Jesus, Robert,' she cried. 'Don't creep up on me like that!' The anger in her voice caught her unawares. She glanced uncertainly at him but he didn't respond. They both looked at the litter of china on the kitchen tiles.

Then Robert turned away from her. 'I'll get the brush.'

Lynda stooped and picked up the larger pieces. Homer Simpson's yellow face grinned up at her, lopsidedly. One of Ciarán's favourites. 'Sorry, hon,' she said as Robert returned from the cupboard in the hall, carrying the brush and pan. 'You startled me.' His face was white, tense. Still he didn't reply. 'Robert? Are you okay?'

He handed her the dustpan full of broken china.

Lynda took it and thought: why doesn't he just put it in the bin himself? It's right behind him. She could feel her defensiveness growing. 'I said I was sorry – and you did give me a fright.'

He looked at her, not understanding. 'What? Oh, no, don't worry about it. No need to apologize. It's not that.'

'Then what?' she said. 'What is it? What's wrong?'

He shook his head impatiently. 'Nothing – just a letter from Danny, that's all. More of the usual bullshit. Nothing for you to worry about.'

'From Danny?' Lynda didn't try to hide her alarm. 'That's *always* something to worry about.'

Robert stooped and kissed her. 'We'll talk later. It's nothing to get upset about. Just Danny being Danny, all over again. Same old, same old.' He shrugged. 'Trust me.' He drained his coffee cup and smiled at her, but it was a smile without conviction. 'Now I've really got to run. Call you later, okay?'

Lynda saw the strain around his eyes, the pulled-down corners of his mouth. She noticed the shadowy bit under his chin that he always missed while shaving. Her stomach went into freefall. But she squeezed his hand. 'Yeah. 'Course. I'll be here all afternoon. Has Danny said anything in particular to upset you?'

Robert shook his head. 'No, no, not at all. I just don't relish hearing from him, you know that. All his "poor me" crap. Danny, the eternal victim.' His tone was impatient.

Lynda's questions hovered in the air between them, but she didn't ask them. Instead, she searched Robert's face for the truth and didn't find it. His silences always made her feel edgy. She had never got used to them. 'Let's talk about it when you get home, then, all right? We'll keep saying "no" to whatever it is he's asking, just like we agreed. Don't you worry about him – and I won't either.' She gave him a quick hug and brushed imaginary specks of dust off the shoulders of his suede jacket. She wanted to hold onto him for a few minutes longer.

Robert missed a beat. 'Yeah, well, I'm certainly not babysitting him again, not after the last time.' He seemed about to say something else, but then changed his mind. 'Look, gotta run. See you tonight.'

She blew him a kiss; he waved from the front door.

'Have a good day,' Lynda called. She watched from the porch as he struggled out of his shoes and into his work boots, holding onto the Jeep's open door as he did so. He fired his yellow hard hat into the back, and settled his briefcase beside him. With one arm slung across the back of the passenger seat, he glanced over his shoulder and reversed down the long driveway. All his movements were swift, confident. Lynda had always admired Robert's physicality: it was one of the things that had attracted her to him in the first place, the best part of thirty years ago. He had towered over everyone else she knew in those days. His longish dark hair and grey eyes had been a striking combination, one Lynda had found irresistible. His body did what he asked of it: tennis, football, pouring cement, sawing wood. There was nothing too much for it. She still loved its solidity, tending now towards heaviness. Predictability made flesh.

Lynda watched the receding headlights, saw that the Jeep's paintwork was almost completely covered by a thick layer of greyish mud. She waited on the front step until all traces of Robert's presence vanished and the car had disappeared down the hill towards the traffic lights.

She stepped into the hallway and walked quickly back towards the kitchen. Once inside, she turned to where Robert had dumped the morning post on the counter under the microwave. Just the usual stuff: ESB bill, gas bill, flyers for yet another pizza joint. Impatiently, she pushed them aside and riffled through the remaining envelopes one more time. She must have missed it first time around. But there was nothing. Nothing from Danny.

For a moment, Lynda looked at the strewn counter with

disbelief. Then she moved over to the sink and filled a glass with cold water. She sipped at it, keeping both hands around the heavy tumbler. It helped to anchor her. Anchored by water, she thought. Not very substantial. Still, it was better than nothing.

She went back out into the hallway and glanced at the bottom stair. But there was no envelope here, either. Sometimes, Robert tossed the post there, just outside his office. He'd leave it, reminding himself to deal with it later. She stood, feeling even more puzzled now. She and Robert kept no secrets from each other concerning Danny. That had always been their most solid, their most united, front.

There was a faint breeze making its way through the flap of the letter box that still needed to be fixed. She must remind Robert, again, that there was a new one waiting to be installed. She wished that she could block off the letter box completely, seal it closed for good. Too much news of Danny had reached them that way over the years. That, and his sporadic phone calls, all of them brittle, all of them needy, sucking her and Robert in again before they even realized it. But it was well over three years since they'd heard from him now, long enough for memories of his last visit home to be, if not forgotten, then at least gratefully put aside.

She decided now not to 'go there' as her children would advise. She didn't care to remember. Instead, she tried to shrug off the images that were flashing by, thick and fast now, all their bells and whistles zinging. She walked back into the kitchen and poured a fresh mug of coffee for herself, put tea and toast onto a tray. Then she made her way upstairs to Ciarán's room.

Time he was up, and out of her hair.

Time she got to work. That, at least, was a distraction.